RICHTON PARK PUBLIC LIBRARY DISTR

3 6087 00146 4317

P9-CDJ-963

THE
COLONEL'S

THE
COLONEL'S
Lady

a novel

LAURA
FRANTZ

Revell

a division of Baker Publishing Group
Grand Rapids, Michigan

© 2011 by Laura Frantz

Published by Revell
a division of Baker Publishing Group
P.O. Box 6287, Grand Rapids, MI 49516-6287
www.revellbooks.com

Printed in the United States of America

All rights reserved. No part of this publication may be reproduced, stored in a retrieval system, or transmitted in any form or by any means—for example, electronic, photocopy, recording—without the prior written permission of the publisher. The only exception is brief quotations in printed reviews.

Library of Congress Cataloging-in-Publication Data
Frantz, Laura.
    The colonel's lady : a novel / Laura Frantz.
        p.   cm.
    ISBN 978-0-8007-3341-4 (pbk.)
    1. Single women—Fiction. 2. Frontier and pioneer life—Kentucky—Fiction.
I. Title.
PS3606.R4226C65 2011
813'.6—dc22   2011010717

Unless otherwise indicated, Scripture quotations are from the King James Version of the Bible.

Scripture quotations marked ESV are from The Holy Bible, English Standard Version® (ESV®), copyright © 2001 by Crossway, a publishing ministry of Good News Publishers. Used by permission. All rights reserved. ESV Text Edition: 2007

This book is a work of fiction. Names, characters, places, and incidents are the product of the author's imagination or are used fictitiously. Any resemblance to actual events, locales, or persons, living or dead, is coincidental.

11 12 13 14 15 16 17   7 6 5 4 3 2 1

For Wyatt and Paul
May you grow to be godly heroes.

And a special dedication to the men and women of our country's armed forces, who, since 1776, have given of their own lives and liberties to ensure ours.

Author's Note

When I visited Locust Grove in Louisville, Kentucky, and came face-to-face with a portrait of George Rogers Clark, I knew I had to create a hero like him. After I read James Alexander Thom's epic *Long Knife*, Colonel Clark was firmly etched in my mind and heart as a true American legend. Only he had a tragic life. After researching, I felt compelled to give him a happier ending. Colonel Cassius McLinn is loosely based on Clark and his heartbreaking struggles as a soldier and private citizen. Roxanna Rowan, while entirely fictitious, is the woman I wish George Rogers Clark had met. If he had, I like to think his life would have turned out a bit differently.

The life of a soldier in any century is difficult. We owe an enormous debt to those who serve. But a soldier who served two hundred or more years ago had very special challenges. Conditions for the army in that era were extremely taxing. The water was often polluted, thus the reliance upon alcohol or spirits. To make this story true to history, I had to include its use and show how detrimental it truly was. The political situation on the American frontier was also quite complex. I have dealt with it only superficially in my story, as it was ferocious.

George Washington is credited with saying, "I have heard the bullets whistle, and there is something charming in the sound." This so describes the fortitude and courage of the Revolutionary War soldiers that I had Colonel McLinn echo the words.

The maxims used in this novel were taken straight from the eighteenth century and were then titled *Rules of Civility and Decent Behaviour in Company and Conversation*. These were the very rules George Washington learned at an early age and followed his entire life. Perhaps this is why he became one of the finest soldiers who ever lived.

Although the Purple Heart did not come into being until 1782, I made use of it earlier in this story. Only three men are known to have been awarded this prestigious honor during the Revolutionary War.

As a novelist, I find it a joy to take the historical record and bring to life the lovely, lost, bittersweet things of the past and breathe new life and hope into them. I attempted to do this with *The Colonel's Lady*. I hope that you, dear reader, enjoy the story.

1

This is madness.

Roxanna Rowan leaned against the slick cave entrance and felt an icy trickle drop down the back of her neck as she bent her head. Her right hand, shaky as an aspen leaf, caressed the cold steel of the pistol in her pocket. Being a soldier's daughter, she knew how to use it. Trouble was she didn't want to. The only thing she'd ever killed was a copperhead in her flower garden back in Virginia, twined traitorously among scarlet poppies and deep blue phlox.

An Indian was an altogether different matter.

The cave ceiling continued to weep, echoing damply and endlessly and accenting her predicament. Her eyes raked the rosy icicles hanging from the sides and ceiling of the cavern. Stalactites. Formed by the drip of calcareous water, or so Papa had told her in a letter. She'd never thought to see such wonders, but here she was, on the run from redskins *and* Redcoats in the howling wilderness. And in her keep were four fallen women and a mute child.

They were huddled together further down the cavern tunnel, the women's hardened faces stiff with rouge and fright. Nancy. Olympia. Dovie. Mariah. And little Abby. All five were looking at

9

her like they wanted her to do something dangerous. Extending one booted foot, she nudged the keelboat captain. In the twilight she saw that the arrow protruding from his back was fletched with turkey feathers. He'd lived long enough to lead them to the mouth of the cave—a very gracious gesture—before dropping dead. *Thank You, Lord, for that. But what on earth would You have me do now?* A stray tear leaked from the corner of her left eye as she pondered their predicament.

The Indians had come out of nowhere that afternoon—in lightning-quick canoes—and the women had been forced to abandon the flatboat and flee in a pirogue to the safer southern shore, all within a few miles of their long-awaited destination. Fort Endeavor was just downriver, and if they eluded the Indians, they might reach it on foot come morning. Surely a Shawnee war party would rather be raiding a vessel loaded with rum and gunpowder than chasing after five worthless women and a speechless child.

"Miz Roxanna!" The voice cast a dangerous echo.

Roxanna turned, hesitant to take her eyes off the entrance lest the enemy suddenly appear. Her companions had crept further down the tunnel, huddled in a shivering knot. And then Olympia shook her fist, her whisper more a shout.

"I'd rather be took by Indians than spend the night in this blasted place!"

There was a murmur of assent, like the hiss of a snake, and Roxanna plucked her pistol from her pocket. "Ladies," she said, stung by the irony of the address. "I'd much rather freeze in this cave than roast on some Indian spit. Now, are you with me or against me?"

The only answer was the incessant *plink, plink, plink* of water. Turning her back to them, she fixed her eye on the ferns just beyond the cave entrance, studying the fading scarlet and cinnamon and saffron woods. With the wind whipping and rearranging the leaves, perhaps their trail would be covered if the Indians decided to pursue them. They'd also walked in a creek to hide their passing. But would it work? Roxanna heaved a shaky sigh.

I'm glad Mama's in the grave and Papa doesn't know a whit about my present predicament.

At daylight the women emerged like anxious animals from the cave, damp and dirty and wild-eyed with apprehension. One small pistol was no match for an Indian arrow. But Roxanna clutched it anyway, leading the little group through the wet woods at dawn, in the direction of the fort they'd been trying to reach for nigh on a month. By noon the women in her wake were whining like a rusty wagon wheel, but she didn't blame them a bit. They had lost all their possessions, every shilling, and hadn't seen so much as a puff of smoke from a nearby cabin at which they could beg some bread.

Were they even going the right direction?

The dense woods seemed to shutter the sun so that it was hard to determine which way was which. When the fort finally came into view, it didn't match the picture Roxanna had concocted in her mind as she'd come down the watery Ohio River road. The place was dreary. Lethal looking. Stalwart oak pickets impaled the sky, and the front gates of the great garrison were shut. Drawing her cape around her, she stifled a sigh. It needed fruit trees all around . . . and a hint of flowers . . . and children and dogs running about, even in the chill of winter.

But not one birdcall relieved the gloom.

As they came closer, she could see the Virginia colors flying on the tall staff just beyond high, inhospitable walls. And then something else came into view—something that matched her memories of home and made a smile warm her tense face. A stone house. She blinked, expecting the lovely sight to vanish. But it only became clearer and more beguiling, and she drank in every delightful detail.

Solid stone the color of cream. Winsome green shutters with real glass windows hiding behind. Twin chimneys at each end. And a handsome front door that looked like it might be open in welcome come warmer weather. Situated on a slight rise in back of the fort, the house was near enough to the postern gate to flee to in times of trouble, though she doubted even the king's men could penetrate such stone. Who had built such a place in the midst of such stark wilderness?

Papa never mentioned a stone house.

Roxanna was suddenly conscious of the company she kept—or rather was leading. It wasn't that she was afraid to be seen with these women in their too-tight gowns and made-up faces, or that she felt above them in some way. Glancing at them over her shoulder, she pulled her cloak tighter as the whistling wind of late November blew so bitterly it seemed to slice through her very soul.

Her skittishness was simply this—she feared the reaction of her father. Stalwart soldier that he was, what would he think to see her arrive in such flamboyant company? He hadn't an inkling she was coming in the first place. But to see her roll in unexpectedly with doxies such as these, and a pitiful child to boot . . .

"Is that Fort Endeavor, Miz Roxanna?" The weary voice was almost childlike in expectancy. Dovie, only fifteen, had attached herself to Roxanna with the persistence of a horsefly in midsummer's heat from the moment they'd met on the boat.

"Yes, that's the fort, or should be," she replied as the girl clutched her arm a bit fearfully. "Best keep moving lest the Indians follow." Roxanna looked to her other side and grabbed hold of Abby's hand. The child glanced up, ginger curls framing a pale face buttonholed by bluish-gray eyes, her dimpled cheeks visible even without a smile. "We'll soon be warm and dry again—promise."

At the rear, Olympia laughed, and the sound tinkled like a tarnished chime in the frozen air. "I aim to be more than that, truly. Or I reckon I'll turn right around and find me another fort full of soldierin' men—or an Indian chief."

Ignoring the babble of feminine voices, Roxanna looked over her shoulder warily as they emerged from the woods. How in heaven's name had it come to this? She realized she was running from discomfort to danger. Virginia no longer felt like home, and she was desperate to leave its hurtful memories behind. But *this* was far more than she'd bargained for.

Oh, Lord, was it Your will for me to leave Virginia . . . or my own?

Every passenger on the flatboat they'd just forsaken seemed to be running from something. Even Olympia had confessed she'd left her life at the public house because she was tired of the lice and the stench of the river and the men who manhandled her. Her sister who had worked alongside her had died, leaving a child behind. To her credit, Olympia wanted a better life for little Abby. The girl hadn't spoken a word since her mother's death a few months before, and Roxanna wondered if she ever would.

"I've heard that in Kentucke, women are so scarce even a fallen one like myself can take my pick of any man I please," Olympia had announced aboard the vessel one evening. "And he'll treat me decent too." She smiled with such satisfaction that Roxanna almost envied her.

"I just want me a little cabin with some chickens and a plot of corn. Seems like that ain't askin' much," Mariah added.

Beside her, Nancy arranged her tattered skirts and purred like a cat with a pot of cream, "I'm partial to a soldierin' man myself."

Dovie's faded blue eyes lingered on each woman, her round face full of expectancy. "Why, Miz Roxanna, you ain't said a word about why you're travelin' to the wilderness."

A hush fell over the group as they huddled about the shanty stove. Roxanna expelled a little breath. "Well . . . my father's at Fort Endeavor serving as scrivener. He's always writing letters telling me how beautiful Kentucke is, how you can see for miles since the air is so clear, that even the grass is a peculiar shade of blue-green, and the forests are huge and still. Not leaping with Indians like some folks say."

"Sure enough?" Mariah murmured as the other women huddled nearer.

"My coming to Kentucke is a surprise. Papa's enlistment is near an end, and we'll be going somewhere to settle, just the two of us."

"Don't you want to find a man—get married?" Mariah asked.

The innocent question stung her. Roxanna lifted her shoulders in a show of indifference. "I'm not so young anymore—spinster age, some say."

The women exchanged knowing glances and began to titter.

"Seems to me you're comin' to the right territory, then. A frontiersman ain't gonna let a gal who's a little long in the tooth stop a weddin'," Olympia said, her smile smug. Reaching into the bosom of her dress, she withdrew a Continental dollar and waved it about. "I bet Miz Roxanna with her fine white skin and all that midnight hair won't last five minutes once she sets foot in that fort."

There were approving murmurs all around. Roxanna smiled ruefully as Nancy reached over and snatched the bill out of Olympia's hand, tossing it into the stove. "That dollar's worthless and you know it. Show me somethin' sound."

Still chuckling, Olympia lifted her soiled calico skirt and took a pound note from her scarlet garter. "Now, who's to wed after Miz Roxanna?"

"I say Nancy 'cause she's so sweet." Mariah sneered, rolling her eyes.

This brought about such feminine howls a riverman stuck his head in the shanty doorway.

"I ain't sweet but I'm smart," Nancy said, tucking a strand of flaxen hair behind her ear. "I'll take the first man who asks me, so long as he ain't wedded to the jug and don't beat me."

Mariah rubbed work-hardened hands together, the backs flecked with liver spots. "I've got a hankerin' for a cabin in the shade of a mountain with a spring that never dries up, not even in summer. If a man won't take me, I'll make do myself, just like I've been doin' since I was nine years old."

Roxanna felt a stirring of pity for every scarred soul around the hissing stove. "Why don't we pray for husbands—for all of you?" she said on a whim, watching their faces.

Olympia smirked and shook her head. "With all due respect, Miz Roxanna, the only experience I've had with prayin' women is the ones who've prayed me and my ilk out of one river town after another."

"I ain't never prayed before," Mariah confessed.

"I like the idea. It ain't gonna hurt none," Dovie said quietly. "Maybe it'll help."

Reaching out, Roxanna squeezed her hand. Despite their worldly ways, these women could be surprisingly childlike, and they responded to any compliment or scrap of kindness like a half-starved cat.

"Praying isn't hard," she told them. "Sometimes when I can't think of what to say, I just remember the words I learned as a little girl." Opening the door of the stove, she added some dry willow chunks. "It goes like this. 'Now I lay me down to sleep, I pray the Lord my soul to keep. If I should die before I wake, I pray the Lord my soul to take.'"

Nancy nodded. "I learned that a long time ago in settlement school back in Pennsylvania."

"Well," Mariah urged, "keep on a-goin'. Might as well add that we're all needin' husbands."

"Maybe we should hold hands," Dovie suggested, reaching for Nancy's. "Once I peeked in at a prayer meetin' and it seemed that was what they did."

Self-consciously they bowed their heads. Roxanna stayed silent as they made their petitions before adding her own at the very end. "Father, You know what we have need of before we even ask. But we ask anyway, knowing You are patient and kind and the giver of all gifts. I ask that You send each of these women a husband—but only men who are honest and kind and good. Help them to be the women You made them to be. Help them to know You." She looked up, eyes searching the shadows. Curled up on a cot against a far wall, Abby was fast asleep. "And please bring Abby's voice back—let her speak again. Amen."

Dovie didn't let go of her hand. "Why, Miz Roxanna, you left yourself out."

Swallowing down a sigh, Roxanna dredged up a half smile.

Truly, some things are past praying for.

"I ain't goin' to bed till you're prayed up," Olympia said, crossing her arms.

They joined hands again, the only sound the stove's popping and water sluicing under the hull beneath their feet. One by one they all prayed again, this time for Roxanna, and it seemed she'd never heard such sincere whispered words. But it was Dovie's petition that lingered the longest.

"Help my friend Roxanna, Mister Eternal. Prepare her a man she can't take her eyes off of and who can't take his eyes off her. And let it be right quick, if it pleases Ye."

2

'Twas the deep lilac of dusk, a dangerous time to be a soldier. Trail-weary, the Kentuckians under Colonel Cassius McLinn's command were only too glad to succumb to a keg of rum at day's end. It was a flourishing finish to a successful winter campaign in Shawnee territory—indeed, one that had ended but hours before when the men had split ranks and ambushed a British-led war party in a matter of minutes, bringing an end to the enemy's planned raid on the frontier settlements.

Colonel McLinn turned away from the barren ridge and tucked his spyglass in a coat pocket, aware of the bound men behind him. Redcoats and redskins made strange bedfellows, he mused. They watched him as intently as he watched them, feathers fluttering and faces smeared with paint and gunpowder.

It had been a mostly bloodless battle. Those were what he was known for. Wars could be won by weapons *and* wits. What was it the *Virginia Gazette* called him? "The gentleman colonel"? The Shawnee knew him as something less stellar—the Bluecoat town burner. He preferred the first title by far but acknowledged he'd earned the second. Swinging round to face his fifty prisoners, he wondered, what did they think of him now?

In the winter twilight he knew he cast a Goliath-like shadow. The tattered, stained skirt of his long leather coat flapped about his thighs in the wind, and his silver-spurred boots were firmly planted on frozen ground. He unsheathed his sword, and the bell-like ring of fine steel lingered in the air.

The prisoners were watching him now, perhaps wondering if he'd live up to his reputation. But which one? He paced back and forth in front of them, eyes on the bare trees behind them, wondering when the woods would give up all his men. Wondering too if they concealed the dozen or so Shawnee and Redcoats who'd gotten away.

Perhaps he'd been wrong to send a small party looking for the escaped enemy. He'd placed thirty soldiers under the leadership of Richard Rowan, though Rowan was more scrivener than soldier. Given this, the men would likely get lost—or frostbitten—before they came back. But with his second-in-command sick, he'd had little choice. And Rowan, weary of desk duty, had been more than willing. Cass had watched the woods swallow his men with a tightness in his chest he couldn't account for. Rowan was like a father to him to boot.

Sheathing his sword, he shoved aside his misgivings as a lieutenant came forward with a pewter tankard. "This'll take the chill off, Colonel."

Within an hour no one was thinking of their missing comrades or the elusive enemy as they huddled about the fires and partook freely of the rum. To a man, they were all pondering the comforts of home. Trestle tables piled high with meat and bread. The gentle swish of a skirt. Downy feather ticks. And Cassius McLinn was thinking of Ireland . . . and the estate he hadn't seen in six years . . . and the fragrant, enveloping arms of Cecily O'Day.

Always, always Cecily.

When daylight had eroded completely, he spotted a flash of movement in the forest. Men—mere shadows—began to emerge with muskets raised. *The escaped raiders!* With a furious, catlike swipe, he reached for his rifle and sighted. In one single, unforgiving blast, he felled the lead man. All around him, his soldiers followed suit, picking off the approaching men like turkeys at a target shoot. There was precious little resistance—a terrifying silence—then an anguished cry.

His own.

They were downing their own men! Fellow Patriots, all. The soldiers still standing were now running back toward the woods in terror. With a hoarse cry, Cass dropped his musket and sprinted across the icy sheen of grass, the soles of his boots like skates.

Oh, eternal Father, have mercy . . .

Richard Rowan lay faceup, his Continental coat flecked crimson from the gaping wound in his chest. He worked his mouth hard, swallowing back blood, one hand grabbing Cass's lapel as he hovered over him.

"Colonel . . ."

Cass fell to his knees and reached for his scrivener, bringing his head off the hard ground. He tried to utter words of comfort—anything at all—but couldn't get past the crushing burden in his chest.

Merciful God, reverse this terrible hour.

Excruciating seconds ticked by, and he cried brokenly, "Richard, I thought—you were—the enemy."

The grip on his lapel tightened. "You have . . . an enemy . . . but it's not me . . ."

Cass blinked, tears spattering onto the gray-whiskered face of the man he held. The very ground seemed to reel beneath the weight of what he'd done. Could Richard smell the rum? Did he know such mistakes were easily made at dusk? 'Twas at twilight—traitorous twilight—that one troop of men was nearly indistinguishable from another.

Strangely, Richard Rowan's countenance held no blame or recrimination. His face seemed to almost clear, and his voice held a stronger cadence than Cass had ever heard. "Take care . . . of my . . . Roxie."

3

"Yep, that's a fort all right," Mariah said between expulsions of tobacco. "The first one I seen for four hundred miles or better. Hope we ain't in for a surprise once we get there."

At this, all five women slowed their steps. Nancy crossed her ample arms above her broad bosom and shot Mariah a disgusted glance. "Now explain to me just what you mean by that."

"I'm just sayin' Fort Endeavor's locked tighter than a double-corked jug, so the flatboat captain said right before he dropped dead. We might have better luck at one of them other stations further downriver."

"Who's in charge of Fort Endeavor?" Dovie asked.

"Colonel Cassius Clayton McLinn," Roxanna answered, wondering if she'd gotten every syllable right. "He's commander of the entire western frontier. I believe he's from Ireland."

An Irish Patriot. There were many of them in the colonies, almost as many as the rebel Scots. She tried to resurrect all that she'd learned of him through her father's letters. Educated at Harrow . . . commissioned as an ensign in the British army before defecting to the colonies . . . awarded a Badge of Military Merit for heroic action at Brandywine Creek. The facts swirled in her weary head before settling and posing yet another question.

Given these sterling accomplishments, what was the colonel doing *here*?

Looking back over her shoulder, she motioned the women on toward the unfriendly-looking fort.

"Reckon they'll shoot at us?" Dovie wondered aloud. "Or even unlock them gates?" The entire garrison was now clearly in view, and Roxanna could make out more winsome details of the stone house on the hill. When they'd rounded the last bend that brought them abreast of the smooth river, now turning from dull green to opal as the sun strengthened, she could hardly contain her relief. She couldn't walk another mile, as the soles of her boots were worn thin as paper.

She guessed Papa would be in the orderly room with the colonel, scribbling his shorthand in myriad ways. Protocol demanded that the sentries at the gates stop them and inquire who they were and then summon her father. Thankfully, her traveling companions were no longer a source of consternation. Somehow, amidst the turmoil of the past hours, they'd united into an unlikely band. Though they'd made it thus far with just the clothes on their backs, they had made it with scalps intact, and this was all that mattered.

"It sure ain't Virginia," Mariah muttered at her elbow.

Roxanna took a last look at the woods and river. Truly, Kentucke wasn't like genteel Virginia. Even locked in early winter, the land seemed to pronounce itself superior in the subtlest of ways—from the curious stands of cane one could hide in to the abundance of springs and staggering girth of giant trees. They had come across all kinds of animal sign as well, and had nearly stared some buffalo in the face. Overhead an enormous flock of pigeons flew, darkening the sky. Kentucke looked, smelled, and felt dangerous.

Yet every step closer was a step away from the past, and for that reason there seemed to be a small sun rising in her breast, just like the one now pinking the sky over the treetops. She hadn't felt hope for so long—or excitement—but she felt it now and was hard-pressed to keep the emotion from telling on her face. It was all she could do not to run to the massive gates and fling herself into her father's arms. Though it wasn't the life her mother had dreamed of for her, it was an honest life.

The end of the road, such as it was, angled through a clearing large enough for military evolutions. The stubble of fallow cornfields and a small outlying orchard spread east. This was, despite its grim facade, a prosperous place, a garrison where soldiers were never idle. Roxanna was relieved to find some signs of normalcy amidst the wildness. A few lean milk cows were fenced in by the fort's east wall, and behind this was a chicken house with an enormous red-tailed rooster strutting about. Yet no sound came from the fort, nor could she see any sentries on the upraised banquette inside.

"Looks deserted to me," Nancy mused as they came nearer.

Roxanna's joy began to ebb. *What if Papa is already on his way back to Virginia? What if his enlistment ended earlier than expected? What if...*

She was hurrying now toward gates slowly swinging open, her boots rubbing holes in the heels of her stockings, her limp so pronounced she winced. The sentries were looking with a sort of awed delight at the knot of weary women approaching. Had they even exchanged a quick wink? Roxanna's eyes wandered to the spacious parade ground within and an astounding collection of barracks and outbuildings.

Olympia began to stretch and adjust her cape to better reveal her soiled, cardinal-colored dress. With her brightly clad as a Christmas package, it was a wonder she hadn't led the Indians after them all the way. Roxanna found it almost comical to watch the exaggerated curtseys that nearly spilled the women's cleavage from their stays, and the stiff bows and fawning faces of the soldiers who'd begun to appear. Like at a stage play she'd once seen in Williamsburg, she stood riveted, hardly noticing the orderly at her elbow.

"Are you with them, ma'am?"

"I—am," she stated, tugging Abby closer. "I mean, I'm not—not really. I've come here to see my father."

The orderly looked relieved. "And who would your father be, ma'am?"

"Captain Richard Rowan," she said in a little rush.

The sudden respect that struck his face was gratifying. "I'm pleased to meet you. Is this your daughter?"

Roxanna looked down at Abby, whose pale, upturned face seemed almost translucent beneath her crown of curls. "No. Abby is in the care of her aunt, Olympia, one of the women from Redstone."

He nodded. "I'm Private Ballard. Is your father expecting you?"

"I'm afraid not—it's a surprise. Is he here?"

Her entreating question seemed to unsettle him. "Nay, Miss Rowan. He's away with Colonel McLinn—on a campaign."

Away. The simple word seemed to snuff out all the high feeling in her heart, and the poise she'd tried to practice took flight. Still, "away" was better than "en route to Virginia." Or worse.

She swallowed hard and was a soldier's daughter again—stoic, composed, practical. "Do you know when they'll return?"

"Nay, miss, can't rightly say. They've been out six weeks or so. The colonel told 'em he'd have 'em back inside the walls of this fort by Christmas Day. And if he says so, he'll do so."

Christmas Day was weeks away. She scanned the fort's interior, noting the collection of tiny cabins squeezed between blockhouse bulwarks at all four corners. Which was Papa's? Wary, she lingered on the gathering crowd of soldiers next, dismissing broad backs and blue Continental coats and tricorn hats till she came to a hands-on-hips black woman, her piercing eyes dark as garden seeds. She stood on the fringe of the crowd as a stocky man in uniform strode past her, assessing the spectacle before him as he walked.

"Ladies," he said warmly, removing his hat to reveal a slightly balding pate. Though dignified, his expression was startled, even a bit bemused. He took in Roxanna at the back of the throng, lingering on her a bit long as if trying to make sense of her puzzling presence. "'Tis ungallant to keep travelers out in this cold. Private Ballard, take these women's belongings to those empty cabins."

Olympia hooted at this, drawing her cloak tighter. "We ain't got no belongin's, beggin' your pardon. We're all poor as Job's turkey."

"Indeed." He looked toward Roxanna as she stood with Abby. "What befell you exactly?"

Taking a deep breath, she smoothed her muddy skirts. "We were upriver about six miles from here when a party of Indians in canoes pushed off from the north shore. The flatboat crew panicked, most of the men were killed, and the Indians climbed aboard just as we'd pushed off toward the south bank of the river." Shuddering at the memory, she covered Abby's ears. "The captain fled with us but took an arrow to the back. We hid in a cave, where he died—"

"Say no more, please." He stood a little straighter, eyes roaming over each bedraggled woman. "I'm Captain Stewart, acting commander of this garrison since the colonel is away. Since this is a military post and not a civilian one, we rarely have visitors. But you're welcome to stay till other arrangements can be made. I'll send a detail out at once to inspect the damage—see if anything's left of the flatboat and your belongings. If you'd care to join me for supper, I'd be happy to hear what brings you to Fort Endeavor. In the meantime, you can retire to your cabins and I'll send an orderly over with hot water and whatever else you wish."

Olympia sauntered toward him and placed a gloved hand on his sleeve, her voice soft and inviting, eyelashes batting like a butterfly's wings. "I'm obliged, Captain. What time did you say supper was?"

"Seven o'clock, ma'am—"

"*Miss* Olympia," she replied, looking his uniform over and obviously finding it to her liking.

For a moment he stood as if lightning-struck, and a murmur of amusement passed over the men. Watching this display of feminine wiles, Roxanna felt a queer pang. Perhaps if she'd tried the same sort of thing with Ambrose, matters would have turned out a bit differently.

Suppertime found them all gathered around a huge trestle table in a cavernous blockhouse, each woman interspersed between officers. The room was big and cold and damp—a cheerless place to partake of a meal. The fare offered was nearly as bland. A sandy-headed lad poured cider into pewter mugs at their elbows, and Roxanna took a discreet sip. The aged brew fizzled and tickled as it went down and nearly made her sputter.

Venison steak, crusty corn pone, and a few scabby potatoes were set before them on wooden trenchers by the black woman Roxanna had seen earlier. She wondered if a supply wagon wasn't overdue. Papa had often spoken about the trouble of getting goods from Virginia in a timely manner and so wrote countless letters asking—nay, *begging*—for provisions.

At one end of the table, Captain Stewart presided, Olympia on his left with Abby, while another captain graced the other end with Nancy, Mariah, and Dovie. Roxanna found herself in the middle between two lieutenants who paid her little attention, fixated as they were on her colorful companions. They'd introduced themselves, but in her befuddlement she'd already forgotten who they were. She'd never been good with names. Strangely, the cumbersome if lyrical moniker of their commander, Cassius Clayton McLinn, wove through her mind like a melody, easily remembered.

Despite the meager food and melancholy surroundings, the

women kept up a lively discourse, the officers seeming to hang on their every word. Olympia was, if nothing else, an admirable actress, her voice projecting to the dark corners of the block-house, every expression laced with drama. No wonder Abby didn't speak, Roxanna thought. With Olympia as her aunt, the child couldn't get a word in edgewise.

Soon the laughter about the table was explosive, as the women recounted their trip downriver and all the mishaps along the way.

Listening, Roxanna became lost in her own silent version of events, none of them remotely amusing. What began as an un-eventful journey in late fall, starting at the Redstone settlement on the Monongahela River, had snowballed into something else entirely. She'd been traveling with a Kentucke-bound family of ten—former Virginia neighbors—when three of the children had suddenly taken ill. A stop was made at Redstone and the family disembarked, their places soon taken by this collection of women.

From the time the Redstone women spilled out of the public house along the rickety waterfront and set foot on the flatboat, one calamity after another began to occur. Soon the polemen manning the vessel began to murmur that the women aboard were nothing but Jonahs sent to sink them. Snow began spit-ting and the boat bobbed along on chunks of ice as the river threatened to freeze.

Two of the crew fell ill and were left at another isolated place. Roxanna's alarm had spiked when the captain broke into the store of spirits and became too inebriated to man the sweep. Toward dusk one snowy eve, a slab of ice snuck under the bow and nearly upended the entire vessel, sending kegs of rum and flour, seed sacks, and crates of chickens flying into the water.

Knowing other boats had sunk in these shallows, she'd gotten on her knees in the tilting shanty and started to pray. Hard. The cursing, seething rivermen, armed with axes and pikes, fought chunks of ice as it collided with the hull, their acid eyes on the

Redstone women as if they'd turn on them next. But then, to her astonishment, the vessel began to right itself and a warm wind kicked up, thawing the road of river. In the end, they'd sailed out upon the river's calm middle, leaving the ice jam behind, the lights of a dozen lamps of bears' oil shining on the water's smooth surface and assuring them all was well.

"Seems like we should celebrate," Olympia announced inside the overheated shanty. She disappeared from sight and returned with a fiddler, and all the women began clearing the space of chairs and cargo to make room for a dance floor.

Standing in a corner by the potbellied stove with little Abby, Roxanna listened as the lively strains of a jig coerced the rivermen inside. Soon the flatboat seemed threatened with a different kind of danger. Was anyone manning the tiller?

No one seemed to care as the men and women were now four deep, leaving little room for the whirling dancers. Roxanna could hardly believe that the same rivermen who had given them such venomous glances but an hour before now pranced and cavorted like long-lost lovers. One man even began doing a dance of sorts on his hands.

If there was a queen present, it would have to be Olympia. Perched atop a whiskey keg, she presided over the festivities, a pewter tankard her scepter, bestowing a sip or two to whomever she pleased. Beside her, the captain allowed it, his gray eyes growing more glazed as he swigged from his own jug. Soon the stench of sweat and spirits was stifling.

Breathless, Roxanna went out onto the deck, Abby in hand, and leaned over the gunwale. The wind that had helped save them was strangely warm, toying with her cape and the inky hair she'd pinned so neatly that morning. Behind them a stranger was at the sweep, whistling along with the fiddling. The sky above seemed wild and untamed, violently black with stars like saber points—so many her head swam. Water burbled beneath the hull, hurrying them ever nearer to Kentucke.

Drawing the trembling child closer, she said, "Everything's going to be all right now, Abby. You needn't be afraid."

But she looked down and saw that her own hands were shaking. She hardly believed her own reassurances. All her senses seemed muddled, as if she'd given in to the whiskey now emanating from the crowded shanty. She was on the edge of her emotions tonight, the strange sights and sounds all around her making her feel lonesome and upended. Perhaps it was wrong leaving Virginia so soon after Mama died and Ambrose jilted her.

Had it been only a year or so ago that all was well? Mama had been in high spirits if failing health. Roxanna was betrothed. Letters from Papa were arriving regularly via post, assuring them he'd soon be home, promising he'd never enlist again. He wanted to be by her mother's side, so he'd written—enjoy his future grandchildren. And then everything began to alter, subtly at first, followed by a veritable avalanche of trouble and heartache.

Now, listening to the Redstone women entertain the men at table, she wanted nothing more than a cup of steaming tea and a quiet corner, thinking of the cabin waiting two doors down. An orderly had taken her there earlier and she'd stood on the threshold to find Papa's tobacco-laced, masculine scent pervading every inch of the shuttered, shadowed place. There he seemed larger than life, even when absent.

She pondered that as she pushed an underdone potato around her plate. Soon Papa would come and they'd sit together around the fire and look at maps and dream of where they'd settle next. Perhaps farther south on the Green River. Or the idyllic valley to the west known as Angel's End. Smiling to herself, she became aware of the officer on her right watching her.

"You've said little since your arrival, Miss Rowan. Not that you've had the chance," he remarked, eyeing the chattering women while sawing at the leathery cut of meat on his plate. "But I see you smiling, so all must be well."

"A journey's end is always a pleasure," she said, reaching for her cider.

"I'm sure your father will say the same once he returns." He took a bite of meat and glanced toward the blockhouse door. "You do know where he's gone, I suppose?"

"Into Indian-infested woods, so Captain Stewart told me," she said quietly, her tone a trifle wry. "'Tis a wonder you didn't go with him."

He chuckled. "Oh, I wanted to—madly. But the dysentery stopped me."

Flushing, she rearranged her napkin in her lap. Papa had had more than his share of this miserable malady and so might she, given the close quarters of this fort. Her smile faded, eyes sweeping around the long length of table, aware of the heightened hum of conversation and heady bursts of laughter.

The acting commander was pouring brandy now, and it promised to be a late night. She was so tired she didn't know if she could string two words together if this kind officer kept her talking. But the serving woman was coming around with a steaming pot of chicory coffee laced with blackstrap molasses, and Roxanna gave her a grateful smile.

What if Papa were to come in right now and I was abed? Best stay up a little while longer. But her eyes, despite the bracing coffee, refused to stay open.

"Miss Rowan, might I have the pleasure of walking you to your cabin?"

She drained her coffee cup and now looked at the man on her left for the first time, forgetting his name, wondering about his intentions. But he was old enough to be her father—was a friend of her father's. Relieved, she blew Abby a kiss, bid goodbye to her supper companions, who were hardly aware of her going, and slipped out into the chilly, star-laden night.

Once inside Papa's tiny cabin, she built up the fire and began shucking off her soiled blue calico dress and the clumsy shoes that helped disguise her limp. The left boot heel was a good inch higher than the other, making her walk with a near-normal gait, if no one looked too closely. But since her trek in the woods, the heel was missing a shoe nail or two and in danger of coming off altogether. Her other pair was aboard the flatboat, perhaps gone for good. Papa had always seen to her shoes. Since he'd soon be back, she wouldn't worry about them.

Shivering, she decided to keep her stockings on, garters and all, along with her shift and petticoat. Her nightgown was missing too, locked in the leather trunk bearing her initials. Captain Stewart had sent out a scouting party as promised to inspect the damage and salvage what they could. She prayed they'd return on the morrow, scalps intact.

Tonight she'd forego the nightly brushing of her hair, given she didn't have so much as a comb. Nor did her father, she discovered—just a rusty razor lying beside a wash basin. The unfamiliar corn-husk tick seemed seeped with cold, and she struggled to bring the thin quilt up to warm her, too tired to say anything but the childhood prayer she'd learned so long ago.

Now I lay me down to sleep, I pray the Lord my soul to keep . . . She lay on her back, looking up at the firelight dancing on the crude ceiling, teeth chattering. *If I should die before I wake, at least I'll leave this dismal place.*

4

The snow was spitting, the wind punishing every man present.
Cassius McLinn stared hard at the glowering sky and ordered
his men to make a bonfire over the burial site. They would
have to thaw the unforgiving ground before they buried the six
soldiers they'd mistakenly shot at dusk. And they'd be making
twin fires this morning, he directed. Two of the prisoners—a
Redcoat and a redskin—had died in the night from wounds
received from yesterday's skirmish, and he vowed they'd not
share the same grave.

His men were watching him warily, watching the herd of prisoners, waiting for orders. He was bone weary—and feverish—
and trying to hide it. He was having to think everything through
twice to surmount the foggy miasma in his brain and hide the
swell of emotion behind it.

"Major Hale!" He looked around for his ailing second-in-
command and found him on the edge of the wood with some
men, bringing in deadwood for fires.

Micajah Hale came running. "Colonel, sir," he said, his pale
face pinched more from grief than the dysentery. His own cousin
had been mistakenly shot in the gloom, and though the regular
hadn't killed him, they both wished he had. Gut-shot he was,
and bleeding to death in the makeshift shelter behind them.

"Make sure the prisoners are fed so they'll be able to march. I'm sending Simmons out with a scouting party to make sure we aren't being followed. We'll set out as soon as we see to this." He gestured toward the struggling fires and stingy smoke.

Turning away, Cass crouched and entered the lean-to where Hale's cousin lay completely still. Was he already gone? Before the hope kindled, it was smothered as the wounded man moaned and moved an agitated hand. "Colonel?"

"Phineas." He said the captain's name as he'd said it a thousand times—but never with such regret. Phineas's dull eyes fluttered open and—could it be?—still regarded him with respect and affection.

"I—I—"

"Don't try to talk," Cass intervened, his own insides wrenched with pain. "Bail o Dhia ort." *The grace of God be with you.* The Gaelic rolled off his tongue effortlessly, though saying it nearly made him wince.

Where was God's grace in *this*?

Phineas's eyes rolled back and he moaned. Reaching inside his cloak, Cass brought out a silver flask and uncapped it, holding it to Phineas's wan lips and letting it dribble down to the last medicinal drop.

"Thankee, Colonel."

Cass put a hand on his sagging shoulder, saw the once-pristine shirt spattered red, and it seemed he could feel the life ebbing out of Phineas beat by beat. Cass's own cold fingers slid to his wrist and found the pulse weak.

"Guess I get to go home—to Eire—sooner than you."

Cass's throat tightened. "Aye, it does seem you're about to be promoted. If the Almighty hadn't beaten me to it, I might have made you a major."

A glimmer of a smile appeared, and Phineas gripped Cass's gloved hand harder. "Ye don't have t' tell 'bout this, Cass . . . 'twas just an accident . . . it might go badly after all your trouble . . . back east."

A blinding rush of emotion made the man before him a blur. Cassius McLinn had never felt less like an officer in his life.

Phineas was shaking now, more from the shock of blood loss, he guessed, than the bitter cold. Taking off his camlet cloak, Cass draped it over Phineas, but before it had been tucked under his chin, Phineas drew a final ragged breath. Unseeing amber eyes stared back at Cass and he moved to shut them. After drawing the cape over his friend's bent head, he half crawled out of the shelter, standing so suddenly he nearly toppled.

The snow was swirling now—his head was swirling—and the icy whiteness was up to the ankles of his boots. If they didn't dig the graves fast, they'd be caught in the belly of a blizzard and not make it back. He knew that was what his prisoners hoped—to be stalled here till word reached the upper Shawnee towns of the ambush and more British and Indians could come streaming down to skewer them.

Striding a bit unsteadily to where twin bonfires blazed, he took Major Hale aside and told him to dig an extra grave. That done, he walked over to the fallen men at the edge of the woods where they'd been laid. Studying the linen sheet covering them and weighted down with heavy rocks, he felt equally burdened. He knew each man simply by the sight of his boots.

At the very end was Richard Rowan. Kneeling, Cass uncovered him slightly, trying not to look at his face. Quickly he moved stiff fingers over the coarse wool of his uniform, feeling like a pickpocket as he searched for any personal items. Richard had had a fine watch once, and Cass had sometimes seen him reach into a hidden crevice of his coat and retrieve something else in a rare idle moment. Something small and silver that snapped when he shut it.

Strange how a body was so heavy once the spirit left. And cold . . . so cold. Cass felt half alive himself, doing this terrible disservice to a man who'd been hale and hearty but twelve hours before. He tried to think of anything but touching the familiar coat in this unfamiliar way. His mind kept returning to Cecily. Always Cecily. And the dress she'd been wearing when he'd last seen her. 'Twas the same color as this Continental coat—but dark blue silk, not wool, its folds slipping through his hands like water . . .

What would she think of him now?

When he'd nearly given up searching, his fingertips felt something smooth and round just above Richard Rowan's still heart. *Forgive me, old man.* In the harsh pewter light, he withdrew a piece of silver on a fine chain. A locket. The sight made his eyes sting, and he swallowed past the knot in his throat.

He remembered Richard had a wife in Virginia who'd died the previous year. For a week or so after receiving the news, he'd been unable to work, and Cass was struck by the depth of his grief—or regret. Soldiers had all kinds of regrets, mostly having to do with being away from hearth and home. Likely this silver locket contained his wife's portrait. Without thinking, he flicked at the tiny clasp and it sprung open in his hand. Just as suddenly, a speck of decency stung him and he moved to close it—but couldn't.

In his palm he held a woman . . . a girl. Not all gossamer and golden like Cecily. Nay, the likeness looking up at him seemed as finely made and enduring as the surrounding silver frame. He felt a strange twist of sentiment. How could an artist contain so much in such a small space—an even smaller face? For a moment he forgot he was kneeling and the wind was whipping the tails of his coat and the snow had frosted the russet queue of his hair.

Hair like black coffee. Eyes like blue trade beads. The oval face seemed entreating even in miniature, the full, unsmiling mouth a brushstroke of rose. There was something terribly alive within that lovely face, something so vibrant and far-reaching it couldn't be confined to a locket. Richard Rowan had never shown him this . . . girl-woman. But he knew who she was without a doubt.

Roxie.

5

Roxanna stood on the fort's frozen parade ground, her pale face tilted toward the same blue sky her father was walking beneath as he came back to her from wherever he was. Though she didn't know just how far he had to go, she had a feeling, with the weather worsening, he'd soon slip past the gates of the fort and swing her off the ground in welcome.

Simply thinking about it made her smile. She felt like a little girl again, awaiting him after a particularly lengthy enlistment, about to search his pockets for a sugar cone or some fascinating trinket from afar.

Two years they'd been apart. So much had happened inside those years. Thinking of it squeezed her heart into little pieces. That was why she stood here in the bitterness of mid-December, stirring a steaming kettle of lye-soaked laundry with a wash paddle. Staying inside Papa's cabin was too dangerous, the solitude resurrecting a host of memories she was desperate to forget. Yet she couldn't help but think of what her genteel mother, born and bred in Williamsburg, would make of this.

You must not act like the daughter of a common soldier, Roxanna. Never forget you have refined and polished roots. I may have married your father for love and cast away my own chances at becoming a Carter or a Randolph, but I'll not let you do the same.

Oh, what high hopes her mother had had for her! Sometimes Roxanna wondered if all the social scheming, the expense of finishing school, had led Mama to an early grave. Lifting a hand, she wiped away a tear as it slashed across her cold cheek. Papa had been a bitter disappointment to her mother. As a daughter, Roxanna had been no better. Though she tried to recall only pleasant things about her former life, there was more gall than good. This was why she must lose herself in work, as Papa always advised—even work that wasn't her own.

Minutes before, the black woman who served them supper each night had been tending to the wash and then disappeared. As Roxanna had watched from her window, studying the unfamiliar moods and rhythms of this strange fort, she soon saw that the fire beneath the huge copper kettle was dwindling and threatening to go out. Snatching up her cloak, she slipped onto the parade ground and began to feed the flames, adding dry wood stacked nearby, aware that the sentries at the gate were watching.

For several long minutes she waited for the woman to return, finally taking up the paddle to stir the dirty shirts and breeches. A sagging clothesline had been strung up between two posts, awaiting the wash to be wrung out and hung. Carefully, Roxanna began to lift each garment out of the gray water and place it in a draining trough till it was cool enough to handle.

She knew her help might not be appreciated, but she'd be doomed if she didn't do something—and she'd not lie abed like her wayward friends in the far cabins. She had awakened in the night to muted laughter and fiddle music but had soon fallen back asleep on the thin pallet made for her father's sturdy frame. Last night it seemed she was the only one abed. This morning it seemed she was the only one who wasn't, save the sentries and the elusive washerwoman.

Forehead furrowing, she thought again of Abby. Truth be told, she missed her, waif that she was. Olympia seemed intent on keeping her shut in with the Redstone women, and that was precisely what troubled her. What was going on behind their doors? Moreover, what would Colonel McLinn say when he arrived to find all this feminine company? Something told her he might not be as welcoming as his affection-starved men.

"Law, Miz Roxanna, you get away from that mess!" The strident voice seemed almost to shout, stinging her with embarrassment as she stood wringing out the first shirt. The sentries turned dull eyes on them, amusement enlivening their cold features.

The washerwoman was behind her now, scolding mightily. "What would your pa say to see you so? Washin' filthy breeches! Ain't no daughter of Richard Rowan gonna scald her hands on soldiers' rags!"

Roxanna kept right on wringing and looked over her shoulder with a half smile. "At least let me finish what I started."

She crossed thin black arms over a skeletal chest, her scowl slipping. "I know you is only tryin' to help me. But it pains me to see a lady doin' such." Casting a backward glance at the silent cabins in the morning shadows, she sighed. "Now, them hussies might need somethin' to do besides cattin' around all night and makin' mincemeat o' soldiers come mornin'."

Flushing at such plain talk, Roxanna took the first shirt and pinned it to the line. But would it dry? The wind gusted and tossed a few snowflakes about as she studied the surly sky before returning to the drain trough. "I don't believe we've met, at least properly."

The woman took up the wash paddle and began to stir idly. "My name's Bella, Miz Roxanna. Just Bella."

"Pleased to meet you, Bella." She took up some steaming breeches and began wringing them free of water. "You already know who I am, obviously."

A wide smile spread over the woman's lined, mahogany face. "Law, but you is just yo' pa in a dress. Nobody had to tell me so."

Pa in a dress, indeed. Roxanna didn't know whether to laugh or cry. "Do you really think he'd mind my helping you this fine morning?"

Bella grimaced and shook her head. "Naw. Reckon I got too many things goin' on all at once. Since them hussies come, Captain Stewart's given me a heap of washin'—and a mess of orders for victuals."

"I'm a fair hand in the kitchen. Love to cook, truth be told. When my mother took ill, the only thing she could keep down was a broth I concocted." This tidbit was tossed out and then Roxanna held her tongue, wondering how it would be received. But Bella pretended not to hear. They continued to work side by side in silence till all the wash was hung and not a dirty garment remained.

When Bella finally turned toward the far blockhouse, Roxanna followed. She was headed to the kitchen, she guessed, the same place they'd eaten last night. Her stomach growled a complaint, and she thought she could smell coffee when Bella opened the door.

Mercy, but what I'd give for another steaming cup sweetened with molasses . . . and an egg and a crust of bread besides.

An amused smile pulled at Roxanna's face as she walked in Bella's footsteps. The washerwoman well knew who shadowed her but didn't say a word, just trooped past long trestle tables in the dining hall, finally slipping through a squeaking door into a cold, dimly lit kitchen. Bella wouldn't ask for her help, she guessed, but neither would she shoo her away. Relief washed over her as she surveyed the friendly fire blazing in the huge hearth and the generous assortment of cooking vessels all around. This was like home, and felt familiar and safe and necessary.

"Shouldn't the men be up and at breakfast?" she asked.

Bella swung a skillet over the flames and huffed, "Should be . . . but ain't." Her lean fingers sliced bacon from a side of pork hanging from a hook in the corner. Tossing the pieces into the sizzling skillet, she poked at them with a long-tined fork. Spying a grinder, Roxanna began to make coffee, marveling at the abundance all around her in light of their meager meal last night.

Strings of yellowish-orange pumpkin slices hung from the rafters like festive Indian necklaces alongside garlands of shriveled-up apples and beans. Bushel baskets of potatoes and onions rested along a far wall beside kegs of flour and other essentials. And there were eggs—at least two dozen of them—big and brown in a wooden bowl atop a trestle table. And in the corner stood a churn.

"I already milked this mornin' and poured the old cream in, but I ain't churned." This revelation seemed more an invitation, and Roxanna wasted no time in donning an apron and taking a seat on a stool, her hands enfolding the smooth handle of the dasher like a long-lost friend. In time Bella went out and left her to all the little domestic details she'd so missed since leaving home.

Once the butter came, she wondered where the springhouse was or if she even needed it, given the cold. Poking around in every corner and crevice, she found a tub of lard and set about making biscuits, eyeing the dried apples overhead and dreaming of pies. Before Bella returned, two pans of biscuits rose to flaky, golden heights, and she began frying eggs in the bacon grease.

Ambrose always said I was the best cook in Fairfax County.

With a sigh, she let her thoughts drift. Perhaps if she'd been better at kissing . . . or bundling . . . or whatever else won a man's heart, she'd be standing in her own kitchen and not this crude one on the far frontier.

She'd come so close to being the wife of the gentleman her mother desired for her. They'd met at a horse race at Thistleton Hall, the estate that bordered their humble home. Soon Ambrose was coming round to court her, taking her and Mama to dine at a fine ordinary or to see a stage play. Twice they were guests at his townhouse in Richmond. Mama was smitten; Roxanna was unsure. And her uncertainties sprang up like poisonous weeds between them, thwarting her mother's best hopes. When she'd finally decided to give her heart away, having convinced herself he was the man for her, Ambrose had found comfort in the arms of another.

Taking a pewter plate, Roxanna slid an egg onto its tarnished surface, buttered the smallest biscuit, and sampled the chicory coffee. Divine.

"Law, but you look like you own the place!" Bella sputtered.

Heavens, I hope not, Roxanna mused. Sheepish, she slid off her stool and presented Bella with a plate, pouring her some coffee and sliding a crock of honey toward her. For a moment the tired eyes that met hers were a deep, damp brown. The silence in the shadowed kitchen stretched on till footsteps could be heard on the other side of the kitchen door. It swung open, and there stood Captain Stewart, unshaven and unpressed, his breeches and fine linen shirt looking sorely in need of a sadiron.

"Cap'n, sir," Bella said between bites of biscuit.

"You're just in time for breakfast," Roxanna told him, taking up another plate.

Heaping it full of food, she moved past him to the dining room where she plunked the plate down at the place he'd occupied last night. He followed meekly and sat as if speechless, watching as she served coffee and left him to his appetite.

"Law, but you gonna work me out of a job," Bella exclaimed when Roxanna returned to the kitchen.

"Just till Papa comes," she said with a satisfied smile. "Then you can have it all back again."

"Maybe I don't want it back," Bella breathed, eyes wide as Roxanna took a chair and climbed up to steal two dried apple strings from the timbers above.

"Idle hands are the devil's workshop. Isn't that what they say?"

"Can I have me another biscuit?"

"Certainly. Take two." Roxanna began measuring out flour and lard for pie dough, thinking she could flesh out Bella's spare frame, if not the remnant of men at the fort. "What shall we make for supper tonight?"

"Best talk to LeSourd—the fort hunter. He'll bring down anythin' you want to cook. Cap'n Stewart's partial to buffalo. But Colonel McLinn likes them beef cattle that come with the supply train."

"I don't see any sign of beef. Or Colonel McLinn. One buffalo, then. That should feed these men—about thirty, did you say?—and us guests." Her forehead furrowed as she added water to the dough. "I'm not familiar with buffalo, though. You'll have to show me how it's done."

"I'll fetch LeSourd," Bella said, going toward the dining room door and pushing it open a crack. "Law, but we got a mess o' men to feed this mornin.' They must have smelled yo' biscuits. If you cook, I'll serve. LeSourd'll have to wait."

The scraping of chairs along the puncheon floor and the men's muffled voices made Roxanna abandon her pie making. "It seems discipline is a bit lax among the men. I didn't hear reveille this morning."

Bella turned away from the door. "Colonel McLinn keeps his men strung tight as fiddle strings, but Cap'n Stewart—well, he ain't cut o' the same cloth. He and the colonel don't see eye to eye so the cap'n gets left behind to man the fort. And things get a little lax."

Expelling a relieved breath, Roxanna said, "So Captain Stewart isn't likely to turn me out of this kitchen, then."

Bella's dark face twisted with a knowing smile. "Naw, Miz Roxanna. He'll leave that to Colonel McLinn."

Pushing open the door to her father's cabin after breakfast, Roxanna surveyed his domain. On the mantel were some twists of Virginia tobacco alongside his treasured clay pipe. A worn wool cape dangled by the door above his boots. Tallow candles,

41

half burned, stood in pewter holders here and there. Taking up a poker, she stabbed at the smoking logs in the hearth as they tried to catch on their bed of sour ashes. At least so tiny a cabin was easy to heat, she mused, cheered again by the thought that Papa's enlistment was ending and they'd soon be on their way. If she could just keep her mind fastened on their future, she'd be able to tolerate her dark surroundings.

She breathed a thankful sigh that her belongings were intact, including her best gowns and beloved dulcimer. The detail Captain Stewart had sent out to the flatboat upriver had returned with her locked trunk and the possessions of the Redstone women, but the cargo of gunpowder, lead, and other valuables was missing, the vessel abandoned on the north side of the river. Where the surviving polemen had gone was anyone's guess.

Though she'd been here a fortnight, she was still disturbed by what she saw. Since Ma's passing, Papa had nearly gone to seed. Dust and spiderwebs decorated the tiny room, and she looked askance at the bed's tattered counterpane and a mountain of ashes that needed hauling from the hearth. This was so unlike her orderly father she winced. An assortment of quills and inkpots littered one small corner desk, a testament to her father's work. But this was white with dust as well, the quills down to nubs, the inkpots dry.

This was why she'd come. During her time as a tutor, traveling from one genteel house to another, she'd sensed he needed her. His letters, written in his characteristic longhand on fine foolscap, never said so, but she'd read lonesomeness and discontent between each and every line. And she, truth be told, needed him. Her Virginia life had become dull, predictable. She had faded to little more than Miss Rowan, a patient, capable tutor of children, invisible at best. To her father, and only her father, did she truly matter.

And so here she was—a surprise.

Laura Frantz

⸙

Bella watched Roxanna slip a darning egg in a stocking she was knitting. "You sure is handy with a needle. How many o' them socks have you made yo' pa? The way you're goin', I ain't ever goin' to have to wash a one. He'll have a new pair every day o' the week all year round."

Sheepish, Roxanna looked at the overflowing basket at her feet. "I can give some to the regulars who need them—the ones who don't have any womenfolk to tend them."

"Oh, there's plenty o' that kind around here. Just be careful who you give 'em to lest they think you come with 'em."

Roxanna managed a halfhearted smile. Bella couldn't possibly know about the broken betrothal—or her age. Past spinsterhood, she was. The reminder nipped at her with fierce little claws, though it was the memory of her mother's reprimands that most haunted.

Roxanna, how many times must I tell you not to slouch so? Proper posture is essential to the female form. No man wants a hunchback for a wife!

I'd never thought to have a spinster daughter. By your age I'd been wed eight years and become a mother three times over.

Are you applying lemon juice to your complexion? Why, you're as brown as an Indian! If I catch you without your bonnet one more time . . .

I suppose you might have a chance with one of your father's soldier friends, though the very idea makes me shudder. Look what marrying beneath one's station did in my case. You must promise me . . .

Roxanna sighed. "I promised Mama I'd not marry a soldier. And I doubt I'd tempt one—or be tempted."

Bella clucked her tongue. "You ain't met Colonel McLinn."

"No, but I've heard about him."

"Hearin' ain't seein'."

She looked up from her knitting in surprise. "Why, Bella, you sound bewitched by him."

"Law, Miz Roxanna. I just wash his clothes and tidy his house. Every woman from here to Virginny is smitten with him. Settlement gals come canoein' upriver just to eyeball him. He's that handsome. Some say the Almighty was so pleased after He made the one that He had to make two."

Twin McLinns? "He has a brother, then?" Roxanna's interest piqued and her needles picked up in rhythm. "Papa never described Colonel McLinn to me except to say he's the finest officer he's ever served under since Light-Horse Harry Lee."

"Hmmm." Bella got up to take the hissing kettle off the fire. "Them's mighty fine words. Your pa was always one to find the good in folks."

The scent of sassafras, brewed strong and pink, warmed the pewter mug Bella handed her. Abandoning her knitting, Roxanna sipped it gratefully, thinking she hadn't been warm since her arrival. She sat opposite Bella in a rare idle moment, and they huddled close enough to the flames to singe their hair and homely dresses. Like a pair of old crows they were, Roxanna thought, drinking tea and trying not to gossip. But the fodder in the fort provided plenty, and it seemed Bella was about to enlighten her further.

"Your pa ain't uttered one bad word against Colonel McLinn?"

"Not one," she answered honestly, thinking back to the letters he'd sent since coming under the colonel's command. "I think Papa considers him something of a son, working with him so closely and all."

"And *all*." Bella's black brows knit together over piercing eyes.

Obviously Bella was itching to spill some secret. Roxanna bit her tongue to keep from uttering the maxim she'd oft repeated to her pupils. *Be not hasty to believe flying reports to the disparagement of any.* She eyed the half-finished sock in her lap, the indigo wool soft as thistledown. She didn't want to delve deeper—indulge in gossip. Truly, Papa had only spoken well of the man.

Bella licked her lips. "Did your pa, saint that he is, ever mention why Colonel McLinn was sent west?"

Sent. It had an ominous sound, particularly for an officer. "Nay."

"Or that he drives his men unmercifully?"

"Nay."

"Or that he holds a court-martial nearly every day?"

"Nay."

"Or that he can curse in three languages?"

"Three?" Roxanna raised an eyebrow. "One should be sufficient."

Bella cracked a smile. "Gaelic, French, and King's English—in case you're wonderin'."

"He's not a God-fearing Irishman, then?"

"Humph!" Bella rolled her eyes. "He don't fear nothin'. Awful arrogant he is. Browbeats his men somethin' awful—and he's a gentleman besides!" She paused in her tirade and stared into her steaming cup. "But they nearly worship him, God forgive 'em, though I don't know why."

Roxanna sipped her tea and tried to tamp down her curiosity—and another maxim that rushed to mind. *Speak not evil of the absent, for it is unjust.* Squelching it, she simply savored her sassafras and said nothing, cowing Bella into a short-lived silence.

Shifting in her chair, Bella expelled a ragged breath. "All I'll say is this—Colonel McLinn used to be one o' General Washington's favorite officers, one o' them Life Guards, watchin' over the general and all for his protection. Till McLinn got in a roarin' red rage 'bout somethin' and Washington sent him west."

Though her ears were burning, Roxanna remained silent.

Bella leaned forward conspiratorially. "You sure yo' pa ain't said nothin' 'bout this?"

"Nary a word."

She sighed. "Well, I wish to heaven he had cuz I'm just about eat up with not knowin.'"

Roxanna leaned over to hide a smile and tucked her knitting into the basket at her feet. "So I gather Colonel McLinn is an extraordinarily handsome Irishman who manages to be quite charming when master of his temper."

"Did I mention he's malarial?"

"Nay, to your credit."

"Well, once in a while he gets real sick and takes to his bed. He ain't easy to nurse neither. I've tried my hand at it a time or two. I'd rather wash his shirts and breeches any day."

"Does he not have a personal physician?"

"That'd be the post surgeon, Dr. Wilbur. But he up and died last spring." Sighing, Bella stood and shuffled toward the door. "Somethin' tells me I ain't gonna get to sit here takin' tea with you much longer. The colonel's gonna come round the bend with all his men just in time for Christmas like he promised. I'd best go on to bed. Guess I'll be dreamin' about roast goose and plum puddin' when I do."

Roxanna's eyes flew to the crude calendar on the cabin wall. Five more days. Tears of joy and anticipation made the numerals a wash of black. 'Twould be the first Christmas with her father in years. He'd simply not had leave since then.

When Bella went out, Roxanna knelt by the trunk that held all her earthly possessions and opened the lid. Inside was the pocket watch she'd purchased upon leaving Virginia, the fine silver chain shining richly in the hearth light. Papa had lost his during the last campaign, he'd written, or had it stolen, as was so often the case. She turned it over, seeing the fine engraving on the back—her initials and the date of Christmas 1779. Lying under this was her best Sabbath dress, the heavy corded linen finely embroidered with flowers that mirrored the blue of her eyes. A straw hat with a clump of forget-me-nots on the brim lay alongside the dress and reminded her of spring and long walks and . . . him. An unwelcome memory rose up as strongly as the lavender sachet within . . .

"Come, Miss Rowan, and walk out with me."

The smooth masculine voice unnerved her, perhaps because he'd been away for so long. She looked up from her damask roses, senses swimming from their sweetness, and felt a flicker of disquiet. Aware that her mother watched from a window, she set her clippers and basket aside and took the arm Ambrose offered, hoping her straw hat was on straight.

"I've just returned from Richmond on business. I apologize for being away for so long."

"How is . . . business?" As soon as she asked, she wished the words back, her mother's latest rebuke ringing in her ears.

'Tis most unladylike to inquire about masculine pursuits.

"Nothing to worry your pretty head about." He smiled at her and patted her hand as it rested on his coat sleeve. "I am a bit discouraged, however. With the war on, things are not what they should be." He hesitated, fixing his attention on a far fence that marked the border of Thistleton Hall. "I've lost a valuable account of late. A British one. Mr. Abernathy is returning to London. But even if he wasn't, he says he can no longer do business with me, given the fact that I have . . . Patriot associations. He recently learned of our betrothal, you see."

"Oh?"

"Of course, I assured him that your loyalties—and your mother's—lie with England."

Her hand slipped from his sleeve. "But that's not true—not on my part. I believe the colonists—the Patriots—have good reason to oppose England. At least based on what little I know. Granted, my mother, being British, is sympathetic to her native country—"

"I don't mean to upset you, Miss Rowan. Let's leave these scurrilous politics to the men who make them. We must speak of other things."

She studied him, looking beyond his thinning, tobacco-colored hair to hazel eyes sharp in their censure. Not once had she ever heard him take a stand and declare his own opinion of anything, not even the war. His views depended on whom he was speaking to, whoever was in the room. Fickle as the copper weathervanes he sold in his Richmond shop, she thought, capable of turning in any direction.

"No need to let business—or politics—interfere with more heartfelt matters," he said stiffly. "Come, we'll walk to the carriage. I've brought you and your mother a little something from the city."

She tried to be effusive about the lovely bonnet he gave her, but her mother was far more enthusiastic about her tin of sweetmeats. Later she learned he'd gotten the gifts after his dalliance with the woman who was now his wife . . .

Roxanna shut the trunk with a bang as if doing so could shut away the memory, but felt she'd slammed her finger in the lid instead. Even the slightest reminder stung, though she'd tried her best to forget. Indeed, she'd come downriver four hundred miles to escape it, all the way to this frightening place. She should have pitched the hat in the Ohio River along the way, but as it was her favorite, she didn't.

Lying down on the freshly made bed, she smiled at the rustle of the corn-husk tick, thinking of the feather one she'd left behind. Truly, her new life here on the far frontier hardly held one reminder of her old one. At home, in their small stone house, she'd had a fine four-poster bed with plump pillows and a calico cat that slept at her feet, rag rugs on polished pine floors, a clothespress scented with rose sachet. All such amenities were missing here. Thinking it left her feeling a bit hollow.

But, she decided, the wilderness was a fine antidote to all her regrets. Soon, very soon, she and Papa would leave this inhospitable place and be on their way to a new home. A new life. She needn't think again of Ambrose or the future she might have had.

6

Wrapping herself in her heavy woolen cloak, Roxanna wandered to the fort's front gate and looked out a loophole to the wide Ohio River. In the twilight of late December, the water was more opal than emerald, the trees along its muddy banks shivering like skeletons in the wind. Try as she might, she couldn't hear a sound. No crunch of marching boots over frozen ground, no shouted commands or chatter of drums, no thud of hoofbeats or clink of canteens.

Just above her head, the garrison's name was embedded in a huge oaken timber. *Fort Endeavor.* The farthest-reaching fort on the western frontier. 'Twas home to some of the finest soldiers Virginia had to offer in defense of the Kentucke territory, or so her father said. Behind her flew the flag of that fine colony, stiff as a starched petticoat in the brisk wind.

Glancing to her right, she could see musket balls embedded in thick log walls. Overhead a cannon jutted like an ugly beak from the parapets just above. Drawing her cape closer, she shivered. There was something terribly lethal about this place, something so at odds with Christmas peace. A few sentries stood watch and nodded to her when she passed, eyes more on her than the river and woods.

Oh, Lord, to be rid of this place for good.

49

Her gaze wandered to the west wall where the Redstone women still slumbered in a far cabin. Except for meals, she'd hardly seen them since their arrival. It seemed they slept all day and caroused all night. She continually worried about Abby and tried to think of a way to befriend the child, but nothing reasonable had yet come to mind. Even if she made the effort, she'd soon be gone. So why try?

Tomorrow was Christmas Day. Bella was busy preparing a feast, and Roxanna had helped her concoct a number of pies and puddings since dawn. LeSourd had delivered not only another buffalo but several fat turkeys now soaking in salt water. At day's end they'd gotten down on their hands and knees and scoured the dining room floor with river sand, then set fresh candles out, along with a barrel of cherry bounce that the colonel was so fond of.

"Colonel McLinn promised his men he'd have 'em back by Christmas," Bella had told her. "My man Hank told me so hisself. He fetches and carries for him."

Hank. Her husband? Roxanna wondered, trying to make note of the name.

Now, pondering the silent woods, Roxanna wagered the colonel and his men were gathered round some distant campfire only dreaming of Fort Endeavor and remembering that promise. And Papa . . . was he thinking of her? Thinking she was still in Virginia, earning her keep as a tutor? Betrothed to Ambrose, perhaps? Or recalling the last holiday they'd spent together years before?

Her thoughts turned to other heartfelt matters, like the Christmas service held at their little country church in Virginia, every pew bedecked with evergreens and ribbon and countless candles. All that seemed a world away, and she missed it with a fierceness she'd not thought possible, though she didn't understand why she should. Aside from church, which had always been her solace, her happy memories were mere crumbs.

Last Christmas had hardly been merry. With her mother ill

and Ambrose distancing himself more by the day, she'd taken Christmas dinner alone. Standing by a rain-soaked windowpane in their quiet kitchen, she fancied she heard a fiddle at Thistleton Hall. She'd missed her father so fiercely then, missed his ability to make the best of whatever situation he was in. If Papa had been home, he'd have opened the window wide, caught her about the waist, and danced to that fiddle as it echoed in the crisp air . . .

Remembering it all, Roxanna leaned against the postern gate and looked west from her peephole toward the frozen woods. The everlasting stillness seemed broken now. Could it be? The forest was coming alive with the anticipated clink of canteens and crunch of boots and other things she couldn't name. Within seconds the sentries on the banquette above stood straighter and looked more soldierly, and even Bella appeared outside the kitchen door.

Time seemed suspended as the sounds crept closer, yet the men making them stayed hidden. Noiselessly, the sentries moved to open the gates. Within minutes there appeared a half-frozen procession of soldiers streaming through the far trees, chests crisscrossed with the white belts of their weapons, each sporting a dark tricorn hat. Her eyes roamed the group hungrily, heart in her throat. The troops were more distinguishable the closer they came and far larger than they first appeared. One hundred . . . two?

Where in this large company was her father? She should have been looking for him, beloved as he was. But she had eyes for one man only.

The figure at the front of the throng seemed to be looking at her even as she looked at him, his keen eyes drilling her from a distance, making her wish she was standing back with Bella in the doorway of the kitchen and not struck smitten at the gate like some settlement girl.

There was something riveting in the way he sat atop his horse, his rich blue camlet cloak flowing to the stallion's belly and touching the tops of his boots. The rigid set of his whiskered jaw and the contrasting queue of copper braid snaking past his collar seemed to shout for attention. Could this be the commander her father had spoken of so highly? She hadn't expected him to be so young or so . . . astonishing.

One long look at Cassius McLinn did more to displace Ambrose in her mind than had six months of crying and trying to forget. He simply collapsed like a paper caricature in the colonel's sturdy shadow. She thought Bella had merely exaggerated the colonel's charms. She never dreamed she'd understated them.

When Roxanna had gathered her wits, she stepped back inside the gate and watched the soldiers file past, shrinking the parade ground in the deepening dusk. They all looked alike to her now in the shadows, and she felt almost dizzy trying to find her father. Voices were sounding everywhere around her, and she spied Olympia and Abby at the door of their cabin with the other Redstone women. Next came a swarm of grim prisoners, a mix of redskins and Redcoats, all tethered together in a long line. Watching them, she felt a chill clear to her bones.

This . . . at Christmas.

She'd seen her share of British soldiers in Virginia, but few Indians. Even bound with chain and hemp rope, these tawny men walked proudly past, a colorful parade of buckskin and buffalo robes, quills and beads and feathers, silver ornaments dangling from arms and ears and ebony heads.

She'd expected to witness some jubilance among the soldiers at being back inside fort walls before Christmas as promised, but not one contented face did she find. No festive feeling suffused the air, no shouts of greeting. Out of the corner of her eye, she caught the Virginia flag being lowered on its staff. Down, down, down it came till it was limping at half-mast. A strange silence swept through the crowd as soldiers began to remove their tricorn hats. Watching, Roxanna remained at the gate as if frozen, her gaze sweeping over the strangely muted group to the steadfast figure of Bella still standing at the kitchen door.

Even from a distance, her dark face looked drawn and distracted. It seemed Bella's eyes were everywhere at once, as restless and searching as her own. Could she not find her Hank? Roxanna had just seen a black man in homespun speaking with another man beneath the flagstaff. Surely this was he.

Bella seemed to be searching for someone else now—and with a start Roxanna realized it was her father. Within moments Bella had crossed the crowded parade ground and placed a hand on Roxanna's sleeve, and it seemed her touch was altogether too firm.

Never had her heart thudded so hard beneath her Sabbath-best dress. Soon it seemed the only thing keeping her upright was the pressure of Bella's bony fingers on her arm. Roxanna hardly noticed the soldiers staring at her in the gloom as if trying to piece together the puzzle of her appearance.

That she was Richard Rowan's daughter there could be no doubt. Nor could there be any doubt that the man now standing before her, towering over her as he dismounted, was Colonel Cassius McLinn. No introductions were needed on either score.

The hard knot of alarm in her throat kept her from speaking. She could only stare mutely at him, his startling azure eyes transmitting a hundred dreadful messages as they held her own. Her gaze shifted, falling to the braided collar of his cape. She watched his throat tighten visibly as if he struggled to say something. It took every shred of her composure to keep from crying out.

Suddenly he spun away without a word, parting the lingering soldiers who stood about woodenly waiting for orders, before disappearing completely into a far blockhouse. For once Bella was speechless. She didn't even acknowledge the black man who came over to them, his face worn with weary lines, eyes bloodshot. He stood with them in a sore circle, saying nothing, hat in hand, and Roxanna felt an appalling dread.

Something terrible had happened on this campaign.

7

Cass eyed the orderly who stood in the doorway of the block-house awaiting his directive. Behind him, another fumbled with flint and tinder at the cold hearth, trying to kindle wood with nervous hands. He wanted to send them out of the room, but he had need of them both—one to summon Richard Rowan's daughter and the other to make a fire in the stone house.

The oak and leather tang of his headquarters, coupled with the candlelit darkness, seemed foreign since he'd been away so long. The fog in his brain seemed only to have thickened on the return march, and by the time they'd reached the ice-encrusted creek that signaled an end to their misery, he'd nearly fallen off his horse. Now, simply removing his tricorn and cloak and placing them on the wall pegs behind him took supreme effort.

How, by the Eternal, would he have the wits to tell this woman her father wasn't coming back?

The shock of seeing her had nearly stripped him of his stupor. Hidden in his breast pocket was the locket that assured him that this was indeed Roxie Rowan. Her face and form had risen up like some specter in a Shakespeare tragedy, demanding he give a reckoning for his sins. He couldn't postpone telling her. If he dallied, someone else on the parade ground might do it—or perhaps she'd already surmised the obvious.

He pinned the orderly at the door with aching eyes. "Richard Rowan's daughter is with Bella on the parade ground. Bring her here."

"Aye, sir."

The heavy door shut, and he stared at its bulk, wanting to sit down. Behind him the fire was finally blazing, and the orderly timidly asked if he needed anything else.

Aye, he felt like shouting. *I need Richard Rowan—hale and hearty—just as he was when I sent him on a fool's errand into the woods!*

He dismissed the orderly and stayed stoic in the stillness. Long minutes ticked by before Richard's daughter stood before him, Bella and Hank flanking her. With a look he dismissed them as well. Roxanna Rowan looked up at him, and then her eyes seemed to make a clean sweep of the dim, damp room. The shock of stale air—the reek of rum and stale tobacco—assaulted his senses after being so long outdoors. Surely it did hers as well.

His massive desk was between them, and he leaned toward her slightly, palms flat upon the polished wood. His lips parted then closed. He'd expected to simply send her a letter. All the way back to the fort he'd composed what he would say, never dreaming he'd have to meet her face-to-face. And now the woman in the locket was looking back at him with that same unsmiling mouth, her lovely eyes doe-like, almost beseeching, her body tensed like she was about to take flight.

Was she trembling?

A rush of pity stirred him. He took in her finely embroidered gown, no doubt worn for her father's homecoming, and his eyes lingered on the blue ribbon in her upswept black hair. But his gaze kept returning to those eyes. They regarded him warily—even suspiciously—making this terrible thing he must do all the harder.

The violent ache in his chest expanded, and his head thudded like it had been grazed with a tomahawk. He was too sick to do this with any semblance of grace. She was staring at him, and her oval face had turned so poignant it only made what he had to say doubly hard because she seemed to be sorry for him—for him having to tell her.

The realization stunned him. Tears gathered at the corners of his eyes and he blinked them back.

She said softly, "Sir . . . you are trying to tell me . . . about my father."

He simply looked at her.

She took a small step away from the desk and held up a hand as if to stop his unwelcome words. "He's not—"

"Miss Rowan—"

"—coming back." She blinked and backed up further, and when he tried to speak again, she whispered, "Please . . . don't."

The simple words were a broken plea that he understood completely. "I'm . . . so . . . sorry." He ground his back teeth to steady his voice, but the Irish lilt of his words seemed to pulsate with anguish. Could she hear his deep regret?

She spun away without another word, and relief coursed through him. Perhaps it was enough, he thought.

For now.

❧ ❧

Roxanna lay on the bed her father had lain on in life, dry-eyed and disbelieving. Her shock and lonesomeness was eased somewhat by Bella's snoring on the pallet near the hearth. She'd wanted to be alone, but Bella had insisted she stay near, if just for one night, and Roxanna had been too benumbed to protest.

I should be growing used to this grieving.

But she was learning that there were all kinds of grief. Ever-present ones like feeling forever unattractive or unaccomplished. Then those that hollowed out an undeniable ache inside, like the loss of a mother who was never satisfied. A broken betrothal . . . a heart betrayed. What kind of grief would the loss of her beloved father prove to be? Taken one at a time these were bearable, but heaped together they were too much.

Father in heaven . . . help Thou me.

The stone house, always welcoming as a woman's arms, now felt like a tomb. Cass passed through the front door, hardly aware of Hank on his heels and the orderlies scattering below to kindle fires. The room at the top of the stairs was cast in deep shadows, and the enormous bed specially made for his tall frame seemed the only furnishing in it. As he walked, he stripped off his coat and soiled shirt, then bent down to unfasten his garters and remove mud-spattered leggings.

My apologies, Bella.

He was in no condition to be tidy tonight. A trail of clothing led from the staircase landing to the threshold of his bedchamber and then to a corner washbasin skimmed with ice. He dunked his head in the chill water, and his feverish brow seemed to sizzle.

He needed help with his boots, and Hank was there with the bootjack, pulling them off before he asked. He was too sick to bathe. Too sick for his usual double dose of whiskey. With any luck, he'd be asleep before the worst of the delirium hit. Perhaps this time the attack wouldn't be so bad and he could begin to make amends to Miss Rowan. As his backside deflated the fine feather tick, he remembered the locket.

His speech was almost slurring now. "Hank, bring me my coat—top of the stair." Hank hurried to obey.

In the light of a single tallow candle, he flicked open the miniature and studied the vulnerable, winsome face within. He'd done the same in the blockhouse before the flesh-and-blood Roxanna came in—only beneath all that fragility was a wall of composure he'd not reckoned with. He'd seen hardened soldiers bear bad news with less grace.

Miss Rowan, I will honor your father's request and take care of you—though you may not want me to.

Under any other circumstance, one would think Cassius Clayton McLinn was trying to woo her. His courting began with a letter, slipped by an orderly beneath her cabin door. She heard its rustle from her bed, though she continued to lie a long time before rising to retrieve it. The sight of the paper brought a queer pang, for it was the same linen paper Papa had used in all his letters to her, only the handwriting on the outside was distinctly different. She could almost imagine the writer taking up a goose quill and dipping it quickly into an inkpot, writing with strong, slashing pen strokes that dominated the page before her.

There, on the outside, he'd penned her name. *Miss Roxanna Rowan.* Twice folded, the letter bore McLinn's indigo wax seal. For a time she could only hold it, preparing herself for what she knew lay within. He was trying to tell her on paper what he had been unable to tell her in person, in private. The thoughtfulness of the missive touched her, only she couldn't read it. Not yet.

It had come early Christmas morn, before the day was touched by dawn, making her wonder if he'd lain awake all night like she. At noon Bella came round with a tray of the finest soldierly fare Fort Endeavor had to offer. Roast goose. Chestnut stuffing. Apple tansy. Mashed potatoes and turnips with a well of gravy. Beaten biscuits and gingerbread. Only she couldn't eat a bite.

"I got me some help in the kitchen," Bella said. "A couple of them Jezebels decided to rouse and help once they heard about your pa."

Toward dusk something else appeared. A small package. This she opened. The lovely contents made her want to weep. She was sitting in Papa's chair by the flickering hearth, having forgotten to light a single candle, yet the exquisite offering in her hands needed no illumination.

Never had she seen so fine a china cup—perfectly white,

so fragile she feared it might crack if she simply looked at it. Around its rim was a lovely thistle pattern, the handle fluted and gold-trimmed and painted with a fleur-de-lis. Instinctively she knew it came from the stone house, not this roughshod fort. But that was not all. A sealed tin of tea was within, smelling of refinement and ease and the olden days under British rule. Did Colonel McLinn know she was partial to tea and not coffee, like her father? Next came a dainty silver strainer with hooked chain for keeping the leaves from the cup. He'd thought of everything, truly.

Bella appeared and watched her from the doorway. Despite her grief, could her friend sense her pleasure? Was this Colonel McLinn's intent? Unable to speak, she simply set the things on the low table next to her and began to prepare hot water, swinging the copper kettle over the flames.

"Come, Bella, and we'll share this fine gift."

Though her voice and hands quavered, she brewed a fine Christmas tea, rich with fresh cream from the springhouse and a crock of honey from the fort's hives. Bella made her take the thistle cup, choosing a common pewter one for herself. They sat in silence and sipped the steaming brew, watching the fire pop and spark, aware of the twang of a fiddle across the parade ground.

With a sigh, Bella drained the last of her cup. "This is the sorriest Christmas I ever spent, with you in mournin' and Colonel McLinn sick over in the stone house and all them Injuns in the guardhouse lookin' like they're ready to burn the place down."

Roxanna set her cup aside, recalling the unnatural flush in the colonel's face and his bloodshot blue eyes. "I knew he was unwell when I first saw him. Is there someone to tend him?"

"Not a soul 'cept my Hank. The post surgeon's long buried, remember?" She stirred from her chair and cast Roxanna a baleful look. "The colonel did send word he wants to see you when you're able—and he's able."

Roxanna eyed the letter. She didn't want to face him a second time, nor did she want to read the letter. But once Bella went out, she broke the wax seal. The fine paper bore the watermark of a Continental soldier, musket in arms, with the legend *Pro Patria* beneath. His boldly penned words seemed to leap from the page, and before she'd finished the first line, her eyes were swimming.

> *My dear Miss Rowan,*
>
> *Seven times I've taken pen in hand yet find I cannot summon the words to express how I feel about your heartrending loss . . .*

The carefully couched words seemed only to finalize the fact that her father wasn't coming back and she was four hundred miles from civilization without a shilling to her name to return her there. Hot tears splashed onto the paper, making the ink spot and run.

> *Your father died in the line of duty, honorable to the end . . . not only a scrivener of the first rank but a fine soldier. I was with him at the last and must convey his concern for you, his beloved daughter. Indeed, his final words were these: "Take care of my Roxie."*

She got up onto the bed where her father's unforgettable tobacco scent still lingered and bit her lip till it nearly bled. Colonel McLinn's letter still lay in her hand, and she turned away from it, perplexed.

He hadn't told her how it had happened. "In the line of duty," he'd said. What did that mean exactly? Indian arrow? British saber? An accident? Perhaps it was better he'd spared her the particulars. He was a gentleman, after all.

And what did it truly matter? Knowing the sordid details wouldn't bring Papa back.

The letter fluttered to her feet, and she gave way to the pain lashing her heart. Sinking down on the dusty hearth stones, she put her head in her hands and wept.

8

Papa's worn Bible on the trestle table seemed to call to her. When she'd first arrived, it had been open to the Psalms. Now it was turned to Ecclesiastes as if moved by some unseen hand. Bella, perhaps? In the dim light of the first day of January, Roxanna leaned over the candlelit page and let the words seep into her worn soul and begin to miraculously mend it.

To every thing there is a season, and a time to every purpose under the heaven: a time to be born, and a time to die.

She'd been very little when Papa had taken her on his knee and told her how it was to be a soldier. He'd served with the British during the French and Indian War, long before he'd joined the American army. 'Twas a hard life. Adventuresome. Dangerous. Deadly. But death hadn't been a stranger to any of them back then. Her brother William had drowned before the age of eight, and baby John had died of a fever. After that, 'twas just her and her parents in their snug stone house, somewhat reminiscent of Colonel McLinn's. There'd been no more children. Papa was often away with the army, and somehow she'd grown accustomed to the lonesome absences, if her mother had not.

She remembered that Papa believed a man was born not by happenstance but by design, that the Almighty fixed one's time on earth like He fixed the stars in heaven. There were accidents, calamities, death. But these were ordained also.

Still, her heart hurt.

Hungrily, she searched the next verse, her sadness tempered word by word. *A time to weep, and a time to laugh; a time to mourn, and a time to dance.* Oh, how she wanted to laugh—and dance! Was there to be only weeping and mourning in her future? If she stayed in this cheerless room and was of no use to anyone, there would be. And she simply must see about Abby.

She dressed in indigo wool, sweeping her hair back with pins so that it warmed her bare neck. Blowing out a solitary candle and banking the fire, she slipped out onto the frozen parade ground, so unobtrusive that not even the sentries took notice. She was drawn to the big blockhouse kitchen, glad to find it empty, the hearth containing a few red embers beneath its bed of ashes. In time she had it blazing and was boiling water, grinding coffee, cracking eggs, and making breakfast. For an army.

An hour later Bella appeared, wide-eyed and grateful. "Law, Miz Roxanna, you can smell them cakes clear to my cabin. I hope you've made a heap o' coffee cuz the men are startin' to rouse."

Dovie and Nancy soon followed, red-eyed and yawning. Had they been up all night? Roxanna greeted them, hardly pausing in her work, glad to find them too tired to talk. She served them cups of steaming coffee and they smiled wearily, peering out the crack in the kitchen door as the dining room filled.

Within minutes Abby arrived in a dirty frock, her curls a rat's nest of red tangles. Relief flooded Roxanna. "Morning, Abby," she said with a smile, handing her a long wooden spoon. "I could use some help. Would you stir the syrup, please?"

Abby nodded, ever solemn, and Roxanna noted how blue-gray her eyes were, stormy as the Atlantic on a blustery day, the dark shadows half moons beneath. Was the women's carousing keeping her awake? 'Twas time—past time—to talk to Olympia about Abby.

This morning she'd heard reveille for the first time since arriving at Fort Endeavor. Colonel McLinn was back, and sick as he was, some semblance of order had been restored in the wake of Captain Stewart's lax command, after a brief period of mourning. Taking a huge platter, she began to stack pancakes half a foot high, eyeing Abby as she stirred the kettle of maple syrup she'd set to warming.

Someone had churned—or tried to—but the butter hadn't set properly and was more a puddle. Roxanna dumped it into the pot of syrup, smiling in approval as Abby stirred more vigorously. Pancake making always reminded her of her mother, who'd been more at home by the hearth than anywhere else in the house. She held on to the image now, saw her mother's bent, graying head intent on her task, nearly tasted the jams and preserves they'd concocted. If Mama had ever been happy, it had been in her kitchen. Distracted by the bittersweet memory, Roxanna poured more batter on a big griddle slick with lard, trying not to wince as Bella bossed Dovie and Nancy.

"Now, snap to it and go round with these cakes, startin' with Major Hale near the head o' the table. Then take the syrup round next and give 'em each a dip, but don't let 'em manhandle the ladle away from you, you hear? Some o' them men are more hog than soldier. There's got to be enough for everybody, remember. I won't have Miz Roxanna workin' those fine hands o' hers to the bone makin' more."

Nancy made a face and took the platter, leaving Dovie the syrup kettle. Still yawning, they disappeared into the dining room. As the door cracked open, the warm sound of laughter and the scraping of chairs filled the cold space. Bella followed with a mound of jowl bacon and a pot of coffee, and Roxanna sighed. Cooking was a pleasure, even for a crowd—when provisions were plenteous, the men were content, *and* she could hide in the kitchen.

Truth be told, all those broad backs and booming voices made her more melancholy than ever, given her father should have been among them. She could hear murmurs of approval and Dovie's high-pitched tone squeaky as a fiddle string. The merry tenor of men's voices grew bolder and less distinct as more soldiers flocked to the tables.

And then the hubbub ground to a sudden halt. All she heard was the clink of a fork as it hit the plank floor and a muted round of respectful murmurs that might have been a greeting. Ears taut, she continued making pancakes—and would do so till Bella told her to quit. She fixed Abby a plate near the warm hearth, relieved when she wolfed down two pancakes and held up her plate for a third.

Bless her heart . . . Hadn't Olympia been feeding her? Where was Olympia anyway?

With a sudden whoosh, the kitchen door opened and Bella swept in with an empty platter and coffeepot, face tense. "Colonel McLinn just come in."

Roxanna said nothing, watching as Bella took a clean pewter cup and began to brew something from a small tin. "It's cinchona bark—good for bein' malarial. But best serve him some of yo' fine coffee too. He ain't eat for nigh on a week, Hank says, so keep right on makin' them cakes."

The feeling in the air seemed different now, and she could hear the distinct lilt of an Irishman, followed by an onslaught of fresh laughter. Was the colonel up to making jokes? She hoped it wasn't about his breakfast! He'd said but a mouthful of words to her, yet she sensed it must be him. Her flush, brought on by the heat of the hearth fire, deepened. Just what had he said to her Christmas Eve?

Miss Rowan . . . I'm so sorry . . .

Remembering made her eyes sting, and she lifted a corner of her apron discreetly. Bella was at her side at once. "Now, you go on back to yo' cabin and get out o' this here kitchen. Most of the men are done eatin' anyway. But best leave out the back door so *he* won't see you."

Biting her lip, Roxanna stood steadfastly and flipped the cakes. "I was hoping you'd ask me to help you do the washing next."

Bella looked aghast. "Law, but you'd best get that out o' yo' head once and for all. The colonel's back, and such a thing won't be done on his watch, let me tell you. If he even finds you in this kitchen, he'll have my hide for supper!"

Nancy returned, bleary-eyed and empty-handed. "We need more pancakes and bacon—and coffee. Quick."

Roxanna heaped another platter high, glancing up as she exited. In the split second before the door shut, she could make out the colonel sitting in uniform at the head of the long table, his broad back to her, the bright queue of his hair bound with black silk ribbon and falling between widespread shoulder blades.

In moments Dovie returned, cheeks pink, eyes on Roxanna. "The colonel sends his compliments to the cook . . . and he says he's wantin' to know *who* the cook is."

Bella moved to stand near her, her voice a strained whisper. "And what all did you tell him?"

"I ain't stupid," Dovie hissed. "I said he'd best ask *you*."

Bella rolled her eyes and slapped her thigh with a dishrag. "Miz Roxanna, you best get on back to yo' cabin."

But Roxanna merely smiled and shook her head, filling the coffeepot again with a steady hand. "Leave Colonel McLinn to me, Bella. This is my doing, not yours, remember."

Bella's dark face creased with fresh agitation. "I never figured on him comin' over from the stone house so soon. You see, the real cook and his helper deserted while the colonel was gone on this here campaign, and Hank ain't had the time or the gumption to tell him. And this ain't the day to do it with a court-martial about to commence and some soldiers set for floggin' and all them prisoners to fret over."

Suddenly a pall seemed cast over the day. Roxanna looked around the overwarm kitchen with mixed emotions. In the fortnight she'd been its mistress, save the week she'd spent mourning Papa's passing, it had made the hours in this wretched place move faster. Would Colonel McLinn now oust her?

She didn't have the heart to return to the cold cabin where Papa's shadow seemed to linger in every corner. And she'd rather be occupied here than having to linger there and wonder about all this bad business involving court-martials and floggings and prisoners of war—and how much like a prisoner she was as well.

She took Papa's watch from her dress pocket. Half past eight. Her mind was already moving to the noon meal—

"Miss Rowan."

Slowly she turned toward the sound. There was no one in the kitchen now save her . . . and him. Cassius McLinn stood in the doorway, arms crossed, a gaunt giant. The ravages of illness highlighted every single feature of his handsome, intense face, and his eyes seemed awash—a glittering lapis blue.

"Colonel McLinn," she returned.

"'Twas a fine breakfast."

She nodded her thanks and nearly curtsied. What was it about this man that made her want to bow and scrape? Her back stiffened. She was no backwoods girl but a daughter of a fine Virginia family with solid British roots.

He came forward and straddled a stool, arms still crossed. "Miss Rowan, do you enjoy feeding an army?"

Surprised by his easy manner, she smoothed her soiled apron. "'Tis better than going into battle, surely."

His generous mouth quirked in a half smile. "It appears you've been there and back." His gaze took in the mess all around them—the batter-encrusted crockery and wooden spoons, a mound of spilled coffee grounds looking like a swarm of ants near his boot, a puddle of sticky syrup dripping down the hearthstones.

A battle indeed.

Her cheeks warming, her eyes trailed after his as he surveyed her domain. "I'll soon have it cleaned up and set to rights," she said spiritedly. "Just in time for the next . . . skirmish."

A flash of amusement warmed his face. "And what is your plan of attack at noon?"

"Soup, bread, perhaps some apple tarts. Unless you order otherwise."

He ran a hand over his clean-shaven jaw. "If I remove you from this kitchen, my men are likely to court-martial me."

She almost smiled. He was treading lightly for her sake, she guessed, because she was in mourning. Taking the stool nearest the hearth, she darted another glance at him and saw that despite his winter-tanned skin, he remained a very ill man underneath. Or was he so grieved by her father's death—

"I want to see you in my office first thing tomorrow morning—say, eight o'clock," he ordered, then amended quickly, "at your convenience, of course."

"Of course," she echoed, wondering if she should offer to make him more of that bitter brew called cinchona. Thinking of it jarred her into remembering the tea he'd sent, and she recovered her manners, folding her hands in her lap. "I want to thank you for your letter—and the teacup and fine things."

And all the gentlemanly sentiment behind it.

"The pleasure, Miss Rowan, was mine." His voice was deep and thoughtful and so formal it seemed they were in some fine Virginia drawing room. "If you have need of anything else . . ."

Only my father, she thought. *And you can hardly remedy that.*

Her eyes grew damp as he stood and cast a long shadow in the dim kitchen. She watched him turn and go, wishing he'd invited her to meet him at the stone house instead. Its handsome facade remained a riddle, looking like it had been plucked from some lush hill in the Virginia countryside and settled stone by stone upon this wild and dangerous ground. It truly reminded her of home.

The home she no longer had.

When land taxes had come due and Papa's soldier's pay came late, the debts had mounted and the creditors had come . . .

Shrugging the painful memory aside, Roxanna tried to dismiss her homesickness, but it made her nearly ill with longing. She'd loved every stone of that house, unassuming as it was. It had been the only home she'd ever known.

In this dim, dismal fort, she couldn't forget Old Orchard, as Papa called their former farm, its expansive windows gracing every wall and drawing the outdoors in, every room resplendent with light whatever the season. Here a loophole just big enough to ram a rifle barrel through had to suffice, the danger was so deep. Aye, this place was fraught with danger and a hint of mystery, the least of which was her father's sudden death.

9

She couldn't sleep a wink between missing Papa and considering the coming confrontation with the colonel. Sometime during the night she plucked her dulcimer from the mantel and sat as close to the fire as she dared, the flannel of her nightgown hardly warming her. Her hair was loose and hung like a mourning shawl about her slumped shoulders as she softly played, casting glances at Pa's open Bible. If she kept her mind on both the Bible and the music, she'd be all right, even in the frigid darkness with soldiers and Indians right outside her door.

Colonel McLinn's fine house was too far away for comfort. Though it was less than a stone's throw from the fort's west wall, she felt they were a continent apart. She wished he was inside this fort with the rest of them, perhaps because she craved the security of Papa's presence. There had always been something so solid and enduring about her father . . . The irony of it stopped her cold. Thus far there'd been no enduring men in her life—not her father, certainly not Ambrose—and no promise that there ever would be. Why would Colonel McLinn be any different?

Forehead furrowing, she looked down at the polished walnut of her instrument, admiring the tiny cut leaf pattern fashioned by Papa's own hand. His gift to her, he said, to while away the long winter hours. She stroked the strings as quietly as she could,

69

mindful of the sleeping soldiers on all sides of her. "Barbara Allen" had been one of Papa's favorite tunes, and she thumbed the notes, tears spilling onto the tops of her fingers. But this was a good grieving. Music, like Scripture, soothed one's soul. She continued on, pouring her aching heart into the music, each note becoming a thing of beauty in the firelit cabin.

Long before daylight, she secured a copper tub from Bella and heated bucket after bucket of water. The tiny cabin was soon as steamy as a midsummer's day, and a cake of rose-geranium soap was taken from her trunk.

Benumbed, she let Bella fuss with her, heating curling tongs so that her hair fell from the back of her head in ebony spirals to her shivering shoulders. She felt like she was going to a ball, but it was only Colonel McLinn she was to see. Bella removed her corded linen dress from the clothespress, and then, wearing French stays that seemed to stifle any remaining emotion and prop her up, Roxanna sat before the fire and waited for Bella to finish weaving a blue ribbon in her hair.

"Law, Miz Roxanna, you look good enough to eat," Bella exclaimed, clucking over her like a mother hen. "Reminds me o' my days seein' to fancy folk in Philadelphia before the war broke out."

"Were you a lady's maid, Bella?"

"Once upon a time I was, before I come down in the world to a mere washerwoman."

"Who did you work for?"

"Well, I was turned out o' the Eustaces' mansion a few years ago. They rightly suspected me o' bein' a Patriot and were afraid they'd be accused o' forsakin' their Tory leanin's. But they was good folks. They freed me after they got religion."

"How did you meet Hank?"

A hint of a smile touched her lips. "I took up washin' for General Washington's troops the same time Hank joined the rebel army. He'd been with the British first and got his freedom, then saw servin' with them was just another sort o' slavery." She set the curling tongs aside to cool and dug in her pocket, producing a small, cracked hand mirror. "I'm glad you don't own a mournin' dress. You'd look just awful in black."

Roxanna took the mirror reluctantly, eyes widening at the sight of her elaborately coiffed hair. "Maybe we shouldn't take such pains—"

"Now hush. Do you want to get out o' these woods or don't you?"

Roxanna looked at her in surprise. She hadn't said a word about her situation, but Papa always vowed her every feeling was written on her face. Did Bella suspect she hadn't a shilling to her name? And no relatives to turn to?

"You won't have to plead yo' cause long before Colonel Mc-Linn, bein' a lady and all. Hatin' this place like he does, he might just take you east himself."

This startling thought did little to ease her. Indeed, her angst seemed to double at Bella's words as she pondered her predicament. Here she sat in the middle of Indian-infested wilderness, with the river she'd just come down frozen hard as a brick, and she must now go begging. Mortification seeped into her very soul as she anticipated pleading her case before the proud colonel.

Bella eyed her with grim sympathy. "You want me to go wi' you, Miz Roxanna? Or just announce you?"

She stood breathless in her too-tight stays. "Neither." Making a fool of herself in front of McLinn was bad enough. She'd not beg before Bella too.

Father in heaven, please prop me up.

❦

Cass pored over the papers on his desk by the light of a dozen candles situated just so against the early morning gloom. But his mind wasn't on the stack of missives from Richmond, important though they were. Some had sat waiting the six weeks he'd been on the winter campaign against the Shawnee and British. Nay, even longer, since the malaria had struck and his second-in-command had seen to things in his stead.

He didn't like to let correspondence linger any more than he liked his own to sit on Virginia's end as it so often did. But he had more important matters to attend to just now. Like the fifty prisoners in ball and chain just beyond the blockhouse door.

And Roxanna Rowan.

Running a hand over his jaw, he rued his lack of rest. She—nay, the locket—had kept him up long past midnight. And then, when he did sleep, he'd awakened to see it lying on his bedside table, the firelight playing off of it so that it glinted and tempted him to take another look. He'd resisted the urge to study that unfamiliar face, not liking what happened to him when he did.

He should have returned the locket to her in the kitchen when he'd found her after breakfast yesterday morning. But the timing hadn't been right, and timing was everything, at least where she was concerned. He was out of his ken dealing with a grief-stricken daughter, composed as she was. There was something about her that made him want to tread as lightly as a skittish colt on cracked river ice—mostly because he was to blame for her fragile state.

Leaning back in his chair, he chewed his cheek as the clock struck seven. Bella was likely in the kitchen making an abomination of breakfast by now. He tried not to recall the fine coffee, feather-light pancakes, crisp bacon, *and* subsequent spike in morale among his men yesterday after a good meal—or the fact that Roxanna Rowan had looked at home in that kitchen. He hated to take it away from her, but he had no choice. He'd not rest till he'd put her out of this wretched place.

"Colonel, sir?" The door opened and the orderly appeared, a willowy shadow behind him. Cass stood as Roxanna entered, struck by the lush lines of her pressed gown and the gloss of her hair as it cascaded over her shoulders in three faultless curls. Bella's work, surely.

He gestured to a chair. "Please, have a seat."

Taking the chair he offered, she sat on the edge of it, her downcast eyes sweeping the enormous desk strewn with maps and spyglass and papers. In the candlelight, he could see faint shadows beneath her eyes that suggested a night bereft of rest, much like his own.

She looked up just then and gave him a timorous smile, her eyes a flash of ocean blue behind their fringe of black lashes. The effect was so winsome yet so artless he felt the heat rise from his neck to his temples. Time to take command of this tenuous situation, he reminded himself. But how to begin?

He sat down and leaned back in his chair, wishing Roxanna Rowan was a soldier and he merely had to issue an order and she'd disappear to do his bidding. Marking time, he began slowly and carefully, inviting her to jump in. "I want to talk about your future plans . . ."

She squared her shoulders, hands folded in her lap. "Yes, of course."

"Bella tells me you are doing better."

"Bella is very kind." She swallowed and looked past him to the elaborate clock across the room with its silver-plated hands and bold numerals. "I must leave this place, of course. But with the Ohio River frozen . . ."

"There are other ways to travel, Miss Rowan."

She darted a look at him. "Through the wilderness, you mean?"

"Aye, I could assign a contingent of soldiers to escort you to Virginia."

"But the weather . . . and the Indians," she began, knotting her hands in her lap and looking down at them. "Truly, 'tis more than this. You see, when the Indians raided the flatboat, I lost my indispensable—"

"Your . . . *indispensable*?"

She flushed. "My handbag—it fell into the river. I have no funds to travel."

He leaned forward. "You have your father's pay, which I gladly give you today. And the journey would be of no expense. But," he admitted, pushing a paperweight atop a pile of correspondence, "it would be . . . complicated."

"Fraught with danger, you mean." When she met his eyes again, he realized they were even bluer than his own.

"Aye," he said.

"With the warring Shawnee."

"Don't forget the British."

Her shoulders sagged a bit, and one curl spiraled down over the rich fabric of her bodice when she tilted her head. "Did you know my father well, Colonel?"

The unexpected question seemed sharp as a saber tip. He fixed his eyes on the buffalo fur hanging on the wall across the room and said, "Your father spent nearly every waking hour sitting in that chair, taking down all I told him. I suppose I did."

"Then you must know he lost his wife—my mother—last year?"

"Aye."

"I only mention it because I have no near relatives."

"Not one?"

"Some distant relations in Scotland. But with the war on, the sea is hardly safe for travel." She lowered her eyes again, and he sensed her profound dismay at all the doors slamming shut before her.

He made himself look away from her tense face. Hadn't there been some business about a man—a betrothal? Like a dream slowly remembered at daylight, he recalled her father's displeasure. Richard hadn't liked the man who'd pursued her. Liked him so little, in fact, that he'd shared his reservations with Cass himself. What was the scoundrel's name? Abe? Amos? Adam?

Ambrose.

The clock struck eight o'clock so loud and long it prevented him from speaking for several moments. Finally he asked quietly, "You have no sweetheart? No intended?"

Immediately he regretted the question. She flushed and seemed to flounder under his scrutiny, her translucent skin turning scarlet. "I—I did. But the betrothal was broken. I meant to tell my father when I came here . . ."

The sudden silence turned excruciating.

"Say no more, Miss Rowan." He got up and went to a corner table where a portable writing desk rested. Lifting it off its stand, he came to her and placed it in her lap.

"Your father's lap desk," he said, yet knew he didn't need to.

The telling emotion on her pale face reassured him she'd not forgotten. She wrapped her hands around it almost lovingly. Steeling himself against his own grief, he leaned against his desk, crossed his arms, and looked down at the planks in the floor, affording her some privacy.

Her voice was a whisper. "You're giving it to me?"

Aye, he nearly said, sympathy gaining the upper hand. As quick as the thought came, he said instead, "It comes with a proposition."

She looked up warily, luminous eyes assessing him so intently it seemed she could peer clear to his soul. He wanted to squirm like a schoolboy but managed to say, "I am, as you know, in need of a scrivener."

"You are more in need of a cook, I should think," she returned softly.

He raised an eyebrow and continued on, weighing the wisdom of her words. "'Twill be difficult to function without your father. There are endless dispatches, treaties, and correspondence to see to, and most of my men are common soldiers, unable to read or write. My officers, though lettered, are needed elsewhere. What say ye, Miss Rowan?"

She looked down at the lap desk, her hands caressing the

mahogany tambour top as if she was toying with the temptation of lifting the lid and peeking inside. "Sir, I cannot possibly replace my father."

He worked hard to keep his impatience down. "No one can *replace* him, Miss Rowan. But he once told me that he taught you all he knew and your writing hand is as fine as his own."

She nodded thoughtfully and rested her hands atop the waxed wood. "He considered it part of my schooling—before sending me away to Miss Pringle's Academy, that is. But a female scrivener in a fort full of men—"

"There is Bella, don't forget." *And the Redstone women*, he didn't say—who would soon be on their way.

"Yes, Bella," she echoed, and then her lovely face turned entreating. "But you can't be serious."

"Deadly serious," he replied, then nearly winced at his wording.

She looked so perplexed he nearly backed down. But what else was he going to do with her? Send her packing? Hold a frolic so some settlement yahoo could woo and wed her? Move her downriver to Smitty's Fort?

He expelled a ragged breath. "Say you will, Miss Rowan. At least until I can send for a replacement scrivener in spring."

When she didn't respond, he circled her chair and sat back down, the desk between them. Her nearness was nearly as unnerving as his offer. For a moment he forgot just what he'd asked her, distracted by her alluring scent. Clean linen . . . talc . . . violets. It nearly made him groan. Cecily had been all satin and spice. He cleared his throat.

Her head came up. "Just till spring?"

"Aye, spring," he answered, sensing she was thawing. "By then the Ohio River will be navigable and the war might be won, leaving you free to sail to Scotland. Or seek a position in the colonies." *Or marry*, he mused.

She leaned forward slightly, the backdrop of firelight casting them in an intimate circle. Her fingers skimmed the desktop. She seemed to be lost in the treasure on her lap.

"I promised your father . . ." he began. At this, she seemed to almost flinch, but he continued slowly, his every word like a vow. "I promised him I would take care of you. And I take any and all promises I make very seriously."

She looked down at the lap desk again, perhaps imagining doing the same work her father had done, he guessed. He willed her to open it and examine the writing implements inside, the side drawers for paper, the containers of ink and sand.

Instead she asked, "When would I begin?"

He smiled for the first time, hope rising and crowding out the tightness in his chest. "Tomorrow. January 3."

"Nay," she said quietly, looking away.

The shadow crept back into his soul. "'Tis too soon."

Reaching her arms around the lap desk, she hugged it closer. "I need sufficient time to think—pray about things first."

He merely nodded, remembering the locket. Should he return it to her now? He began to reach inside his coat pocket then stopped. Would a woman want a likeness of herself? Aye, a vain woman. Vain she was not. Perhaps the lap desk was enough for now.

"There's another cabin available should you decide you want to move there," he told her. *Away from the memory of your father*, he thought.

If only he could do the same.

Even now he felt the chill of the woods, the snow on his boots, and relived the fatal moment he'd fired his musket and Richard Rowan had crumpled in the clearing. A thousand times he'd fired that shot in memory, both asleep and awake, as if attempting to change what he'd done.

How long before one of his rum-soaked men spilled his terrible secret? How long before he could bear to tell her himself?

The Irish lilt of his voice thickened slightly when he said, "And how much time might you—and the Almighty—need?"

"I shall ask Him," she said softly, rising gracefully despite the bulk of the desk in her arms. "And then I will tell you my decision."

He might have been amused if the situation hadn't been so serious. Taking the desk from her, he walked her to the door. "Then I shall anxiously await your heavenly answer."

An orderly helped carry the lap desk to the cabin that was solely hers, if she wanted it to be. As they walked across the parade ground, she glanced at the empty structure by the officer's barracks that Colonel McLinn had mentioned and weighed the wisdom of moving. The garrison hummed with activity this morning, men with muskets guarding the herd of prisoners behind a rail fence that was attached to some half-face shelters at the far west end. More soldiers were tending fires and stirring huge kettles of mush as they prepared to serve breakfast to the captives.

Roxanna walked slowly, eyes on the men trapped behind that fence, still in ball and chain. How did they sleep or do anything at all? The Indians still looked as proud as when they'd marched past her Christmas Eve—seeming impervious to the cold, buried in buffalo robes, while the British soldiers shivered in their scarlet uniforms, pale faces pinched.

"What will happen to these men?" she asked the orderly who hefted her desk.

"They'll soon be marched to Virginny," he replied around a mouthful of tobacco. "All but two of them redskins."

She let her eyes roam. Which two?

Her thoughts were diverted by the sight of a regular leaning against the wall of the smithy, pipe in hand. Dovie was with him. Roxanna raised a hand in greeting before slipping inside her cabin, shutting the door soundly and setting her precious cargo on the trestle table. Unhooking her gown, she loosened her stays and donned a worsted wool dress, thoughts returning to the matter at hand.

She could stay and work . . . if she wanted to. Trouble was, she didn't want to.

Not with Colonel McLinn acting as her commanding officer, so to speak. Did she even recall what her father had taught her? Opening the top of the lap desk, she found a few loose papers, an almost dry inkpot, and a sharpened quill. She set aside the little jar of pounce before dipping the quill into the black ink, writing in abbreviated form as fast as she could remember how.

Colonel Cassius McLinn has asked me to serve as his scrivener till spring in lieu of my father on this 2nd day of January, 1780. Under the circumstances, I have decided to . . .

She paused, teeth on edge, and imagined herself in the Windsor chair beside McLinn's massive desk, taking down every word that he told her, forcing herself to look away from his riveting form to attend to her task, trying not to make a mistake and raise his redheaded ire. Then she thought of her father's pay, now to be hers, and how much it was needed as she headed toward an uncertain future.

Oh, Lord, what would You have me do?

In the evening shadows of the blockhouse kitchen, Bella stared at her, the gap between her front teeth looking more pronounced in the candlelight. "You said what, Miz Roxanna?"

"Oh, Bella, please don't look at me like that." Setting down her spoon, Roxanna fumbled with the napkin in her lap. "I've little choice but to find employment—just till spring, mind you."

"Mercy! You won't last till spring with Colonel McLinn!" She took a gulp of cider, her pewter cup clinking atop the table as she set it back down. "Yo' pa was a saint for servin' as scrivener these past two years, but I disbelieve he'd want his daughter to do the same."

"I start at eight o'clock in the morning. And I'll *not*," she said, hating the rush of heat to her cheeks, "be alone with him. He has an orderly or two. As chaperone."

"Hmmm. Somethin' smells."

Roxanna sighed. "He merely made me a kind offer."

"'Kind' and 'the colonel' don't mix."

"Well, what else will I do all day in this fort? I'm sure to be stockade-crazy come spring if I don't."

"You'll be colonel-crazy if you do."

"Bella! You're not helping matters—at all."

Bella began to chuckle, though her face remained dark with concern. "I knew I shouldn't have left you alone in that room with him. He works quite a spell."

"I told him no at first . . ."

"I bet your 'no' didn't last five seconds."

"I said I needed time to think and pray."

"And what did his high and handsome self say to that?"

Roxanna finished the last of her soup. "He simply said he'd be awaiting my heavenly answer."

Across from her, Bella seemed to have lost her appetite. She set her own spoon down. "Law, best start ringin' those weddin' bells. You look enraptured already."

10

Roxanna awoke the next morning to reveille, her heart and head pounding from the jarring noise of fife and drum. After shrugging on a dressing gown, she made tea at the hearth, pouring the steaming brew into the exquisite thistle cup given her by Colonel McLinn. Despite the sunlight sliding through the shutter cracks, Papa's shadow seemed to hover in every corner. How would she ever heal, coming back to this lifeless place day in and day out? Perhaps it would be better to take up residence in another cabin.

Perching on a cane-bottomed chair, she let the cup warm her cold hands, eyes on the mantel clock. Only six. Two more hours till she faced McLinn. Why did it feel like a court-martial instead? Glancing at her father's writing desk in a dark corner, she realized she'd need to sharpen some quills, check the ink and sand and paper again—ordinary rag linen as well as fine Dutch bond. She felt the familiar tug of excitement when using a fresh sheet and sharpened pen—yet it jarred sourly with her grief.

Taking the desk onto her lap, she wondered what she should call him. "Colonel," she guessed, or "sir." Would he even like her work? Bella had indicated he was exacting, hard to please. Withholding a sigh, she opened the tambour top, took stock of all the implements, and found them in good order. Good soldier that he was, Papa had been exacting too.

Her fingertips brushed the smooth, dark lines of wood, familiarizing herself with what was now hers. When she'd been small, Papa had always kept a sweet or two hidden in an interior drawer, away from the casual eye. He'd called it his secret compartment, and only the two of them had known how to press the tiny hidden spring that surrendered its contents.

She finally found it through her tears, half hoping to discover a piece of sugar candy. But the drawer divulged something else entirely. No sweets, only a little leather-bound book, its cover smooth and its edges worn. She swallowed down her disappointment and opened it. Papa's fine Gothic hand dominated the page, and her eyes lingered on a telling line.

April 1, 1779, Thursday. In this isolated, forgotten outpost, intrigue swirls on every side . . .

Before she'd finished the first sentence, a chill danced down her spine. She snapped the book shut, stunned by the strong feeling of the words within, knowing it was a private journal not meant for a daughter's eyes. Quickly she put it back and shut the secret drawer, then returned the desk to the corner. Truly, this task as scrivener was already beyond her ken, and she hadn't even begun.

Thoughts swirling again, she dressed in the most demure of her dresses—a serviceable gown of brown tabby silk, the sleeves and bodice ruched and beribboned in matronly fashion—before pinning up her hair, every ebony strand, wishing for the curling tongs Bella had wielded so well. Before she'd laced up one worn black boot, she heard a sob outside her door and then a timid knock.

Dovie peered in, Abby in her wake, a look of abject misery marring her comely features. "Oh, Miz Roxanna, somethin' awful's happened." She shooed Abby inside and shut the door, swiping at her wet face before sinking down atop a chair by the door. "Colonel McLinn's turnin' us out—in this bitter cold—with nary a goodbye to our sweethearts. Just sendin' us away with the clothes on our backs and not a shilling to our names . . ."

Her voice trilled higher as she recited a litany of complaints against the colonel with hardly a breath between. Roxanna opened her arms to Abby, who nested in her lap like a kitten, leaning her tousled head on Roxanna's chest. Dismay pummeled her as she listened. She wanted to close Abby's ears to such talk and give her a bath and clean clothes and a secure future. But all she could do was listen patiently, waiting for the finale that finally came with a pitiful request.

"Now, we know you have the colonel's sympathy," Dovie said. "Might you say somethin' to him about his rough treatment? Buy us a little time? Just so we can make other arrangements?"

"Of course I'll speak to him," she said reassuringly, holding Abby closer and glancing toward the clock. Half past seven. Time enough to plead Dovie's case. Dread knotted her stomach, and she swallowed down a sigh. "You'd both best go to the kitchen and get some breakfast. And pray. I don't know if I have the colonel's sympathy, but I'll do what I can."

Two orderlies were already at work when Roxanna knocked on the blockhouse door. Colonel McLinn looked up from his work as she appeared, lap desk in arms. Standing, he cut a fine figure in the candlelight that danced in the manifold drafts airing out the stale room. She'd always thought the Continental uniforms dashing with their buff and blue, far more so than the British scarlet and white. On this particular Irishman, she admitted grudgingly, they rose to new heights.

With an inward wince, she looked away. Bella was right. She'd been a fool to take this on. And Papa had been no wiser tying them together on his deathbed. She was hardly an impression-able schoolgirl. And McLinn was no fledgling officer. The fine lines about his eyes cast him over the age of thirty, and the confidence he wore like a cloak aged him older still. Pleading for the soiled doves in the far row of cabins was not going to set well with a seasoned officer, she feared. But since he had been fond of her father, perhaps he'd honor this one request.

"Miss Rowan," he said in greeting.

"Good morning, Colonel McLinn." Compared to his sonorous lilt, her voice seemed whisper thin in the suddenly still room.

He glanced at the corner clock then gestured to the Windsor chair. "You're early. I like that in my staff."

She took the chair and settled the lap desk like a hedge be-tween them. "Actually, I've come ahead of time to discuss some-thing with you."

He sat back down and seemed to sear her with his astonishing eyes. Too blue, she decided, meeting them reluctantly. Like the Virginia sky in July. The firelight just behind him was making his hair a halo of reddish-gold, emphasizing his broad shoulders and the dimple she'd just noticed in his left cheek.

Lord, have mercy . . .

"What say ye, Miss Rowan?"

She swallowed, schooling her thoughts—or trying to. "I've just learned that you've bid the women from Redstone farewell."

"Aye, so I did."

The room stilled. She was aware of the orderlies pausing in their work, and she lowered her voice to a near whisper. "That is not setting well with at least one of them. I've come to ask you to reconsider."

To her surprise, he almost smiled. Leaning back in his chair, he folded his arms across his chest, and she saw the flash of a signet ring on his right hand. "On what grounds?"

Her gaze wavered, and she looked down at her lap desk. "It *is* winter. And they have nowhere to go."

"This isn't a civilian station, Miss Rowan," he said amiably. "They should have thought of that before they left Redstone."

"Foresight is not everyone's gift, Colonel. Perhaps if you gave them some time to make other arrangements—"

"Other than the fortnight I've already given them, you mean." She held back a sigh. "I wasn't aware of that."

"Now you are. Need I remind you that I'm commanding a garrison here, Miss Rowan? *Not* a tavern?"

She looked up at him, stung by his condescension. "I need no reminding, sir. But since you're commander of the entire western frontier, it would seem you could find a more suitable solution than sending destitute women into the cold with an Indian war on." Out of the corner of her eye, she saw the orderlies move away, as if expecting some sort of a ruckus. "And there *is* a child to consider, as you know." At this, his jaw tightened ever so perceptibly, but she rushed on regardless, her tone quiet and respectful but firm. "I've heard Smitty's Fort is at full capacity and Fort Click is no better."

"You've heard correctly," he returned, surprising her. "What is your recommendation?"

"You might employ them. Bella could use a hand in the kitchen and laundry."

"In return for room and board, you mean?"

"Yes, just till spring, of course."

He was smiling now, leaning forward conspiratorially, Irish charm oozing. "I would like to hear your scheme for keeping them locked in their quarters at night and not out carousing with my men."

Oh my. Her fingers did a nervous dance upon the tambour desktop, and she faltered under his scrutiny. "I—I—"

"Any other recommendations, Miss Rowan?"

She smiled a triumphant smile and stilled her hands. "Yes. Reward the women—and the men—for good behavior by having some entertainment at week's end. I've heard a fiddle or two since I've been here. And I have a dulcimer. Surely a frolic now and then would help while the winter hours away."

He contemplated this for a few solemn seconds before looking toward the orderlies who'd been listening hard and pretending not to. "Hobbes? Wilkerson?"

They stood at attention, nervous smiles playing across their faces. "A fine plan, sir. Compliments to the lady here, sir."

He turned back to her. "And may I have the pleasure of the first dance, Miss Rowan?"

She gave him a slightly wide-eyed stare, while his eyes narrowed and crinkled at the corners, full of mischief.

Mercy . . . he does work quite a spell. Her poise dissolved and she shook her head. "I'm afraid I don't dance, sir."

At once all the *joie de vivre* left his handsome face. Abrupt as he was, she half expected him to press the matter. Astute as he was, she was surprised he hadn't noticed her limp.

He waited until the orderlies were across the room rummaging through some maps before he said, "Do you not *want* to dance, Miss Rowan?"

She looked down at her lap. "'Tis not a matter of wanting, Colonel, but being unable."

There, she had confessed it. Tears gathered at the corners of her eyes as a host of memories flooded her. The only man who'd ever danced with her had been her father, and with him she'd felt she had no infirmity at all. But Ambrose . . . Ambrose had been embarrassed to dance with her.

"'Tis too soon," he murmured, averting his eyes and studying the papers strewn across his desk. "I apologize. But later, should you change your mind, the offer stands."

He didn't understand, of course, thinking grief held her back. But she was in no frame of mind to set him straight, as if anyone could, imperious as he was.

As the clock struck eight, she opened the desk and prepared her quill, swirling it in the pot of ink and awaiting his directive.

He shuffled through some papers, moved a spyglass, and took something an orderly offered him. Spreading it upon the desk, he anchored it with a surveyor's tool and a small cannon ball, and she saw that it was a detailed map of Kentucke and the infamous middle ground of Ohio.

He shot her a quick glance. "First letter will be to the acting commander at Fort Pitt."

It seemed like a cage of butterflies had been sprung open inside her at his curt command. All her father had taught her seemed to take wing and fly right out of her head. She gripped the quill tighter, and a drop of ink soiled the rag linen paper beneath. A flicker of alarm pricked her, and then she remembered it was only the original, not the official copy she would craft for him later.

He began, "Sir, I have received your letter of the seventeenth of September. The present state of affairs at this frontier outpost in regards to the hostiles is thus . . ."

The symbols and abbreviations she'd once learned as a sort of game at her father's side returned to her in a small flash flood. Occasionally, the colonel would pause to peruse his map, allowing her to catch her breath. He had a natural eloquence that was easy to follow, and his low voice . . . Oh my, but it seemed to her like silk and leather and cream. Thinking it, she scribbled the wrong symbol then crossed it out.

Before she knew it, the clock struck eleven and an orderly was bringing in a tray of hot coffee and beaten biscuits. The colonel looked up in surprise and glanced at Roxanna as she sifted sand over the last letter in order to dry it.

"It would seem Bella is concerned I not overwork you."

She returned her quill to the inkpot. "Perhaps she is worried I will overwork you."

His mouth curved in a near smile. "I suppose this calls for a truce."

They both looked at the tray awkwardly, as if unwilling to

make the first move. Suddenly she was overcome by the realization of how intimate simply sharing a cup of coffee could be. Taking a cup, she made a fuss of stirring in cream and honey and timidly took one biscuit.

As she sat across from him, all her insecurities returned to her tenfold. She'd never before taken coffee with a man. A true gentleman. Discomfort needled her and nearly made her hands shake. Coupled with the fact that he was looking at her in that intent way of his, as if she was undergoing inspection and had a button undone or a spot on her kerchief . . .

He leaned back in his chair. "Would you rather be in the kitchen, Miss Rowan?"

She looked up, thinking he was teasing, but found his face tense. "I . . . nay," she replied.

He picked up one of her letters. "Your writing hand is finer than your fa—" The last word was bitten off, and a pained expression crossed his face. "I apologize."

"I don't mind if you mention him," she said quietly despite the sting of grief. "He's never far from my thoughts."

Setting the letter down, he stirred cream into his cup but didn't take a drink, nor did he look at her. "I lost my own father prior to leaving Ireland and enlisting under General Washington."

As a Life Guard? Wasn't that what Bella had said? Or in the field? There was something mysterious about his coming to Kentucke . . . something about a red-roaring rage and his being sent west. But she could hardly mention that. Sympathy nudged her. "I'm sorry about your father. Did you come to Kentucke from Virginia?"

"Aye, I did. Next month marks three years."

She took a sip of coffee and found it strong even with cream and sugar. "You've done a great deal since coming here—the stone house and orchard, this fort."

"My orders were to build a garrison that couldn't be breached. I had the stone house built as well, knowing it would outlast this post. It sends a clear message to the Indians that we're here to stay."

She thought of the enemy British and Indians marching east to Virginia at dawn. All but two. Though she'd not seen those remaining men yet, she felt a wary fascination. They were heavily watched and kept in the guardhouse. She wondered about the colonel's reasons for detaining them, if they might not be important to his cause, whatever that was.

"You're a long way from home, Colonel McLinn. May I ask what makes this war your war?"

He looked at her then, so keenly she wanted to wince beneath his blue gaze. "Half the Continental army is Irish, Miss Rowan. There are twenty-six Irish-born generals serving under Washington, not to mention lesser officers like myself. We're committed to ending the tyranny of England whenever and wherever we can. If not in our homeland, then here."

She nodded, shamed at her ignorance of the world at large and the war. Mama hadn't allowed her to read the *Virginia Gazette* or indulge in politics. What little she'd gleaned came from her father's letters and her time spent tutoring. "So England has long been the enemy of Ireland."

"Aye, not only Ireland but Scotland and other parts. Now we have a chance to fight back."

"My father mentioned you have an estate in Ireland."

"Had. The Crown confiscated our ancestral lands when I joined the Americans. But 'tis a loss well worth bearing for liberty's sake."

She detected a bite of bitterness beneath his gentlemanly tone and imagined there to be far more to his losses than the privation of his estate. But she warmed to the conviction in his voice, and her eyes moved from his face to his uniform coat, lingering on the fine gold epaulets atop his wide shoulders, the eagle insignia on his left collar, the blue riband worn across the breast between his coat and waistcoat. Yet for all her looking, she failed to find the distinction she sought.

Where, she wondered, was his Purple Heart?

"You've done a day's work all in one morning," he said abruptly, returning his cup to the tray. "After this you're at your leave. I have to interview the Shawnee prisoners, and I don't want you present."

She merely nodded and finished her coffee, tucking the biscuit discreetly into her pocket for Abby and seeing a flash of amusement cross his face as she did. He missed nothing. Little wonder his men couldn't get away with the slightest infraction.

"I'll finish the correspondence in my cabin and have it ready for your signature in the morning," she said, lifting the lap desk and wishing he wouldn't ask an orderly to carry it for her, which he promptly did. She hoped he wouldn't forget about the Redstone women, and then discarded that notion as well. She'd worked with him for a wee three hours, long enough to know he overlooked little.

"Good day, Miss Rowan," he said, standing till she was beyond the blockhouse door.

An icy blast of air sent stinging particles of snow into her face and threatened to pull her hair free of its pins. Her eyes moved to the quarters where the Shawnee were being held, then Olympia's cabin just across. She could see Abby's pale face in the square of window, and her heart twisted. After she'd finished her correspondence, she'd invite Abby to the cabin. Waving a hand, she moved on.

Just outside the kitchen blockhouse, Bella's wash stood at stiff attention on the sagging clothesline. Smoke from a dozen chimneys hung over the parade ground like a dirty linen shroud. Everything was cast in shades of gray—somber, bleak, distressing. Despite her high feeling about her morning's work, thoughts of her father crowded in and snuffed out her satisfaction. She felt her mood plummet with every step.

All I need is a cup of tea. And a good cry.

She thanked the orderly at the cabin door and slipped inside, surprised to find the fire blazing and Bella stabbing it fiercely with a poker.

Whirling, her dark eyes exclamation points, Bella sputtered, "Why, I thought you'd not be shed o' McLinn till midnight!"

Roxanna set down the lap desk and hung up her cloak. "Bella, you don't have to fuss with my fire—not with all the other work you have to do."

"It was the colonel's doin', tellin' me not to let yo' fire go out while you were workin' with him over in the blockhouse."

Truly? Hearing it, she felt a tad lighter in spirit, touched by his concern. "I have some good news. The colonel's decided to let the Redstone women stay till spring—if they're willing to work."

Bella snorted then scowled. "I doubt even McLinn could get a guinea's worth o' work out o' any o' them doxies, or even thought to try. I bet this is yo' doin'."

Sheepish, Roxanna ladled water from a bucket into the teakettle and hung it over the fire. "I thought you'd be glad. You could use the help."

Bella perched on the edge of a chair and eyed the porcelain cup Roxanna set out. "So how did it go with the almighty McLinn this mornin'?"

"Well enough that I don't believe a bad word said about him."

Her lips pursed in a pout. "Well, the honeymoon ain't over yet. I give it till the end o' next week."

"So far I find him a prodigious worker, uncommonly astute, impeccably mannered—"

Bella glowered. "I don't know a one o' them words. He's dangerous as a keg o' powder, and you'd best see him for what he is."

"I think you need a cup of tea," Roxanna said, pouring the hot water through the strainer and watching as pink liquid sloshed into the fine cup. "Sassafras." Taking the biscuit out of her pocket, she placed it on the table. "For Abby."

"I thought this cup was for you," Bella protested as Roxanna handed her the steaming brew.

"I just had coffee at headquarters, remember?"

Bella took the cup, peering at Roxanna with fresh intensity. "Maybe McLinn's smitten."

The notion was oddly pleasing, if ludicrous. Roxanna resisted the urge to roll her eyes. "Why would you think that?"

"Cuz he's behavin' hisself."

"Soldiers and naval men prefer blondes, Bella. Isn't that how the popular military saying goes?"

Bella looked down at her steaming tea. "I did hear somethin' 'bout an Irish lass o' his."

Roxanna sat down opposite her, surprised by the tight feeling blooming in her chest. "I expect he has someone waiting somewhere."

"How 'bout you?"

"Me? I was betrothed . . . once. But he married another."

"Then you is free."

Free? Roxanna's eyes roamed the dark cabin walls with its sole stingy window, the savage woods just beyond. "I don't feel free locked inside this fort. I think everyone outside these walls is free, but not me . . . not us."

Bella pondered this and sipped her tea. "Hank tells me there's trouble brewin' on account o' them two Indians McLinn's got locked in the guardhouse over yonder."

Roxanna held back a sigh, having wondered the same. "Did Hank tell you what the colonel plans on doing with them?"

"McLinn ain't one to blat his brains out even to his second-in-command."

"And who would that be?"

"You mean you ain't met him? He's never far from the colonel's side. His name's Micajah Hale. Major Hale." When Roxanna didn't answer, Bella pursed her lips. "You ain't heard a word I been sayin' for a full five minutes. You thinkin' 'bout that little gal again?"

"I am," Roxanna admitted, sitting down opposite Bella and digging in her knitting basket.

"I don't know for the life o' me what that child is doin' with such women."

"'Tis simple, really. Olympia is her aunt. Her mother died not long ago of a fever."

"Oh, I know all 'bout that. Who's her pa?"

Roxanna lifted her shoulders in a slight shrug. "Some passerby, Olympia said. She was born and raised in a tavern in Redstone, remember."

"Why don't she speak?"

Roxanna sat back, a half-finished rag doll in her lap. "She's missing her mother, I suppose."

"I bet that child's seen things no child should. Olympia sure lords it over her, hardly lettin' her out o' her sight." Bella's dark eyes landed on the doll and shone with rare sympathy. "I been watchin' how you try to draw her out . . . get her to smile."

"I thought maybe this doll would help. Why don't we have a little tea party—just the three of us? I imagine Olympia is sleeping and wouldn't even miss her—"

Behind them the door cracked open as if on cue, and two inquisitive blue eyes fastened on Roxanna. She turned toward the sound and her smile widened. "Why, Abby, come in!"

Looking furtively over her shoulder, the child slipped inside, hovering as if unsure of the invitation. Roxanna said quietly, "I have something for you—two things, actually."

The light of curiosity sparked in her face and she took mincing steps across the small cabin, eyes on the biscuit Roxanna gestured to. "I can make you a little tea with cream and honey too."

Bella got up to fetch another cup as Abby slid onto the bench beside Roxanna. Taking a bite of biscuit, she lowered her eyes to Roxanna's lap.

"I've almost finished your doll, but I need to know what color you'd like for her hair." Rummaging again, Roxanna held up a hank of cochineal-dyed wool and then one of yellow and brown. Lovingly, the little hand stroked the red in silent communication.

Was her mother's hair red? Roxanna wondered. "Red it is, then," she said, wishing she could elicit a smile. But the little face was locked tight, pale as frost beneath her unruly red cap.

"I had me a doll when I was young and in Virginny," Bella said, setting Abby's pewter cup in front of her. "My mammy made it for me."

Roxanna looked up from braiding the doll's hair, touched by her poignant tone.

"I wished I still had it sometimes. It was nothin' but corn husks, but I loved it."

Abby chewed the last of her biscuit, then took a sip of tea. When Bella offered her the honey spoon, she licked it almost daintily, her chin spotted with sticky drops.

Roxanna softened at the whimsical sight. *Why on earth is such a beautiful child in such a forbidding place?* she wondered for the hundredth time. She made a mental note to mend Abby's worn frock—the calico was so tattered in places it was nearly transparent. But she'd have to speak to Olympia first, as she was so touchy about anything concerning Abby.

While they sipped their tea, Bella began to talk about supper and LeSourd's foray for turkeys and the overdue supply train. Roxanna listened absently, eyes drifting to her lap desk, the thought of her father's journal worming its way into her thoughts. Shifting uncomfortably, she tried to dismiss it, but the cryptic words seemed burned into her brain, kindling the need to look again and unravel its mystery.

In this isolated, forgotten outpost, intrigue swirls on every side . . .

With some difficulty, she returned her attention to Abby and wondered what would happen to the girl. Though Olympia hadn't said, Roxanna guessed the child was about five years old. Time she learned her letters. But to what avail? This was no safe Virginia village, but hostile wilderness. Folks weren't concerned with schooling, just survival. She could well imagine Colonel McLinn's reaction if she were to broach such a civilized topic.

Unbidden, he seemed to lurk in the corners of her mind, making a mess of her yarn.

Oh, Lord, please help Abby. And me. And all the broken people in this broken place.

11

Cass stood with Micajah Hale as the two Shawnee prisoners were brought in, their chains clinking with a lethal rattle that cast him back to the twilight eve when he'd ruined Roxanna Rowan's life. The fact that a head chief of the Kispoko Shawnee now stood before him seemed less a coup than hollow victory. The young chief had to duck his head to enter the blockhouse door, and the flash of black eyes seemed to probe the dim room for an escape before assessing and dismissing each officer. At last his icy gaze leveled on Cass and lingered like a predator fixed on its prey.

Cass met the dark eyes without wavering, knowing he was as revered and feared among the Shawnee as the young chief was among Kentucke's settlers. It was this Indian, backed by the British, who'd destroyed a Kentucke fort and two stations and taken a host of white prisoners. Cass's task was to arrange a prisoner exchange, if it could be done. In retaliation for the destruction this Shawnee and his warriors had wrought, he had crossed the Ohio River with his men the previous summer and destroyed five Shawnee towns and six miles of corn.

Lately it seemed almost a game of sorts between them, albeit a dangerous one. Only now Cass had the upper hand. He wondered how long it would last. He wouldn't turn his back on the man for the slightest second, even guarded. He motioned for the regulars escorting them to seat the captives on a long hickory bench in the center of the room.

His translator, a bearded half blood named Jim Bear, surveyed his kinsmen through squinted eyes. Despite their being confined in the guardhouse and in chains, they'd not been denied the basic necessities. They were clean and well fed. He didn't want to alienate them completely before forcing their cooperation, if they could be forced.

The older Shawnee was looking around in undisguised curiosity, but the younger chief had turned inward, almost brooding, and Cass stepped in front of him, motioning for Jim to begin.

"Ask him his name."

The Shawnee translation was swift, even musical, and completely unnecessary. Cass well knew his name was Five Feathers, not simply owing to the eagle feathers affixed to the silver disc above his left ear. Tales of his misdeeds had spread clear to the colonies and beyond. The *Virginia Gazette* even carried a regular column about his exploits, which, Cass rued, needed little embellishment.

Jim Bear repeated the question, but the answer was a stony silence.

Cass moved to stand in front of the two Indians, hands clasped behind his back, and addressed them directly in English. "Do you know why you're at Fort Endeavor?"

Jim repeated the question in Shawnee, and there was a protracted silence. Finally the older Indian answered slowly and Jim translated. "Why has the red-haired chief brought us here?"

Why indeed? The question—coupled with their name for him—nearly elicited a wry smile. They were here so he could ascertain if the captives from the burned-out forts had been tomahawked, assimilated into the tribe, or sold to the British in Detroit for bounty. Equally vital was his learning which British officer was behind the attacks on the settlements and supplying the Shawnee with what they needed to do it. But he'd start small.

Cass crossed his arms and fixed his eye on the clock across the room. "I mean you no harm by bringing you here. Just as an enemy can come peacefully into a Shawnee town and remain unharmed, so too you can come here and expect fair treatment."

Jim Bear took his time with this, speaking as much to the younger Shawnee chief as to the elder. But Five Feathers sat as if deaf, his tawny face so impassive his fearsome features seemed cast in stone. Cass felt a spasm of impatience. He hadn't the time to waste with silence. He looked toward the regulars who had escorted them in.

"Increase their rations and give them both a gill of rum." *A goodwill gesture,* he didn't add, thinking it might do little good at all. As they left he said to an orderly, "Send for Miss Rowan."

Within minutes the orderly returned. "She's not in her cabin, sir."

"Check the kitchen, then."

Sheepish, the young private shut the door, and for a few seconds the cold weight of remorse and grief rushed in to fill the empty space. Cass eyed the crystal decanter of brandy on a corner table and then the clock. A quarter till three. Too early yet to take the edge off his emotions.

When the door creaked open again, he tamped down an incapacitating rush of regret as Roxanna entered the room, her arms full of papers, the orderly trailing behind with her lap desk. Shoving the memory of Richard Rowan aside, he recalled the gown he'd last seen Cecily wearing. Not the simple, spinsterish brown Roxanna wore, but an extravagant silk the hue of a ripe peach with a ribbon of the same winding through her honeyed hair . . .

"You sent for me, Colonel."

Even with his desk between them, he could see a slight dusting of flour on her cheek and chin. His mouth quirked wryly and he said, "You've been baking."

She colored slightly. "Yes."

"*What* have you been baking?"

"Pumpkin pies." At his intensity, she cradled her papers in one arm and lifted a hand to smooth away the flour, her eyes hugely blue in her pale face. "Fort Endeavor had a fine garden last year, Bella tells me. Pumpkins, anyway." His gaze slid to the papers she held, and she added, "These need your signature before folding and sealing."

He leaned across the desk and took them from her, resisting the sudden urge to brush the remaining flour from her face. Had she ever been properly courted by a man, he wondered . . . kissed? Kissed by a man who knew how to do so? Thinking it, he nearly forgot the matter at hand. The sheaf of papers held a hint of . . . was it violet? He found the documents impeccably transcribed, the elegant slant of each letter as appealing as the one who penned them.

Sitting down, he took up his own quill and scrawled his signature in bold black six times across as many documents. As the ink dried, he watched her settle the lap desk on her knees and take up her quill, though she didn't look at him. Since she'd arrived, she seemed to be trying *not* to look at him, he realized.

Perhaps the sight of him pained her as much as her presence did him. Their distressing situation only strengthened his resolve to quit his post. Since the eve he'd shot her father, he'd been a hairbreadth away from resigning his commission. Every morning of the past three years he'd considered it, hardly believing he was still in this crowded, filthy fort with two hundred surly, affection-starved men and half as many horses, in constant danger from illness and Indians, and with repulsive rations to boot. This was his punishment for a crime he hadn't committed. General Washington had sent him west, saying it was his salvation. Sometimes he wished they'd simply hanged him instead.

"Colonel McLinn . . ."

The gentle voice brought him back, and he grabbed for the

first rational thought he could, saying tersely, "Next letter will be to the Continental Congress. 'Dear Sirs: It is proposed to carry the war into the heart of the country of the Shawanoe, to burn their towns, destroy their next year's crops, and do them every mischief which time and circumstances will permit. This I have done with less than two hundred able-bodied men, few supplies, and no reinforcements.'"

She was scribbling hard and fast, her head tilted just as Richard Rowan's had often been. He could see so much of her father in her earnest face. Then suddenly she stopped writing.

He hesitated, hardly able to speak past the crushing soreness in his chest. "Do you need me to repeat anything?"

She kept her eyes on the document. "Nay, I do not care to hear it again."

There was a sharpness to her voice he'd not heard before, and it set him further on edge. He continued on, "'Presently I have two chieftains in custody with which to enforce compliance with the last treaty made at Fort Pitt, ensuring the Shawnee bring in every Kentucke captive they have in custody prior to the next council to be held in September this year.'"

The orderlies were back—and Micajah Hale, freshly shaved and impeccable in blue swallowtail coat, linen stock, and buckskin breeches. Cass gave him a cursory nod and ran a hand over his own shadowed jaw, rebuking himself for not shaving properly. Finished with dictating, he made introductions, looking on as Micajah took Roxanna's hand and brought it to his lips.

"I think I may be in need of a scrivener myself, Cass," he said lightly, lingering a little too long on her upturned face, which was, under his scrutiny, turning a becoming pink.

"Then I suggest you send for one," he replied drily. "Perhaps you'll have better luck with couriers than I."

"Still smarting over that last dispatch? I'll wager that missive never made it past the Licking River." He smiled down at Roxanna, his affable demeanor belying his ominous words. "Perhaps

Miss Rowan will turn our fortunes and keep a courier alive with her correspondence."

"With six deaths, I doubt it," Cass replied, crossing his arms and leaning against the edge of the desk as Roxanna sifted sand over the ink to dry it. Her lips parted and she seemed about to say something, then hesitated. He couldn't resist asking, "What say ye, Miss Rowan?"

She gave them both a gentle look laced with warning, her voice as beguiling as any Virginian's could be. "I say, speak not of melancholy things as death and wounds, gentlemen, and if others mention them, change the discourse if you can."

Micajah's rumbling laugh filled the cold space. "Pardon, Miss Rowan."

Duly chastised, Cass bit the inside of his cheek, wondering why he'd asked her to serve as scrivener in the first place. She was a bit of a prude, he guessed, sour over being jilted—and now in mourning. Mentally he raced through the ranks of his men, wondering who could serve as scrivener in her stead. Facing her day after day, being reminded of what he had done, was more than he could bear. And then to have her rebuke him . . .

She was intent on the document now, funneling the sand back into a jar and presenting it for his approval. He took it and forced himself to play the officer and gentleman. "Miss Rowan, forgive my lapse in judgment. I've nearly forgotten all rules of civility and decent behavior since coming to this godforsaken place."

She smiled up at him, so wide and winsome it was like a sunrise coming up in a cold, dark place. "All is forgiven, Colonel McLinn."

All. Even the unforgivable act of killing your father.

She seemed to be waiting for him to smile back at her—to speak—but Micajah was doing just that, saying in his infernally charming way, "Perhaps God hasn't forsaken this place, Cass, and has sent an angel to remind us of our manners."

"I need no further reminding, Major. And I doubt even an

angel could stomach this miserable outpost." He swirled the quill in ink, venting his angst in a particularly aggressive signature across the immaculate paper. Any solicitous thoughts he'd once had of the Almighty had dissolved in the hail of lead that cost Richard Rowan his life. He'd be hanged if he trusted in Providence again.

He looked up to find her eyes still on him, but all the light in her face had gone out. She was regarding him just as she had the day he'd tried to tell her of her father's death—with an uncanny solemnity and concern, as if she could sense his inner turmoil. He didn't like that dissecting look, and he deflected it by putting on his tricorn and turning away.

"If you'll excuse me, I'm late for a court-martial—as are you, Major Hale."

He felt her eyes on his back as he exited, aware that Micajah lingered, probably to make amends for his bad behavior. He cursed under his breath—in Gaelic—as he went out. She wouldn't understand Gaelic, he guessed, and could utter no rebuke about that.

Roxana lay her quill down and stared at the bold signature looking like black lightning on the page with its forceful zigzag pattern. *Colonel Cassius C. McLinn.* Major Hale had gone out after him, though he'd looked like he wanted to stay on with her. *Better to obey than a court-martial*, she thought. Bella had told her that two regulars had been caught stealing rum—and since the men didn't take kindly to having their allotment of the stuff swiped, the resulting punishment was expected to be severe. Not only that, the men had been forbidden to "make water" against the pickets, and a cat-o'-nine-tails would mete out a reminder.

Sighing, she wondered how she'd last till spring. 'Twas but January. All the thankfulness she'd felt upon arriving here safely was now nearly snuffed out in this dark, forbidding place. Yet what could she do? If couriers couldn't make it out of Kentucke, what hope would she have of leaving? To combat the dreadful thought, she tried turning it into a prayerful plea.

Lord, deliver me . . . You're the only one who can. And please deliver the colonel from whatever demons are driving him.

She opened the lap desk, trying to dispel the image of his fiercely handsome face that followed on the heels of her prayer. Across the room the orderly worked, oblivious to her presence. Pressing the tiny spring that released the hidden drawer, she removed the journal and opened it for the second time. Should she read . . . or shouldn't she? The question had tormented her since she'd first discovered it. Giving in, her eyes fell to her father's fine hand. The ominous entry she'd previously read led to a second equally cryptic one on the next page.

June 19, 1779. Today Cass announced his intention of a winter campaign into Ohio's middle ground. Reinforcements from Virginia supposed to arrive any day. Another courier gone.

July 4. Celebrated our separation from Mother England with bonfires and a shooting match. No sign of reinforcements yet. Feel there is one loyalist spy among us . . . but who?

A spy. She steeled herself against a shiver and sought solace in a new thought. 'Twas old news, all of it. Last July seemed so distant. Surely they'd have found out the spy by now. She'd not raise an alarm by making foolish accusations.

Quickly she returned the journal to its secret drawer. Her eyes roamed over the colonel's huge desk cluttered with maps and documents, a small cannon ball, compass, and spyglass, yet all still seemed to retain some semblance of order. He knew where everything was instantly. Not once had she seen him rummage for anything. And he trusted her enough to leave her alone in this room with only one orderly present.

That she was in a man's domain there could be no doubt.

Crowded into the cold space was an abundance of crude puncheon benches and tables. Tin lanterns and grease lamps hung from dark beams overhead. Shadowy corners were decorated with maps and powder horns, bullet bags and dispatch cases. A massive buffalo hide was pegged to one wall beside a sagging shelf stuffed with drill books. She wanted to sink her fingers into the thick fur, it looked so lush.

At the creak of the door, she nearly jumped. Captain Stewart entered, as disheveled as Major Hale had been tidy. Olympia never seemed to mind the captain's disarray, she'd noticed, and had declared herself his paramour. He drew up a bit stiffly and gave a little bow.

"Miss Rowan, I wanted to thank you for speaking on behalf of the Redstone women. Olympia tells me they're to stay on. For the winter, anyway."

"'Twas the colonel's doing, actually. And Bella could use the help."

"Ah, yes. She's already put them to work in the laundry and kitchen. I expect everything will run a bit more smoothly and we can look forward to a fine frolic at week's end."

"Yes, a fine frolic," she echoed. He looked so gleeful she almost felt sorry for him. "Do you like to dance, Captain?"

"I'm a bit of a toe stepper," he confessed. "But a few of the officers have graced some of the finest ballrooms in the colonies. I trust you'll be there—with your dulcimer?" At her surprise, he added quickly, "I've heard you playing nights—not enough to disturb anyone, mind you, when I've been up and around myself."

Up and around with Olympia, she gathered. With Colonel McLinn sleeping at the stone house, more than a little nocturnal mischief was being made within Fort Endeavor's walls. Thinking of Abby, Roxanna held back a sigh.

"Till Saturday, then, Captain," she said with a slight smile, wondering if McLinn would keep his promise . . . and the Redstone women would behave.

12

Despite dressing in the somber little cabin with all its secrets and shadows, Roxanna felt an unexpected spark of excitement as she pulled on her stockings, securing them to her garters and smoothing her petticoats into place. Bella had insisted she dress her hair in long spirals once again with the curling tongs, weaving in a bit of silver ribbon among all that glossy black to match the fine Irish lace fichu about her shoulders. It dressed up the sedate lines of her dove-gray gown and made her look less mournful.

"Now, I know yo' missin' yo' pa, but he'd want you to look mighty fine while you're playin' that there music box he made you." She pulled a stray string from Roxanna's skirt and sighed. "Law, but I hope all them men behave when you womenfolk walk in. With the colonel there, they won't make too much mischief. And then there's the child."

At that mention, Abby peeked out from behind Roxanna's full skirts. A smile pulled at Bella's dour mouth as she surveyed the dress she'd made Abby. 'Twas a lustrous yellow satin with a quilted petticoat, gotten from her secret stores in the stone house.

"Why, you look bright as a sunbeam," Roxanna whispered as Abby fingered the lacy bows of her bodice.

105

Despite the compliment, no answering smile graced the small face, and her blue-gray eyes seemed huge in the shadows. Earlier, Olympia had finally given her over to their care, intent on beautifying herself for the dance without the child underfoot. Taking advantage of the moment, Roxanna asked if she might teach Abby her letters.

"Letters?" Olympia paused in affixing a beauty mark to her cheek. "What for?"

"I think Abby would like to read . . . write her name."

Olympia tucked a strand of graying hair behind her ear and made a face. "No sense in makin' a silk purse out of a sow's ear."

"But I thought you wanted a better life for Abby," Roxanna said quietly, as stung by her callous comment as by the sudden sadness in Abby's eyes.

"Who'd teach her?"

"I would. Before coming here, I was a tutor to children just Abby's age. I have a hornbook in my belongings, some story cards."

"I'll study on it," Olympia said, fussing with her powdered hair, clearly bored with the subject.

Pondering it now, Roxanna took Abby's hand and crossed the snow-dusted common with her dulcimer in arm. They entered the large blockhouse dining room that served as a makeshift dance hall and marveled at the change. Dovie and Nancy were putting fresh tapers in all the candelabras, and a fire crackled in the river rock hearth. Benches lined the log walls, and there was even a small platform where the musicians would sit.

She found Bella leaning over a barrel in the kitchen, a rapturous look on her bony face. "Bella, are you imbibing?" Roxanna couldn't help tease.

"I sure is," she said, waving a ladle. "Would you like a little sip?" Roxanna stepped up as she made another pass over the shiny liquid. "None o' that flip or mulled wine for McLinn, but genuine cherry bounce."

Roxanna's delight faded as grief crowded in. Papa had dearly loved cherry bounce. She and Mama had made many a gallon from their own orchard in days past. *Here's to old times*, she mused, in a sort of silent toast. She took a generous gulp and her eyes widened. "Why, Bella, that's the best bounce I've ever tasted!"

A rare smile softened Bella's countenance. "Let's hope the colonel says the same. I was nearly scalped pickin' all them cherries downriver at Smitty's Fort. Hank helped me. He and the colonel planted a fine orchard back of the stone house here on the hill, but the trees are young yet, and what little we get the birds gobble up."

Roxanna longed to learn all she could about the colonel's private retreat but stayed busy helping set out an assortment of cheese, bread, and tarts alongside cider and the coveted bounce. As the soldiers began assembling, she kept a close eye on Abby, easily spied in her yellow dress. Soon Micajah Hale was beside her, a fiddle tucked under one arm.

"The evening improves already," he said, eyeing her dulcimer appreciatively. He removed his uniform coat to better play his instrument, revealing a pristine linen shirt and brocade weskit, his sandy hair tied back with silk string. Small pockmarks pitted his cheeks and chin, evidence of the scourge so common to soldiers. She thought how waifish he was when compared to his commanding officer.

Around them the air seemed to crackle with excitement. Bella had wisely left the blockhouse door ajar, and the room was filling with every conceivable soldier but Colonel McLinn. Micajah gestured to a seat and Roxanna took it, glad to be off her feet. Two more fiddlers gathered round and Hale made polite introductions, all the while looking at her, she noticed. Slightly ill at ease from the attention, she listened to their small talk but found her eyes trailing to the blockhouse door again and again.

Would the colonel not come? Were the comforts of the stone house so great?

She'd seen smoke rising from the twin chimneys just as the sun had set and the stately walls had flamed with warm crimson and gold light. She imagined him sitting feet to the fire in a deep wingback chair, perhaps smoking a pipe, far removed from the filth and cramped quarters of Fort Endeavor. She felt curiously let down, though the Redstone women were a blessed distraction, making a grand entrance in dresses she'd never before seen.

Each preened like a colorful songbird—Olympia bright as a cardinal in red wool, Mariah in canary yellow, Nancy a bluebird in rich indigo. Dovie brought up the rear. Clothed in pink linen, she looked even younger than her fifteen years. Tonight they were the belles of the ball, though Roxanna wondered how they would hold up with such an abundance of partners. Then, remembering the impromptu dance aboard the flatboat, she sensed the night might be long indeed.

Micajah began tuning his fiddle—fine maple from the sheen of it—and she dared to ask, "Shouldn't we wait for Colonel McLinn?"

He stopped his adjustments and gave her a smug smile. "If we wait, we might not have a frolic at all." Seeing her confusion, he added, "The colonel rarely partakes of any sort of amusement. I wager he feels it beneath him. A cramped blockhouse hardly compares with a Williamsburg ballroom."

With that, he struck a spritely tune, and the twang of the fiddles nearly drowned out the dulcimer. Roxanna soon lost herself in the merry music and rhythm of the reel, looking down at her hands as she played, almost able to forget where she was and her uncertain future. Less than an arm's length away sat Abby on a stool, watching her pluck the strings as if transfixed, her riotous curls alight in the fire's backdrop.

When at last Roxanna looked up again, it was the colonel she saw straight across from her, broad shoulders filling the width of the door frame, fiery head ducking beneath the lintel. The fiddlers began a new tune, and she fell in a bit behind, thoughts askew.

Ah . . . one simple look . . . but what a memory it made.

He was in full dress uniform and clean shaven, his hair pulled back in still-damp strands and caught with the usual black silk ribbon. She saw a flash of white teeth as he laughed and joked with his officers, and she felt a deep gnawing to know what it was he found so amusing. In blockhouse headquarters, he was often tense and solemn, his smiles tight, as if her company somehow grieved him. This was a side of him she'd not seen.

Across the way, Bella was bringing out the cherry bounce for him to sample, and his satisfaction was so apparent her own dark face creased with a smile. The lively strains of the gavotte filled the large space, and she looked up again to see the colonel escorting Mariah into the middle of the melee. Mariah smiled up at him as he placed one hand upon her waist and led her out with the other. How gallant—and surprising—Roxanna mused, given his reservations about the Redstone women.

Truly, Captain Stewart had not lied. Colonel McLinn had indeed graced some of the finest ballrooms in the colonies. Partnered with him, even Mariah seemed to shine. Roxanna wondered how it felt to be held so, to be turned about like one was light as thistledown. Her best shoe with its extra-tall heel seemed almost to ache as she watched them, and when she looked back down, the polished wood of her dulcimer was a watery brown.

She shouldn't have come—her emotions were too raw. Every poignant note seemed to prick her, though she played as stalwartly as she could. She was more than ready to stop when the musicians took a short rest and Micajah brought her some cider. Abby had slipped away to the food-laden table, eyeing the apple tarts. A hundred or more voices hummed inside the timbered room now six people deep. There was precious little room for dancing, yet the men showed little inclination to quit—perhaps not till the clock struck twelve and turned into the Sabbath.

"You don't have to play all night," Micajah told her. "Though you play very well." He tucked his bow under one arm and sat beside her, fiddle in one hand and cherry bounce in the other. "'Twas a brilliant idea you had suggesting this. I've gotten more work out of the men this week than most. And aside from that court-martial, there's not been one breach of behavior."

"Everyone seems to be enjoying themselves," she said, letting her eyes roam over the crowd again. "Even Colonel McLinn."

Surprise crossed his face. "I wasn't sure he'd come—or stay. Once he leaves fort walls for the day, he doesn't often come back. Likes to shut himself away in the stone house."

"'Tis a beautiful place."

"A bit grand for Kentucke, some say. He calls it *Sithean*—that's Gaelic for 'fairy hill.' The only way he could abide coming to the frontier was to build a bit of home here."

"He must miss Ireland, then."

He shrugged. "Oh, I don't know. He rarely speaks of it. He does have ties there—some relatives and an Irish beauty by the name of Cecily O'Day. I suppose Bella has told you about that. No doubt you've heard of Liam McLinn."

Roxanna brushed a speck of dust off her dulcimer. "Bella mentioned he has a twin."

"Aye, so he does—one who just happens to be an officer in the British army. When Cass joined the Americans, it caused a bit of a fracas. As heir, he lost the family holdings when the British learned of his betrayal. But it hardly mattered. Liam was already wreaking havoc making free with their inheritance. He spent some time in Dublin's Marshalsea Prison for debt, but slippery as he is, he escaped and came here." The relaxed lines of his face tightened. "General Washington calls him Lucifer McLinn—on account of all the trouble he's caused." Seeing her blank expression, he added, "Don't you read the papers, Miss Rowan?"

"Just the *Virginia Gazette* . . . occasionally."

He grimaced. "Liam McLinn is a staunch loyalist and spy. And one of the greatest threats to the Continental cause there is. He's done untold damage masquerading as his Patriot brother in the colonies. Once he nearly had Cass hung for treason."

A chill touched her spine. "What?"

"A group of New York Tories led by Liam formed a secret organization to assassinate General Washington. Fortunately, the plot was uncovered, and forty or more conspirators were arrested, including one of Washington's beloved Life Guards."

"Colonel McLinn was also a Life Guard, wasn't he?"

"Aye. Liam tried to implicate him, but there wasn't enough evidence to send him to the gallows. Fortunately, Washington never believed ill of him. A close friend of the colonel's, Captain Thomas Hickey, wasn't so lucky. He was hanged. After that Washington sent Cass west."

"To remove him from the danger and speculation, you mean? So no one can confuse him with his brother?" The prospect was so stunning—and intriguing—she cast aside her self-imposed rule to mind her own business.

He nodded and downed the last of his bounce. "Now Washington merely has to point west when an ugly rumor arises. Having Cass here makes it that much easier for Continental forces to catch the real loyalist McLinn."

Cass. She found herself lingering on the name, liking its softness, so at odds with the man himself. Behind them the fiddling commenced again, and Micajah left her side to resume playing. She found her heart racing inexplicably, her pulse keeping time to the music. Her thoughts were in such a troubled jumble she decided to sit this tune out, searching through the crowd till she located the object of their discussion.

The colonel was standing in front of Abby now, and she barely came up to his thigh. Her head was tipped back and her lips parted as if in a sort of wonder. Around them all had stilled, even the music, every eye on the commander and the child. Roxanna watched as he made a small bow. Though no expression crossed her face, Abby put one foot behind the other and gave a surprising curtsey.

A ripple of amusement passed through the gathering. Cass held out his hand and Roxanna held her breath. Would he even charm a mute child? Pensive, Abby studied him before extending her own small hand. He took it, and the music began again, but not before he'd stood her little feet atop his polished boots.

Around and around he danced with her, holding on to her hands, her feet firmly planted atop his own. And she was . . . *smiling*. Still mute yet smiling. Even Olympia seemed a bit awed, standing with Dovie and Captain Stewart in the shadows. It seemed something of a miracle. Roxanna swallowed past the tightness in her throat and returned to her dulcimer, trying to sound the right notes, the picture of Abby and the colonel lingering.

The dark log walls and press of perspiring men receded as her thoughts winged across a continent to Ireland and an Irish beauty named Cecily and a twin called Liam McLinn. *Lucifer* McLinn. She regretted that their trouble went deep, pitting brother against brother. Family rifts were common enough with a war on, but one involving an enemy twin seemed extraordinary somehow—and doubly dangerous.

An hour passed in a sort of haze. Suddenly weary, she waited for the right time to bid the musicians goodbye, then slipped into the empty kitchen unnoticed and hastened out the small side door that led to the springhouse and parade ground. But before she'd pulled it shut, she heard a heavy footfall. Cold moonlight cast the colonel in a long black silhouette directly in her path.

"Miss Rowan, I believe you're in need of an escort."

In the silence, his voice was deep and clear and lilting, and her soft response was lost as the music started up again. He held out his arm, and she had little choice but to take it, startled when he brought his other hand to bear on hers as it rested on his wool sleeve, its warm width covering her cold fingers like a glove. She was acutely conscious of his height and how, unlike the diminutive Dovie, she was eye level with his epaulets. There was something different about him tonight, and it struck her as hard as the cold. He was gallant . . . charming . . . almost mellow. Perhaps on account of Bella's fine cherry bounce.

He said quietly, "I wanted to thank you for the evening's entertainment."

She nearly slipped on an icy patch, but he caught her and she stammered, "Th-thank you for allowing it." Hugging her dulcimer tight with her free arm, she noticed he walked the long way to her cabin, along the north barracks, as opposed to simply crossing the parade ground.

He looked down at her. "You're leaving early." She opened her mouth to mumble an excuse, but he went on easily, "But then, so am I."

She looked over the far pickets and up the hill where warm light beckoned in every window of the stone house. *Home.* She wanted to keep walking right out the fort's gates and up the rise and over the threshold into a warm paneled room where she just knew a wingback chair waited before a crackling hearth.

The ache in her chest expanded till she could barely breathe. "What will you do when you get there?" The wistful question was uttered before she realized what she'd asked, and there was no wishing it back.

She could hear the smile in his voice in the darkness. "Read. Smoke. Badger Hank into going to that dance."

She hadn't noticed Hank was missing. Only Bella had been there.

He stopped abruptly and turned to her. "What will you do when you get here?"

They'd come to her cabin door, and she hadn't expected him to echo her question. It took all the poise she possessed to simply say, "Read. Have a cup of tea." *Cry.*

He released her arm. "Are you in need of some books, Miss Rowan? *Tristram Shandy*, perhaps? Some Samuel Johnson?"

She nearly raised an eyebrow at his recommendations. *A touch scandalous*, she thought. For a moment she sensed he might invite her to the stone house. Bella had said he had a fine library. "I have the good book, Colonel. 'Tis enough for now."

"The offer stands should you have need of anything else—or want to move to another cabin." He hesitated and she thought he might say more, but he simply finished with a disappointingly curt, "Good night, Miss Rowan."

He opened the cabin door, and she went inside and set her instrument down. Still breathless, she cracked open the shutter to watch his retreating back and heard the crisp crunch of snow under his boots. An extravagant moon illuminated every nuance of the scene unfolding before her. The sentries at both gates saluted as he passed, the saber tips of their muskets a flash of silver in the deep darkness.

He was moving toward the little sally port along the north wall of the fort. Bella had pointed it out to her, and she'd been struck that it was barely big enough for a man's girth. A secret escape, if you will. Two regulars fell in behind him without a word, and the trio disappeared behind the high north wall, only to emerge on the moonlit hill leading to *Sithean*.

Her heart gave a lonesome leap as they reached their destination. Before he'd taken the first of three steps to the front door, it opened wide in welcome and Hank's voice rang out. Cass disappeared inside and then Hank took his leave, coming back down the frozen hill with the two regulars and entering through the sally port.

A knowing smile touched Roxanna's lips. Colonel McLinn hadn't had to do much badgering. Hank made a beeline for the blockhouse and Bella's cherry bounce.

❧ ❧

The Sabbath yawned gray and quiet. Since the army chaplain had died in the fall, no services were held, Bella told her. If they had been, Roxanna wondered how many would attend. She smelled strong coffee brewing all the way across the parade ground, but not a soul came for breakfast save little Abby, wandering across the cold common in her fancy quilted petticoat, clutching the doll Roxanna had made her.

I must fashion a day dress for her from one of my own, she decided. And so she set to work, assembling her sewing supplies, knowing Bella would feed Abby once she slipped into the kitchen. Truly, Bella seemed fond of the little girl.

It wasn't till dinner that anyone stirred save the sentries. When Colonel McLinn appeared through the sally port at dusk, Roxanna wondered what the commander of the entire western frontier did on an idle Sabbath day. She kept busy helping Bella in the kitchen while the Redstone women prepared to serve. It had become their habit to eat in the confines of the kitchen before the men crowded into the dining room.

Bella stood watch over a venison roast turning on a spit while Nancy mashed the potatoes. "These need a mite more salt, just like the gravy," Nancy said, reaching for a salt gourd.

"Careful," Bella cautioned. "Our salt's runnin' low—same as everything else around here."

"I thought the colonel sent out a salt-makin' party over a fortnight ago," Mariah said.

"He did, but they ain't back yet. Makin' salt's a bad business even in the dead o' winter. We'll have to stretch what we have another week or better till they get back."

Roxanna set the trestle table for their own meal, thinking they were becoming woefully short of many things, even cornmeal. Fort Endeavor grew mostly corn, the now fallow fields barely visible under a skiff of snow. Bella bragged that some stalks were so tall they seemed to touch the Kentucke sky. But plowing and planting were months away. She'd be gone before anything was harvested—or so she hoped.

They sat down together, all six women and Abby. Joining

hands, they said a prayer, then passed bowls and made small talk, all the while waiting for the men. Roxanna noticed each woman seemed to be listening for a certain voice in particular. She'd often done the same with Ambrose, waiting for his warm baritone to fill the long hallway of her house back home. Beside her, Olympia kept an eye on the door adjoining the dining room. She still claimed an officer, Captain Stewart, while the others had settled on the less refined regulars.

"That was some frolic, Miz Roxanna," Mariah said between bites of bread. "But it's a shame you didn't dance."

"She's mournin' her pa, remember," Olympia reminded her.

"Oh, it's more than that, really," Roxanna confessed, filling Abby's mug with milk. "I'm a bit lame in one leg."

"Lame? How?" Dovie asked.

"I fell out of a tree as a child and had a bad break that didn't mend properly. I'd like to dance but don't manage the steps well."

"I noticed you limpin'," Nancy murmured. "Though you hide it right well."

Olympia grew sly. "Now, say you were to dance with someone who knew what he was doin'. I'll wager you wouldn't feel lame at all."

The women tittered around the table, and Roxanna felt heat inching up her neck. Beside her, Bella drew up like an injured hen. "No matchmakin' is goin' to go on in my kitchen, you hear? You'd best hoe your own row."

"Now listen here," Olympia snarled, rebellion in her eyes. "Miz Roxanna shouldn't have to sit and watch the rest of us make merry, is all I'm sayin'."

"Well, you is always sayin' too much."

"Ladies, please," Roxanna intervened.

A strained silence settled round the table so that only the snap of the fire was heard. This was Bella's domain, but Olympia, strong willed as she was, liked to overstep her bounds, even in the most trivial ways. The ill feeling between them seemed to simmer and set the rest of them on edge. Roxanna wondered if she'd been wise asking for them to stay on. Yet where would they be otherwise? And there was Abby to consider.

Roxanna finished her meal, eyes trailing to Dovie's untouched plate beside her. As the others got up and prepared to serve in the dining room, she said quietly, "Abby, will you take round the bread?" The child stopped chewing and slid off her stool. When she'd disappeared, Roxanna continued in hushed tones, "Dovie, are you ill?"

The girl averted her eyes and picked up her fork halfheartedly. "I ain't got much appetite here lately."

Mariah turned around, arms full of pewter plates, and hissed, "You might as well tell her. She'll see for herself soon enough."

At once Roxanna knew. She'd had too many friends shunning their supper plates on account of this condition—all of them wed. But Dovie seemed reluctant to share her secret, simply whispering, "I'm scared Colonel McLinn will turn me out if he knows."

Roxanna's mind raced as she scrambled for the name of the young soldier she'd last seen her with. "Is Private Dayton the father, Dovie?"

She gave a little shrug. "I ain't sure."

Swallowing her dismay, Roxanna asked, "Would you like him to be?"

"I like him the best of them all. And he says he's goin' to ask the colonel if he can marry me. But his enlistment ain't up till after the baby comes."

"When will that be?"

She furrowed her brow, and the sprinkling of freckles across her nose turned her touchingly childlike. "September or so, by my count."

Disbelief coursed through Roxanna. So soon? They'd been at the fort less than two months.

Bella ceased stirring the gravy and eyed Dovie sternly. "You'd best 'fess up right quick and call for the preacher. The colonel don't have no tolerance for loose women."

Dovie turned watery eyes on Roxanna. "Will you speak to him, Miz Rox—"

Bella's spoon clanged against the side of the kettle. "Don't you go beggin' a lady to air your dirty laundry with McLinn—"

"Now, Bella . . ." Roxanna dug in her pocket for a handkerchief and turned back to Dovie. "If Johnny's willing to ask the colonel for your hand, I think he must care for you and want to make things right."

But Bella shook her head dolefully. "Johnny's likely to get fifty lashes and a court-martial for his trouble. Now, there's more than one way to skin a cat. Old Granny Sykes over at Smitty's Fort can fix you up a tonic—"

"Bella! No!" Roxanna stood, plate and mug balanced precariously in one hand, the other on Dovie's shoulder. "Babies are a gift, not . . . garbage."

Bella had the grace to look sheepish, eyes averted. "I'd sooner take a tonic than face McLinn." With that, she went out, the door slapping shut in her wake.

Roxanna sat back down. "Despite Bella's rather vocal opinions, Colonel McLinn is an honorable man. And I'm sure he'll listen to Johnny's proposal. Besides, a wedding and a baby are some of the finest things this life offers. I've often wished for both myself." The admission made her own eyes water, and Dovie passed her back the handkerchief.

"I'm still prayin' you'll find your man, Miz Roxanna," she said, squeezing her hand. "And I promise not to send for Granny Sykes."

13

Reveille sounded at daybreak, followed by roll call and drill, rousing Roxanna as she lay on her corn-husk tick. She'd overslept this morning simply because she had stayed awake most of the night imagining, among other things, what the interior of the stone house must be like. In drowsy dreams that both delighted and disturbed her, she had crossed the threshold of that house looking for Colonel McLinn but had come awake before she'd found him. Now the ache of it lingered and made no sense.

Beyond her shuttered window, the breathtaking day held a hint of spring. She crossed the sunny parade ground without a cape, holding her skirt hem out of the muck and melting snow. Soldiers stood in formation around her, and sentries removed the huge cross timbers of the front gates, which slowly groaned open. She'd no sooner touched the handle of the blockhouse door than the colonel opened it, his sturdy frame filling the rough-hewn space like an impenetrable wall.

"Miss Rowan."

"Colonel McLinn." This morning the name seemed a mouthful, and she was reminded of her nocturnal musings. Flushing, she felt almost relieved to find him here—hale and hearty—when she'd missed him so mournfully in her dream.

"I've left some things on my desk for you," he said, fastening the gold braid of his collar. She took in his rich camlet cloak to avoid meeting his eyes, startled to see Abby just behind him. Had she come in of her own accord? He didn't have time for a child, mute or no . . .

Seeing her surprise, he said wryly, "Miss Abigail has just provided me with half an hour's entertainment."

"Oh?" was all Roxanna could think to say.

"I'm teaching her to play chess."

"Chess?"

"'Tis not our first game, ye ken."

At this, her eyes widened and she looked again at Abby, who peeked out from behind her opponent's cloak with a winsome smile. Her expression was so merry, so full of mischief, Roxanna nearly laughed.

"She seems determined to take my king and might well do so in future. Don't be fooled. Beneath that tangle of red hair is a formidable mind. She even demands her prize before we play."

Abby held up her treasure, a tiny cone of loaf sugar, as proudly as if it were gold. And gold it nearly was, Roxanna thought, thinking of their depleted stores. Abby was wearing the dress she'd made her, and the green wool was a nice counterpoint to her unusual eyes and ruby hair. But it was her smile that struck Roxanna nearly speechless. She seemed so relaxed, so at ease with her giant guardian, Roxanna was amazed.

A sudden voice from behind made her turn. Micajah Hale stood watching them, bemused as well. As the colonel moved past her onto the parade ground, his second-in-command took her arm. "It's not quite eight o'clock, Miss Rowan. Perhaps you'd like to join us for a bit of shooting practice. I'm in charge of an elite rifle company, and we put on quite a show."

Taking Abby's hand, she stepped away from him. "Thank you, Major Hale, but the noise of the guns . . ." She softened her refusal with a smile and escaped inside, relieved to find the room empty. A fierce fire blazed in the huge hearth, and she moved toward the colonel's desk, stifling a sigh. He'd posted her orders on a handbill of sorts, only she found his handwriting a puzzle. Like the man himself. Little wonder he needed a scrivener.

Perplexed, she took up a magnifying glass and studied the jumble of bold letters till they made sense, then sat down to do her work. Abby sat beside her, sucking on her sugar lump, in dire need of a bath. Roxanna studied her a few moments later as she looked up from her work, seeing so much potential, even if Olympia didn't. If the child could manage a game of chess . . .

With sudden resolve, she decided to go ahead with Abby's schooling. She would deal with Olympia later. Hurrying back across the parade ground, she retrieved her hornbook, a slate, and stylus. Within an hour, Abby was making a painstaking row of As and Bs.

Pleased, Roxanna kissed her cheek. "Oh, Abby, your aunt will be . . ." She paused, nearly wincing at the sudden thunder of guns. Knowing Olympia probably wouldn't care, she amended, "I'm so proud of you. Colonel McLinn would be proud too, as he likes fine penmanship. Your letters are straight as soldiers."

Abby's face lit up and then darkened as she looked warily toward the window.

"All those men make quite a commotion," Roxanna lamented. "To your tender ears, especially."

She cracked open the shutter to find the air full of smoke, the acrid smell stinging her senses. It seemed Fort Endeavor was low on everything but powder and lead. Companies of men were now moving beyond fort walls to the broad level leading to the river.

"Colonel McLinn is drilling again. You'd best stay inside, Abby, and keep making your letters. If not here, the kitchen, perhaps. I'm going to see what all the fuss is about."

Abby nodded dutifully and returned to her letters. Though reluctant to leave her alone, Roxanna went out and shut the door. She met Bella in a warm puddle of sunlight near the front gate.

Shivering in her tattered cape, Bella flashed Roxanna a wide, gap-toothed smile. "Law, but that gate ain't been open in months. The scoutin' parties must have brought back a good report."

"No Indian sign, you mean?"

She nodded. "No Redcoats neither." Looking down, she dug in her pocket and handed Roxanna some tow linen. "Best put it in your ears, same as me."

They moved beyond the shadow of the long front wall, ears plugged, enjoying the expansive view. The river wound in a serpentine shimmer of ice beyond far banks. On their side of the Ohio, all was clear and level, the trees trimmed back to allow for orchards and fields of corn. Crowning the rise at their backs was the stone house, a golden nugget on the sun-drenched hill.

Giving in to a wild reverie, Roxanna saw not the fetid fort, but the grand house with a long porch . . . a summer kitchen . . . a smokehouse . . . full-grown fruit trees . . . a scattering of giant oaks and elms for shade. Just as it had been in her dream. But the sudden storm of a hundred guns stole away her musings, and she turned back in time to see the two Indian prisoners being led through the gates, unchained but under heavy guard.

How proud they looked—and how wary.

The feathers in their dark hair fluttered in the wind, as did the long fringe of their buckskin tunics and leggings. Each wore calf-high, fur-lined shoepacks, and a blue trade blanket was draped around their shoulders. The younger of the two was looking everywhere at once and then, hawk-like, directly at Roxanna. Feeling a twist of pity and then fear, she shivered and moved into Bella's shadow.

Bella murmured, "They've been brought out here to be impressed with all the noise and fuss. And if there's any more like 'em over on that side o' the river, they're welcome to watch as well."

Fortunately, the far bank was well out of musket range a mile or more away. This morning, at least, the surrounding brush and trees simply held an icy sheen, harboring no enemies. Or so they hoped.

"My, ain't the colonel in fine form today." For once Bella's voice wasn't sharp with sarcasm but touched with respect. Reluctantly, Roxanna turned in his direction, the music of fife and drums in her ears.

For a few disorienting seconds she felt she'd been cast back to that twilight eve when she first caught sight of him on his white horse, the wind whipping the edges of his Continental cape so that the scarlet lining was visible, his tricorn shading his handsome features.

From the river's edge his voice boomed loud as a cannon. "I want a *feu de joie* from east to west."

A running fire of musketry? Roxanna wondered what he meant.

The men scrambled to do his bidding, forming a tremendous line of sunlit silhouettes, muskets raised. Roxanna watched as the colonel rode to the far right of the long column, shouting another order before taking off at full gallop, just abreast of each exploding gun. Startled, she stepped back and stuffed the linen further into her ears, heart pounding louder than the accompanying drums.

Surely this was no show to impress the two Indian chiefs. Nay, this was . . . suicide . . . assassination. A spy—*the spy*—might still be among them. The paralyzing realization made her take a step back as she realized her part in it all. She hadn't told the colonel about the journal, and one of these men might mean him harm. Unwittingly, he'd placed himself in the line of fire. If only she'd gone straight to him with her suspicions—

Oh please, God, no!

At the end of the long line, he whirled about on his winded, excited stallion to the roar of his cheering men. Even Bella clapped her hands as Hank moved to stand beside her. Whirling, Roxanna grabbed up her skirts and ran for the gates.

The icy mud churned and seethed beneath her boots, flinging ugly spatters across her clean dress. By the time she reached her cabin, she was shaking, haunted by the explosive crack and smoke of muskets, feeling she was as small as Abby and fleeing a fire-breathing dragon instead. Shaking, she stood before the warm hearth, acutely aware of the lap desk behind her. How easily the enemy might have shot him. With so many guns, who would ever know who'd fired the fatal shot?

The night before, she'd stayed awake reading every single entry written in her father's flowing hand, dismayed to discover each as cryptic as the last. There was an enemy, he'd said, but never had he alluded in name or physical description as to who that might be. He'd come close, but then, as if he sensed someone might discover his suspicions, had actually torn out the last few pages, leaving a puzzle she couldn't possibly piece together.

A savage hurt took hold of her, and she fumbled for her handkerchief, dampening it thoroughly by the time a knock sounded on the door. Bella? There was no use pretending with Bella. Balling her hankie into a fist, she took a deep breath.

The door swung open to reveal Colonel McLinn. He had to duck his head to clear the lintel of the door frame and didn't wait for an invitation to enter in. Stunned, she took a step back on the dusty hearth stones, singeing her skirt hem in the hungry flames. The smell of scorched wool filled the closed space between them. Taking her firmly by the shoulders, he maneuvered her away from the fire.

She was acutely aware of her childish tears—and the stern, undeniably irritated way he was regarding her—and felt like crawling underneath the trestle table. *Oh, Bella, where are you?* She'd never been completely alone with him save his escorting her back to her cabin and was suddenly struck by how intimidating he truly was. He towered over her, seeming to shrink the cabin to the size of a snuffbox. Worst of all was his silence.

Her mouth felt full of cotton when she mumbled, "You might have been killed."

"'Twas a simple military maneuver, Miss Rowan."

Her chin came up. Was he making light of her fears? "Nay, not simple, Colonel."

Not with an enemy on the loose.

His eyes, hard and blue as stained glass, softened ever so slightly. "I've been a soldier a long time, and it's hardened me. I apologize for frightening you. I didn't . . ."

He hesitated and she filled the silence. "You didn't see me."

"Aye, I did. But I kept on. And I'm truly sorry." With that, he sat down on the bench in front of her, a humble footnote to his apology.

Still shaky, she sank down at the opposite end, hands knotted in her lap, sensing he had more to say. It was sheer work not to look at him. He was no longer the commander here in her tiny cabin but just a man with a mercurial charm, contrite and brusque by turns . . . and terribly appealing.

Eyes down, she waited for him to leave but instead felt the sudden warmth of his hand as he reached over and brushed her damp cheek. The gentle gesture only made her eyes fill again.

He said apologetically, "I have no handkerchief."

Startled, she revealed the one she held, its lace edges damp and wrinkled. His hand fell away and his gaze skimmed the dark walls as if seeing them for the first time. "Miss Rowan, you don't belong here. Not in this cabin, not in this fort."

"Nor do you," she replied softly. "You belong on a battlefield somewhere in the east, helping win the war."

"I've been on a few battlefields. And we were winning for a season. But now . . ."

She said nothing, waiting for him to finish, wondering if he'd tell her about the trouble that brought him west. Wanting him to.

Instead his eyes turned wintry again. "You might as well know I'm considering resigning my commission in the near future."

He shifted on the bench and his knee brushed hers. "But not until I see you safely settled."

Somehow this didn't bring the solace she craved. Thinking how she'd just turned tail and run from the guns still shamed her. "I don't want you to make your plans around me. Nor do I mean to keep you from military maneuvers or anything else. If there's an opportunity for you to leave this place, I urge you to take it."

"And where would that leave you?"

She balled up her hankie again and avoided his eyes. "Colonel McLinn, I'm nearly nine and twenty, more spinster than schoolgirl. My father was wrong to bind you to that promise." She paused, resurrecting something Olympia once said. "And given all the solitary men on the frontier, I'm sure making a match here would be as easy as falling off a log."

"Aye, I'm sure any of my men would gladly wed you, Miss Rowan. Not that any of them would pass muster. As for the locals—frontiersmen, trappers, and convicts—you can put that out of your head. Your prospects here are bloody few."

Her shoulders straightened, and she locked eyes with him again. "I'd much rather talk about your prospects, Colonel. My father once told me he considered you the finest commanding officer he's served under since the French and Indian War. He followed you to the frontier because of it. If you can leave this place for a better one, I suggest you do so and not give my situation another thought."

"You underestimate me, then." Leaning back slightly, he crossed his ankles and folded his arms. He was the commander again, challenging her, staring her down, forcing her to retreat. "What kind of an officer—and a gentleman—would deny a man's final request to see to his only daughter?"

Oh, they were back to her father again. There was no undoing that final promise.

Stifling a sigh, she made the last appeal she could. "You

aren't ultimately responsible for me, Colonel. God is. Even if you were to renege on your promise, He would not." She got up and crossed to the corner where the lap desk rested. Opening the top, she touched the spring that released the secret drawer. She took out the leather-bound book and sat down beside him.

"There's another reason you should leave this place. You may have an enemy within these very walls. My father felt your life was—perhaps still is—in danger." She leafed through the worn pages with nervous hands, head bent in concentration. "When I saw you riding in front of all your men and all those muskets, knowing at least one of them might mean you harm, I couldn't stand there and watch . . . so I ran."

Passing him the journal, she took a long, unhindered look at him as he contemplated the offering. Hands in her lap, she stifled the urge to reach out and ease the tense lines of his brow, smooth away his every worry. The heady scent of bergamot mingled with the sharp but subtle tang of lye and sent her senses swimming. She could no longer remember what Ambrose looked like, or smelled like, or was like. All she knew was Cassius Clayton McLinn.

All she wanted began and ended with him.

Hank had laid a fine fire, full of snap and fury, and its bold light flickered over the blue paneled walls in such a merry dance it nearly shifted Cass's pensive mood. Of all the rooms in the stone house, the study was his favorite. Here some of the finest craftsmen in Kentucke had left their mark. He took in the deeply recessed bookshelves, the elegant moldings and cornices, and the polished walnut floors, feeling the filth of Fort Endeavor recede with every step.

Removing his linen stock, he made for the wing chair nearest the hearth and eyed the tilt-top table bearing a crystal decanter. Hank hadn't forgotten his brandy, but he'd forgotten to have

Hank help him with his boots. Scowling, he looked down to find he'd left a muddy trail across the needlepoint rug, and ground his back teeth in frustration. Bella would have an unholy fit.

But Roxanna wouldn't.

He pictured her standing beside him, hands pressed together in quiet delight. Somehow he knew she'd simply shake her head and smile at the mess he'd just made. Or scold him just a bit. Thinking it, he roamed the cozy room with new eyes—her eyes—and felt a deep appreciation. The colorful gros point rugs, the walnut spice cabinet with its little silver key, the blue brocade chair that was twin to his own, the multitude of leather-bound books lining the walls—they would all work to woo her, given he wanted to.

He'd had the house built for many reasons, mainly as a statement of permanence and to put up river travelers. In fair weather, when the Indian threat wasn't too high, an interesting assortment of courageous guests spilled onto the Kentucke shore. Most sought refuge in the fort, but military men like Generals Hand and Lafayette, and visiting dignitaries like the Spanish governor in Missouri territory, preferred this. And they all said the same thing—the house badly needed a mistress. But he was too preoccupied to play host . . . or wed.

He'd come close on one occasion. But Cecily O'Day wouldn't have lasted in the wilderness. Nor the colonies. Though the daughter of a British general, she hadn't the stamina or spirit of her colonial cousins. Women like Kitty Greene, who'd been at her husband's side at Valley Forge. Or Martha Washington, with her long-suffering cheerfulness. Or Lucy Knox, with her ebullient humor.

Unlike Roxanna Rowan, Cecily would never have entertained the notion of coming downriver four hundred miles into the very heart of danger. Nay, Cecily seemed a hothouse flower in comparison. 'Twas well their foolish passion ended when it did. A few kisses. A few letters. And then she'd wed another. Lately he'd given it little thought.

Aye, he had other things to think about. Like the enemy. And who Richard Rowan thought posed a threat. Ignoring his boots, he took a chair and withdrew the small journal from his waistcoat pocket. Since leaving Roxanna's cabin this morning, he'd carried the book about with him as he drilled his men, ever conscious of its subtle weight, his curiosity at fever's pitch.

Shelving all correspondence for the time being, he'd given her the rest of the day off, wagering she'd disappear into the blockhouse kitchen soon after. At supper he'd been rewarded with roast turkey so succulent it fell off the bone, buttery spoon bread, and apple tansy, followed by coffin pie and strong coffee.

"Maybe you should let yer scrivener work nights, Colonel, and keep 'er in the kitchen days," one of the regulars joked.

"And I'll remind you to keep a civil tongue in your head, Private, or you'll find yourself on double duty," he shot back with a scowl.

He'd lingered longest at table and then, when the room was empty, he'd gone into the kitchen to thank Roxanna, only to find Bella and the Redstone women up to their elbows in dirty dishes—and no sign of Roxanna Rowan.

With a sage look, Bella said, "If you've come to thank Miz Roxanna for the fine meal, she's done gone to her cabin."

Disappointed, he'd left out the sally port, acutely aware of the guard flanking him. Hank threw open the door just as he'd done nearly every night for the past two years or better, bridging the darkness in welcome. As he did, a recurring thought struck Cass hard as a fist. What if the enemy opened the door instead? What if he came face-to-face with a British bayonet? Or an Indian arrow?

Now Richard Rowan's journal seemed heavy in his calloused hand. He thumped it absently across one knee of his breeches while he reached for the decanter of brandy with his other hand, pouring half a glass. The liquid disappeared in two swallows.

Would that this traitorous talk could vanish as easily.

Eyes fixed on the fire, he court-martialed each of his men in his mind. Micajah Hale, though cross-grained and vain, he trusted with his life. Patrick Stewart was too lazy to make much of an enemy—and too busy wenching to turn loyalist spy. As for Jehu and Joram—the Herkimer brothers, both captains—he'd safely turned his back to them more than once. They'd served as fellow Life Guards before reenlisting under him at Washington's urging.

His remaining officers seemed unswervingly loyal, intelligent, and refined, expert marksmen and swordsmen like himself. Not once had they given him pause. As for the rest, he kept them in order with verbal threats and frequent lashings. They were a rough, ragtag lot as regulars went, but he liked most of them and they in turn respected him.

He opened the journal, recalling how Roxanna had done the same, only her hands had been shaking. He'd gladly take the blame for her trembling and her tears, racing down the line as he'd done and scaring her out of her usual composure. She hadn't known it was his usual way of doing things—with a hint of danger to ease the boredom and keep the men sharp and on edge.

August 18. Another courier missing. Cass down with malaria.

August 23. Suspicions grow. A crucial document concerning the Ohio campaign is missing. Hesitant to tell Cass just yet.

September 4. Rec'd letter from Roxie. God be praised—the westbound courier came through. Cass preparing for winter campaign.

The terse words—and the scrivener who'd so carefully penned them—returned his grief to him tenfold. He read on with wet eyes, a swelling remorse in his chest. But 'twas more than this, truly. 'Twas a feeling of his own impending doom, born out of an Irish sixth sense that he couldn't shake. He'd felt it shadow him since coming to Kentucke, and he felt it now, pressing down on him like a leaden weight.

September 17. News out of Detroit troubling. The British are paying even larger bounties for settlement scalps and supplying tribes with weapons and munitions to drive the Kentuckians out.

October 6. Official papers not as I left them. Documents seem to be disturbed. Feel a foreboding . . . must tell Cass.

Cass read each entry through once, twice, three times, increasingly perplexed. Richard Rowan had not been a man whose suspicions were easily aroused. Meticulous, exacting, of excellent memory and sound judgment, Richard Rowan hadn't the time or temperament to dream up danger.

At the back of the journal, Cass noticed there were several missing pages and then a final entry almost eerie in its brevity. In the same fine hand was written:

Psalm 140. Deliver me, O Lord, from the evil man: preserve me from the violent man; which imagine mischiefs in their heart; continually are they gathered together for war.

He shut the words away and stared into the hearth's fire. The matter was imminently simple. If Richard Rowan thought there was an enemy within fort walls, then there *was* an enemy.

14

In the dank winter's chill, Roxie knitted as Bella peered closer in the dim confines of the tiny cabin. "Them baby things for you or Dovie?"

"Bella!"

Bella chuckled, her dark face lit with amused mischief as her bony fingers caressed the tiny yellow cap and stockings. "No need to get uppity now. There's just all kinds of talk swirlin' since Colonel McLinn abandoned his men at maneuvers and come to yo' cabin like he did. You know what folks are startin' to call you, don't you?" She darted a sly look her way. "'The Colonel's Lady.'"

Roxanna returned to her knitting, trying to keep any surprise or pleasure from showing on her face. "He simply offered me an apology for frightening me."

"Some say he's smitten and was offerin' a proposal."

"So who are you going to believe, Bella?"

"I believe," she said with a smug smile, "that he was makin' you an apology, but what he was wantin' to do was offer you a proposal."

"I beg to differ," she said, feigning disinterest. "He doesn't seem the matrimonial sort."

"I ain't talkin' 'bout *that* kind of proposal."

Tying off the loose strings of the knitted cap, Roxanna refused to take the bait. "Since his apology, I've hardly seen him except for meals. That should shush any nonsense about his being smitten."

"He's been drillin' his men nearly night and day and ain't had no time for dictatin' to you. Hank says come spring he's goin' to push hard into the middle ground against them Redcoats and redskins and is gettin' in fightin' shape to do it. Maybe even go as far as Detroit and scare ol' Hair-Buyer Hamilton out o' his lair."

"Sounds ambitious," she said, thinking of all he'd confided right here in her cabin.

Had he changed his mind about resigning his commission since she'd given him Papa's journal? Or had he simply shared his plans with her to see what she'd say? She felt such a surge of curiosity, borne out of a week's waiting, that she'd almost followed him out the sally port to the stone house but an hour ago. The fact that she'd yet to plead Dovie and Johnny's case gave her a ready excuse. If she showed up on his doorstep in the winter dark, he'd have had little recourse but to let her in. But Bella had been her salvation, coming in just as she'd put on her cape.

Restless, she watched Bella's gnarled hands hitch the teakettle to the crane over the flames. Getting up, she set out the thistle cup and saucer and a plain pewter mug. "Sassafras or Bohea?"

"Sass," Bella replied. "I can't stomach that Bohea without sweetenin', and we just run out."

Roxanna poked around in a corner cupboard for some sugar of her own. "A supply convoy's due any day, isn't it?"

"Overdue. We'll be eatin' powder and lead shortly."

"Not with all the game in the woods, surely."

"There ain't nearly as much game as there used to be. That's one of the reasons them savages are so fired up. We're sittin' on their sacred huntin' grounds and drivin' all their eats away."

Roxanna's thoughts turned to the Shawnee in the guardhouse, encased in leg irons yet still able to raise the hair on the back of her neck. She wouldn't ask Bella if she knew the colonel's plans for them. It wasn't any of her business, and she didn't want to encourage Bella to gossip or relay anything Hank might have told her in confidence. Nor would she dare mention a spy. But she couldn't stop herself from asking about something a bit more benign.

Taking a seat, she said quietly, "Bella, tell me about the stone house."

"The stone house? If I tell you, mebbe you'll want to be up there on the hill." She paused, lips pursed in contemplation. "I been ponderin' that. I heard all them rumors 'bout General Washington and Kitty Greene dancin' the night away for hours on end back east. Here lately I been worryin' mebbe the colonel will follow suit and try to make you his mistress."

Roxanna swallowed down a too-hot sip of tea as if to brace herself. "That's utter nonsense about Colonel McLinn. *And* Kitty Greene and General Washington. He's a happily married man who simply has a penchant for dancing. I believe we were talking about the stone house."

"All right, then," Bella grunted. "What exactly do you want to know?"

The question was tempting as treacle. The stone house had assumed such lofty proportions in Roxanna's mind that she'd begun to think of it as McLinn's castle. 'Twas so grand, so out of place in the wilderness. So reminiscent of home. "I was just . . . well, wondering what's beyond that handsome front door."

"In the foyer, you mean?" At Roxanna's nod, Bella got a rare glint in her eye and seemed to forget all about her tea. "Law, it's like steppin' into somebody's dream. Don't know if I can do it justice. First there's a fine walnut floor runs all the way to double back doors. And a curved staircase as high as the heavens along one wall. On the third floor is a ballroom, long and fancy, with painted paper walls—sorta lavender and pale green flowers and leaves. But my favorite room's the kitchen. It's got runnin' water piped from a spring beneath the house and lots of clean, white cupboards, pretty as you please."

Hearing it didn't quell Roxanna's curiosity as she'd hoped but stoked it into a still-sharper yearning. Her knitting needles stilled. "And the study or sitting room . . . does it have an abundance of books and wingback chairs?"

The startled look on Bella's face would have been amusing if Roxanna hadn't been so serious. "Law, Miz Roxanna, did McLinn let you in? Or you been peekin' in them winders?"

"Of course not."

"The study's the room the colonel spends the most time in, lest he's sick in bed with the ague or down here at headquarters. It has all them books and chairs you're talkin' 'bout. How'd you know?"

Bending over her basket, Roxanna took out a skein of yarn dyed a deep indigo. "I've a good imagination, is all. And the colonel's house reminds me of our own back in Virginia, only ours wasn't nearly so grand. 'Twas simple stone and had a sitting room with a few books and a fine fireplace."

"Did it have a gros point carpet and a sugar chest with a little key?"

Roxanna cast a wistful look her way. "Nay, just some braided rugs and Windsor chairs."

There was a conspiratorial hush, and then Bella said in a near whisper, "I can sneak you in—show you around—when the colonel's gone."

For a moment Roxanna almost gave in. Then she thought of coming face-to-face with Cass in the confines of his house, uninvited and speechless. The excruciating prospect nearly made her squirm. "Best wait till the master of the house invites me."

"McLinn don't invite nobody! Well, maybe his officers now and again."

"What about those river travelers you've been telling me about?"

"The ones without lice and the like? There's just a few of them, mostly military men. He puts them up, and me and Hank dance attendance till they're gone again." With a quick grin she bent down and lifted the hem of her homespun skirt, removing something from her shoe. Taking it out, she flashed it in the candlelight. "A gold piece from General Hand. He give it to me just before he went back east awhile ago."

Her delight was so contagious Roxanna chuckled. "Then you'll no doubt welcome him back again."

"Oh, he'll be comin' round again once the Injun trouble dies down. Hand and McLinn get on like a house afire. He and General Washington are the ones who sent the colonel out west in the first place. Word is they consider guardin' the frontier a plum assignment even if the colonel don't."

"I imagine he wishes he was back east fighting in the war—or still serving as a Life Guard."

"Better that than fightin' redskins and Redcoats right here, that's for sure." Giving in to a wide yawn, Bella drained her cup. "Enough talk about McLinn. What are *you* goin' to do?"

The simple question seemed to weight the air between them. For a few seconds Roxanna was at a loss for words. How could she explain her changing heart to Bella without sounding smitten? "I don't rightly know. And until I do, I need to keep busy. I'd like to help put in a garden." Roxanna glanced at her trunk, recalling how hard it had been to get here in the first place. The memory of hovering at the mouth of the cave and looking down at the finely fletched arrow in the flatboat captain's back returned with cold, crimson clarity. "I'm praying about it all."

Bella's face twisted in a grimace. "Law, but it'll take a heap of prayin' to get out o' this place. Mebbe you should start a weekly meetin' with them Redstone women and pray us all out o' here."

Roxanna sighed. "I've already tried, but they have, um, other matters to attend to."

"All them men, you mean," Bella nearly growled. Giving the fire a final poke, she went out.

The twin candles on the mantel flickered from an icy draft,

returning Roxanna's thoughts once again to the stone house. No doubt there were few drafts on the hill. With walls two feet thick, Colonel McLinn would be warm indeed sitting in his wingback chair before his own solitary fire.

Pulling herself out of her chair, she crossed the room and peered through the shuttered window, glad Papa's cabin had been so perfectly placed. From here she could easily see the stone house over the fort's northwest pickets. Tiny pinpricks of golden light limned the two first-floor windows. The study, she guessed. Leaning her head against the cold casement, she gave in to the temptation to think about him again.

Since Ambrose, she'd resigned herself to joining the family line of spinsters—those six Scottish sisters on her father's side who had one broken betrothal after another, or none at all. Perhaps her growing attraction for Cass, as she'd begun to think of him, hinged on a sort of desperation. With him she felt girlish, attractive, alive. If only because she was one of the few eligible females within fort walls.

Pushing away from the window, she tried to think of a Scripture—anything—to supplant the intense image of him burned into her brain. Clear blue eyes hard as marbles one minute, then without warning, thawing and turning tender. Hair so glossy it couldn't be confined in a tidy queue but like red silk slipped through. Continental coattails flapping and calling attention to every heart-stopping detail of all the rest of him. Little wonder settlement women risked danger and hung about the gates in warmer weather, or so Bella said.

At least she'd not be here to witness *that* spectacle, thank heavens. A telltale warmth crept into her cheeks.

Why did she suddenly wish she would be?

15

Cass eyed Richard Rowan's journal where it lay on the middle of his desk, surrounded by such a stack of papers it was barely visible. Across from him stood Micajah Hale, tricorn hat twirling in his gloved hands in a rare moment of tension. Try as he might, Cass couldn't keep his mind on the major's attempts at conversation. Hale was hemming and hawing in such an infuriating way Cass was tempted to bring his fist down atop the polished wood to startle him into coherency. But he was little better this morning, he mused, his mind taking myriad rabbit trails yet always returning to the half-buried journal and its cryptic entries.

Finally he could stand it no longer. Leaning forward slightly, he leveled his senior officer with a less than gracious gaze. "Blast it, Micajah! Come to the point!"

Micajah's composure crumpled like a spent cartridge. "With all due respect, Colonel, you don't make it easy for a man to state his case."

"Seems you could have stated it a quarter of an hour ago when you first walked in. Miss Rowan will be here soon, so I advise you to start talking."

A tide of red inflamed Micajah's fair face as he sat down hard in the nearest chair. "Miss Rowan is the very reason I'm standing here making a fool of myself."

At this, Cass came to full attention. The furious fire that hardly seemed to thaw the blockhouse's chill now seemed to burn his backside. Reaching up, he ran a cold finger around the overly warm linen folds of his stock. Tight as a noose it felt.

Breath pluming in the bitter air, Micajah finally said, "I've come to ask your permission to court Miss Rowan."

Cass leveled him with another hard look. "You've been drinking."

The petulant jaw tightened. "I'm stone sober and dead serious."

"I commend you for coming to me about the matter—but why would you?"

Standing, Micajah jammed his hat on his head, only to take it off again. "Why? Because your former adjutant, her father, made you her guardian of sorts."

Aye, guardian indeed. Cass rued he'd ever shared Richard Rowan's dying request—with Micajah or even Roxanna. Guilt drove a typically closemouthed man to stupid confidences. Yet here his second-in-command stood, offering a sensible solution to his dilemma. Micajah could well woo and wed her, thus relieving him of his own responsibility to both her and her father. And in so doing, Cass could resign his commission and return to Virginia now or Ireland at war's end, without so much as another guilty pang.

Yet he heard himself saying quietly and with conviction, "You're not the man for her, Micajah."

Stiffening, the major resumed sitting, his expression an unattractive mix of defiance and disbelief. "I say, sir, you're making this harder than it ought to be. Why not let Miss Rowan decide?"

"Why? Because she's grieving and not likely to make a wise decision where you're concerned."

"But—"

"If that's not reason enough, let's look at the facts. You've two broken betrothals and a wandering eye. Although your enlistment is about to end, you have few prospects and a mountain of debt."

Twisting in his chair, Micajah seemed about to have an apoplectic fit. "With all due respect, Cass, you'd do well to look to your own situation before maligning mine."

Ignoring this, Cass continued, his Irish lilt intensifying in his irritation. "Miss Rowan is pure, intelligent, sensitive, and extremely religious."

Everything you're not, he didn't add.

A satisfied smile slid over the major's flushed face as if they'd reached some sort of agreement. "Aye, she is indeed—all the qualifications for a fine wife. I've often thought the right match would improve my lot in life . . . yet you'd interfere."

There was a peevishness to his plea that Cass didn't like, and it only hardened his resolve. Standing, he looked over the major's head to a sole window, catching a glimpse of Roxanna crossing the frozen common.

He said with sudden finality, "I'm assigning you to a woodcutting detail till you can clear your head of her."

The air was so taut with tension it seemed to snap. From the look on Micajah's face, Cass might as well have said he was court-martialing him. The major spun away without a word, nearly colliding with the orderlies and the object of their heated exchange as she came in. Cass noticed the look that passed between them and searched for something that might indicate Roxanna's attraction for him. He found her greeting merely polite, and Micajah's a bit too hearty.

He felt a twist of something he couldn't name and didn't care for. When she approached his desk, he tried to fight the feeling that she nearly always elicited of late and he could no longer shove aside—a wave of pure, unadulterated delight. Her presence seemed to settle his blistering mood, and the intensity of moments before ebbed.

He motioned for an orderly to help her with her cape while another rested her desk on the edge of his own. A whole week he'd been away from her, drilling his men, while she'd sought refuge in the kitchen, turning out one mouth-watering meal after another despite the lack of provisions. Not only this, but it was reported she had been visiting the sick in the infirmary, remembered the names of the least of his men, and had started some sort of a sock distribution campaign.

"Good morning, Colonel McLinn." The soft slur of her words, coupled with her winsome, warm smile, nearly made him forget where he was.

For a few stunned seconds he groped about for a rationale to explain away her effect on him. He guessed his sympathy for her was simply coloring his judgment. That and the fact he'd been without feminine company for too long. The plain truth was he could never let his feelings go forward, because the sight of her would always remind him that he'd shot her father.

"I'm sorry to call you out of the kitchen." *Back to Bella's unimaginative rations*, he thought wryly.

"I'm ready to transcribe," she told him, eyes falling to the center of his desk where her father's journal lay. A flash of something inexplicable crossed her pale face, then skittered away like mist.

Reaching out, he moved a sheaf of papers and buried the book. "I have to interview the Indian prisoners this morning, and I'm in need of an official transcript. But I realize this might be asking too much of you. Major Herkimer could serve in your stead. He sometimes worked with your father."

"Nay . . . I'll stay."

He simply stared at her in relief, expecting more than a simple *nay*. After Micajah's unending petition, he could have leaned across the desk and kissed her. Still, he wondered if she might change her mind in the face of the two intimidating captives. Turning to an orderly, he said, "Bring in the two Shawnee."

"Where would you like me to sit?" she asked, expressive blue eyes sweeping the room with its assortment of benches and chairs.

"Well behind me," he replied, removing a long, colorful belt from a desk drawer. Seeing her interest, he draped the wide swath of beads over his coat sleeves for her to admire. "It's wampum."

"What does it mean?"

"It's a sort of historical record, keeping account of treaties and battles and the like. This was taken from one of the burned Shawnee villages."

She reached out a hand to touch the shiny, mysterious pattern of blues and reds and blacks, a bit awed, he thought. "'Tis sacred," he told her, "and highly prized."

The door groaned open and they both looked up. A lanky man in buckskins entered, dark hair plaited and clubbed and tied with whang leather, hazel eyes swinging from Cass to Roxanna.

"Miss Rowan, this is Ben Simmons, my principal scout—and translator."

They exchanged a greeting, and Roxanna seemed surprised when Simmons said, "I was real sorry to hear about your pa. He was a good man—the best."

Their eyes met briefly in wordless understanding while Cass looked on. Recalling that deadly day nearly locked his voice in his throat. He said with difficulty, "Ben's the best scout in the Kentucke territory. Only he's too humble to admit it."

Simmons flashed him an appreciative look. "That's some compliment, considering it's from the finest commanding officer on the frontier."

"The only one, anyway," Cass murmured, eyes on the door swinging open again.

Wary, he realized something was amiss even before the orderly took him aside. The older Shawnee—the one who liked to talk—was ill and refusing to leave his pallet, asking for a medicine man. But this perplexing turn of events seemed less significant than watching the interaction of Roxanna Rowan and his favorite scout as they continued their conversation in low tones. He knew Ben Simmons as well as any man, and he sensed his friend had more than a passing interest in the woman who stood before him.

The orderly said tentatively, "Colonel, sir . . . do you still want the other Shawnee brought in?"

"Aye, I do," he replied absently, his mind churning along with his emotions, neither having to do with the matter at hand.

He crossed to his desk and lay the wampum aside, recalling what he knew about Simmons and his tragic past. Bits and pieces came back to him, gleaned over their two-year acquaintance.

Simmons's wife and child had been killed by a group of Shawnee raiders several years prior. Hardened as he was to the realities of war, Cass felt his insides twist at the gruesome memory. It had made his own forays into Indian territory all the easier, easing any guilt he felt about desolating the Shawnee. He merely burned their towns and crops, he reasoned. He hadn't killed their women and children.

Within a few minutes, the sole Shawnee was ushered into the blockhouse, and a hush fell over the room. In the face of so many armed men, Cass asked that his leg irons be removed. Then, like the director of a stage play, he assembled all the players. Roxanna took a seat in back of him yet still near enough to clearly hear Simmons interpret from where he stood. Half a dozen regulars were interspersed about the room, and a guard was posted outside the door.

He glanced at Roxanna again and noticed that her features had leached to the hue of raw linen. Had she never seen an Indian up close, he wondered? Though captive more than two months, the younger Shawnee had lost none of his hauteur but retained an aura of undiminished vitality and extreme hostility. Though he'd grown thinner, he remained one of the finest Indians Fort Endeavor had ever seen.

Cass didn't blame Roxanna for staring. No doubt the Indian

had caught many a Shawnee maiden's eye in the middle ground. If only he was as communicative as he was commanding. So far he'd not uttered a single meaningful word, save a few flawless English epithets aimed at the guard. This was why Cass had resorted to using wampum. Wampum for words. He had to know who among the British in Detroit was inciting the Shawnee and other tribes to raid the Kentucke settlements. Until he knew, he couldn't cross the Ohio and quell the growing trouble.

After a tedious half hour, Ben Simmons took Cass aside and told him it was hopeless. It was then that Cass reached for the wampum on his desk. He draped it across one arm, the ends of the belt nearly touching the floor and shining in a kaleidoscope of color. At once the Shawnee stiffened. Cass could feel an unmistakable dislike thread the air between them.

"Tell him the belt will be returned to him when he tells me which Redcoat chiefs are sending the Shawnee south into the settlements to do their fighting for them."

Simmons translated, and behind them Roxanna leaned over her lap desk. Cass could hear the persistent scratch of her quill as it met paper between the long, tedious silences. After more pointed questions and few answers, Cass called for a break and sent for the doctor downriver at Smitty's Fort to attend to the older chief.

As the door opened and closed behind the courier, an orderly appeared bearing a cloth-draped wooden tray. 'Twas Bella's not-so-subtle reminder that he tended to overwork everyone around him, Cass mused. Roxanna rose and took the tray, bringing him a cup of coffee. A cluster of apple tarts crowded a small pewter plate, and he eyed them appreciatively, wondering if she'd made them.

A feeling of wonder—and raw alarm—settled in his chest as he watched her take the second cup and cross the quiet room. Steam swirled around the pewter rim as she set the coffee down on the bench beside the uncommunicative Shawnee. Without a word she motioned that it was meant for him. The fiercely fixed stare that had been unbroken swiveled to take in the offering. For a moment Cass feared the warrior would overturn the bench, coffee and all, and the image of Roxanna's terrified reaction made him tense. He set his own untouched cup down on his desk, ready to intervene.

She was reaching into the folds of her dress, and the Shawnee's ebony eyes followed her every move. Removing something from her pocket, she extended her hand and passed it to the chief, indicating he could put it in his coffee. Ever so slowly he took the small chunk of loaf sugar—perhaps the last in the fort—touched it to his tongue, then dropped it in the pewter cup.

Around the room the regulars were elbowing each other, but Cass didn't share their amusement. There was something so inexplicably poignant about the scene it crowded out his irritation at her audacity. When she sat back down, Cass tried to pass her his cup. Smiling up at him, she simply shook her head and took an apple tart instead, passing the plate around the too-still room. The Shawnee sat and drank his coffee, his eyes returning to her again and again from some far-off place.

Watching, Cass felt a tingling wariness. He'd erred greatly having her present for the translation. Realizing he might have placed her in danger, he dismissed them all save Roxanna and an orderly. She had pocketed the pastry, he noticed, and was reading over the barren transcript, which he hoped would yield something more substantial tomorrow. He'd have better luck with the older Shawnee if his malady wasn't serious.

Alone with her, he started to caution her, to reprimand her for a breach of prisoner protocol. But this time, before he could rebuke her, a spasm of guilt checked him. He was often so abrupt with her, upbraiding her nearly as much as he did his men. He made a mental note not to have her present when the Shawnee came again.

"Are we finished, sir, or do you have something else in mind for me to do?"

Her softly spoken question returned him to the present, and he stopped thumbing through a sheaf of papers to look at her again.

"Nothing more," he said, "till tonight." Her eyes widened slightly in question, and he added, "You are coming to the wedding, are you not?"

"Oh . . . that."

"Aye, that," he said, forcing a smile.

The matter of Dovie and Johnny had been such a simple one to resolve, yet she still seemed surprised by his swift agreement. It wouldn't do, he'd agreed, to have an illegitimate child when a father was willing and waiting. And the couple did seem to care for one another. Word of the wedding had spread like wildfire about the fort, adding a festive feel. The Redstone women were elated. Dovie would be respectable at long last, Olympia crowed with a sort of envy, and the rest of them would get a fine frolic to boot.

Cass escorted Roxanna to the door and took her cape off a peg. The subtle scent of violets enveloped him as he settled the indigo wool about her shoulders and leaned forward to open the door. They said not a word to each other as they crossed the slippery common, his hand on her elbow to keep her upright. Around them the smithy, magazine, and quartermasters were seething with activity, but he hardly noticed. At some hazy point in the last twenty-four hours, Cecily O'Day had ceased to exist, and he no longer rued her passing.

16

Muted fiddle music could be heard from the east blockhouse, and Roxanna tapped one stocking-clad foot in time to the music. A jig, she guessed, wondering if Dovie was an anxious bride. Behind her, Bella put the finishing touches on her hair, softening the unrelieved black with a length of fragile ecru lace that made it seem snowflakes had fallen and lay frozen amidst her upswept crown of curls. She'd had a bath before the crackling hearth and now felt nearly woozy from its warmth. But for Bella's chatter.

"It'll be some miracle if Dovie can keep from losin' her supper durin' the ceremony," she said, setting aside the brush. Turning to the table, she fussed with a sadiron and a petticoat's stubborn wrinkle. "She's been awful sick on account o' that babe."

"The midwife from Smitty's Fort gave her some raspberry tea. Maybe she'll remember to drink some beforehand."

"I reckon my cherry bounce will do the trick if it don't. Now close yo' eyes."

The excited trill of her tone alarmed more than delighted Roxanna, but she did as bid, squeezing her eyes shut and waiting for the familiar feel of her best linen dress.

"Hold up yo' arms so I can get it o'er yo' head without messin' with yo' hair."

The rustle of silk slipping into place made Roxanna's eyes fly open. Bella began hooking the snug bodice from behind, expression smug. Looking down, Roxanna found herself draped in pale lemon and lace, the luster of the gown catching the candlelight and revealing tiny embellishments of ribbon and rosettes, much like the cockades on the officers' tricorn hats.

Speechless, she rested careful hands on the lace sash about her waist and took in the lush lines of the skirt, feeling she'd been caught in a delicious dream. But then practicality took over. "Bella, I'm not the bride. Dovie is."

Clucking, Bella soothed, "I done took care of Dovie. Now turn around so I can see how it fits. I had a time takin' in the waist, though the hem looks to be just right."

As Bella bent to search for stray threads and smooth the flounced sleeves, Roxanna allowed herself a forbidden thought. *I feel like a bride.* After all, yellow was the preferred color for brides in the colonies. Even England. The winsome if wayward notion of a waiting groom—in a Dutch blue Continental coat with a light blue riband running across his chest and a honeymoon in the stone house—worked its spell, and she put a hand on a chair back to steady herself.

"Law, Miz Roxanna, you woolgatherin' again?"

Again. Lately she'd gotten into the intoxicating habit of daydreaming, and Bella, astute as ever, was quick to call it what it was.

"Yes," she confessed, aware that the telling flush she saw in the mirror had nothing to do with the gown and everything to do with *him*.

"Mind tellin' me who you thinkin' 'bout?"

"Abby," she said in a little rush, for there was some truth to it.

"Aw, I hear she's sick with that fever goin' round. She should be better come tomorrow. It lasts 'bout three days then goes."

"I brought her some broth earlier. She took a few spoonfuls."

"Now, never you mind about that child. She be fine. I'm goin' to bring her a little weddin' cake later on." Bella studied her with a motherly eye. "You still rememberin' that promise you made to yo' ma? The one 'bout not marryin' a soldier? She didn't say nothin' 'bout dancin' with 'em, did she?"

"No," Roxanna answered. "But I can't dance, remember."

Bella examined a flounce and acted like she hadn't heard. "Now I wouldn't let any o' them regulars tromp on my toes. But any o' them officers would do fine." She glanced at the mantel clock and grimaced. "Best get on over to the kitchen and bring out my bounce."

Roxanna watched her go, a tight feeling in her chest. *Oh, Lord, it is a wedding I want. And I do feel like a bride tonight, albeit an old one.*

Most of her friends in Virginia had been wed by the age of eighteen. And she'd stood up with one after another, soul-sick with longing, just like she was about to do with Dovie.

Going to the corner trunk, Roxanna rummaged for her best handkerchief, pushing aside a vial of violet water till she found one of fine linen bearing her mother's initials. Before she straightened, a decisive knock sounded on the door, and another knot ripened in her already tense stomach. Remembering the last time she'd been surprised with not Bella but Colonel McLinn, she opened the door carefully to find his towering frame filling it completely.

All the air went out of her as he cleared the lintel log and stepped inside. "I've come to escort you to the wedding, if you're ready."

If . . . If you only knew.

Their eyes met for a fleeting instant, in which she tried to take in as much of him as possible, thinking it might stem her perennial need to look again. She'd already made up her mind to leave the festivities early if she could, as soon after the ceremony as possible. She needed some solitude to right her wayward heart with a cold dose of reason. Since Papa's passing, she sensed she was trying to fill the great void in her life with a man, any man—even Cass. And he, feeling intensely responsible for her, was determined to do his duty. Like escorting her tonight.

He reached for her cape hanging by the door with an endearing familiarity, and they went out into a night of wind and snow without another word. And there, waiting in the blockhouse before the blazing hearth, stood an entirely altered Dovie in royal purple brocade, her hair pinned up like Roxanna's, looking happy if wan.

Casting a glance about, Roxanna realized McLinn was to stand up with Johnny just as she stood with Dovie, but they were all standing—a hundred fifty or more soldiers and the Redstone women, even Bella and Hank—as there weren't nearly enough chairs.

She searched for a pastor or magistrate, but there was only a newly enlisted regular by the name of Graham Greer making his way through the throng, bearing a small black Bible. With a start she realized he was the official.

The ceremony was as short as decency allowed, and she felt benumbed by its familiarity. *Dearly beloved*, indeed. She'd heard it a dozen times or better. Her favorite part came when Graham Greer intoned, "You may kiss the bride." Johnny did, long and lusty, to the rousing "huzzahs" of every man present save Colonel McLinn. She was a bit taken aback by the couple's show of passion, but the colonel grinned broadly, a hint of extra color showing beneath his winter tan.

At last the dancing and cherry bounce could begin in earnest. An ear-splitting reel complete with fiddles, fife, and drum rocked the large room, and immediately Micajah Hale stood before her. She smiled and shook her head in polite refusal, unable to make herself heard above the music and foot stomping. Bowing, he left her alone and commandeered Mariah. Seeing another officer heading her way, she began backing up toward the kitchen.

She waited till the colonel led the second set with Dovie before making her escape. Out the back door she went, wishing she'd brought her dulcimer. As it was, she had no excuse to stay on. She couldn't dance, yet the dress she wore seemed a vivid calling card to do just that, and she didn't like all the attention.

As she hurried along, a silver sliver of moon penetrated the sleet and cast an eerie light on the stone house. Turning her face aside, she wished the music was as easily shut away. The old tune "Liza Jane" followed her clear across the parade ground, every sweet note seeming to hammer home Papa's passing.

As she reached her door and fumbled with the latchstring, a keen relief settled over her. Colonel McLinn needn't bother with escorting her back to her cabin tonight. She was tired, in need of rest. Yet once inside, she realized she couldn't possibly undress without Bella's help due to the double row of hooks down her back. She decided to check on Abby again but found her sleeping, the fever finally broken, and Nancy watching over her, half asleep herself.

Returning to her cabin, she lit twin candles and sat back from the hearth, afraid a spark might burn the lush skirts of her gown. She could hear a flourishing finish to another poignant song, and her heart squeezed tight, a tear trickling to her chin. She wiped it away with her hankie, waiting for Bella.

Long minutes passed, and she tensed at the crunch of boots on snow. Soldiers on guard duty? A passing regular? Steeling herself, she readied for the knock. When it came, she summoned all the composure she could muster and opened the door, hiding her handkerchief behind her back. Colonel McLinn ducked inside, clutching the cape she'd completely forgotten in her haste to leave the wedding frolic.

He hung it from its peg by the door, which he shut firmly behind him. *Captive*, she thought. Her fickle emotions did such a strange dance she didn't know which was uppermost. Pleasure? Embarrassment? Surprise? Something told her he had no great desire to be at the wedding frolic either and this was his escape.

Gesturing toward the hearth, she said a bit breathlessly, "Please . . . come in."

He hesitated—was he reluctant?—before crossing the tiny space in three strides and taking a chair facing the fire. She sank down on a stool, watching the orange and yellow tongues of flame leap and curl around the charred burls of oak Micajah had left under her eave.

A brooding silence settled between them. He finally broke it by saying, "You're much too lovely—and well dressed—to be sitting alone by the fire, Miss Rowan."

The compliment, coupled with his gentle rebuke, made fresh tears well in her eyes. Blinking them back, she said, "It seems silly to attend a dance when one can't dance."

He gave her a sidelong look. "Because you're in mourning?"

"Because I'm"—she took a breath—"a bit lame."

His eyes swiveled back to her and stayed put till she looked at him again. "If you can walk, Miss Rowan, you can dance."

A flicker of panic warmed her insides as she realized where he was headed. Bella's wary words came rushing back. *Maybe the colonel will try to make you his mistress.* She said quickly, "Perhaps another time."

"Why not here? Now? With no one watching?"

The faint but unmistakable strains of a slow country dance seemed to back up his startling invitation. He stood and moved his chair out of the way. Firelight spilled into the empty space, gilding the floorboards a rich gold. She had little choice but to stand up on unsteady legs and obey the . . . order.

She dared look up at him, the lace of her bodice rising and falling in a breathless rhythm a mere three inches from the gilt buttons of his Continental coat. He was entirely too close . . . so close she caught a hint of cherry bounce on his breath. Wetting her lips with the tip of her tongue in an agony of anticipation, she felt one firm hand rest against the hollow of her waist and the other enfold her fingers in his own.

With more grace than a man of his stature should possess, he began moving her over the flickering floorboards, their shadows an intimate silhouette on the rough wood walls. In moments, every taut fiber of her being began to soften. At long last she was indeed dancing . . . and she'd never felt less lame in all her life.

Oh, Papa, if you could see me now . . .

He was so adept a dancer, so in control, there was never a chance for her to misstep. She simply followed his lead, knowing from the gentle pressure of his hands whether to go backward or forward or sideways. The music ended and was replaced by a distant, rousing reel, but neither of them seemed to notice or care.

Every turn they took about the tiny cabin seemed to shake loose a dark shadow. In the two months she'd known Cassius McLinn, he'd never been nearer than he was tonight, so close it seemed she almost touched his soul. Here in her humble cabin, he was no longer the curt commander but something more. She sensed his deep enjoyment of the moment . . . the music . . . holding her . . . and caught a glimpse of the man he truly was. Or who she wanted him to be.

"Roxie . . ." He had come to a stop and was looking down at her.

Startled, she met his eyes. "No one's ever called me that . . . save my father."

"Do you mind?"

"I—nay, Cass." His name slipped off her tongue like she'd been saying it a lifetime, though the surprised pleasure on his face told her otherwise.

The lapse seemed an open invitation for him to come nearer. Slowly he skimmed his knuckles along the oval of her cheek before twining his fingers in the richness of her hair, dislodging some of Bella's carefully placed pins.

At his touch, a woozy rush of pleasure overcame the last remnants of her reason, and she did what she'd dreamed of doing since the first day she'd met him. Reaching up, she skimmed the glossy sheen of his hair, starting at his temple and sliding toward his broad back till her fingers found his silk queue ribbon. In a whirl of wonder and yearning, she pulled it loose. Her reward was a flash of brilliant red falling free about his wide shoulders, softening his intensity yet kindling his need of her. She saw it in his eyes instantly.

Oh, Lord in heaven, what have I done?

Never had Ambrose looked at her in such an all-consuming way . . .

Frightened, she drew back, even as his hand fell away. Her dress . . . the dance . . . the candlelit confines of the cabin . . . all had cast such a spell she felt far removed from who she truly was—a soldier's daughter, a bit desperate for attention, her fear of spinsterhood shadowing her—till she'd snapped to her senses at the last second.

"Roxie, I—"

She shook her head, her voice a plea as she took another step away. "Please . . ." She swallowed, spilling her heart out in a few words as she backed up further. "I don't want to fall in love with you."

The answering anguish in his face made her wish the words back. Turning on one heel, he crossed the room with furious haste and went out, leaving the door open wide in his wake. Before she could bend down and pick up the slip of silk ribbon, Bella appeared, her face taut with apprehension. She stood in the open doorway, the icy wind rushing in and lashing them like a whip.

"Law, Miz Roxanna, I ain't seen the colonel so riled since his men spilled a shipment of muskets into the river last spring."

Stricken, Roxanna said, "I—I forgot my cape—the colonel was returning it to me . . ."

Bella stared at the length of ribbon in her hand. "Looks like the colonel forgot something hisself."

Feeling caught in a trespass, Roxanna believed she would

burst if she didn't confess everything, yet her throat was so tight she couldn't speak.

Coming up behind her, Bella said wearily, "It's gettin' late. Let me help you out o' yo' dress and then you can sleep the Sabbath away."

The Sabbath? Her eyes flew to the mantel clock that proclaimed it half past midnight. The colonel had been in her cabin for some time, yet it had felt like mere minutes. Had anyone but Bella seen him come in, then leave? She waited for a reprimand about being alone with him, but Bella was strangely silent, her dark fingers plucking the combs and pins from her coiffed hair. Roxanna shut her eyes, feeling his hands instead, trying to reconstruct the events that had led to his doing so. The ease with which she'd touched him in return—nay, not simply touched but *untied* his wealth of hair from his neatly bound queue . . .

Oh, Lord, forgive me.

Confusion muddied her shame. With Ambrose, it had been enough to have him hold her hand or kiss her cheek. She'd wanted nothing more from him—she'd needed nothing more. Her feelings for Ambrose had been tepid, not feverish, compared to what she felt for Cass. Tonight he'd awakened in her a hunger she didn't even know she had . . . made her wonder in the span of a few breathlessly passionate seconds if being his mistress might not be better than being a spinster . . .

Bella went out without a word, leaving Roxanna to her own tangled thoughts. Candles snuffed, she sat before the fire, riddled by guilt, stuttering another conflicted prayer, this one suffused with a breathless thanks.

Knowing there are men like Cassius McLinn, thank You for sparing me a lifeless marriage to a man I only pretended to love.

His ambitious stride, long by any standard, now doubled in his fury. The guard could hardly keep up with him once he passed through the sally port and gained a firmer foothold uphill. He had a hair-trigger temper at times—and this was one of those times. They gave him wide berth.

Hank threw open the door and then got out of the way. Cass pushed past him with such vehemence the silver sconce glittering on the lowboy in the foyer was nearly extinguished. Up the smooth staircase he went, unable to stem the thought of her, his heart already pulling him back down the hill to apologize and make amends, but mostly to take her in his arms again.

His bedchamber seemed empty as a tomb. As he lowered himself into a wing chair before the flickering fire, Hank's sturdy shadow darkened the door frame. Without a word, the steady black hands tugged off one ice-encrusted boot and then another, ready to whisk them below stairs to be cleaned and blacked.

"Care for some brandy, sir?"

"Nay, whiskey." Glancing at the clock mounted above the door, he grimaced. A double shot of whiskey on the Sabbath should do. Though he barred his men from the same.

Aye, what he should do was get rip-roaring drunk and drown out the feel of Roxie Rowan's silky skin and hair beneath his fingers and her poignant, heartfelt plea.

Please, I don't want to fall in love with you.

How in heaven had it come to that? He'd simply meant to return her cape. Instead he'd left all his wits at the door and succumbed to the unparalleled sweetness of her presence. Standing before him, with the fire gilding her gown and skin, she seemed the answer to all his angst and regrets. In the span of five minutes, he'd forgotten all about spies and overdue supply wagons and stone-faced Shawnee. Even Richard Rowan. Simply being in the same room with her gave him a measure of peace.

That she'd been crying was obvious, and it brought out every protective instinct he had, reminding him he was to blame for her sorrow. A father's loss was hard to bear. On the heels of the loss of a mother and a broken betrothal, it might well be unbearable. He wanted to comfort her—and find comfort. One dance was all he'd wanted.

Running a hand through his unbound hair, he drew a steadying breath, listening to Hank's footfalls on the stair and his rumblings in the kitchen far below. Aye, he was to blame for letting the situation turn so tender. He'd sensed her resistance, yet he had taken advantage of her and was furious with himself. The only puzzling aspect of the evening was when she'd turned his hair loose from its tie.

"Whiskey, sir." Hank moved gingerly into the room and set the glass on the table before the hearth. It glowed amber and gold and held the subtle tang of oak. He finished it in two swallows.

Best be done with this Roxie Rowan business. Starting tonight, he'd make sure he never had occasion to be alone with her again. There was nothing to be done but honor her poignant plea.

As the whiskey flowed through him like fire and did its mellowing work, he wondered what she'd done with his black silk ribbon.

17

I must put a hedge around my heart. No more long looks in his direction. No wishing for what cannot be. When I think of him, it must be to pray for him . . . and pray only.

He was, she reminded herself, already promised to an Irish beauty—Cecily O'Day. Having been on the receiving end of another woman's wiles, she'd not cause Cecily hurt. Nay, she'd not tempt Colonel McLinn, as if she could, nor be tempted.

Standing before Papa's small shaving glass, she took note of the black smudges beneath her eyes, evidence of a near-sleepless night. Since Cass had left her cabin, she'd been in such a tangle her turmoil showed on her pale face. She still felt the effects of his parting fury yet didn't know why her words had made him so angry. Could it be because he wasn't used to being told no? Perhaps Bella had been right and his intent was to make her his mistress. Confusion filled her to the brim and overflowed. The mere thought of facing him, even with a desk between them, gave her a fierce headache.

'Twas twenty minutes till eight. Draping a plain linen kerchief about her shoulders, she fastened the ends above her snug wool bodice with a cameo, then gathered up her waist-length hair and subdued it into a chignon with a multitude of pins, all the while thinking of him. Penitent, she breathed a prayer for both of them, bypassing the cape hanging forlornly by the door. There would be no forgetting it again, as she'd not be wearing it, not this morning anyway.

Head down, she crossed the common to Olympia's cabin to check on Abby, letting herself in when there was no answer to her knock. Olympia stood by the hearth, expression sorrowful, and Roxanna's gaze was drawn upward to the loft, where two large black boots were suspended from the ladder. Cass? No wonder they hadn't heard her knock. The sound of giggling, high and musical as a song, spilled into the cabin from above. Wonder washed through her. If Abby could laugh so effortlessly, why couldn't she speak?

"The colonel just got here, and she's better," Olympia said, drying her eyes with a handkerchief. "Seein' her sick brought back memories of her ma . . ."

"I'm so thankful," Roxanna murmured, backing out the cabin door. "Let me know if you need anything."

She hadn't expected him to be here, but it touched her to think he was as concerned about Abby as the rest of them. Somehow the gesture seemed even to have softened some of Olympia's hostility toward him.

Turning away, Roxanna hurried to the work awaiting her. The blockhouse door was ajar, and she took a steadying breath as she stepped over the threshold. A dozen eyes swiveled in her direction, followed by a respectful murmur among the men. The regulars were present with the younger Shawnee chief, and Ben Simmons was warming his hands by the hearth. Both orderlies were busy in a far corner, sorting through a collection of maps.

"Mornin', Miss Rowan."

"Hello, Ben."

Aware of his eyes on her, she began checking the supplies in her lap desk where it rested in a corner, noting she was low on ink. Hopefully a quantity would come in with the now-overdue supply train. If not, she could try to make some of her own.

As she sorted and straightened papers and quills, sand and inkpots, she felt she wasn't tidying her lap desk at all but someone else's. Pages of correspondence seemed to be out of order, and the customary neatness was missing. Alarm shot through her. Nay, things weren't as she'd left them Saturday last. She must tell Cass . . .

Ben was at her elbow, and she sensed his impatience. "Seen the colonel, Miss Rowan? Doc Clary is here, wanting to report about the sick Shawnee."

"Colonel McLinn is with Abby," she said. Closing the tambour top, she tried to push down her suspicions. "How is the older chief?"

Passing a hand over his beard, he murmured, "Pewter poisoning."

Eyes widening, she tried to recall what she knew about the malady. "Best feed him on a wooden trencher, then."

"He's too sick to eat off a wooden plate or otherwise. What we don't want is a death on our hands. Word is there's plenty of Shawnee sign about the fort. Guess they don't like the fact that two of their headmen are in here. I figure they're aiming to get 'em out."

She suppressed a shudder, her gaze moving from the brooding, bearded face of Ben to the smooth-skinned Shawnee on the bench in the middle of the room. Feeling a twist of sympathy override her fear, she let herself linger on him long enough to note his hostility, then checked the time on the watch she had purchased for her father. Half past eight. At least when Cass came she'd not be alone with him. The room was chock-full of men.

She looked up from the watch and felt the Indian's eyes on her. Though he'd been looking elsewhere in quiet defiance when she'd come in, his gaze was now fixed on the timepiece in her hand. Once again she was struck by the beautiful simplicity of his buckskin clothing and the array of eagle feathers in his shoulder-length hair. Just as she was about to lower her eyes and look away from him, he gestured to her with a dusky hand.

Leaving Ben's side, she crossed the room and sat down tentatively on the bench beside him, placing the pocket watch in his weathered, outstretched palm. A flash of childlike curiosity crossed his face, followed by open wonder. He held it to his ear, then turned it over and traced the engraving. Sensing his delight, she couldn't help but relax. He turned to her with a slight smile, revealing even white teeth, the sober lines of his face softening. Looking directly at her, he spoke in his strange tongue. She felt a flurry of confusion and raised her shoulders in a slight shrug.

Ben drew near, his voice touched with surprise. "Miss Rowan, he's askin' you what it is."

Remembering the protocol of translation she'd observed thus far, she looked only at the Shawnee, bypassing Ben altogether. "It's a watch . . ." Tongue-tied, she struggled to explain it in a sensible way. "It's a device for marking the passage of white man's time."

Ben interpreted and the Shawnee looked satisfied, then a bit surprised when she asked, "How do your people mark time?"

Ben interpreted and there was a thoughtful pause. "The seasons move my people forward. Nature is more reliable than the white man's method—and shows the Creator's splendor."

She smiled in understanding, a bit awed by his eloquence. "Like the first leaves of spring, you mean. Or the coming of the first snow."

He nodded and closed the face of the watch, only to flick it open again.

"You may have it if you like," she said quietly.

At this, Ben seemed to balk. She looked at him and read stark displeasure in his face. Undaunted, she turned to the Shawnee and repeated, "A gift."

Fumbling in her pocket, she withdrew a tiny key on a ribbon fob. "I nearly forgot. This is how you wind it." Taking back the watch, she inserted the key into the silver facing and gave a turn, then held both out to him, murmuring again, "A gift."

It was a full minute before Ben gave the translation. When at last he did, the Shawnee's eyes shone with amused mischief. Leaning nearer Roxanna, his inky hair falling forward and obscuring his smiling mouth, he said in perfect King's English, "Good trade."

Hearing the words so plainly spoken, she felt such a swell of delight that she laughed. Clearly pleased, he removed a slender string of white wampum hidden beneath his buckskin sleeve and held it out to her. Taking it, the offering warm from his skin, she nested it in her palm, admiring its glossy perfection.

When she thanked him, Ben refused to translate. He seemed increasingly agitated, perhaps on account of the elbowing, grinning regulars who ringed the room, muskets at their sides. Were so many men truly necessary?

Turning back to him, wondering if Ben would cooperate, or if the Shawnee knew more English than he let on, she asked, "What is your name?"

Gesturing to his headdress, he filled the silence with more of his mellifluous Shawnee.

Ben stood in sullen silence, and she finally turned to him. "What did he say, Ben?"

"His name's Five Feathers." Beneath his beard glowed the red of blatant embarrassment. "And he says he knows who you are."

"Oh?" She looked at him, expectant.

"The woman of the red-haired chief."

The . . . *what?*

Heat engulfed her cheeks and touched the tips of her ears—she could feel its fiery journey all the way to her toes. An unmistakable titter went round the room and she pinned her gaze on Ben. "Please tell him I am *not*—"

But the words were lost as the blockhouse door opened. The ensuing silence told her just who had entered even before he'd circled the bench and stood before them. She kept her eye on a wide crack in the puncheon floor, unable to look at Cass, their midnight parting flooding her with fresh angst. Even as she studiously avoided him, she sensed he was taking in every single detail of the scene before him—from the timepiece in the Shawnee's hand to the wampum in hers, the regulars' rapt attention, even Ben's bristling. He said nothing, and she realized that this was a subtle tactic he used to force others to fill the silence. Not surprisingly, Ben obliged.

"I'm afraid you've missed all the excitement, sir. Miss Rowan's done more in ten minutes than we've done in ten weeks. If you'd waited a bit longer to come in, no telling what information the chief here might have given her."

"Scrivener . . . chef . . . diplomat?" The quiet question seemed an invitation to look at him, which she would not do. "Miss Rowan's talents seem without end."

Heart pounding, she got up from the bench and turned her back to them, leaving Ben to confer with him in low tones before Cass dismissed the regulars and the Shawnee.

"I'm just saying our Indian appears to know more English than he's letting on," Ben murmured behind her. "He came alive when Miss Rowan gave him the pocket watch. Told her his name and everything."

Ben's whispered words seemed to point an accusing finger, and she felt upended once again. She heard Cass's quiet dismissal of him and felt a sudden shadow fall over her. Slowly she turned to face him. He looked, she realized, like her father used to—before he gave way to one of his rare rages. Only the colonel would give her no quarter, she guessed.

Though his voice was low and calm, it was steel-edged and brooked no argument. "Miss Rowan, are you in the habit of dispensing personal possessions to savages?"

The accusation stabbed her, as did the slur. "*Savages?* Nay—"

"Aye, *savages*—one in particular who won't simply take your watch but your life—*and* your virtue. I don't want you within twenty feet of him."

She hesitated, feeling dwarfed in spirit, struck by how stern he was when he'd been so tender with her in her cabin. "Perhaps he wouldn't be quite so savage if he wasn't treated as such."

The freshly shaved jaw tensed. "He's treated like any other prisoner according to the Articles of War, Miss Rowan."

"I was merely showing him a kindness."

"A kindness." The words held a hint of mockery.

"Yes, a kindness."

He leveled her with a look. "Then let your kindnesses be few and far between. You're under my authority, and I'll not have you gifting a sav—a *man*—who has been the death of countless settlers. Is that clear?"

She glanced away from him, her gaze brushing the orderlies' backs as they performed their tasks across the room, no doubt straining to hear their every word.

"Do I make myself clear, Miss Rowan?"

She raised her chin. "Ask me politely, Colonel McLinn."

Surprise sparked in his eyes, nearly thawing their coldness. Amusement and exasperation pulled at the corners of his mouth. She felt a little surge of triumph at catching him off guard.

"Miss Rowan," he replied, his stern gaze unwavering, "I didn't achieve the rank of colonel by being polite. Do I make myself clear?"

In answer, she simply smiled, softening her refusal to curtsey or salute or do whatever he expected of her. Breaking her gaze, he moved to his desk and said, "We'll continue our conversation later. I have more pressing matters outside the gates."

His terse tone sent fresh alarm through her. Before she could question him, his officers entered, their faces reflecting varying degrees of concern. Micajah Hale was at the front, eyes darting first to Roxanna, then the colonel, as if mulling how much to say. She took a chair along one wall, wondering if he would send her out.

The major spoke quietly, but she could hear every ominous word. "There's a delegation of Shawnee waiting down by the river. They're professing peace and say they want to see you."

"How many in their party?" Cass asked.

"Thirteen," Joram Herkimer replied.

"Thirteen men and one woman, you mean."

Herkimer flushed at the oversight. "Aye."

"Which suggests this is a peaceful party."

Micajah balked. "With all due respect, sir, we don't know that for sure. Up on the banquette, the men have seen some movement in the trees beyond the postern gate that suggests a far larger group."

Herkimer added, "They've agreed to leave their weapons at the gate—the thirteen, anyway—if we let them in."

Cass folded his arms across his chest. "Then let them in."

Roxanna's eyes fastened on him and stayed there, needing an anchor amidst the swirling undercurrents of tension. As his officers checked their weapons, he removed two belts of wampum from his desk—one a glossy, eye-catching black and the other a stark white—both far longer than the ones he'd displayed before.

At his direction, the orderlies flew about the room, moving chairs and tables, clearing his desk of all but the wampum. Turning toward the mantel, he took down a long clay pipe and some twists of tobacco in preparation for she knew not what.

There wasn't a hint of unease about him, which seemed to riddle all his men. Sensing this was a significant event, she began to pray open-eyed and silently, thinking of the other Kentucke stations that had fallen under similar circumstances, remembering how many had been killed, the captives taken north. This might well be her final glimpse of him if things turned treacherous. Given that, heaven wouldn't begrudge her one last look, surely.

He was impeccably dressed, the elegant lines of his inky stock folded about his neck, ruffled shirt peering past layers of weskit and deep blue coat, swallowtails falling in elegant lines around breeches and blacked boots. Another black silk ribbon caught back his fiery hair.

Just like the one she'd hidden beneath her pillow.

It seemed the only safe place, well away from Bella's probing eyes and questions. She'd thought briefly of returning it to him, then tucked the thought away. He wanted no further reminder of their last liaison any more than she did, surely. And now with fresh anger simmering between them . . .

"Miss Rowan, I don't want you present." His Irish lilt reached to her across the room, polite and deferential and terribly distant.

She shifted in her chair. "'Twould seem, sir, that under the circumstances, you need a scrivener more than ever."

"Meaning?"

Their eyes met. "Rather, you need every one of your men." *In case things turn ugly*, she didn't add.

He hesitated as if debating whether having her with him might be safer than having her away from him. "Very well. I want you over here, then." Moving her Windsor chair behind the bulk of his desk, he waited for her to claim it and settle her lap desk on her knees.

She said with far more composure than she felt, "'Tis hardly the time to be telling you this, but I'm dangerously low on ink."

Pulling out a drawer, he revealed a startling supply of his own ink alongside an ornate pistol. Handing her both the ink and the gun, he advised her to put the latter in her lap desk. "If matters turn treacherous, don't hesitate to use it, provided I can't defend you myself."

"Is it—loaded?"

He nearly smiled at her naïveté. "Aye, Miss Rowan. And if you're feeling timid, just pretend it's me you're aiming at and I'll wager you'll have no misgivings at all."

18

Shivering, Roxanna replenished her ink and hid the pistol just as the door opened wide to admit a startling retinue. As the Shawnee party filed in dressed in flashing silver and calico, stroud and skins, she watched Cass in profile. He seemed to be assessing and categorizing each one, face firm but not unfriendly, hands clasped behind his back. She felt a swell of pride as respect overrode her fear, and she realized he'd placed her well in back of him to protect her if things went awry. For the moment it even softened her anger over their heated exchange moments before.

A half-dozen Indians faced him, ebony eyes rising from the belts of wampum—one denoting war and the other peace—to his grave, thoughtful face. But Roxanna was no longer looking at stalwart soldiers or stoic Indian chiefs. Astonishment peppered her like buckshot as her gaze came to rest on the first Indian woman she'd ever seen. For a few heart-stopping seconds, she realized every officer stood transfixed.

Even Colonel McLinn.

The woman stood wrapped in a red trade blanket, her lustrous hair spilling in an ebony waterfall to her knees. Finely sculpted features glowed tawny with health, and she kept her eyes down with a becoming modesty, the fringe of her lashes long and black. Small shells and silver rings glittered from the outer edges of her ears and mirrored the jewelry about her neck. Tall and graceful and astonishingly lovely, she seemed the daughter of a chief. Or perhaps a chief's wife.

Cass drew his sword and laid it across the desk between the wampum belts. The stillness seemed excruciating to Roxanna as she sat motionless with her quill, sensing this was just the start of a long ceremony fraught with protocol. Perhaps she'd been rash to ask to stay on—but 'twas too late to change course in midstream.

Across from them, the tallest Shawnee came forward with an elaborate feathered pipe in his hands. Cass circled the desk to stand before him, and Ben Simmons retrieved a live coal from the hearth. Clouds of rich smoke perfumed the air between them, wafting back to Roxanna on a cold draft. The pipe was then passed to each Indian before Cass spoke.

"Since you have initiated this meeting, I want to hear why you have come. Did the bad birds of the British send you like they have sent so many of your warriors to fight their battles for them? Or are you here of your own accord to talk truth—and peace?"

Roxanna held her breath at such plain speaking, scanning the dark, impassive faces as Simmons translated.

The chief with the pipe spoke again, his face creased in thoughtful lines. "We do not come with British cannon or dressed as Redcoats, as you can see. The gifts we bring the red-haired chief are not from Detroit. We come to hear the truth of why the Bluecoats make war with their father across the great water and in turn make war on us. Since you have come into our country, we have had no peace. We have also heard you will soon cross the Ohio River and trouble us further, like the Long Knives before you."

As she pushed the quill furiously across her paper, Roxanna was thankful for the frequent lulls in the translation, if only to rest her hand and try to make sense of the proceedings.

"I do plan to come into your country again, if only to find out who among the British are sending Shawnee into the Kentucke settlements to spill blood and take scalps," Cass said. "My quarrel is not with you but the Redcoats. Burning your towns and destroying your crops is distasteful to me. I know the whole of your people are suffering because of the greed and evil of a few bad birds among the British. If you tell me who these Redcoats are, I will bypass the middle ground and go straight to them, sparing your people much turmoil."

A second chief spoke, his wrinkled face bearing a hundred hard lines, his silver-streaked hair wrapped in otter skins. "We only know of the soldier chief Hamilton in Detroit. He is the one paying our young warriors for Kentucke scalps. You speak of someone else?"

"Aye, I do. I've learned that Hamilton has at least one British officer working among your people, particularly your young braves, bribing them with rum and muskets and goading them to violence. I mean to find out who that is."

The next hours unfolded like scenes from a tedious play, and Roxanna's hand cramped from holding the quill so tightly. She wished they would stop and smoke again but sensed this would not happen till meeting's end, if then. Words flew like sparks between the colonel and the Shawnee—hot, colorful, alarming. Yet her grudging admiration for Cass grew. Not once had she caught him in a lie, though Indian politics, as Papa had often said, was fraught with deceit. Nor did he ply them with drink and gifts to bribe them.

As the clock struck four, the delegation passed outside, into light and fresh air. The Shawnee had brought Cass gifts so generous she was surprised. A fine black stallion prancing just outside the door. Pouches of the finest, most fragrant Indian tobacco. A heavily fringed deerskin coat with a stunning array of painted quills in an artful pattern across the back.

Standing by the shuttered window, Roxanna watched the exchange on the parade ground, aware of the beautiful Shawnee woman still in the room with her. The woman lingered by the hearth, eyes roaming over this strange domain of white men, much as Roxanna's ranged over the colorful assortment of Indians outside. A bleak February sun was stabbing through the clouds, catching the copper of Cass's hair so that it seemed to flame. He had since returned his sword to its scabbard but was still wary, she sensed, though amiable and assured in outward manner.

He swung himself up on the stallion's bare back and, to the obvious delight of the chiefs, took off at a gallop and cleared the low-lying magazine that held Fort Endeavor's precious powder stores. Dismounting beside the flagpole, he removed his uniform coat and gave it to the chief who'd served as spokesman for the group. The Shawnee donned it proudly, particularly taken with the proliferation of gilt buttons and ornate braid. Cass likewise shrugged on the deerskin coat, clearly as pleased with the gift as the Shawnee chief now sporting his.

The only sticking point in the whole affair, Roxanna reflected, was the Shawnees' refusal to divulge who among the British was inciting their warriors to raid the frontier settlements. Discovering this was Cass's burning mission, and he'd not once let up in trying to achieve it, using a clever arsenal of verbal tactics. Listening hard and transcribing till the pain in her wrist rivaled that in her head, she was tempted to believe the Shawnee truly didn't know. Cass, she sensed, felt they simply weren't telling.

The only significant piece of intelligence he'd elicited was that the British were planning a joint attack on the remaining Kentucke forts at some shadowy point in future, complete with cannon, in a concentrated effort to drive the settlers back over the mountains once and for all.

"And do your chiefs believe that the British, if successful, will return the hunting grounds of Kentucke to you?" he'd asked them with characteristic candor. "If so, the Redcoat lies are as thick as flies. They want this land as their own. After they drive the settlers out, they will drive you out."

Simmons translated the forceful words, and there was a profound silence. *Peace, peace . . . there is no peace.* Unbidden, the Scripture came to Roxanna's mind in all its desolation. Like the Israelites of old, the Shawnee would one day find themselves without a country once the British and Americans finished fighting each other.

Returning to her chair, she funneled sand back into a jar and looked at the now dried pages of shorthand. Later she would spend hours copying them into official transcripts to be sent to Virginia and beyond. She waited for the men to come back inside, acutely aware of the Indian woman as she walked about the large room, the fringe of her tunic swaying with every graceful step.

The trade blanket she'd worn like a cape now lay in a red puddle on the floor before Cass's desk. Without it, she was even more astonishing, her doeskin dress snow white, the blue beadwork breathtaking. Her waist was wrapped in a fur belt, its slimness a startling contrast to the lush curves of her hips and chest. She looked, Roxanna thought with something akin to envy, like an overripe pawpaw waiting to be picked.

When the officers and Indians returned, they again gathered around the desk to smoke. The party wanted to be on their way by dusk, Simmons told them in translation, despite Cass's invitation to stay and eat. Roxanna breathed a prayer of thanks. With the commissary so low, Bella would be hard-pressed and in a fury feeding any more guests.

Thankfully there were few closing remarks. Roxanna put down her quill, only to pick it up again when the eldest of the chiefs stepped forward. "We believe you have spoken the truth here today. Though we have never met before now, we have heard of your exploits as a warrior and chief. The Redcoats fear your shadow will fall over them in the north as it has our people in the middle ground. To show you that we are prepared to turn from the British and bury the hatchet and walk the path of peace, we present you with a final gift."

Quill idle, Roxanna waited for Cass to respond to the translation. He hesitated, and she sensed an undercurrent of fresh distrust. The officers were darting nervous glances around the room in search of the promised gift—or perhaps a surprise ambush. Cass stood facing the Shawnee party, strangely silent. Roxanna's attention swung from him to the Indians as tension crackled in the cold air.

The older Shawnee's eyes seemed to shine with goodwill. "The Great Spirit has revealed to us that peacemaking comes from the melding of body, soul, and spirit. Only then can two peoples truly understand each other. It would be a good thing for the blood of the red-haired chief to flow in our veins. Strength and peace will be shared between us. To achieve this end, I give you my daughter."

Roxanna's transcribing ground to a halt. The room grew so still she heard naught but the sudden thrumming of her heart. Frontier politics were often unpredictable and dangerous . . . but *this*? Simmons had mistaken the translation, surely. Gripping her quill so hard she thought it would snap, she heard Simmons murmuring something to the chief, who simply repeated his offer of before.

How, she wondered, could such a gift be graciously refused? And what did this beautiful woman, capable of winning any man's heart, think of her father's outrageous offer?

Stricken, Roxanna looked up, the sympathy welling inside her turning to stark dismay. Though her head was lowered demurely, the Indian woman's comely features were nevertheless suffused with pleasure at the prospect of such a liaison, a beguiling half smile playing across her lips.

And Cass . . .

Her heart constricted while he stood there, broad back to her as he turned toward this flesh-and-blood gift, the buckskin jacket making him seem taller and even more appealing. Dropping her eyes to the papers on her desk, she waited for his refusal. When it didn't come, she looked up at him entreatingly.

He raised a long arm, the fringe of his sleeve swinging forward with an easy grace, and laid a hand on the woman's shoulder. "What is your name?"

Her response was simply a lovely echo of all the rest of her, softly and gracefully articulated, and when she lifted her dark eyes to look up at him, they held an enticing invitation.

"Falling Water," Simmons finally said in a breathless sort of wheeze.

Addressing the chief, Cass said, "I accept the gift of your daughter—and I thank you."

Stifling a gasp, Roxanna pressed her back against the hard rungs of her chair. The sudden movement jarred the lap desk, spilling the inkpot and staining the moss green of her skirts a deep indigo. The quill followed, fluttering wildly to the floor like a wounded bird. She hardly heard the satisfied response of the chief in translation. Within moments they were exiting the room, Indians first, officers following, then Ben Simmons and finally Cass and his prize. Numb, Roxanna sat as if bound to the chair. Visions of copper hair turned loose from its tie, tawny arms, and flashing black eyes made her clench her jaw so tight tears came to her eyes.

Alone in the room, she felt a sudden desperation seize her. Ignoring the mess she'd made, she rushed to the window and unlatched the shutter to take in the scene outside. Twilight was falling fast, casting the parade ground in purple shadows. The front gates were groaning open to allow the Shawnee to pass, and the officers had fanned out around them, ever wary. High above, the banquette was crowded with armed regulars. But Roxanna couldn't look away from Cass—and *her*.

She leaned into the window, the crude bulk of the shutter creaking as she sagged against it. She felt like she was five years old, sitting on the lofty branch of that old oak, secure one minute then slipping the next. Down, down, down she'd fallen, legs folding under her like broken sticks, left foot shattering. Then, and now, all the breath flew out of her, and she couldn't speak or cry or do anything at all. Mere bones had broken then. 'Twas nothing like her heart, which, though she'd forbidden it, had fastened itself to Cass.

She watched in silent agony as he turned to the Indian woman and held out his hand. Without a moment's hesitation, she entwined her fingers in his. The intimate gesture was done with such a touching familiarity that fresh pain sliced through Roxanna's heart.

Oh, Cecily, to be in Ireland, unable to see your beloved like this . . .

He was walking toward the sally port now as he did every evening, the guard flanking him, leaving the fetid fort far behind. Everyone—to a man—was watching them go, all those remaining lost in a cloud of bewilderment or blatant envy.

Up the greening hill to the stone house they went. Hank was not there but here, standing with Bella near the flagpole, the new American flag with its stars and stripes outstretched in a stiff early evening wind. At the entrance to the stone house, Cass opened the door and let the Shawnee woman in before shutting it firmly behind them.

Roxanna leaned her head against the shutter, a great emptiness rushing in to rival her hurt. What would they say when alone with one another? How would they make themselves understood? The innocent questions pushed her pain deeper still, and then the wisdom of her twenty-eight years took root. Some things needed no interpretation.

Lovemaking was the same in any language.

19

Wrapping the fragile thistle teacup and saucer in a piece of linen cloth, Roxanna buried it in her trunk alongside her other treasured things. It was nearly midnight now, and her righteous indignation of hours before had eroded into a childish desire to run away. After shunning supper, she'd drawn in the latchstring to avoid visitors, praying for solitude. Sometimes Dovie or Nancy would stop by—and always Bella. But tonight, strangely, Bella had not come. Nor had Abby, up and around again, free of the fever. If Roxanna had any regrets, they concerned leaving Abby.

Her whole world felt upended and queer. Habit pulled her to the window as it did night after night, and she gave in to the impulse a final time. Saying good night to the stone house had become her bedtime ritual. She loved the way the moon, when it shone, turned the stone a pearly white, noble as a castle wall, and how a solitary candle, star-bright, always flickered from a second-story oriole window. His window, she guessed. And now . . . hers.

Tonight she couldn't bring herself to open the shutter and look. If she had, she would have stared into utter blackness. The moon was hidden behind a bank of clouds, its light snuffed like a candle. No longer was the stone house a thing of beauty and

175

grace and peace. When Cass had taken the Shawnee woman inside, it had become a place of dishonor.

In the ensuing hours, her hurt had hardened to anger. All the admiration she'd had for him as an officer and a gentleman had turned to ashes. Oh, she wasn't so naive that she didn't know officers sometimes relieved their loneliness in discreet ways. Even Bella had hinted he was in need of a mistress. But a commander, especially one assigned by General Washington himself, whose reputation extended to every tribe and settler from east to west, had an example to maintain. And in the space of one afternoon, he'd thrown it all to the wind.

Stomach careening, she recalled the eve he'd recently shared with her. When they'd danced and he'd taken the liberty to touch her, brushing her cheek with his fingers before twining them in her hair, she'd sensed his deep loneliness—and her own. Fearing both, she'd told him she didn't want to fall in love with him. And his response had been a barely tamped-down fury.

Pressing cold fingers to her aching temples, she tried to make sense of it all. Oh, but she had so little knowledge about men— or how war was waged on the frontier. But why bother? It only mattered that she get away as soon as possible.

She lay down, but sleep would not come. The parade ground outside her walls had assumed a ghostly quiet, and her prayers seemed to reach the ceiling and go no further. In the wee hours, she finally found her only solace—repacking her trunk. But even this brewed a fierce battle inside her. Twice she took out the gifts he'd given her—the thistle teacup and saucer, the silver strainer, his heartfelt letter telling her of Papa's death, his black queue ribbon—intent on leaving them behind, only to return them to the trunk again.

She slammed the lid, buckled the leather straps, and waited for the sound of Hank's wagon as he readied for his weekly trip to Smitty's Fort. He went for supplies at the sutler's there, Cass said, and to gather reports from militia leaders as to what was happening at the various frontier stations in regards to the Indian trouble. Roxanna thought him quite brave to make these forays, sometimes with a few regulars but mostly alone. Bella reassured her that the Indians had a fearsome superstition about Negroes and usually gave them wide berth. Remembering it made her feel slightly less skittish about accompanying him today.

Finally hearing him, she hurried out, but only after she'd penned a terse letter. Never again would he be simply Cass to her, but Colonel.

Colonel McLinn,

Circumstances forbid me to continue in your service. I am on my way back to Virginia, beginning today. You are henceforth relieved of any and all responsibility for me.

Sincerely,

Roxanna Rowan

Leaving the letter on the trestle table, she rushed onto the parade ground, straight into the path of the oncoming wagon. Seeing her in the chilly dawn mist, Hank slowed the team to a stop and applied the hand brake, his dark face full of questions.

"I need a ride to Smitty's Fort. My lap desk and trunk are just inside."

He scratched his gray-whiskered chin. "Miz Roxanna, last I heard, Smitty's Fort was full up."

She clasped her gloved hands together pleadingly. "Perhaps there's room today. I don't mind sharing quarters—living temporarily with a family . . ."

His brown eyes reflected a wary resignation. "You tell the colonel 'bout this?"

The quiet rebuke ruffled the prim edges of her composure. "I doubt he cares about such mundane things this morning." The hasty words brought a new wave of hurt, and she looked down at the mud thawing beneath her boots, fighting tears.

"Bella's gonna be plenty put out wi' me—and you."

"Hank, please. I don't want a scene. I have some shillings . . ."
The words died out and revealed the depths of her desperation.

Looking over her head to the stone house, he tried a different tack. "It's a mite dangerous outside them gates. You know
how to use a gun?"

Feeling a small measure of success, she reached inside her
cape pocket and produced her silver-mounted pistol. Eyeing it,
he nodded and jumped down, heading toward the open cabin
door. In moments her trunk and lap desk were hefted into the
empty wagon bed, and he helped her up onto the rough seat.
She noticed his own musket tucked beneath them as the wagon
wheels groaned and lurched forward, past the sentries and
through the front gates.

They followed the river on a rutted road that had been worn
from woodcutting details and Hank's frequent forays to the
fort a few miles distant. As they rode, he was quieter than
usual, remarking only about some sign of spring—the tightly
furled buds of a passing dogwood or the throaty chant of
tree frogs.

'Twas the first of March, Roxanna remembered. Benumbed,
she didn't look back. Time to be moving on, no matter the danger. Fort Endeavor had brought her nothing but heartache. And
regret. She'd never even asked where Papa was buried. Somewhere in the wilderness was all she knew.

⁂

So this was Smitty's Fort. Half the size of Fort Endeavor, it
had no military presence aside from a small militia, not even
a flagpole flying the familiar Virginia colors. The stench of too
many people and animals trapped in too small a place, and not
one house of necessity but two, added to the aura of dirt, dung,
and despair.

While Hank did business with the sutler, Roxanna approached

a woman smoking a clay pipe outside the blacksmith's shop and learned that a cabin had just been vacated. "Old man Horner up and died two days ago. I ain't poked around his place myself, but you'd best take it right quick if you've a mind to."

Roxanna was afraid to ask just what he'd died of, saying simply, "I was hoping to join up with a party who might be going over the mountains to Virginia."

The woman ran appreciative eyes over Roxanna's fine cape. "Ain't nobody been comin' or goin' with the Indian scare on. Best talk to Marcus Calloway. He heads up the local militia and might know when another party could head back that way."

Half an hour later, Hank had deposited her trunk inside the deceased's cabin and built a welcoming fire. Now he stood in the doorway looking decidedly grieved. Behind him the sun sent feeble spokes of light into the dark interior, exposing a dozen spiderwebs threading the rafters and a good quarter inch of dust below.

"It ain't too late to come back wi' me, Miz Roxanna," he said for the fifth time, fur felt hat in his hands.

A barb of alarm, of feeling she'd run ahead of the Lord's will for her once again, nearly made her reconsider. "Thank you, Hank, but I can't. Please tell Bella and the others goodbye for me. And . . ." Tears sprang to her eyes and strained her voice. "And Abby."

Nodding, he turned to go but left the door wide open. Spying a grease lamp on a small table, she snatched a piece of straw from the bottom of a broom and kindled it, lighting the grease-soaked wick. The feral smell of bear's oil made her wrinkle her nose. Though the slant of the sun told her it wasn't yet ten o'clock in the morning, she was midnight weary. Sleep would be a welcome escape.

Finding a bed wrench beneath the sagging rope springs, she tightened each one, eyeing the corn-husk tick with growing concern. An army of bed bugs scurried for cover as light settled on the soiled linen ticking. Unbidden, an image of her tidy cabin just a few miles distant seemed to mock her.

Taking her quilt from her trunk, she wrapped herself in its familiar folds and settled into the room's only chair—a worn rocker—and tried not to think of the rat she'd just seen darting into a corner hole.

Lord, I didn't mean to run away from You. Just him.

Cass angled the razor over the long, lean slope of his jaw, the basin of water on the scrolled stand beneath him offering up a plume of bayberry-scented steam. After shaving, he cleaned the blade and laid it aside, drying his face with a towel. With Hank away at Smitty's Fort, the house was particularly quiet, the morning's calm broken only by the throaty trill of a robin beyond the window.

Darting a glance in the shaving glass, he blinked bloodshot eyes that bespoke a near sleepless night—for all the wrong reasons. Only Ben Simmons was privy to the truth of the last hours. All the rest believed he was busy courting a chief's daughter, albeit a very beautiful, informative one.

Opening a shutter, he peered past panes of glass that bubbled and streaked in the morning light and surveyed the stalwart lines of Fort Endeavor. A flash of red near the sally port caught his eye. Bella was mounting the hill, her calico kerchief bright as a beacon. He knew something was wrong simply by the cast of her features. Always dour and forbidding, they seemed even fiercer this morning. Surely the woman was descended from some Ethiopian warrior line. The guard could hardly keep up with her. She clutched a paper in one hand, and he realized she bore news. Bad news.

His gut gave a slight wrench. Abby? Was she ill again? Or Roxie . . .

Without another thought of being in his shirtsleeves, he went below to meet her.

Roxanna stirred from under the covers, a delicious drowsiness receding as consciousness pushed her awake. The large square room was filled with light, for someone had left the shutters open. A hint of oil paint lingered in the still air. As she lay back on the bank of goose-down pillows, her eyes drifted upward beyond the exquisite crewelwork canopy to Wedgewood-blue walls. The color rested her, reminded her of the Atlantic and the Virginia shore.

It was midday—the clock over the door told her so, but a few moments passed before she remembered why she was abed at such a busy hour. Smiling, she expelled a half-amused, half-indignant gasp as a furious little foot jabbed her beneath the rib cage. This was why she was upstairs, her baking left to Bella in the kitchen far below. Rolling onto her side, she cradled the bulk beneath her bed gown with impatient arms.

Come out, wee one. Only at your appearance will we know if your hair is to be a Rowan black or a McLinn red . . .

Roxanna jerked awake. Had she been dreaming, then? If so, the dream was so sweet she didn't want it to end. Stiff from sitting so long in the rocker, she opened her eyes, only to close them again in protest, the fine canopy bed far preferable to her present surroundings. But the rudeness of the room was too jarring, and she came fully alert.

With a cry she spied her trunk by the door, the lid open, linen undergarments and shoes spilling out. Her scrivener's pay, a princely stack of shillings bound in an embroidered handkerchief to hasten her to Virginia, was missing, the cabin door ajar. Robbed? Hands trembling, she flew to the trunk and dug deep for the treasured teacup and letter and hair ribbon, her frantic actions revealing the state of her heart. Each lay unharmed at the bottom of the trunk and she breathed a prayer of thanks, then remembered the reason she'd fled Fort Endeavor—and her dream.

The two collided in a sickening rush—the latter so sweet, the former so base she sat down on the closed trunk and let a cold, hard numbness overtake her. She'd been dreaming about McLinn in a way she was ashamed to even recall, wed and abed, lying upstairs in a room she'd never seen but that had felt like home to her. Only the stone house wasn't hers—'twas the Indian woman's. She herself was at Smitty's Fort, not only homeless and fatherless, but suddenly shillingless. Closing her eyes against the tears welling there, she leaned her head back, the soft knot of her chignon pressing against the rough log wall.

Lord, forgive me for my foolishness. I commit myself to You anew. Please deliver me and rescue me from the error of my ways.

She'd not yet said "amen" when the door swung completely open. Sitting beside it, she looked up, eyes widening.

Oh, Lord, Colonel McLinn is not what I meant!

Still, the tremendously tall figure filling the door frame, immaculate in buff and blue, cross belts and weapons in place, seemed every inch the rescuer. She fought the urge to fall headlong into his arms in relief, nearly forgetting the trouble that sat squarely between them.

He didn't look at her or speak but surveyed the threadbare bed, the table and rocker, the glowing remains of Hank's fire. His intense expression said he found it all lacking. She felt an acute embarrassment, as if she were somehow to blame for her sorry surroundings.

"I've come to escort you back," he told her.

His ironclad tone nearly made her waver. "I'm not going back."

He gave her a disgusted look. "You've just been robbed and you're in the quarters of a dead man. Why would you want to stay?" He reached inside his coat and withdrew her hoard of shillings.

What?

Startled, she stood and faced him, watching as he deposited the money atop a table. His striking face was as resolute as she'd ever seen. She was going back, every hard line seemed to say, if only because he wasn't going to waste time debating the matter when he had better things to do.

Folding her arms, she took a steadying breath, unable to resist one needling remark. "I'm sorry you came all this way, as I'm aware you have more pressing matters to attend to."

His ice-blue eyes seemed to spit at her. "Sarcasm and innuendo don't become you, Miss Rowan. I suggest you say what you mean."

"You know full well what I mean."

"Aye, I do, but I'm not going to discuss it with you—*and* them." When he stepped clear of the doorway, she was astonished to see a small crowd gathering outside.

Their blank, bleak faces, hungry for any sort of amusement, showed not a smidgen of remorse for eavesdropping. Heat rushed to her cheeks, and she looked away. If it was a lover's quarrel they wanted, they were to be sorely disappointed. Turning her back to them—and him—she folded her arms, fighting tears. The groan of the hinges and the ensuing shadows assured her he'd shut the door. It took her a full minute to realize he was no longer in the same room with her. He'd left.

Confused and frantic, she flung the door open wide again. He stood looking down at her, but the crowd had dispersed. *How had he accomplished that?* she wondered.

"So you do want to talk to me," he said.

Bested—and humiliated—she looked up at him through damp eyes. She wasn't sure just what she wanted. A stony weight settled in her chest as she motioned him in. When he shut the door soundly, yesterday's spectacle returned to her in all its color and confusion.

The colorful chieftains and ensuing haze of tobacco smoke. Melodious Shawnee flowing from their mouths like music. Hours of translation and transcribing. And then the gifts—a horse, an elaborate buckskin jacket, a beautiful woman. She felt anew her own careening emotions, like she'd been riding in a carriage for far too long and lacked air. Her head and stomach swirled in such tandem she thought she might be sick.

She took the rocker while he straddled a bench facing the fire, a hand resting on the hilt of his sword. Even a few feet away from her, he was so physically imposing she seemed to be cast in his shadow. But he was a bit hesitant, she thought, as if as disinclined to talk and as tired as she.

Finally he said, "What are you running from, Miss Rowan, without so much as a by-your-leave?"

She bit her lip. "I couldn't stay—after yesterday."

"After the gift giving, you mean—that and the incident in your cabin."

The incident. It was more carefully put than anything he'd ever said.

"Yes." She looked down at her hands awkwardly, surprised he'd risk discussing so delicate a matter.

"Things aren't always what they seem in matters of love—and war. Yet you think me so base you believe the worst."

The accusation made her want to crawl beneath the bench. "What else was I to think?"

"I never meant to demean you that night in your cabin, ye ken. And I took the Indian woman in the house to question her, not seduce her."

Hearing it so plainly stated, she felt herself go crimson again and said nothing.

"You're not even going to ask me what I asked her?"

"Nay." She fixed her gaze on a crack in the floor, wishing the whole excruciating matter would melt away.

"Falling Water is not simply a chief's daughter. She's the daughter of the war chief of the Shawnee nation. As such, she is privy to all matters of war and the men who make it, particularly the British. I couldn't risk the chief's ire by refusing her outright."

Slowly her confusion began to clear. She looked at him entreatingly. "You hoped she'd tell you who among the British are provoking the Shawnee raids on the settlements?" At his nod, understanding washed over her, along with the realization of how she'd misjudged him. "And did she tell you—even when the chiefs would not?"

"She told me a great deal more than I thought she would."

"How do you know it's the truth?"

"It confirms the intelligence coming out of Detroit and other places in the middle ground."

She grew quiet, pondering it all. The respect she had for him was flowering again, save one final question. "Colonel McLinn, you are a man of considerable charms. May I ask how you were able to convince her to divulge such valuable information?"

"I have her lover in custody."

"What?"

"The younger Shawnee chief—Five Feathers. I told her she could see him, take care of the old man."

Shame tugged at her. "I—I thought—"

His dissecting stare told her he wasn't going to let her escape so easily. "What exactly did you think?"

She took a deep breath and said in a little rush, "I thought you were an unprincipled officer whose loneliness finally got the better of him."

His smile was tight, even wry. "I am lonely. And I'm tired of fighting Redcoats and redskins. But my honor is still intact."

The honest admission—and her own rash judgments—made her more woozy. "Please . . . forgive me."

"Aye, I will," he said in measured tones, removing his tricorn. "If you'll return to Fort Endeavor with me."

She swallowed past the knot in her throat. "I think you'd be glad to be rid of me, thinking so ill of you."

He looked away from her into the fire. "The truth is Fort Endeavor needs you."

Confused, she shifted in her seat, darting a look at him.

"I need you," he amended quietly. "Not just your services as scrivener. I need your goodness and gentleness and strength. Sometimes I think you're the only one I can trust, even above my own officers."

There was a degree of humility in his words that warmed her like the fire they sat beside. But his sudden honesty was also unsettling, making her recall matters she longed to leave behind. "You're thinking of Papa's journal. I didn't want to show it to you—make you suspect your own men. Maybe he was wrong."

"Your father wasn't one to make rash accusations. I know I have an inside enemy working to aid the British. I don't know who it is yet, but I'm narrowing the field. And I need your help."

"Help?" she echoed. "What can I do?"

"Stand by me. Believe in me." His eyes sought hers again. "Maybe even petition Providence for me."

"I will pray for you—I *do* pray for you," she said, feeling a new tenderness toward him. Yet her erstwhile words seemed to echo even now and push them apart. *Please, I don't want to fall in love with you.* Looking away, she made herself say, "'Tis nearly spring. I need to be thinking of leaving."

He gave an agitated move on the bench. "How can I, in good conscience, let you go? I can't even keep a courier alive."

She folded her hands in her lap, facing the truth of it, yet holding on to hope. "I'll come back to Fort Endeavor with you today. And I'll help you in any way I can. But I want to leave at the first opportunity."

"Just promise that you won't go away again without telling me."

Surprised, she darted another glance at him. Today he seemed so . . . different. Suddenly it seemed what they weren't saying to each other was the only thing she heard.

When, she wondered, had she lost her heart to him?

Simply sitting beside him in this dusty, infested, fire-lit cabin was so excruciatingly sweet she couldn't speak.

"Promise me, Roxie," he said again.

The way he said her name—low and slow and sweet—was like nothing she'd ever heard. She could feel his eyes on her in such a way it was as if he was tracing the oval of her face with his fingers. And all her halfhearted talk of leaving turned to ashes.

"I promise."

20

They left Smitty's Fort, he on the black Shawnee stallion, she on a borrowed mare. Her trunk, entrusted to the sutler, would follow when Hank returned to the fort later that day. Once outside the gates, she looked around, her high feeling of reconciliation—of being rescued—eroding like river sand. The ubiquitous guard that shadowed Cass was missing, though the brilliant sunshine made light of her fears. How could anything evil exist in the face of such bright beauty?

"Stay abreast of me," was all he said.

She rode between him and the river, and the reason soon came clear. If an arrow or musket ball erupted from the brush, he'd buffer her. Was that his thought? But once he fell, what then? Her pistol packed small comfort, though he was fully armed, the sash of his sword a bold blue, with more weapons hidden beneath his uniform coat. Somehow the fact that they'd just discussed a spy made their traveling alone doubly ludicrous.

"Why," she asked a bit breathlessly, "did you come without a guard?"

He eyed her beneath the shadow of his tricorn, every angle of his face wary. "I didn't think you'd appreciate being returned to Fort Endeavor like a prisoner."

"I *am* a prisoner, Colonel McLinn."

"So are we all, Miss Rowan."

She studied him as she bumped along atop the unfamiliar horse, trying to keep up with him. "To be honest, I'm nearly shaking in my boots. Yet you seem so fearless. 'Tis a curious trait among you Continental soldiers."

He smiled, his eyes crinkling at the corners. "I've heard the bullets whistle, and believe me, there is something charming in the sound."

"I don't fancy being under fire myself."

"What do you fancy?"

Their eyes locked, and hers skittered away to the safety of the river. *Robust men in buff and blue. Cherry bounce. Fireside dances in dark cabins. Stone houses.* "Safety and civilization and peace."

"You have a dim view of Kentucke, then. Your horizons need expanding."

With a touch of his spurs, he turned away from the river. She had no choice but to follow, praying all the way as the forest's green shadows swallowed them. Her straw hat was nearly swept off her head by a low-lying branch, but she pushed her fears down in the face of his stalwart shoulders and intrepid profile.

Colonel McLinn . . . please, she almost begged in a plea to turn back.

Yet no matter how frightened she felt, there was no denying the exhilaration of riding free. Was this what he'd meant about the charm of whistling bullets? Every nerve taut, every sense stretched? Embracing every breath, knowing it might be your last? This was what life would be like with him, she thought—never quite comfortable or safe, always with an undercurrent of danger.

They crossed a little rippling creek with bluish-gray stones that reminded her of Abby's eyes. Robins and cardinals exploded in song, raising the fine hair on her arms and the back of her neck.

She darted a look around. "Why do I have the feeling we're being watched?"

"I have scouting patrols in these woods," he said easily. "Eze-kial Click and his cronies move about freely—not to mention Indians."

Freely . . . yet hidden.

They climbed a greening rise where dogwood was about to bloom and mountain laurel showed a subtle peek of their scarlet splendor. Everything seemed to be waiting for spring—she most of all. Below in an open valley was a small cabin puffing smoke, near a patch of garden ground and a newly plowed cornfield. A far cry from the stone house, she thought, yet a promising start. As they skirted the hill, a woman came out onto the porch, half a dozen children scampering around her. A man was building a fence in a stump-littered clearing, musket propped against a post.

Awe threaded her voice. "Do they go on, day after day, oblivi-ous to the danger?"

He pulled his tricorn lower. "Not oblivious, just in spite of. This family—the O'Hares—is from Ireland. There are many like them hidden in these hills and hollows. They come here for freedom—a chance to realize a dream."

"And you're here to defend that dream."

"Well said, Miss Rowan. Even if it's not quite so noble."

"My father said you're the reason these settlers stay on—that without a strong military presence, the British and Indians would have a field day and overrun the Kentucke territory."

His expression was patently resigned. "I'm here because I'm expendable and cost General Washington a great deal of time and trouble in the colonies. No one else wanted the command."

"No one else was qualified, you mean. You're the only American officer I know of who's been awarded a Badge of Military Merit for valor in battle, for nearly losing your life. Yet you refuse to wear it. Why?"

"Who told you about the Purple Heart?"

She hesitated, steeling herself against a rush of emotion. "My father."

A flicker of distress marred his calm. He was looking pensively at the ground with such disregard for their surroundings she sensed he was about to tell her something momentous.

She stayed quiet, willing him to speak, knowing he couldn't confide in or unburden himself to many. A new thought assailed her. Might the Lord have brought them together not for love but for simple companionship, however brief? She said quietly, "You are in need of a friend, Colonel McLinn. Let me be that friend."

His head came up, and there was such unmistakable anguish in his eyes she nearly winced. And then his demeanor hardened and he was unreachable—and unreadable again.

"We must move on," he told her with a jerk of his reins, turning away.

With a confidence akin to a surveyor's knowledge of the land, he led her through thick stands of cane, past steaming mineral springs to a stony ridge rich in wildlife, with eagles soaring high above Fort Endeavor and the Ohio River. God's view, she thought, looking down at soldiers performing all the routine functions she was so tired of. She spotted Bella near the kitchen, a splash of sunny yellow in the weary canvas of military life.

When they finally came down from their perch, she felt her senses quicken. Beneath the close confines of her linen dress, perspiration ran in itchy lines. Not from the heat, as there was none this chilly March day, but from sheer trepidation—from the danger she felt pulsing all around them. Though she didn't want to return to the fort, she felt far safer within its walls.

The damp earthiness of the woods receded as she moved into a sunlit clearing just ahead of him. And then her hearing sharpened at a sudden *thwack*. Jerking her head around, she saw an arrow protruding from a near tree. Gasping, she watched as Cass turned and fired his pistol into the brush they were exiting before slapping the rump of her mare. It shot forward into the fort clearing, nearly toppling her. Everything in her screamed danger as she bent low, her hands tight about the reins, her thoughts full of him.

A second sound pierced her panic. 'Twas a musket ball, and its whistling brought every soldier on Fort Endeavor's banquette to full alert. A volley of answering gunfire exploded from the pickets above her head as if welcoming the two of them in. Just ahead, the postern gate cracked open to admit her—and then him. Chest heaving, she nearly fell off her horse. He simply dismounted beside her, a model of calm, though his tricorn was missing.

"Are you all right, Miss Rowan?"

Their eyes met, and she was astonished to find that his were unmistakably enlivened.

"Nay, Colonel McLinn." The words came out in breathless snatches, revealing her turmoil. "I have heard the bullets whistle, and believe me, there is nothing charming in the sound."

"I apologize for the close call."

Her thoughts were swirling, wondering who had meant him—them—harm. Reaching out, she felt for her mare, hoping to lean into its silky side, but a regular was already leading it away, and it was Cass's coat sleeve she gripped instead. She was so close to fainting that dark spots danced in her vision. She barely heard his order to bring some cherry bounce to restore her senses but felt him pick her up as effortlessly as she'd seen him do Abby. Into headquarters they went, away from probing eyes and wagging tongues.

The blockhouse was blessedly dim and empty, and there she could nurse her shame in private . . . but for him. Depositing her gently in her Windsor chair, he took a seat beside her. She drew back a bit as he began untying the chin ribbon of her hat. There was something so intimate about his doing so that she wanted to squirm. In seconds he had the hat off and in her lap. She examined the wide, pansy-draped brim with its glossy leaves and ruched ribbon and felt her mouth form a perfect O—as perfect as the hole made by the musket ball that had passed through the hat's crown.

Oh, Lord, was I one breath away from death?

His steady voice settled her. "Was it a favorite?"

"Nay," she said shakily, thinking of Ambrose.

"'Twas a fine target," he mused ruefully.

"Am I very pale?"

"Paler."

"I've never fainted in my life."

"There's always a first time."

He leaned near again—so close she shut her eyes, overcome by wooziness of a different kind. His searching fingers were in her hair—reminding her of the night in her cabin, taking liberties no man ever had—all in search of half a dozen hat pins . . . or a lead ball? He took her hand and deposited the pins in her palm just as Bella came in.

"Law, but you is white as washed wool," Bella exclaimed, passing her a cup of cherry bounce. Her keen eyes ran up and down Roxanna, lingering on her hat. "But I reckon I'd be the same if I had a hole in my hea—*hat*."

Clucking her tongue, Bella went out and Roxanna sipped the bounce, feeling an instant fire that all but paled next to the one the colonel had just kindled in her.

"Would you like some?" she whispered, offering the cup, thinking he looked a bit shaken himself.

He took it a bit absently, downing the remainder. A tense silence ensued—so protracted she felt on tenterhooks. He seemed on the verge of revealing something just as he had in the woods. Sensing it, she held her breath. And then he got up and went out without a word, leaving her alone in the chill and gloom of the blockhouse.

21

Within a fortnight, a convoy of keelboats came downriver, making good time in the watery spring rush, bearing a wealth of supplies to the half-starved outpost. Tucking his spyglass in his coat pocket, Cass trudged up the muddy bank a quarter of a mile or more to where the regulars waited with wagons. It was too soon to fire a volley and welcome the vessels in. Though they were well beyond the reach of Indians and river pirates this close to the fort, other watery dangers awaited. Just six months before on this very spot, he'd watched a scow, loaded to the gills and almost to shore, become impaled on a snag and sink with crew, cargo, and all else.

Contemplating it, he looked over his shoulder and took in a far more pleasant prospect. Beyond the fort's west wall, on the gentle rise of ground leading to the stone house, stood Roxie, hoe in hand, her cranberry-colored skirts swirling around her ankles in the fickle mid-March wind. With the Indian threat so high, he'd assigned a double detail to guard her, and they stood at the garden's four corners, acutely aware of his scrutiny and making a show of looking at the river when they'd been looking at her moments before.

He didn't blame them, starved for feminine company as they were, but he didn't fancy the way it made him feel. He'd have to keep a careful watch on her once the polemen came ashore.

These free-spirited Frenchmen, whom he liked well enough, became absolute devils when drunk, their antics so spectacularly sinful they made his most hardened soldiers blush.

Shading his eyes against the blinding glaze of green water, he watched the lead boat round a final bend before its brown bulk came sharply into focus. This particular vessel was a floating fort—loopholed and armed with four one-pounders—and coming straight at him. He heard a litany of French profanities as the captain lost a setting pole in the shallows, but after several more precarious minutes, they dropped anchor and came ashore, the regulars helping place the gangplanks.

"Bonjour, mon colonel!"

"Bonjour, Captain. Any trouble coming downriver?"

The wiry Frenchman shot Cass a grizzled grin. "Ah . . . nothing that a well-placed cannon couldn't cure. *C'est la vie.*"

Grinning, Cass took the bill of sale and perused it as they began rolling out barrels. Micajah stood at his elbow, ready to assess the condition of the long-awaited supplies. Half an hour passed in mutual satisfaction, and Cass left him in charge so he could return to the fort. But the sight of Roxie in her garden proved too great a temptation, and he veered toward her.

She was kneeling, the bright circle of her skirts looking like a discarded blossom atop the freshly tilled ground, the tilt of her straw hat eclipsing her pale features. He felt his heart give a sudden lurch when she looked up at him, her delight so plain that he felt almost smothered with guilt.

He'd shot her father and she didn't know. He carried her locket in his breast pocket and she didn't know that either. He should confess the former and return the latter, yet if he did, she'd never again look at him in that winsome way she had, and it would be like shutting all the sun out of his dreary life. Recently, after their hair-raising return from Smitty's Fort, he'd nearly confessed everything. And then feeling nearly capsized by his emotions, he'd changed course.

He dismissed the guard, and there were just the two of them in the little sunlit meadow, and for a moment he was nigh speechless. Ever since he'd gone after her—had contemplated her bullet-ridden hat and how close he'd come to losing her—she'd gained a firmer foothold in his head and heart, and nothing could shake her loose. She'd begun to matter in ways he couldn't explain and was increasingly uncomfortable with. The sooner she could go east, the better.

Standing, she smoothed her skirts, proudly pointing to the rows she'd just planted. "Peas. Beans. Melons. Squash. Soon, Colonel McLinn, you'll have a fine table."

He shot her an apologetic glance. "And you'll hear no more of my complaining about the lack of provisions."

A smile tugged at the corners of her mouth. "Good humor makes even one dish of meat a feast, or so my father often said."

"Aye," he answered thoughtfully. "Scripture runs along the same lines. Something about a merry heart being good medicine, if I remember."

Surprise softened her features. "Good medicine, indeed." Looking toward the river, she asked, "How are the supplies coming?"

Swinging his gaze from her to the keelboats, his answer was cut off by Micajah's sudden shout. "Colonel, sir!"

Not wanting to leave her alone or be alone with her, he motioned for her to come with him. She abandoned her hoe and they walked down to the bank, his hand on the soft ruffle of her sleeve.

Micajah stood over an open barrel, clearly perplexed. Beside him, the keelboat captain's features hardened as he sampled the contents, then spat onto the muddy ground. Immediately Cass rued inviting Roxanna along.

"Pardon, mademoiselle," the Frenchman apologized, seeing Cass's features darken. "But thees barrel ees no good."

Cass caught the stench of spoiled meat from where he stood.

Running a practiced eye over the casks of brined beef and thinking of the ten or more men lying ill in the fort for want of good meat, he felt a tremor of fury. He'd been in worse straits, down to half a cup of parched corn and a fragment of jerky as a daily ration, but this was sheer stupidity.

Counting the casks, he measured his response, swallowed down the oaths in his throat, and forced cordiality into his tone. The keelboat captain and Micajah were eyeing him warily, awaiting his usual tirade, no doubt.

With a broad-shouldered shrug, he said evenly, "Green casks sour the brine and spoil the meat."

Micajah's skittishness faded to bewilderment as he gazed at the paper in his hand. "Even an idiot knows to pack supplies in seasoned wood. Who filled this order?"

Roxanna leaned over the open barrel in dismay. Of everyone present, she well knew the straits they were in from working in the kitchen. Game had become so scarce of late that they'd been anticipating this shipment all the weary winter like manna from heaven.

"They're likely all the same," Cass said evenly, aware that his second-in-command was now regarding him with far more interest than the ruined meat. But he was past the point of exploding now, and glad for the opportunity to further addle the men, he said with as much affability as he could muster, "We'll light a *feu de joie* for our French friends—have some feasting and dancing and an extra gill of rum for every man."

At this, Micajah almost gaped. Slapping him on the back to keep his mouth from hanging open, Cass turned and winked at Roxanna. "What say ye, Miss Rowan?"

Smiling, she looked up at him. "I say, dance on."

❦

Roxanna stood before the mirror in chemise, stays, pocket hoops, and petticoats, determined to style her hair in an inconspicuous chignon and not give way to the elaborate curls Bella insisted on. Moments before, Bella had disappeared so quickly she'd left the door slightly ajar, and raucous noises spilled through the crack from the parade ground just beyond. Roxanna crossed the cabin and shut the door, senses full of ribald laughter, French jests, roasting venison, and the unmistakable essence of whiskey and rum. The golden twilight held such a spring-like warmth she expected to see fireflies studding the shadows. Already the twang of fiddles beckoned and promised to relieve the outpost's monotony. Thanks to the weather, the frolic would be held outside, not in the crowded blockhouse.

Sliding the last pearl-headed pin into the glossy knot of hair at the nape of her neck, she turned in time to see Bella enter, arms full of something splendid and silky. Her dark face lightened with a flash of white teeth. "I've brought you another dress from the stone house."

"From your secret stores?"

"They ain't so secret. A big ol' flatboat bound for New Orleans sank within swimmin' distance 'bout a year ago. I couldn't let all that fancy cargo go to waste, could I?"

Roxanna started to protest, but when Bella held up the gown and shook it out, the words died in her throat. No doubt Bella had spent a few hours she didn't have altering it to fit Roxanna. The dress was utterly breathtaking, too breathtaking to turn down even if she'd wanted to.

Reaching out a hand to touch the copper silk skirt, she said, "Bella, if I didn't know better, I'd think you were matchmaking."

"Ain't it a fine gown? Look at that blue silk petticoat peekin' out underneath! Hank says he likes to see the colonel's eyes light up when you walk in all gussied up."

"Bella!"

"Law, I didn't say it—Hank did! But he didn't have to tell me so. I done noticed it myself."

Biting back a retort, she let Bella drape the gown over her

bare shoulders, dismayed to find the neckline so low. As Bella hooked the back, Roxanna took a deep breath. "Colonel McLinn simply likes to see something besides buff and blue. Put me in a room full of colonial belles and he'd not notice me at all."

Or alongside an Irish beauty like Cecily O'Day . . .

Bella's answering chuckle was a deep rumble in her throat. "You got some charms them spoiled belles don't know nothin' about."

Oh? "Name one," Roxanna said softly.

"Namely the fact you don't know you have any. Pure as spring water, you are. Skin like new milk and all that snappin' black hair. Why, your eyes are bluer than McLinn's."

Warmed by the heartfelt words, Roxanna didn't like the re-minder nevertheless. Since she'd returned from Smitty's Fort, she and the colonel seemed to have arrived at some unspoken agreement—formal but cordial, with mutual amnesia over their tête-à-tête in her cabin. Yet the thought of him always seemed to be hovering, intense and intimidating and totally unpredictable. He'd winked at her by the river's edge—a meaningless gesture, truly—but it was done with such spontaneous charm she felt herself give way. And that she must not do.

Finished with fastening the back, Bella moved to smooth the ruffled sleeves. "You is right 'bout the colonel bein' at them fancy balls. Word is he was mighty popular back in Williamsburg and Philadelphia. More than one lady lost her heart to him when he stepped into the room."

Ignoring this, Roxanna pulled upward on the décolletage of her gown, the copper silk flashing in the candlelight. "Bella, 'tis simply sinful to expose so much skin."

"Law, you sound like somebody's mother," she quipped, bring-ing something out of her apron pocket. "I almost forgot. This here goes around your bosom and hides what shouldn't be hid."

A length of fragile lace settled about Roxanna's shoulders like a blue cloud, a twin to the blue petticoat far below. Still, she was self-conscious about stepping outside. She could hear Mariah's distinctive laugh and a fife trilling an excited tune.

Taking a step toward the door, she was startled by a decisive knock. Suddenly stiff-limbed, she was hardly aware of Bella stepping around her to open the door. There was no longer any need for anyone to tell her how the colonel's eyes lit up at the sight of her. She saw it plain, and the realization sent little tremors of alarm and delight through her.

"Miss Rowan." Not once had he called her Roxie since that day at Smitty's Fort.

"Colonel McLinn." Never would she call him anything else, the slip of calling him Cass still stinging like a nettle. If she gave way to it now, there would be no going back.

Beneath his Continental coat was a silk waistcoat of the same blue shade as her petticoat and embroidered with identical silk thread. *Bella!* Flushing furiously, she wondered just how much fabric Bella had cut from her gown to make him this.

"It would appear," he said, eyes glinting with good humor, "that you're as well dressed as I am."

She tried to smile. "Yes, we have Bella to thank for that." *Or trounce.*

But Bella had disappeared, having shut the door firmly behind her. He took a step nearer, and she was struck afresh by his immense physical vitality. Though she was tall and willowy in her own right, he made her feel tiny, even dainty. The exquisite hue of his waistcoat turned his eyes a richer blue, and his next words made the bottom drop out of her stomach.

"You look like a bride."

A bride. Your bride? Anyone's bride? Thoughts whirling, she grasped for a bit of levity and returned the compliment. "And you, sir, look like a groom." When he said nothing, she prattled on, "'Tis kind of you to come for me."

He gave a slight bow. "I nearly had to beat a path to your door to do it."

She laughed. "All those men, you mean."

"Aye, all those men." Going to the door, he swung it open, and all the amusement faded from her face. A long, snaking line of soldiers and Frenchmen stood in various stages of intoxication, waiting to dance.

"Oh my . . ."

He offered her his arm and she took it, wondering how, after only one dancing lesson with him, she'd make it through even a few jigs and reels. But she did, dancing first with him and then with others, some too inebriated to notice her missteps. By the end of an hour, she was flushed, thirsty, and winded—and having the time of her life.

Only recently the fort smithy had fixed her best slippers, replacing a worn sole and making them seem like new. She tapped her feet in time to the music as Dovie rested with her on a bench near the edge of the bonfire. Wearing her purple wedding dress, the bulge of baby just beginning to show, Dovie said merrily, "Miz Roxanna, you're sure the belle of the ball tonight. Ain't you worn out?"

"Just thirsty," Roxanna replied with a smile, sipping the cider Cass had brought her.

She took in the revelers—even Bella and Hank were doing a jig—and lingered on Cass now paired with Abby. With the moon full and high and the brilliant backdrop of bonfire, she could make out the sentries up on the banquette above, the restless milling of the horses in the far corral, even the Shawnee standing in the open door of their cabin. Falling Water lingered there, observing the white men's mischief, the younger chief beside her, their silhouettes distinct. The older chief remained out of sight in the cabin the three of them shared.

She wondered what would become of them and if Cass had finally learned who among the British were behind the Indian raids into Kentucke. She knew he'd been meeting with the three Shawnee in the orderly room adjacent to the blockhouse, but she didn't know what success he was having. He hadn't wanted her present, he'd told her, to ensure her safety. If worse came to worst and the fort fell in future, she would know little of such matters and might escape with her life.

Yet this seemed less alarming than the fact that a spy was in their midst, working to undermine the Americans' hold on the Kentucke territory. Her eyes roamed over myriad men, weighing and dismissing them one by one. A feeling of uneasiness—even dread—took hold. Beside her, Dovie was a blessed distraction.

"I've been meanin' to tell you what Johnny and I've decided to call the baby."

Roxanna looked at her friend's shadowed features, fighting the tight feeling in her chest, forcing lightness when she felt none. "I think naming a baby must be a fine thing, Dovie. Tell me."

"If it's a boy he'll be John Cassius Dayton, after the colonel and Johnny, of course. And if it's a girl, it'll be Roxanna Marie after you and my ma."

Roxanna gave her arm an affectionate squeeze. "I'm honored, Dovie—and I'm sure the colonel will be too. Autumn is when you're due, isn't it?"

"September or thereabouts." Dovie's youthful face showed little pleasure. "I don't know where any of us will be by then. Johnny says the colonel's bent on takin' the whole middle ground soon if the Redcoats and redskins don't overrun us first. I'm thinkin' it ain't a good time to be bearin'. Sometimes I wonder if I'll even get to hold my baby."

Roxanna lapsed into silence, struck by Dovie's somber mood. She didn't want to sound trite, but all she could think to say was what she'd been consoling herself with of late. "Only God knows the future, Dovie. Best pray and leave it all to Him."

With a sigh, Dovie turned probing eyes on her. "What are you goin' to do? Once you get shed of this place?"

"I'm not sure. I keep praying about that too. Since it isn't safe to leave, I have to be content with staying here till I have some clear direction."

"Abby will be mighty put out when you go," she ventured shyly. "Not to mention all the rest of us."

Roxanna managed a halfhearted smile. "Someday soon you and Johnny will move onto your land and have a fine farm like you've been dreaming about. Colonel McLinn and his army will likely go east and I'll return to Virginia, and we'll forget all about this place."

If there was peace . . . *if* they survived the danger. She shivered at the memory of their return from Smitty's Fort, of finely fletched arrows and whizzing musket balls.

The reel ended abruptly, returning her to the sights and smells swirling around them, but the frolic failed to ease her trepidation. The future loomed long and lonesome, and Fort Endeavor was but a small stop along the way to a place she wasn't sure of.

But You know where I'm going, Lord, so I'll try to rest in that.

She looked up from the coppery sheen of her skirt to see both Cass and Micajah Hale coming toward her. But another officer took Cass aside, and it was Micajah who reached her first. Lip and brow beaded with sweat from the exertion of the fiddling, he gave an exaggerated bow and stammered, "M-may I have the n-next dance?"

Nodding, Roxanna stood and took his hand, closing the distance between them. She looked over his shoulder and caught Cass's eyes on them as he led her out and they joined the melee of swirling couples. She'd not seen Micajah in some time. He was often outside fort walls, and when he returned he seemed to distance himself from her.

"I wasn't sure you'd dance with me," he said in her ear.

"Why?" she said lightly. "I've danced with almost everyone else."

His smile was tight. "Your guardian seems to think I'm not good enough for you."

Guardian? She opened her mouth to reply, then shut it, stung by the sharpness of his tone.

He rambled on, speech slightly slurred. "The colonel assigned me to a woodcutting detail the past month or so. But I'm back, and like it or not, I'm taking my turn."

She knew about the woodcutting foray, as she had a rick of neatly stacked logs under one eave—but she hadn't known the reason behind it till now. Had Cass assigned him that duty to keep him away from her?

The music swelled and then ebbed, and she said, "He's only fulfilling the promise he made to my father—being responsible for me."

His head bobbed up and down in terse agreement, but there was a cynical twist to his mouth she'd not seen before. "I know. I was there when it happened. But I doubt you'd leap to his defense had you been."

As the words washed over her, her mind grappled with all that he implied—none of it respectful or enlightening, just frightening and confusing. He was slightly intoxicated, she knew, and drunk men often made ridiculous statements. But had he been there when Papa died? Had he seen him fall or make his dying request that tied Cass to her?

As she tried to gather her thoughts and ask, the set ended and he returned her to where he'd sought her out, leaving her abruptly for another drink. 'Twas just as well, she thought. She'd get few straight answers, tipsy as he was.

Sinking down on the bench, she glanced at the moon and judged it was nearly midnight. Since giving her pocket watch to the Shawnee, she was always guessing the hour. The frolic seemed a bit frantic now, pulsing with a reckless hilarity that had a slightly mutinous feel. Out of the corner of her eye, she saw a regular stagger too near the bonfire and almost keel over into the orangey-red morass. Two Frenchmen stripped to their breeches erupted in a fierce fistfight by a keg of rum. The Redstone women showed no signs of slowing down, not even Dovie, and Roxanna wondered if she should be dancing so much with a baby on the way.

Several more disorderly minutes ticked by, and then Cass was at her elbow. She was only too glad to follow him into the shadows near the sally port, thinking he was remarkably self-possessed when two hundred or more men were unraveling all around him.

Facing her but keeping an eye on the revelers, he simply said, "I want you to go with Bella and Abby to the stone house tonight."

Her lips parted in surprise—could he sense her delight? But then her mouth went dry. "Are you expecting trouble?"

"Nay, I always remain in the fort after a romp—to keep order." He smiled down at her as if to ease her anxiety. "To stop the rowdies from burning down my post, ye ken."

"Do you need to stay in my cabin?"

He shook his head. "I've a cot in the blockhouse." Reaching out, he touched her sleeve, and then his hand fell away abruptly. "I'll rest better knowing you're up there on the hill and not here."

Touched by his show of concern, she said, "Of course . . . I understand."

But would Olympia release Abby to their care? From the sight of her with a half-dozen admirers, it seemed she had other things on her mind. Through the shadows, Roxanna saw Bella emerge from the melee with the guard, toting a small haversack filled with what they'd need to pass the night, Roxanna guessed. Abby trailed behind, clutching her rag doll. Could Bella sense Roxanna's pleasure at so inviting an escape?

Her smile was so wide it communicated she did indeed, a hundredfold. "Ready, Miz Roxanna?"

Out the sally port they went, every step a fulfillment of Roxanna's dream as they left the madness far behind, the guard fanning out about them. Up ahead, candlelight winked from every window, and Hank was waiting, door ajar in welcome.

Home.

Simply thinking the word unleashed an avalanche of emotion. By the time she'd trod the smooth yet unfamiliar door stone, Roxanna had to dash away a tear with a discreet hand, unable to say what so moved her. Even Abby looked around in awe. 'Twas the first time she'd been inside as well.

Across the threshold and into the foyer they went, lost in a world of gleaming wood and thick rugs and the heady bergamot and leather scent that was the essence of Cassius Clayton McLinn. It almost seemed she'd stepped into his arms, his presence was so palpable. Looking back over her shoulder before Hank closed the door, she dismissed the hope that he'd followed them. The fort glittered like a lit firecracker on the dark riverbank, and she could still hear raucous laughter above the fiddling.

Given the late hour, Bella promptly took them up the sweeping staircase. Roxanna tried to take in as much as she could—great gulps of beauty and refinement—her eyes eventually falling to the floral carpet. On the landing was an oriole window that would make a fine lookout by day, she thought, or a starry one by night.

Setting foot on the second floor, she saw another less elaborate stair spiraling toward a third story. Holding a sconce high, Bella hesitated, and the candles cast light to the far corners of the hall, illuminating a painting of deep green hills and a glen—Ireland?—above a walnut sideboard with matching chairs. A hint of oil paint threaded the still air, oddly reminiscent of her dream.

"The colonel didn't tell me which room to put you in, but I picked the blue room, and Hank's made a fine fire."

Roxanna stood in the middle of all that austere elegance, slippers sinking into the lush carpet as Bella set the sconce on a highboy and turned down the bed. Next she began unhooking the back of Roxanna's gown. "You'll sleep like the dead after all that dancin.'"

Roxanna looked toward the shuttered windows. "I don't hear the frolic now."

"You won't—not with stone walls two foot thick." She gave a low chuckle. "Law, but ain't the colonel full of surprises? When he told me to fetch yo' things cuz he wanted you up here tonight, I was almost as surprised as when he hightailed it out o' here to carry you back from Smitty's Fort. I figure he'll be askin' to marry you next."

"Shhh!" Roxanna glanced at Abby, who appeared lost in thought as she caressed a figurine on a low table. "Little jugs have big ears, remember."

Still chuckling, Bella led her to a dressing table and began picking the pins from her hair. Distracted a moment by the ivory-handled comb and brush set, Roxanna finally fixed Bella with solemn eyes in the oval mirror, her voice a whisper. "Once upon a time, I remember you warning me away from Colonel McLinn. I don't understand your sudden change of heart."

Bella rolled her eyes. "It ain't my change o' heart but *his*. Since you come it's like he's found religion or somethin'. I can't tell you the last time I heard him cuss or seen him knock the no-good out o' his men, or any o' them other shenanigans he's known for."

"Gentlemen always mind their manners around ladies—or should."

Bella sobered. "There you go again, explainin' away everythin'. Ain't you ever seen a man in love before?"

"Nay," she whispered, thinking of Ambrose for the first time in a long time with complete detachment, even distaste. Her brow furrowed. "He's attached to a lady in Ireland, remember."

"Well, she ain't here!" Scowling, Bella began brushing her hair till it fell in silky waves to her waist before subduing it in a sooty braid.

From somewhere—the foyer downstairs?—came the enchanting chime of a grandfather clock. Oh, but this house, Bella's flattering words—they worked quite a spell. Her infatuation was soaring. Being here only added to Cass's appeal and chipped away at her resolve to simply regard him as a friend.

She groped for sure footing, saying the first thing that came to mind. "Would you like to say a bedtime prayer with me, Abby?"

The child nodded solemnly as Bella removed her party dress. Stripped to her shift, she climbed onto Roxanna's lap. Taking Abby's small hands between her own, Roxanna gave in to the wild wish that this was her little girl and the stone house was home. If so, which prayer might she teach her?

"By day, by night, at home, abroad, still are we guided by our God. By His incessant bounty fed, by His unerring counsel led. God bless Abby and Bella and Hank, and Colonel McLinn and all his men. Olympia, Dovie, Mariah, and Nancy too . . ."

Within minutes, Abby was asleep in her arms, and Bella helped settle the child onto the trundle bed.

Finally divested of stays, chemise, and all else, Roxanna donned a thin linen nightgown and climbed the polished bed steps to the high feather tick. Feeling suddenly at sea in such a grand, unfamiliar house, she whispered, "Bella, where will you be?"

"Me and Hank have a cozy nook in back of the kitchen fireplace below." With that, she went out, as if knowing Roxanna wouldn't need a thing.

Settling back against the headboard on the bank of pillows— six to be exact—Roxanna pulled the finely worked coverlet up to her chin. The blue room was lovely and inviting, but it was the side door that drew her, the one adjoining her room to . . . his?

The temptation to turn the knob and peer further into his world left her nearly breathless. She looked down at Abby sound asleep. With Cass at the fort and Hank and Bella below, who would know?

Climbing out of the just-warmed bed, she crossed the carpet, her hand—and her heart—aching to enter in. Torn, she leaned her head against a painted panel, the knob cold and forbidding beneath her hand. What if it was the room in her dream? The one with the immense canopy bed and the clock mounted over the door? Such whimsy made her almost smile, and her hand moved from the knob to her slim waist. Nay, it was no more the room in her dream any more than she was carrying a child.

Such foolishness sent her back to bed, though sleep was a long time in coming. The feverish night swirled through her mind with such intensity it seemed she'd never left the fort. Her dances with Cass seemed the only ones she remembered. But it was Micajah's words that punctured all the high feeling in her heart with the finality of an Indian arrow.

I was there when it happened. But I doubt you'd leap to his defense had you been.

What exactly had he meant? 'Twas wrong to speak disparagingly of one's commanding officer. He almost sounded like a turncoat . . . a spy. She tried to push the ominous words away, but they were quickly supplanted by other unwelcome things—the striking earnestness in Cass's face when he'd asked her to go to the stone house, the seemingly insignificant way he'd touched her sleeve in parting, communicating a dozen heartfelt messages.

To her hungry heart, anyway.

Turning over, she laid her aching head on a cool pillowslip and tried to sleep, but the tumult of her feelings blazed like a firestorm inside her. Adding fuel to the fire were Bella's convicting words. *Ain't you ever seen a man in love before?* Had she? Nay. And deep down in the depths of her being, she believed she never would.

22

The blockhouse window was open, and at dawn the pure, un-adulterated trill of a cardinal roused Cass from what little sleep he'd had. Running a hand over his whiskery jaw, he abandoned the coffin-hard cot, wondering if Bella was in the kitchen making coffee. Coffee was likely all the two hundred or so inhabitants of Fort Endeavor could stomach after their rum-infested feast the night before.

For the first time in his military career, he felt a spasm of guilt for overseeing such debauchery, if only because he was still stone sober this morning. He pushed open the blockhouse door, and the chilly spring air assaulted him, reeking of rum and blatant excess. Buffalo bones, clothing, and pewter tankards littered the parade ground and deepened his discontent.

He leaned against the door frame, crossed his arms, and tried to reconcile who he'd been with who he was becoming and why he had any qualms at all. Cold logic told him it was madness to keep men under such tight rein without giving them their head now and again, as he'd done last night. Any less meant mutiny, and he'd already court-martialed thirteen soldiers for desertion since coming to Kentucke.

Yet in the ugly aftermath this morning, he was troubled enough that he reached for a limp haversack and began picking up the mess, knowing his men were too dissolute to be of much use, glad Roxie was still abed on the hill and couldn't see the disorder.

The thought of her asleep in his house—her lush hair spilling across a pillow in whatever bedchamber Bella had put her in—was enough to keep the most pious man awake. Pious he was not, yet her winsome goodness made him want to be better than he was.

He was tired this morning, not because of the night's devilment, but because he hadn't been able to dislodge her from his mind in the darkness. And now, at daylight, she was still with him, hair falling down from its pins as it had been when she'd last danced with him in her fetching copper dress. So lost was he in the thought of her that he hardly heard Hank approach from behind.

"Colonel, sir."

Cass swung round, haversack half full, grinning at Hank's obvious amazement at seeing him in his shirtsleeves and breeches, picking up garbage to boot.

"Bella's done fixed yo' breakfast, sir. Why don't you go on in and let me see to this mess?"

Trading the sack for the steaming cup of coffee in Hank's hand, Cass said, "Since it's such a fine morning—and I'm still sober—I thought I'd come out."

Glancing at the clear blue sky, Hank nodded. "The Almighty's made a fine mornin' all right, maybe on account of yo' behavin' yo'self."

Still grinning, Cass gestured to the hill. "How are things at the house?"

Grinning back, his teeth a stark white in his ebony face, Hank said, "Well, sir, you'd best ask Bella 'bout that. Word is Miz Rowan's sleepin' like a baby on that fine feather tick in the blue room. Abby too."

The blue room . . . the one adjoining his. His disappointment at not being able to show her the house himself was keen. He was forever reminding himself to distance himself from her, to take every caution and not be alone with her. Because being alone with her reminded him of her father—and her perplexing plea returned to him like an endless echo.

Please, I don't want to fall in love with you.

The poignant words had burned themselves into his brain like a brand, and it had taken some time for him to sift through the meaning behind them.

She was, he hardly needed reminding, in mourning, upended by a broken betrothal, without a home, in hostile territory, unable to leave. What woman, under similar circumstances, would want a romantic entanglement? Her bruised and broken heart would have little left to give, even if she'd wanted to. And at times he sensed deep down in his soul that she did want to. Little things had given her away. A lingering look. Her unmistakable delight when dancing with him. The painstaking efforts she made to please him with pen and paper.

Turning his hair loose from its tie.

But he had little choice except to respect her wishes and simply fulfill Richard Rowan's dying request. Until she left, he was her guardian and she was his scrivener.

Other dire reminders skirted his conscience and pushed his pain deeper still. Not only had he killed her father, he'd destroyed the secure future she hoped to have. Even if he confessed, the guilt of it would follow him to his grave. There was simply no undoing that bitter winter's twilight.

"Colonel, sir. Here she comes."

Hank's voice pulled him out of his reverie. He spied her leaving the stone house, a willowy shadow on the sun-dappled hill, making her way to the fort with Abby in hand. The guard followed at a respectful distance, saber-tipped muskets gleaming in the pale morning light. She paused to take in her garden, then the river where the keelboats lay at anchor, before turning and looking toward him. The ever-expanding ache in his chest rivaled any earned by a musket ball in battle.

Please, I don't want to fall in love with you.

Aye, he could honor that. But she'd not said anything about him falling in love with her.

❧ ❧

Roxanna set aside the quill she'd been sharpening and returned her penknife to her pocket. She'd been thinking of her garden with its prim rows of peas pushing through all that rich Kentucke soil and what a punishment it was to remain indoors on such a day. But at least the blockhouse window and door were open this Monday morn, letting in the light and a welcome breeze. Sometimes, as if sensing her restlessness, Cass would call a halt to their work and she'd go outside to pull weeds or just glory in being beyond fort walls, even with the guard on her heels. But today he seemed to have forgotten all about her.

Tucked in a corner with paper and inkpots and sand, she'd been making final copies of letters to the Continental Congress and the acting commander at Fort Pitt regarding the coming campaign into Ohio. Across the wide green river of the same name, which the Shawnee called *Spaylayweetheepi*, he would go at some undetermined point in future, and everything they did now seemed caught up in that end.

Since the keelboats had come and gone, their days had been an unceasing routine of correspondence and dispatches and details. By sending couriers on differing routes, Cass had managed to keep them alive and reestablish a chain of communication previously broken. But it seemed they all held a collective breath nevertheless when fresh messages were tucked in dispatch cases and the men rode away.

Looking across the suddenly still room, she almost smiled to see Cass leaning forward in a cane-backed chair, Falling Water seated beside him, Ben Simmons shadowing them from behind and translating. They were studying a map, their backs to her, discussing winsome rivers and valleys and ridges that few, if any, white men had ever seen. Having picked up some of the mellifluous Shawnee tongue, Cass could communicate a bit with Falling Water directly, and his efforts often brought about her small, delighted smile.

Sometimes it seemed to Roxanna that she'd tell him anything he wanted. And who could blame her? The tan, intense lines of Cass's face—and his astonishing blue eyes—seemed to shift more rapidly than the weathervane atop the fort commissary. Brooding one minute, animated the next, he had a mercurial charm that was both disarming and endearing. She wondered if this was a common Irish trait.

From the corner, the clock struck the hour of three, but he paid no attention. He'd already met with the two male prisoners that morning. Out of leg irons but still well guarded, they came in separately. First the older chief, fully recovered and garrulous again, and then the younger, less talkative but clearly pleased at having his sweetheart in residence. Roxanna watched them make eyes at one another with a kind of awed envy.

Save the Sabbath, the three Shawnee had met with Cass in the orderly room every day for a month. Sometimes she wondered if his strategy was simply to wear them down in order to glean the information he wanted. His officers were less patient, probably weary of fort walls, she guessed, and wanting to finalize plans and begin the campaign. He conferred with them often, asking them their opinions and insights.

"They've given us plenty to go on," Micajah had told him the day before. "More than I ever dreamed you'd drum out of them. But how can you be sure they're telling the truth?"

"Because I bring them in separately, ask the same questions, allow them no time to confer, and see if they give me the same answers."

The officers pondered this, poring over the detailed maps on the table, till Joram Herkimer finally said with a sort of suspicious wonder, "They've practically handed over the key to their territory, telling you about every valley, river, Shawnee town, and the like."

"You glean a great deal from asking the right questions," Cass replied. "But most of it comes from how you ask them."

Still, Micajah looked perturbed. "They've still not told you who Hamilton's second-in-command is out of Detroit? The one plying them with trade goods and sending their warriors to raid the settlements?"

Cass shook his head slowly, eyes on a particularly detailed map. "Nay, but I'm coming closer."

There was a murmur among them, and Major Herkimer said, "I wish you'd allow some of us to be present when you question them."

"Why? To make them feel they're being bamboozled?" Hard azure eyes shot down the notion. "I'll not give the appearance of a court-martial."

Micajah leaned against the mantel, eyes roaming to Roxanna as she worked across the room. "When do we move?"

"July at the latest."

Her head bent over her work, Roxanna felt nearly woozy. The thought of marching north in deep summer when the mosquitoes and flies and chiggers were the thickest would be punishment enough, but to make war in wool uniforms with sixty-pound packs . . .

Cass traced a path on the map with a forefinger. "Our intent is to avoid the peaceful Shawnee towns and push north toward Detroit. We'll strike Shemento's band if we have to, as he's closely allied to the British. The other chiefs are declaring their neutrality, if only to spare their women and children another hard winter."

A glimmer of satisfaction shone on Micajah's face. "So your reputation as the Bluecoat town burner is having some effect."

A shadow passed over Cass's features. "I'm not proud of past tactics. Burning villages amounts to making war on women and children, and I've decided to try a far different tack. I'll not have an army of firebrands and brutes."

At this, a few of them looked shamefaced, and Roxanna sensed surprise and tension in the air. Returning to her work, she found the letters dipping and swaying in a wash of black ink as she tried to contain her swelling emotions. She was hardly aware of the officers ending their discussion and leaving her alone with Cass and the orderlies.

Brooding again, he stared into the low fire a few moments before turning in her direction, giving her time to compose herself. Still, her unsettled feelings lingered. He was leaving. Though he'd said little of what was ahead, the campaign he'd soon wage was fraught with danger, and as she'd learned firsthand in December, not everyone came back.

His shadow fell across her lap desk, but she didn't look up for fear he'd see the tears in her eyes. "I've nearly finished this final letter, and these documents are ready for your signature."

Straddling a chair, he took the sheaf of papers from her and said nothing. It was the closest he'd been to her in two weeks, and she breathed in the scent of the stone house—and him—for the two had become inseparable in her mind. Since she'd fled to Smitty's Fort, he seemed to be so careful, so formal with her, never being alone with her for even a few moments, always having others present.

If he'd ever been even slightly infatuated with her, she knew he wasn't any longer. His interest had dissolved like the pearly mist that hung over the river most mornings, and its leaving had stolen something from her. She should have been glad. Friendship was all she could offer—or receive. Because of Cecily, first and foremost. Because he was a man in an intense season of doubt. About himself. His position. Providence. Yet despite everything, she felt blasphemously discontent, and so full of yearning she ached.

"Fine work," he said in low tones, "considering you'd rather be in your garden."

Reaching the bottom of the page, she sprinkled the wet ink with pounce. "There's still time yet."

He leaned closer. "I caught you smiling to yourself earlier, and since it couldn't be anything you overheard me saying . . ."

"I was thinking of my peas." Carefully, she funneled the pounce back into the jar, his nearness making a stew of her insides. "And I meant to thank you for having that fence built to keep the animals out. Those Kentucke rabbits especially seem to have a penchant for all things green."

"So do my men. Best keep an eye on them."

She almost smiled—and then a rush of hot tears surprised her a second time. Panicked, she dropped a piece of paper. As they bent over, their hands and heads collided, and she felt she was swimming in leather and Indian tobacco. He was wearing the buckskin jacket instead of his usual uniform coat, and it made him look more rugged frontiersman than gentleman soldier. 'Twas a wonder she could keep her head on her shoulders and do a smidgen of work . . .

He retrieved the paper, and she murmured her thanks, determined not to look at him. And then, giving sway to his poignant request for her support at Smitty's Fort, she did look, alarmed by the shadows she saw beneath his eyes. "Are you . . . all right?"

He hesitated. "Aye, and you?"

Nay. She couldn't answer—at least honestly—so she said nothing.

A commotion at the door made them both turn to see Joram Herkimer enter again. "The scouting patrols are back, sir, and ready to give a full report."

With a nod, Cass stood. "Bring them in."

Taking the scrap of paper she'd dropped, she retrieved her quill and dipped it in ink. Still tearful, she scribbled the only encouragement she could muster before pressing the note into his hand as she went out.

Praying for you.

23

On her knees that night, Roxanna felt the hard, cold, hickory planks through her linen nightgown as she knelt by her bed. Since childhood she'd prayed thus, like her mother and father before her, and it provided a warm if sometimes bittersweet tie to her past. No other position felt quite right, though she knew all that mattered was the posture of one's heart. Try as she might, she couldn't imagine Cass on his knees. It seemed as far-fetched as her lying abed in the stone house, in that wondrous dream, about to bear a child.

Her first petition was unceasingly the same. *Lord, deliver me from Fort Endeavor.* Being penned within its walls day in and day out was deepening her melancholy over her father's death, her fatal attraction for Cass. Still, she'd promised to pray for him. The hastily scrawled note that said she'd do so was uppermost in her mind, though he might not appreciate her petitions.

Lord, soften his arrogance and temper and intemperate habits. Make him a man after Your own heart . . . because somehow, against my will and surely Yours, he's stolen mine.

Early the next morning, Abby came and shook Roxanna awake. Rolling over on the thin mattress, she took in Abby's

219

tearstained face and sat bolt upright. "Abby, have you had another bad dream?"

The little girl nodded and crawled into bed beside her, which did little to ease Roxanna's anxiety. *Oh, Abby, won't you speak?* Lying back down, Roxanna wrapped her arms about the child's slight form, gratified when her even breathing assured her she was slumbering again. Lately Abby had been coming to her cabin more often, and Olympia didn't seem to miss her. In the mornings before work, Roxanna continued to school Abby in her sums and letters without interference. But she worried unceasingly about the child wandering around in the dark when no one else was about save the sentries.

Before Roxanna could fall back asleep, Bella appeared, kerchief askew, eyes bright in the dawn light as she pushed the door open. "Law, but I been worried to death 'bout that child. Between her sleepwalkin' like a ghost and McLinn sick . . ."

Roxanna pushed herself up on an elbow. "The colonel—sick?"

"Aye, been up all night, Hank says. Can't keep nothin' down and is in an agony wi' his stomach."

"Is it the ague?"

Bella shot her a chilling glance. "Not this time."

"Maybe the dysentery, then."

"Naw . . . worse." Bella slumped in a chair. "Somethin' ain't right here lately. Somebody's been goin' through the kitchen disturbin' things."

"What?"

"I know it sounds foolish, but somebody's out to make mischief and now the colonel ain't well. Somethin' smells."

A coldness crept into Roxanna's spirit. Bella didn't know about the spy. No one did except Cass and herself. He hadn't even confided in his own officers. "Are you saying someone means the colonel harm?"

"I think somebody's set to hurt him, all right. Mebbe poison him. The cinchona I keep in the kitchen in that little tin looks different somehow. I give him some after supper last night as he didn't look right to me, like he might be gettin' the ague again. And now . . ."

"Perhaps he's simply exhausted," Roxanna said, trying to fit all the pieces of this strange puzzle together. "Do you truly believe he's been poisoned?"

Tears glittered in Bella's eyes, and she raised her apron to dash them away. "I know it's so. And I'm sore afraid I'll be blamed for it."

"Bella, I know you wouldn't do such a thing."

"Naw, I wouldn't. But somebody would, and they're right here in these walls. And that scares me to death." She heaved a sigh, damp eyes hardening. "I 'spect it might be one o' them doxies, in and out o' the kitchen like they is. That Olympia bemoans the colonel so."

Roxanna's mind spun with all the possibilities. Perhaps this spy—this man or woman, whoever they were—was no longer content simply rummaging through papers. Perhaps it had become a different sort of game. A dangerous, even murderous one.

Slipping free of Abby's sleeping form, Roxanna began to dress with unsteady hands. Bella sat with surprising lethargy, and Roxanna sensed her fear. Without saying a word, she slipped out and crossed the empty parade ground at a near run. Knowing reveille would soon sound, she wanted to be well out of the way.

The spring dawn was arriving in a red fury, the sky so strangely fiery Roxanna nearly winced. *Red sky at night, sailor's delight . . . Red sky at morning, sailors take warning.* The little rhyme only intensified the fear now crawling all over her, raising gooseflesh as she entered the dim kitchen.

The cinchona tin rested above the hearth on the mantel. Taking it down, she noticed the kettle was already steaming over the hearth's fire, as Bella had been here since first light. Uncapping the tin, she sniffed the contents. The cinchona, unpleasant in any form, seemed no different now. Reaching for a pewter cup, she measured out the amount she'd seen Bella use previously and then added hot water. Bitter tendrils of steam stung her nostrils. She waited for a few minutes, weighing the wisdom of what she was about to do, senses taut.

A spy, she thought, was nothing but a poltroon, slinking around doing damage in the dark. Taking the cup, she took one sip, then two. Never having tasted the medicinal tea, it was all she could do not to sputter as she swallowed.

The back door creaked open and Bella stood there, wild-eyed with worry. "Law, Miz Roxanna, what on earth you doin' with that cup?"

"Praying it's not poisonous, Bella."

Bella rushed forward, hands outstretched, looking like she would dash it to the floor. Quickly Roxanna downed the hot liquid and set the empty cup on the table.

Bella looked stricken. "Lord have mercy! If it made McLinn sick, strappin' man that he is, it might well kill you!"

"So be it," Roxanna said. "'Tis better to know one way or another. Poison or not."

She was indeed sick. Horribly so. Within half an hour, she was retching into the chamber pot beneath her bed. With Abby safely ensconced in the kitchen with Bella, Roxanna drew the latchstring in and wanted to die. Surely Cass felt the same. The malignant brew, tainted with whatever caused such misery, lingered on her tongue and seemed it would never leave her. Bella came by and maneuvered the door open, trying to get her to sip water and take an antidote for her roiling stomach, but Roxanna couldn't keep the remedy down either.

"I'm goin' to send Hank downriver for Dr. Clary," Bella whispered, nearly wringing her hands. "The colonel forbade it for hisself, but he's liable to court-martial me if I don't fetch him for you."

But Roxanna shook her head weakly. "No one need know."

With Cass ill as well, she would hardly be missed. There would be no working at headquarters, anyway. A heavy rain was now pounding on the shingled roof with such fury it rivaled the smithy's hammering. Few were about on such a day, as the parade ground was now a seething pool of dark, ankle-deep mud. She lay on her bed, stripped to her shift, the quilt half covering her between bouts of retching, her mind rife with dark thoughts.

Oh, Lord, let me die in this place, then I'll be free. No more worries about spies or Abby or a bleak future. No more fighting my attraction for a man who loves another . . .

Toward twilight she slept. But it was a nauseous, dreamless sleep punctuated with stomach pain. She came awake to shadows—of someone replenishing the fire that had almost burned out. Bella? And then someone was lifting her head, stroking the tangled hair back from her face, and murmuring whispered words in Gaelic.

She shot upright, pushing against the hard shoulders that loomed over her, fear spiking as she grappled with the shadows.

"Roxie—Roxie, 'tis only me."

Cass? She grabbed his coat sleeve with frantic hands, a bit out of her head. He sat down on the bed and gathered her up in his arms as if she were a child. Like Abby, she thought woozily. Like Papa had with her so long ago. Weak, she succumbed to the heady scent of him, gave in to the unfamiliar feel of his arms and solidity of his chest as he cradled her.

"You need water," he said, but he didn't reach for the cup Bella had close by. He simply stroked her hair and kept murmuring soothing words till she was still.

Ashamed to be seen so, she tried to turn away, face to the wall, but he wouldn't relinquish her. He held her tighter, his breath warm against her ear.

"Roxie, what have you done?" His voice held an uncanny

tenderness, so poignant her heart ached. "Why, love, why? If anything should happen to you . . ." He broke off as if aware he'd tread too far. Fumbling with the cup, he brought her head around so she could drink. She managed a few swallows, chest sore from heaving, skin all ashiver.

He bent his head, murmuring Gaelic words that made no sense yet left an unmistakable impression. He was praying for her. Pleading for her. Petitioning the Providence he disdained on her behalf. Though he wasn't on his knees, she sensed his soul was.

Tears slid down her cheeks, but she was too weary to push them away. Finding her embroidered hankie lost in the bedding, he dried her face, and she succumbed to the warmth of him and slept. In time Bella came, but Cass didn't leave her. Nor did he go when Dr. Clary examined her, poking and prodding and shaking his head.

"I'd issue a statement—an order—saying there's an enemy within fort walls. Every man is suspect," he said vehemently. "Every man is to watch every man. Anything even slightly suspicious is to be reported at once."

Roxanna listened as through a foggy curtain. Across the room, Bella was regarding Cass with a look akin to horror as the implications dawned. "We'd best keep locks on every tub and barrel we got," she moaned, moving toward the door. "And the kitchen is wide open right now, just ripe for more mischief."

She shut the door with a thud that was hardly heard above the pounding rain. Dr. Clary tried to leave, but his horse couldn't manage the muck of the common, so he sought refuge in the kitchen, saying he'd drink coffee till the weather cleared.

When Roxanna awoke, she found everything altered. Cass had hold of Abby, dwarfing the rocking chair alongside her bed. Pushing up on one elbow, she surveyed them in the firelit shadows. Abby was, in repose, so sweetly innocent with her coppery head upon his chest. His eyes remained closed, long lashes dark against his tanned skin. Roxanna traced the strong planes of his face with her loving gaze as her fingers could never do, and bit her lip to stem the desire.

He was asleep, she guessed, having worn himself out being so sick, the lapel of his uniform coat bearing a slight wrinkle from the weight of Abby's head. The buttons marching up and down his chest glinted in the flickering light. Abby stirred and settled against him again, and then, when she'd drifted off, he opened his eyes and looked over at Roxanna.

"You've come round," he said quietly, "at last."

The gravelly warmth of his voice made her stomach pitch, but in an entirely pleasurable fashion. "So have you," she murmured.

"'Tis the sweetest day I've spent since taking command of this post."

Because she was better, she wondered? As was he?

"'Tis the wettest, surely," she whispered back at him, her head beginning to clear.

The crack and snap of the fire was the only sound other than the rain pelting the roof. Absently, she wondered where Olympia was, if she'd been searching for Abby. The thought of anyone finding them like this roused her. Roxanna looked down in dismay at her disarray and then at Cass.

Oh, to be like Abby, so at home in his arms, unkempt and uncaring.

Tying the strings of her chemise, she turned her back to him, putting on a dress. He averted his eyes, profile grave as he looked toward the shuttered window.

"I appreciate your concern—my father would appreciate your concern." She swallowed hard and tried to steady her voice. She felt an overwhelming need to excuse him from her care—it was making him beholden to her in ways she'd not anticipated. Cecily O'Day was here in this room, or so it seemed, shadowing her every thought. Surely she lingered in his.

Unable to bear it a second longer, she blurted, "I—I know . . .

rather, I've heard . . . there's someone else." He looked back at her then, and she nearly lost all her nerve. "In Ireland . . ."

Silence. She could hear the easy rhythm of Abby's breathing as she slept . . . the fire's sputtering as raindrops snuck down the chimney . . . her own frantic heartbeat.

He studied her thoughtfully. "There's no one else, Roxie. Once there was. But no longer."

She sank down on the edge of the bed, momentarily forgetting her sore stomach, her heart was so full.

"Cecily couldn't conscience being wed to an American officer, so she married a British one. I came face-to-face with him at Brandywine Creek. But she wasn't the woman for me. I know the truth of that now."

Surprise—elation—washed through her. His tone, in the telling, was flat—uncomplaining. Cecily was a part of his past. 'Twas long over. But the way he was looking at her, his eyes misty and warm, seemed to suggest that she—Roxie Rowan—was his future.

Oh, Lord, could it be?

When the door opened abruptly, she nearly jumped an inch. Bella brought in a tray of steaming soup and bread, her voice a rasp on the rain-laden air.

"You three best rouse yo'selves and eat. No one tampered with this here soup, I can tell you. The good doctor and I stood watch over it ourselves."

With that, she went out and left them to their simple supper. No one said another word. 'Twas a sweet day indeed. Cass was well. Her prayers for his protection had been answered. For just a few fleeting moments she'd given in to the notion that he cared for her, that she was more than just a burden brought about by her father. And that he, during his own angst-riddled prayer for her healing, might have opened his soul to heavenly matters when it had been battened down before.

The rain eased the next morning, but Cass sent a message by Bella telling Roxanna he'd be meeting with his officers and she could stay abed. Despite Roxanna's protests, Bella insisted she bring her meals to the cabin till she'd fully recovered, so she simply slept, wondering who had tainted the cinchona and how they'd ever find out.

The lull gave her time to ponder her predicament anew. Spring was no longer just a distant thought. Spring had come, and with it was the reminder that she must be making plans, like it or not.

And yet what of Abby? Cass? Even Bella? What would become of them once she left? Her heart was now tied to this impossible post in inexplicable ways. In a strange twist of fate, she realized the people within these inhospitable walls had become her family. A speechless wisp of a girl. An embittered colonel. A caustic ex-slave. And a motley assortment of soldiers.

"Woolgatherin' again?" Bella had a knowing light in her eye when she returned to the kitchen, Abby in hand.

"Aye, about leaving." Not about him. Certainly not about the sweet memory they'd made in the sickness and stillness of the cabin. Nor his amazing revelation about Cecily. She felt the heat bloom in her cheeks even as she set the memory aside, knowing Bella missed nothing. Had the women been talking about her—and Cass—before she'd come in?

"You'd best get that notion 'bout leavin' out o' your head," Bella cautioned, handing her a rolling pin before turning to crank the spit of roasting meat at the flickering hearth. "Ain't you heard the news?"

Looking up from the dough tray, she found all eyes on her. News? She'd heard no news, as she'd been confined to her cabin and Bella had shooed everyone away. Now, within the too-warm kitchen, she realized everyone was unusually quiet. Their strained silence boded trouble, and Roxanna braced herself. Across from her, Olympia was glowering and Dovie's lip was quivering and Mariah, armed with a knife, was poking ham in a pan like she was at bayonet practice. Roxanna cast a look to the far corners. Where was Nancy?

Leaning into the trestle table, palms down, she fastened anxious eyes on Bella. "What has happened?"

Bella wiped greasy hands on her apron. "Six regulars run off last night, and Nancy's beau, Billy, was one o' 'em. When the colonel got wind o' it, he sent a party out after 'em. Found 'em at daylight near Drownin' Creek, the whole lot o' 'em tomahawked and scalped—"

Roxanna clamped her hands over Abby's ears as Dovie ran sobbing from the kitchen. "Where's Nancy?"

"Right now she's in her cabin and won't come out for nothin', not even the necessary. She was wi' Billy when the Indians struck, but she run and hid in some cane and got away."

At the end of the table, Olympia sat down hard on a stool, eyes full of fire. "And do you know what the colonel said when the search party come back?"

Nothing soothing, Roxanna guessed.

Olympia rushed on, voice warbling with rage. "He said the Indians saved him the time and trouble of a court-martial and he didn't have to waste any lead or rope enforcin' it."

Roxanna nearly flinched. Desertion was a serious offense . . . but so was a callous comment. Her flush of moments before gave way to a cold numbness, though Bella's dander seemed to rise.

Taking up the rolling pin, she shook it at Olympia. "Don't you go blamin' Billy's sorry ways on McLinn. He and his ilk got what was comin' to 'em. Looks like even them Injuns knew they weren't worth marchin' to Detroit. I hope they divide them scalps in half and collect a double bounty."

"Bella!"

But Olympia had already stormed away, Mariah in her wake, and the sweet feeling that had followed Roxanna to the kitchen was in tatters. Heaving a sigh, Bella said in resignation, "Law, but it'll be a long day wi' you and me and all them men to feed, though one o' you makes three o' them hussies when it comes to workin'. They're too busy primpin' and lookin' at themselves in pewter plates and the like." Sighing, she patted Roxanna's arm. "Don't you worry none 'bout Nancy. She'll likely have her a new beau come mornin'."

Under any other circumstances, Roxanna might have chuckled. Knowing Nancy, she'd grieve Billy's loss keenly for a short time, then take up with another regular as Bella suspected. Roxanna admired her resiliency, if nothing else. "I'll take her some supper later . . . see how she is."

Bella skewered the meat with a long fork till the juices ran. "She's lucky the colonel let her back inside this fort. Word is she aggravated Billy t' leave, said she wanted to go back to Redstone and get shed o' all this danger."

"I can't blame her for that." Roxanna began to knead the dough, giving Abby a lump to play with. "I've often wished the same myself."

"Ain't nobody goin' nowhere. Guess you ain't heard about them river travelers either."

"Nay."

"Well, a couple o' flatboats were just ambushed upriver. Seems like the Injuns dress up like white folk and call for help along the bank, then kill any settlers who come ashore. That and this spy bidness is 'bout to kill me. Enough's enough, I tell you."

Roxanna feigned a calm she didn't feel. Turning the tray over, she began rolling out dough to make biscuits, glad to occupy her hands with a simple, steadying task, thoughts atumble.

Oh, Lord, You seem to be hemming me in instead of setting me free.

For an hour or more, not a word was uttered. Bella resumed preparing the meat, and eventually Dovie and Mariah returned to help before the officers came in. Probably to stem Cass's ire should he find them missing, Roxanna mused. She watched the kitchen door swing open to reveal a long trestle table topped with glittering candles, Cass at the head. Seeing him again after being so sick sent little shimmies of pleasure sifting through her, so at odds with their dire circumstances.

As in the kitchen, there was a somber mood in the dining room tonight. The officers, usually keeping up a steady run of table talk and laughter, spoke in low tones, if they spoke at all. But at least supplies were adequate and they had a good meal to cheer them. Besides all the biscuits for the regulars, Roxanna had made spoon bread for the officers, its golden top rising like a sun-kissed cloud in its iron kettle.

"Law, but you spoil that man," Bella whispered as Dovie took the creation into the dining room. "He'll soon be movin' you to the kitchen o' the stone house if you ain't careful."

Roxanna kept her eyes down, though her insides turned to wax at the thought. "Now *you're* woolgathering. I merely meant to make them all a little something to take their minds off the trouble. Besides, it was Papa's favorite dish—and a favorite of General Washington's as well."

Bella sniffed. "It'll likely just remind McLinn of where he *should* be instead of where he's at."

Would it? Roxanna watched the door swing open once more as Mariah hefted a pitcher of cider to the table. Though he'd never spoken of it, she knew Cass wanted to be serving under Washington again. Bella had told her he was waiting to be called off the frontier and returned to duty in the colonies. Micajah had mentioned there'd been some sort of trouble with his British-allied brother that brought him here, perhaps kept him here. Having escaped charges of treason, Cass was sent west by Washington. In her opinion, being made commander of the entire western frontier seemed a high compliment. To him it was a curse.

Forehead furrowing, she plunged her hands into the dishwater and scrubbed a skillet clean, eyeing the mantel where the cinchona tin used to be. She scarcely noticed the muted voices of the women serving behind the dining room door or that Bella had slipped out to the springhouse. But she sensed she wasn't alone. Slowly she turned and her heart gave a little lurch.

In the quiet kitchen smelling of baked bread and roasting meat and melting candles, 'twas just the two of them—and Abby. Cass was regarding her solemnly, feet shoulder width apart, hands clasped behind his back, as if he was about to issue an order.

"I'm sorry . . . about the trouble," she said, thinking of the deserters.

"There's no trouble. Not with you here safe and sound."

She felt the warmth of his words reaching out to her, as if the present formality between them was nothing but a sham. "I'm much better," she said, moved by the emotion in his face. "Thank you for praying for me . . . for comforting me."

"'Twas all too easy." He moved to stand nearer but didn't touch her. "I'd rather be with you here, such as it is, than anywhere else on earth."

His voice was but a whisper, yet it resounded to the far reaches of her mind and heart. *As I would,* she nearly said, but tears—and a sense of caution—kept her from it.

He swallowed hard, the cords in his neck taut as rope. "I keep wondering why . . . why you . . ."

Her nerves were on tiptoe now, waiting for him to finish.

"Why did you drink the tainted tea?" He looked down at her, his face weary and grieved. "Are you so bereaved about your father—"

She shook her head and recalled reaching for the cinchona tin, confusion filling her.

"Do you hate it here so much—"

Reaching up, she stemmed his words with her fingers. "I—I

couldn't stand the thought of you hurt—of someone doing you harm." But that was only the partial truth.

I couldn't bear the thought of being without you.

The thought wrenched her with alarm, and she pulled her hand away. Their eyes locked and held fast. Hers were a bit desperate, she knew—his were haunted. He looked like he was using all the self-control he possessed to keep from pulling her into his arms. She wanted nothing more than this, but he couldn't—and she couldn't—

Oh, Lord, a way of escape . . . please.

With a forceful shove on the serving door, Mariah hurried in, shattering their closeness. Roxanna glanced at Abby still playing with her dough, crafting letters on the trestle table, the dusting of flour on her face making her appear more waifish. Suddenly she got down from the bench and slipped her hand into Cass's own, giving him a heart-melting smile. As Roxanna looked on, her heart was nearly rent in two.

Oh, to be like Abby, oblivious to intrigue and danger, able to love her towering commander with unabashed devotion.

24

Cass sat alone in headquarters, watching the April rain splash the crude pane of the blockhouse window, a copy of the *Virginia Gazette* before him with news—old news now—of war exploits in the east. He was so far removed from the conflict he sometimes felt he was reading about a different country, and that the men he'd rubbed shoulders with—Washington, Jefferson, Lafayette—were mere shadows half a world away.

Day after day, he waited here in this wild place to be recalled to the heat of battle, but the call never came, and it seemed he continued to hold the Kentucke territory and tried to expand her boundaries for men who'd forgotten all about him.

He pushed aside the paper and looked down at the manual of arms on his desk, thinking of all he'd learned at Valley Forge when Baron von Steuben had unified a dangerous mix of malcontents into a fighting force for General Washington. He'd been one of them. The memory seemed edged in glass, sharp and painful and permanent as any wound he'd earned in battle.

In the years since, he'd tried to hold on to the good things, those shining moments amidst all the misery. There were blessed few. His rapid promotion from major to aide-de-camp to Life Guard was but one, followed by the Purple Heart he'd earned at

Brandywine Creek. And then the hero's welcome he'd received upon arriving at Washington's headquarters soon after.

Lately each honor seemed as tarnished and unsavory as a copper spittoon. What had they amounted to in the end? A fetid outpost on the fringe of civilization and a king's ransom of spirits to dull the pain of past and present. And now he was attempting to ferret out a spy, having put the entire garrison on alert to that end.

Reaching inside his breast pocket, his fingertips touched the locket and scrap of paper lodged over his heart. *Praying for you.* The ink was now smudged, he'd read it so many times. He wondered exactly what she prayed. He recalled his own agonized petitions when he had sensed her slipping away from him in the shadows of her cabin. Stripped bare of all pretense and unbelief, he'd begged the Almighty to make her well. And this time He'd answered.

Simply put, he couldn't bear the thought of losing her. She was his first thought upon waking, coming to him each morning in that misty haze of half consciousness that had once left him dreading the dawn. She'd consoled him by bringing the peace and light of her presence to this dreary post, allowing him a reprieve from the near-constant foreboding that shadowed him night and day. Somehow, inexplicably, she'd returned his thoughts to the Almighty. Most miraculously of all, she'd uprooted the bitter memory of a woman he'd once thought he loved and who no longer stood between them.

Yet despite these hard-won victories, he was far from realizing a relationship with her, as he still hadn't confessed what lay so heavy on his soul.

A soft knock on the door made him shift in his chair. Roxie. He stood, swallowing down the keen disappointment he felt when he saw the orderlies on her heels. He'd not been alone with her—hadn't let himself be alone with her—since they'd spoken in the kitchen a few days before, thinking it would somehow stem his gnawing need of her. Yet the hold she had on him was steadfast. And today she wasn't making it any easier.

The clean lines of her blueberry dress only called out all the lush lines of her, making her appear even more alluring, the soft chignon at the nape of her neck teased into stray wisps by the wind. As she passed to her lap desk in the corner, she gave him a fleeting half smile, and he did the same, wanting to send the orderlies out, but he felt so addled he couldn't think of a good reason to do so.

Instead he called for Ben Simmons and asked that the three Shawnee be brought in, a routine he was all too weary of. Turning to Roxie, he asked for a transcript of the meeting. Today he was going to do something unusual, and he wanted a record so there would be no confusion as to what had truly happened here.

He pondered his predicament as the Indians came in on silent, moccasined feet. The more time he spent with them, the more his understanding of their predicament deepened. Their complex codes of honor, their innate honesty, their childlike ability to be completely in the present—all worked a curious spell. The brutal fact that six of his men had just been ambushed by some of their tribesmen failed to gain a bitter foothold. He knew of soldiers who'd committed like atrocities and thus forbade any of his men to so much as lift a scalp.

He'd had the two chiefs in custody since the winter campaign and was becoming increasingly uncomfortable with their presence. He sensed their longing to be free, to return to their people across the Ohio River, to tell of their time with the red-haired chief and all his soldiers and artillery on lands held sacred by the Shawnee. He knew they would say that the Kentuckians had come to stay. That alone would do far more than waging war ever would.

Taking up a graphite stick, he marked a heavy X in upper

Indian country on a large map rolled out on the desk, clearly visible to each one of them as they gathered round, their feathered heads bent in concentration.

The words, though long practiced, still felt unrehearsed when he said, "I am prepared to let you go free—today—if you provide me with the information I need." He paused, feeling their surprise—and elation—though they remained outwardly stoic. "My scouts have recently brought back reports that the British have built a fort here along the river you call Maumee."

The older Shawnee nodded sagely, one finger tracing the path of the water to the lead marking. Falling Water and Five Feathers exchanged glances. After some hesitation, she said in careful Shawnee, "In the last Papaw Moon, the Redcoats came into our country telling us the hair buyer—Hamilton—wanted to show us a new soldier chief he had made."

Cass looked down at her as Simmons interpreted, thinking how little the Shawnee gave away unless he showed direct knowledge of it. "Have you seen this man?"

Her intelligent eyes were grave. "*Mattah.* But I have heard of him. This man is so tall, some say, he seems to block the sun. And his hair is the color of his coat."

Out of the corner of his eye, Cass saw Roxie's quill go still. Even before all the words were translated, he felt a hard, cold numbness overtake him.

His hair is the color of his coat.

His *red* coat.

There could be no mistaking the description. Though he'd had his suspicions based on new intelligence coming out of Detroit, nothing could staunch the pain of its confirmation. Like the gouging open of an old wound that had never fully healed, he felt a torrent of breathtaking things. Disbelief. Dread. Remorse. Revulsion.

It took all the strength he possessed to keep the tight knot of turmoil now expanding in his chest from reaching his face.

"You've not seen this man, but you have heard of him—therefore, you must know why he has come into your country."

Falling Water nodded thoughtfully and met his unwavering gaze. "I think you also know why he has come."

"Aye, I do," he replied, his voice so low it was almost inaudible. "But I want to hear it from you."

Five Feathers spoke with authority, revealing a deeper knowledge than Cass had anticipated. "This new Redcoat chief gives our people presents and bounties for making war with the white faces in Kan-tuck-ee. By building a soldier fort closer to the Shawnee towns, our warriors do not have to go to the hair buyer in Detroit."

Cass pondered all the implications as he listened to Ben's translation. In time, once Liam had established himself as a generous and warrior-like agent among the tribes, he would launch a combined force of British and Indians to come against the Kentucke settlements, with cannon and artillery that could breach fort walls.

Ominous murmurs of this had already crossed the river and reached him, but till now he'd thought Hamilton too comfortable in the lair he'd built for himself in Detroit to make war so far south, simply goading the Shawnee to do it for him. But Liam . . . Liam would warm to such a challenge, and Cass knew this was precisely why he'd been given the position.

Swallowing down the bile backing up in his throat, he tried to think of something—anything—that would anchor him. Taking his eyes off the map, he looked across the room to Roxie. The pale lines of her face were composed, but she was studying him as she'd not done for days, and her eyes held a hint of alarm. Did she know about Liam, he wondered? Her intensity told him she did indeed.

Turning to one of the orderlies, he sent for Micajah Hale. When he appeared, Cass began making final arrangements for the Indians. They had risen from the bench and were watching him with a feral fascination.

"Supply them with three of our finest mounts, tobacco, and enough provisions for their trip north across the river," he told him. Micajah opened his mouth in surprise, then shut it as Cass continued, "Return their weapons to them outside the postern gate and let them go."

As Simmons translated, the somber mood of moments before lifted. Cass could feel the Shawnees' gratitude and saw that Falling Water's eyes were shining with joy. Releasing them was a goodwill gesture, but in truth he had no reason to keep them. They'd told him what he wanted to know—and, within the last few minutes, what he didn't.

Ever cautious, he watched as Five Feathers crossed the room to Roxie, pausing before her Windsor chair, dark palm outstretched. In his hand Cass saw the watch she'd given him and the little key that wound it.

"Good trade," he said in careful English.

Smiling now, she looked up at him and reached around her lap desk to draw the white wampum from her pocket. "Good trade," she echoed.

With little ceremony, the room emptied of all but one orderly and Cass—and Roxie. Feeling drained and chilled, Cass continued to look down at the maps, whose curled edges were weighted with a pistol and compass and surveyor's tools. Just a few feet away, she was finishing her work, capping the inkwell and readying the transcript of what had just transpired. From a far corner, the clock seemed to shudder as it tolled ten times. *Still morning*, he thought dismally.

"You're excused, Miss Rowan," he said, hating the formality.

She looked up, surprise sketched across her lovely features. "There's nothing else, sir?"

Turning back to the map bearing the large *X*, he said, "Nay, there's nothing more to be done this day."

Nothing, he decided, except to exit through the sally port, climb the hill to the house, and leave the fetid fort far behind.

Leaning on her hoe, Roxanna looked up the greening hill of bluegrass to the stone house, wondering for the hundredth time how Cass was faring. In the last day she'd seen no sign of him. Only Hank entered and exited, with the ever-present guard stationed outside. Since Cass had freed the Shawnee and learned of his brother's activity in the middle ground, she'd had a dreadful foreboding she couldn't shake.

Knowing Liam McLinn was just across the Ohio, doing as much damage to the Kentuckians and the cause of liberty as he could, had kept her awake nights almost as much as the memory of Cass leaving the blockhouse in a stew of gloom. Though his stoic face betrayed little, she could feel that his soul was besieged—and felt it still. No one had to tell her what he was doing inside that handsome but forbidding building on the hill.

Now at twilight she prayed silently as she finished her gardening, hoping the door would swing open wide and he'd walk out to join his officers for supper. But all that caught her attention were the spring peepers and whippoorwills in the distant tree line and the restless shuffling of the guard as they kept watch around her.

Oh, Cass, you're just drinking yourself into a deeper tangle.

Taking up her hoe, she whacked at a stubborn weed encroaching on her peas, upending its spidery root from the dirt. Would that she could set Cass to rights as easily. Anger ticked relentlessly inside her. She could feel its heat in the rhythm of her pulse, all the more maddening because she was powerless to help him.

Lately he'd seemed to be turning a corner, and she'd glimpsed in him a kinder, gentler side. Since the cinchona poisoning, she'd detected a marked shift in him, a softening toward spiritual things. Though he never gave voice to his thoughts, she sensed the difference, and thankfulness suffused every part of her. There was, she felt, a fine man beneath his hardness. Her father had known it too. Finally her heartfelt, persistent prayers for him seemed to have found answer.

And now this.

Giving the green tendrils of peas and beans a final drink of water from her bucket, she thanked the guard as the last rays of sunlight touched the cold stone of the house on the hill. Turning her back on its beauty and returning to the fort, she felt like someone had thrown a black blanket over her. She was captive in this dark place—mired in her deepening feelings for Cass—and Liam McLinn was another dire reminder of the consequences that awaited her if she tried to leave.

She passed Nancy on the parade ground, heartened to see her on her way to the kitchen, another regular escorting her. The possessive way she clutched his arm and her bright smile reassured Roxanna that mourning Billy was indeed a thing of the past. High on the banquette above, the soldiers were changing guard, and muted talk and laughter erupted all around. With Cass holed up, discipline had dwindled and two more men had been caught stealing rum from the commissary. Everything unsavory within these high walls seemed to seethe and ooze in his absence, and she'd never felt less safe in all her life.

Too pent up to eat, she made tea at her own hearth, shunning the fine china cup for a plain pewter one and grating a brick of bitter Bohea instead of the fine, loose Congou he'd given her. A knock at the door sent her hopes soaring, but when Bella appeared, her buoyant spirits fell to her feet.

Bella's dark face was knotted with concern. "I've brought you some supper. I know my cookin' skills are lackin', but you ain't hardly missed a meal yet."

"Thank you, Bella, but I can't eat a bite. Female trouble, I'm afraid." True enough, she thought, though *colonel trouble* was more accurate.

Nodding in sympathy, Bella turned toward the door with the

tray, muttering, "I'd best send somethin' to Colonel McLinn. He's finally risen from the dead, Hank says."

Roxanna stopped stirring her tea, hoping her relief—and delight—didn't show. "Why don't you let me take him his supper?"

A flash of horror crossed her face. "Law, Miz Roxanna, you been drinkin' too? The only livin' thing McLinn lets near him after one o' his spells is Hank, and poor Hank has to tiptoe to do it."

Inexplicably, the warning only hardened her resolve. Taking the tray, Roxanna said with more bluster than she felt, "Sometimes not even a colonel gets what he wants."

Bella studied her with alarm. "You feelin' all right, Miz Roxanna?"

"Never better."

"Well, best stop by the kitchen and take him a hot plate. This un's likely cold—"

"Army regulation is being on time for meals, is it not? If it's cold, the colonel himself is to blame. He's lucky he gets a meal at all."

Bella took a wary step back. "Law! What's got into you?"

"Fire and brimstone, I guess," Roxanna said over her shoulder, crossing the threshold into the gathering gloom. "If I'm not back by midnight, best come after me."

Cold johnnycake was palatable, but underdone potato, overdone elk, and greasy gravy were decidedly not. Yet Roxanna bore her burden with a steady step despite her slight limp, saying to the guard once she reached the stone house, "Please knock for me, as my hands are full. I'll not take no for an answer."

When Hank's drawn face appeared in a crack of light through the barely open door, she bustled in. The foyer unfolded before her in all its austere elegance, a sconce banishing the shadows lurking in the far corners. For a moment she felt small and overawed by its polished grandeur. *Oh, Lord, don't let me falter.* Yet she'd come up here without having the slightest idea what she'd say, only the burning desire to say something.

Yellow light pooled beneath a closed door to her right. His study? The sitting room? Without a word, Hank knocked lightly and she listened, stomach swimming. Why *had* she come? The answering growl behind the door seemed more ogre than McLinn, but she steadied her tray and entered in.

He was standing by an open window, looking down at the fort, his back to her. The sight of him in shirtsleeves, his uniform coat cast over a chair back, lent an unsettling intimacy to the scene. Her breath seemed to catch and not release, and all her poise took flight. Setting her burden on a table, she heard Hank shut the door, hemming her in. Slowly, Cass turned, the light calling out a dozen unkempt details about him—red-bristled jaw, buff trousers and boots, ruffled shirt open at the neck and lacking a cravat, lank hair loose and missing its ribbon tie.

Behind him the fire snapped and sent a plume of sparks past the dog irons onto delft tiles. The room reeked of tobacco—and brandy—and nearly made her wrinkle her nose. Instead she laced her fingers behind her and said, "I've brought you some supper."

"And a double helping of condemnation as well, aye?"

"You're welcome," she said coolly.

His stiffness melted into a half smile. "Thank you."

Looking away from him, she tried to puzzle out what color the walls were beneath the shadows, her eyes drawn to the twin wing chairs angled before the fire—just as she'd imagined them to be. And the books! The surrounding shelves seemed about to burst, rivaling the library at Thistleton Hall . . .

"Have a seat. Or are you needed back at the fort?" The steady lilt of his voice told her he was no longer intoxicated, just irritated.

She moved to the wing chairs and hesitated. "Which is yours?"

"Both," he replied wryly. "I sit in one and put my feet up in the other."

She nearly smiled. "I'll take the one that bears your backside, not your boots."

He gestured to the one on the right and she sat, sensing an undercurrent of bewildering things between them. Tension. Pleasure. Promise. Hope. She gazed upward to the curved mantel and painted panels and corniced ceiling while he leaned back in his chair, eyes on the fire. For a few agonizing minutes they sat in tense silence, and she did what she'd seen him do to his men—she said nothing and simply outlasted him.

"So, Roxie, why have you come?"

Despite his gruffness, she warmed to the thawing in his tone— and his familiarity. 'Twas Roxie tonight, not Miss Rowan. Not Roxanna. Pleasure seeped past her dismay. "I've come because I'm concerned about you, Cass—and I'm getting a crick in my neck from looking up the hill."

He turned amused eyes on her. "I'm sorry about the crick in your neck, but I'm glad we've finally dispensed with formalities. Hearing you call me *colonel* and *sir* was making me feel like an old man."

"So how are you . . . truly?"

He passed a hand over his whiskers. "I'm *truly* dissolute."

He looked it, though she'd rarely been around anyone who drank and wasn't familiar with its effects.

Meeting her gaze, he said, "You're looking at me like your father used to after one of my binges."

"He used to say liquor ruined many a good soldier."

"Aye, so he did. He also said, 'Let your recreations be manful, not sinful.' But to his credit, he never spoke in judgment or malice. Just concern. Like a father to a son."

Yes, he'd known her father well. Hearing it brought his beloved memory back with such bittersweet ache she felt for her handkerchief.

He moved to stir the fire with a poker. "I'm sorry. I don't mean to hurt you by mentioning him."

"I'd rather he be remembered than forgotten."

"I'll not forget . . ."

She waited for him to finish, but he left off, a look of such poignancy and pain on his face she felt doubly stung. The very air seemed weighted, and Micajah Hale's words returned to her with a blunt force that nearly took her breath.

I was there when it happened. But I doubt you'd leap to his defense had you been.

Micajah had witnessed her father's death. Yet this wasn't what had upended her but the acrid bitterness of his tone. Dare she ask Cass about that fatal day? Here . . . now?

Chilled, she gathered her composure. "Since we're speaking of hard things, I want to tell you I know about Liam."

The telling vulnerability in his face vanished. "Bella told you, I'll wager."

"Bella and Micajah. But I'd rather you tell me so I can hear the truth of it firsthand."

"'Tis not a pretty tale, Roxie. And I'd rather spare you the details."

Their eyes met, and she found his sharp with irritation. But she wouldn't back down, feeling the subject of Liam was what festered inside him and needed lancing. "Speaking of it might do you some good."

"Or it just might drive me to drink again."

"No man should have that kind of power over you, especially a brother."

"He's hardly that," he said quietly yet with heat. "Rather the devil disguised as such. His intent has always been to send me straight to hell. And now, being Hamilton's minion, he might well do it."

Turning to a tilt-top table beside his chair, he retrieved a paper and passed it to her. She'd seen British handbills before—they were common enough in the colonies—but this one preached a coming wilderness war, advising the Kentucke settlers to abandon the Patriot cause and pledge allegiance to the king if they valued their lives.

"I've heard what British soldiers and Indians do to Patriot posts," she murmured, passing it back to him.

"I'll not let them take Fort Endeavor," he said, crumpling the handbill in his fist and tossing it into the fire. "I'll meet them in the middle ground, army to army, to spare as much settlement blood as possible."

"When?"

"As soon as we're able. I'm waiting for reinforcements, if they materialize, which I doubt. If they don't come, we'll march regardless. If we succeed in overrunning them in the middle ground, we'll move on to Detroit."

She turned to look at him again, and it seemed an icy hand gripped her heart. "It sounds . . . ambitious."

"Aye."

Knotting her handkerchief in her lap, she tried to make sense of what she could only call a sickening premonition. There were but two hundred men at Fort Endeavor, yet countless British and Indians in the middle ground. She saw an empty chair across from her and felt suffocated by such a sense of loss that she bit her lip to keep herself in check. If he went, her heart and head insisted, he wouldn't come back . . .

He studied her, every angle of his face taut. "I will tell you this. It's one thing to face an honorable enemy but another thing to deal with cutthroats and savages. Liam McLinn has earned the nickname of Lucifer by shooting men in the back. That is what I'm up against, and that is why I've been holed up in this house trying to forget."

"Trying to forget how dismal your odds of winning are, you mean?"

"Aye, to put it bluntly."

They fell into a sore silence, one she longed to mend but

couldn't. From the hall she could hear Hank's soft tread as he climbed the stairs.

"I'd best go," she said, though she didn't want to. She felt at home here, away from the filth of the fort. She couldn't blame him for seeking refuge in this house, though she abhorred his drinking.

He said a bit more gently, "Your father was often in this room. It seems right having you here."

"Bella will wonder if I tarry."

"Let her wonder, Roxie. Let them all wonder." His tone was so mellow, so inviting, she felt her dilemma play plainly across her face. "I won't offer you a drink, if that's what you're worried about."

Her eyes drifted to the brandy decanter on a far table, drained of all but an inch of amber liquid. "Perhaps a cup of tea."

He got up and disappeared out the door, shutting it soundly behind him. The idea of him—so often brusque and stern and commanding—fetching anything lightened the heavy mood of moments before and almost made her smile. She ignored the nagging bite of warning that bade her go. She should leave now, before he returned. Yet this inviting room and all its amenities begged her to stay. There was no denying she was hungry for companionship. Comfort. Beauty. Surely there was no harm in lingering a while longer.

25

A delicious anticipation spread through her once she yielded. Free to look about, she let her eyes trace every lovely line of the room, from the intricate stitching in the floral carpet beneath her feet to the rich ivory curtains at the casement windows. Blue walls, she noted. A rich, Williamsburg blue.

The door opened, and Hank appeared, bearing a tray with a thistle cup and saucer that matched the one in her cabin, as well as a plump porcelain teapot and a dizzying assortment of tea. Hyson. Singlo. Sassafras. Mint. Even a pitcher of cream, a sugar bowl, a dainty silver spoon—and a plate of Bella's beaten biscuits.

"Would you like anything else, Miz Roxanna?" Hank asked as he moved the tilt-top table nearer and set the tray where the handbill had lain.

She smiled up at him, thinking how pleased he looked to have her here, his furrowed face melting into relaxed lines. She felt equally delighted. "Oh, this is wonderful, Hank. Nothing more, thank you."

Truly, she felt like a fine lady sitting in some fancy Virginia drawing room—or in a safer, more hospitable Kentucke years from now, when the war had been won and the Indian threat had lessened.

"The colonel'll be back shortly," he said, going to a corner chest and withdrawing a cribbage board and cards. These he placed on a second table. Seeing her surprise, he added, "Your papa was fond of playin' games in this room. He gave the colonel this here board right before—" He broke off and shot her an apologetic glance. "Right before that last campaign."

She took the cribbage board wonderingly, its polished lines all too familiar with its ivory pegs and Patriot markings.

"I think it'd please your pa to no end if he could see you here beatin' the breeches off the colonel like he sometimes did," Hank murmured.

"Is the colonel any good?"

He grinned. "He and your pa used to go round and round and stay up half the night tryin' to outdo each other. And if memory serves, he said somethin' 'bout teachin' his daughter to play as good as he did."

"But I haven't played in years. Not since Papa's last leave."

"I bet it'll come right back to you—and it'll surely put a smile on the colonel's face. Mebbe make him forget all 'bout his achin' head."

Head or heart? she wondered. The door opened again, and Cass came in just as Hank let himself out. She kept her eyes on her steaming tea, stirring in cream and sugar, her heart doing absurd palpitations in her chest as he rounded the chair and sat opposite her again.

He eyed the cribbage board and playing cards. "Was this your idea or Hank's?"

"Does it matter?" she asked, looking up, unable to stop a smile from stealing over her face at the sight of him.

Though still in shirtsleeves, he wore fresh, pressed linen, and his combed hair had been returned to its customary queue. His face was clean shaven and smelled of bergamot, not brandy. She was glad he'd taken time to do these things, yet any gentleman should clean up in feminine company. And since she was the sole female present . . .

"Do you want to play cribbage, Roxie?"

No, I want you to lean over this cribbage board and kiss me.

Unbidden, the bold thought seemed to leap between them and make itself known. He was looking at her so intently she almost squirmed under his scrutiny.

"Only if you do," she managed.

She returned her attention to her tea, taking a sip and looking up just enough to watch his long, tanned fingers shuffle the cards with an easy grace. Best tuck away any blasphemous thoughts of kissing. At least any bestowed by him. Ambrose had kissed her just once, in a wisteria arbor back in Virginia. She could hardly remember the kiss, just how clumsily it had been given and how disappointed she had felt afterward. For days. And she knew, somehow, that if Cassius McLinn were to kiss her, he wouldn't be clumsy or awkward in the least, and she'd not be left disappointed . . . just wanting more.

He dealt the cards and said quietly, "A shilling for your thoughts."

Taking another drink of tea, she looked up over the rim of her cup. "They're hardly worth that."

"Oh, I'll wager they're worth a good deal more."

"I'm simply trying to recollect the rules of the game."

"All you need to remember is that it's a fifteen-two game, and you score the most points when your cards add up to fifteen. The first to reach a hundred twenty-one wins."

"I recollect that Papa and I used to play for a prize."

His hands stilled from placing the ivory pegs. "Such as?"

She grew solemn. "If I win, you must abstain from all spirits for at least a fortnight. Not a drop."

"Not a drop," he echoed, eyes warm with amused light. "And if I win?"

She gave a little shrug and set down her cup. "Ask for whatever you wish."

He grew thoughtful, all levity gone. "'Tis customary in Ireland for a man to take his pick of any woman present and kiss her as his prize."

Lord, is he able to read my thoughts?

Unable to meet his eyes, she felt the heat bloom in her face again. "The stakes are quite high."

"You can lower them, ye ken."

The heady thought of losing was too sweet a temptation to resist. *Forgive me, Lord.* "I'll not back down," she told him, picking up her cards with an unsteady hand.

For a moment she feared, worldly as he was, that he could peer clear into her soul and sense her crumbling resistance toward him. Sitting there, staring at her cards without really seeing them, she knew they'd begun something far more dangerous than a simple game.

They started to play, he quietly confident, she bluffing and biting her lip till they were neck and neck. From somewhere in the shadows a clock struck ten times, but he seemed not to notice. He was ahead . . . she was ahead. And then suddenly she fell behind.

Her heart began to dance about and turn her breathless. If he kissed her, *where* would he kiss her? In this room? Would he simply lean over in his chair till he reached her? Or would he stand, arms about her like they were going to dance? Oh, the only thing that mattered was *how* he'd kiss her. Perhaps he'd simply brush her cheek or forehead chastely and be done with it . . .

It had been too long since she'd played the game. And he was the most maddeningly attractive opponent she'd ever had. Small wonder she was losing. She couldn't keep her mind on cribbage or anything else . . . just him.

"One hundred twenty-one," he said, moving his pegs to the finish.

She felt herself wilt. "Congratulations," she said softly without looking at him, turning her remaining cards facedown on the table between them.

Reaching over, he extinguished each candle with his fingertips till there was only the fire's golden glow. For a desperate moment she wanted to run. He stood, and with one firm, calloused hand he brought her to her feet.

'Twas just one kiss, she reasoned, certainly the last before full-fledged spinsterhood. Surely the Almighty would forgive her that.

Amidst the sweet confusion of her feelings came the realization once again of how feminine he made her feel. Though he towered over her, he seemed less intimidating out of uniform. Ever so slowly, he laced his other hand through hers, bringing her arm gently behind her back, anchoring her to him. He was so close, the firm line of his chest was flush against her snug bodice. Drawing in a deep, silent breath, she felt a bit faint and fastened her eyes on the fine stitching of his shirt.

"Roxie . . . how can I kiss you if you don't look at me?"

His tender tone turned her heart over. She obliged, tilting her head back slightly and looking up at him in the firelit darkness. When he bent his head and his mouth met hers, she gave a little sigh, her lips parting slightly in surprise and expectation. He kissed her with the same sure decisiveness with which he did everything else, his mouth trailing to her cheek and chin and ear, returning again and again to her mouth and lingering there, his breath mingling with her own.

She felt adrift in small, sharp bursts of pleasure. Was this how a man was supposed to kiss a woman? Tenderly . . . firmly . . . repeatedly? His fingers fanned through her hair till the pins gave way and wayward locks spilled like black ribbon to the small of her back. In answer, her arms circled his neck, bringing him nearer, every kiss sweeter and surer than the one before. Soon they were lost in a haze of sighs and murmurs and caresses.

The clock struck again, and the somberness of the sound and the lateness of the hour brought her back to the blue room on this cool spring evening, the forgotten cribbage game on the table beside them, her hair spilling down, the skin of her neck and shoulders heated from his kisses. How they'd stayed standing . . .

⟡

With a sudden wrench, Cass pulled free, though his hands lingered on the soft slope of her shoulders. He sensed her sharp surprise and regret—but it paled beside his own. 'Twas all he could do to stem his need and let go of her. She was trembling and looking up at him with such a winsome vulnerability it seemed he held her very heart in his hands.

"Roxie, I—" The words were punctuated with pain. His throat constricted as he worked to say what he should have said from the first. He had no right to kiss her, declare his love for her, with such a fatal secret between them. But the practiced apology—his confession—seemed to stick in his throat. "I have to tell you something. But you won't want to hear it any more than I want to confess it."

In the firelit shadows her eyes turned a drenching blue—entreating, almost pleading—so unlike the day he'd first stood across from her in the blockhouse. Then, and now, he struggled and looked away, only to look back at her, nigh speechless. There was simply no way to soften the bitter truth.

Say it, man, just say it . . .

"Roxie . . . I shot your father."

The horrific statement unleashed a firestorm of memories and emotions inside him. Gunshots falling like hail in the icy woods. Crimson flecking Richard Rowan from head to toe. His own anguished cry to cease firing. The crushing irreversibility of it all.

I shot your father.

It seemed to echo endlessly in the elegant room and deepen the darkness. Slowly, she began backing up, out of his reach, a look of utter disbelief—nay, horror—marring her lovely, tear-streaked face.

"'Twas a terrible mistake at twilight. I couldn't see clearly and I thought—your father—I thought he was the enemy." He stumbled on, eyes wet. "God forgive me. Please . . . you . . . forgive me."

But she simply stared at him, lips parted in a sort of stunned wonder. He read unmistakable revulsion in her gaze and felt a deep, gnawing ache that he'd caused her such hurt. Stricken, he watched her frantic fingers try to return her hair to its chignon with the few pins remaining, the rest scattered on the rug at his feet. Wordlessly, she spun away, opening the door just enough to slip through, almost colliding with Hank in the foyer.

He watched her go, fighting his anguish, wanting to go after her. The room's emptiness in her wake was barren as a winter field, blowing cold clear to his soul. He felt frozen, mired in a melee of emotions he couldn't stay atop of. On the eve of his own demise, he had cast love away, and its loss meant more to him than his own life.

Dear God, what now?

Shame—and a knot of emotions she couldn't name—fell over Roxanna like a fever, but it was too late to simply slip out. The guard snapped to attention as she hurried through the front door, two regulars falling in alongside her to return her to the fort. She nearly fell on the rain-slick stoop, vaguely aware that a storm was rising around her, stirring the night air, mirroring the tempest inside her.

Oh, Lord, help . . .

She didn't look back, didn't see the lithe shadow at one casement window watching her go. Her chest was heaving like she'd run a race, so hard it hurt. Rain pelted down, mingling with her salty tears. She brushed them away with shaking hands, trying to staunch the pain of Cass's confession. All the while a strange numbness was taking hold, enabling her to keep walking, to lift the latch of her cabin door, enter in, and shut herself away.

Going to the washbasin, she splashed cold water on her flushed face, took up a linen towel, and tried to remove all traces of him. But his beloved, traitorous scent still clung to her skin, her hair, her bodice. She wanted to be rid of his shocking words as well, told to her at such an impossibly tender time. Yet they resounded in her head and heart, bruising her again and again.

Roxie . . . I shot your father.

The dark room, lit by a dying fire, seemed to tilt and spin. She had to work hard to draw a needed breath, to stop her shaking. Her eyes darted to the mantel and landed on the thistle cup, the delicate saucer beneath. Wounded by the very sight, she reached for it with trembling hands, wanting to hide it away and bury all her anguish alongside it.

The lovely china—the sentiment behind it—seemed hopelessly tainted. Once she had looked at it lovingly, had counted it her most treasured possession. But in the span of a few horrifying moments all that had changed forever. With a sob she raised her arm, flinging both cup and saucer against the far cabin wall and watching them shatter into countless pieces.

Just like her heart.

Cass came down the hill after Roxanna, hardly feeling the driving rain. Without the guard, he ducked through the sally port in such haste he nearly toppled the sentry standing watch. 'Twas a wretched night on all counts, the only light that of a few stingy lanterns shining in barrack windows. Mud was pooling around his boots, making it seem he was treading in molasses instead. Her shuttered cabin seemed leagues away.

At last he reached her door, feeling for the latchstring and finding it drawn in. "Roxanna, open the door!"

The heavy oak wall seemed symbolic of their separation, cutting him afresh. Never again would her eyes light up when she looked at him. Nor would that beguiling half smile, saved solely for him, warm his sorry soul. Though she'd tried hard not to love him, he knew she did. And he'd just undone all that they'd ever meant to each other, every complicated strand, impossible as it all was. He'd just handed her a reason to hate him.

"Roxie, 'tis me—Cass. Open the door!"

Frustration tugged at him, bade him to do something rash. He could break the door down if he wanted—but to what avail? Somehow he sensed she was hovering on the other side, hearing his every word. He bent his head, arms outspread as he grasped the rough sides of the door frame and waited.

His guilt-ravaged voice reached out to her again. "I cannot leave till we talk, ye ken. Let me in."

Overhead thunder rumbled, deep and discordant, and a flash of lightning rent the sky. The rain began to fall in great sheets, wetting his shirt back so that it lay against him like a second skin. Cold water ran down the back of his neck, chilling him and fueling his angst. Banging a hard hand on the door once more, he felt a desperation he'd never known as a new thought curled like black smoke in his brain.

What if she . . . hurt herself?

What if his confession, coupled with her grief and love for him, made her rash? The day she'd drunk the tainted tea returned to taunt him. He'd never fully understood why she'd risked her own life in the wake of nearly losing his. Till now. If she hurt herself—if she died by her own hand—he died with her. Life meant little without her . . .

His fist grew sore from beating on the wood. He was a broken, sodden mess—half dressed, his voice hoarse from shouting, making a spectacle of himself before the sentries on the banquette above. But he didn't care. Nothing mattered but that she was safe and sound. The image of her father's pistol, kept in her cabin, shattered what was left of his composure.

"Roxanna—for God's sake—open the door!"

Though his voice held strong, he'd never felt so defeated. The weight of it rolled over him till he felt he was sinking in the mud, mired in utter helplessness. Pushing away from the door, he looked across the blackened parade ground to the kitchen, where a light still lingered.

Bella.

At any other time, Cass might have wondered why Bella sat by the hearth's fire at nearly midnight, cradling a cup of tea in her bony hands. When he came into the kitchen, dripping water onto the plank floor, his boots more mud than leather, she stared at him as if he were naught but a ghost. Excruciating seconds ticked by as he crossed his arms and tried to herd his thoughts into a logical formation.

"'Tis Roxie," he said with difficulty.

Her eyes narrowed to suspicious slits. "What do you mean, sir?"

"Earlier tonight she came up the hill to the house. I bade her stay . . . things were said."

"Where is she now?"

"In her cabin. She won't come out."

"She disobeyed your orders to open the door, you mean."

"Aye."

"And you want me to keep an eye on her, make sure she don't do nothin' rash."

He simply nodded, running a hand over his wet jaw, wondering just how much Bella knew. Had Hank told her about Richard Rowan's last day? He remembered Hank was standing near him when he'd fired that fatal shot. Did Bella know that he loved Richard's daughter beyond all reason? And that was why he stood dripping wet in a cold kitchen, nearly begging her to help set things right?

"I'll do what I can, sir," she said, rising and setting her cup aside. "You'd best go on back up the hill."

26

'Twas Monday and Cass had come down the hill early, surprising the sentries and even Hank. He slipped through the sally port and entered the dark, chill blockhouse, sending the orderlies scrambling to kindle fires and candles long before dawn. That done, he could see that someone had taken advantage of his rum-soaked revel to rummage through his desk, disturbing the carefully placed documents he'd planted for that very possibility.

He reckoned he deserved the trespass given his lapse, but it was maddening that he still hadn't an inkling who was spying—even after a poisoning. Blast, but the man deserved some sort of medal! If the British had an operative in this post, he was a believable one and aroused no suspicions. In the dark about the spy's identity, Cass knew his only recourse was to plant false information to confuse and thwart.

Turning to the fire, he kicked the front log with his boot and contemplated the day ahead of him. This dreary April morning, he had an unknown enemy within fort walls, a known enemy in the middle ground, a shortage of fresh meat, two regulars awaiting court-martial for stealing rum, men stacked like firewood in the infirmary from a mysterious fever, no post physician, unceasing spring rains, and a courier who hadn't come back.

And the only thing he could think of was the woman whose heart he'd rent in two.

Since she'd fled the stone house Saturday night, the ensuing hours seemed to echo with regret. He thought the Sabbath would never end, the only respite being Bella's word that Roxie was in her cabin sleeping. Visions of violet-scented shoulders and pitch-black hair and the sweet, almost honeyed taste of her kept him wide awake almost as much as his latent confession. Both bruised his thoughts, nearly driving him to her door a second time. But something kept him at bay. She needed time. Time to sort through the bitter truth of what he'd told her. Time to compose herself. Time to extend forgiveness—or not.

As the ebony hands of the corner clock stretched to eight, he found himself as tightly wound. She'd never been late, not once, and for a few tense moments he feared she wasn't coming at all. He didn't blame her. If she never entered headquarters again, he well understood her reasons.

Going to the window on the pretense of opening it for fresh air, he saw her walking briskly across the common, head down, every lovely curve of her snug in sky-blue linen, a little lace cap covering the gloss of upswept hair he still ached to thread his fingers through.

Returning to his desk, he stayed standing, leafing through the correspondence that needed answering, keenly aware of the moment she came in. As she crossed in front of his desk with a demure, "Good morning, Colonel McLinn," he felt disbelief take hold. Her careful manner seemed to return them to last week, before he'd embarked on his drinking spree, making their tumultuous hours of Saturday eve no more substantial than river mist.

"Miss Rowan," he acknowledged, overcome by the lingering scent of roses in her wake.

When she'd settled her lap desk on her knees and looked his way again, he saw that a slip of hair had come free of its pins, framing her face so fetchingly it took all his nerve not to set it right. The thought of the handful of hairpins he had dislodged in his ardor and now had in his breast pocket nearly made him groan.

So this was to be his penance for all that had passed between them. A forced cordiality was not what he'd had in mind. She was going to punish him with the coldness of her presence. And he was powerless to do anything about it.

"First letter will be to Tom Jefferson of Virginia," he said in low tones, the bulk of the desk between them. "I have a court-martial at nine o'clock, which should give you sufficient time to compose three copies."

She simply nodded, eyes down. He tried not to look at her, but it was his habit to do so, if only to gauge how well she was keeping up with the dictation. Today she'd have no trouble, he wagered. He felt like a musket ball had lodged in his brain. The tables had turned. 'Twas his heart she held in her hands, and it remained to be seen what she would do with it.

As soon as Cass left the room, Roxanna drew a bracing breath. If not for the orderlies still milling around, sorting through maps and perusing ledgers, she'd have put her head down on her desk and wept. An able actress she was not. Papa always said she wore her feelings on her sleeve, and the last hour had been a veritable battle to keep them hidden. Hurt and anger kept gaining the upper hand, but underneath was a far more encompassing and troublesome emotion. How, she wondered for the hundredth time, did one hide the things of the heart?

Despite everything, each time he moved, her eyes ached to follow him. Whenever he spoke, her ears strained to catch the lilt in his voice. This morning he was immaculate in uniform, and the scent of him—clean and spicy and invigorating—reminded her unceasingly of his warm arms. Surely he'd noticed her unsteady hand and the uncommon number of mistakes she'd made in dictation. Blessedly, he'd left the room and she could rectify her errors in secret. At this rate, she didn't know how she'd last through the day.

Weary, she sat in her Windsor chair, second-guessing her decision to arrive for work this morning, yet pleading a headache and keeping to her cabin hardly seemed a refuge. Bella was coming by more than usual, and Roxanna felt certain Hank had told of her bolting from the house, hair askew, looking like she'd just been made love to. For once Bella held her tongue and hadn't asked her outright what had transpired. Mayhap she didn't have to. Cass's coming to her cabin—banging and shouting loud enough to raise the dead—had informed the entire fort, surely.

She finished the three copies he'd requested, using an unprecedented amount of paper. She got up and threw her blunders into the fire, which crackled hungrily as she placed the correct copies on his desk for his signature. Till he returned, she could replenish her inkpots and sharpen a new quill.

She looked about restlessly, wondering about the sudden commotion on the common. The orderlies stopped their work and went out, shutting the door behind them but leaving the window open wide. In moments Abby entered, looking like she'd been rolling in the corral with the horses.

"Oh, Abby, I'm glad it's you," she said, tamping down her dismay over Abby's appearance as the child moved to a table where a game of checkers awaited. "Would you like to play?"

But Abby simply looked up, eyes shining with unshed tears, and pointed a finger toward a window.

"Are you frightened, Abby?" Returning her penknife to her pocket, Roxanna crossed to the window and closed the shutter. "Two of the soldiers were caught stealing and must be punished. Colonel McLinn wants to make sure it doesn't happen again."

The red head bobbed in silent understanding, and Roxanna knelt and put her arms around the child, sensing more was bothering her than soldiers meting out justice beyond the window. But how was she to know? Was Olympia mistreating her? Or simply neglecting her? Without a voice, Abby remained an unplumbed mystery. Roxanna held her close for several silent minutes, not only to comfort Abby but to seek comfort herself.

"Why don't you draw a picture or practice writing your name? You're making your letters so nicely."

While Abby sat down with slate and pencil, Roxanna moved to peer through the shutter. Every soldier had assembled to watch an enlisted man, stripped to his breeches, being tied to a post near the flagpole. She turned away and shut her eyes as a great many lashes were meted out by Micajah Hale. That done, the next offender was brought forward. This time it was Cass himself who took a sword and broke it over the second soldier's head.

The humiliation of each act was palpable. Watching it seemed to shrink her spirit, reminding her of the harsh realities of military life and the man who enforced them.

What, she wondered as anger thrust through her sadness, would the punishment be for an officer who'd shot down a fellow officer? And withheld the bitter fact? Pressing a trembling hand to her mouth, she bent her head and tried to pray, but all that filled her mind was the memory of him holding her, of how treasured and secure she felt before his shattering revelation.

Oh, Lord, forgive me for hating him . . . and loving him too.

27

With the cabin door ajar, Roxanna could hear the spring peepers, something she'd always considered a happy sound, heralding humid days and honeysuckle-scented nights and summer's return. But today hadn't been full of fine things, just military discipline and endless drills that bespoke Liam McLinn and the coming confrontation in the middle ground. Cass hadn't returned after the court-martial that morning, sending an orderly to tell her she was no longer needed, as he'd be busy with maneuvers.

Strangely, the dismissal had wounded her to the very core, and she felt herself sliding further toward melancholy. She knew he was trying to avoid her. Since he'd told her about her father, she sensed his deep distress and sorrow in their every exchange, perfunctory as they were. Yet his remorse failed to cool her turbulent feelings. They trailed after her, destroying the sweetness they'd once shared, reinforcing the fact that she was naught but a bitter spinster, after all. Heavy-hearted, she escaped to her garden in the tepid sunshine under guard, the wide, empty river yet another reminder of her predicament.

Now at day's end, she sat and listened to the thwack of a bat on the parade ground as some of the men played base-ball, her fingers almost frantically working her yarn as she knitted more socks. Supper was over and she'd hardly eaten a bite, aware of the Redstone women's eyes on her as she pushed her cornbread and beans around her plate. But it was Bella she worried about, sharp eyed and sharper tongued. It was only a matter of time before Bella began poking around, asking questions she couldn't answer.

"Miz Roxanna, can I come in?" Dovie stood in the doorway, her growing bulk half hidden beneath her hands.

"Yes—please," she said, forcing lightness into her tone. "I'm tired of knitting and would love some company."

Dovie looked about shyly. Most of the time Roxanna came to visit her. "Johnny's playin' ball on the common, and I'm restless as can be. Since we can't walk out with the Indian threat on, I figured I'd talk to you."

Roxanna got up. "Would you like a cup of tea? I have some raspberry leaves if you need them."

"I ain't feelin' poorly no longer. But sassafras would suit me fine." Drawing nearer the hearth, she began working the edge of her apron a bit nervously, eyeing Roxanna as she hung a kettle from the crane.

Roxanna tried to smile, spying a shard from the thistle cup beneath one of the hearth's dog irons. The sight tore at her, and she worked to keep her tone light. "I think motherhood suits you."

Truly, Dovie looked lovely. Her new dress was becomingly cut, and her face held a luminousness Roxanna hadn't noticed, eclipsing the hardness of before. "This baby's got a mind of its own, let me tell you. But I ain't here to talk about me, Miz Roxanna."

The telling words nearly made Roxanna drop the tin of tea. Someone was whispering about her and Cass, then. What else could it be?

Setting two cups on the table, she said casually, "Not me, surely?"

Dovie perched on the edge of her chair. "I ain't one for fancy talk, so I'll just say it simple. Me and the other women noticed you ain't been yourself lately. I know you're still missin' your pa and all, so I've been prayin' for you."

Roxanna added sassafras roots to the kettle through a haze of tears. "I appreciate your prayers, Dovie, more than you know."

"Well, there's a man who's wantin' to meet you. He's a friend of Johnny's. One of the regulars." Roxanna looked at her in surprise, and she hurried on. "Now I know he ain't an officer or anything—"

"Rank doesn't matter to me, Dovie."

She nodded. "That's what I thought you'd say. His name's Graham. Graham Greer."

Graham. Roxanna liked the sound of it, feeling flattered in the wake of being deceived by Cass. She poured steaming water into the waiting cups. "He's the man who married you, am I right?"

Dovie nodded. "He's not been here long but comes from Fairfax County, same as you. He has a farm there but joined the army after his wife died last year. He's a believer too. And he says he's goin' to ask Colonel McLinn about holdin' Sabbath services."

Truly? The mere mention buoyed her spirits. She'd often wished for a preacher since coming to Kentucke, thinking the fort needed a civilizing—*saving*—influence. Contemplating it, she passed Dovie the cup.

"Right now he's busy helpin' out in the infirmary. There's a passel of men down with a fever and Dr. Clary's tied up."

They sipped their tea in silence, Roxanna wondering if Dovie was happy with Johnny but reluctant to ask her outright. It wasn't easy living in a garrison with little privacy and less cleanliness. Roxanna craved the comforts of the stone house like she'd been born to it, and even now her thoughts turned traitorously to the hill.

"Miz Roxanna, I don't know how to ask you this, but there's a rumor goin' round . . ." She shifted in her chair, and a rare tinge of pink touched her cheeks. "It's about you and the colonel. The colonel, anyway. Some folks are sayin' he's . . ."

Ashamed to look at her, Roxanna fastened her eyes on her cup.

"He's smitten with you. Graham told me real quiet-like that he's a bit afraid of Colonel McLinn and don't want no trouble where he's concerned."

Taking a swallow of tea, Roxanna tried to collect her scattered thoughts. "Dovie, you know what happened to my father." She paused, the loss keener now than it had ever been. Somehow knowing the whole truth only made it doubly difficult. "Before he died, he asked Ca—Colonel McLinn to look after me. Any attention he pays me is simply out of respect for my father."

Dovie nodded, looking more satisfied than Roxanna felt. "That explains it, sure enough."

"Naw it don't." Bella's voice seemed to boom from the open doorway, holding a challenge if Roxanna ever heard one. She wanted to wince but made herself turn and greet her with what little composure she had left.

Bella drew up a stool and sat, arms crossed. "It ain't got nothin' to do with your pa and you know it. And I know it. And anyone with half a head knows it."

"Bella, please." The tears burning Roxanna's eyes reinforced her plea.

Dovie suddenly stood, her tea unfinished. "I'd best be goin'," she murmured. "Lately the baby's been makin' me awful tired . . ."

Cradling her warm cup and breathing in the sweet scent of sassafras, Roxanna heard Dovie shut the door as she went out. Across from her, Bella's countenance softened, but it did nothing to ease the sting of her harsh words, or the frank ones she uttered next.

"That man is in love with you, Roxanna Rowan. Why don't you see it?" Roxanna said nothing, eyes averted, as Bella continued in hushed tones. "Hank says he ain't had a drop of liquor since you left the other night."

Hearing it brought a warm rush of surprise. *Not a drop?* Those were her exact words to Cass. Yet she'd lost the game, not he.

She hardly expected him to honor her request, particularly in light of his confession. If he'd ever needed reason to drink, 'twas now. With forced calm, she simply said, "Colonel McLinn is a complicated man."

"And *you*," Bella replied, "is a complicated woman." She opened her mouth to say more, and Roxanna tensed.

Don't ask me about Saturday night, Bella. I don't want to lie to you.

"You look sorta flushed. You ain't comin' down with that fever, I hope." Bella reached out a hand and palmed her forehead, coming away with a *tsk*. "If you get sick again, the colonel will be beside hisself, for sure."

"I'm not sick," Roxanna said, though she felt it.

Bella's sharp eyes remained on her face. "I guess Dovie told you 'bout Graham."

Roxanna nodded. "I think she's trying to do a little match-making."

"Law, least we agree 'bout that. You need to be married and have you a husband and a lap baby and all the rest. But you can forget 'bout Graham. He's still grievin', and he ain't the caliber of the colonel nohow. It's McLinn who needs to wed you and bed you and give you that baby—"

"Bella!"

"*And*," she said with vehemence, "it's *you* who needs to open your eyes to the truth and let 'im." A slow, satisfied smile settled over Bella's face. "There ain't a problem with either one of you that a whole lot of lovin' can't cure."

Roxanna took a measured breath and tried to steady her voice. "Colonel McLinn is far above my humble station. He has never declared his love for me and he never will. I'm merely a distraction in a fort full of men. Besides, the army is going to war in the middle ground soon, as you well know. That's hardly conducive to marrying and having babies."

"Oh, but it is," Bella breathed. "The stone house is beggin' for a weddin' and honeymoon. It would be a fine send-off for a soldier, if you ask me."

"I didn't ask you," Roxanna said with sudden spark. Setting her cup aside, she looked Bella straight in the eye, finding anger far preferable to tears. "I want you to put down any such nonsense. And if you hear the like, try to stop it. Colonel McLinn is under tremendous strain preparing for this campaign. I'll not add to it and neither should you."

All the levity left Bella's face. Roxanna looked away, hardly believing she was defending Cass.

Folding her arms, Bella drawled quietly, "McLinn ain't the onliest one under strain. You won't hardly eat or talk here lately. What's come over you?"

Feeling all thumbs, Roxanna got up and began putting the tea things away, afraid Bella would notice the missing thistle cup. "'Tis the same as it's ever been. I'm homeless and husbandless. My family—what little I have left—is an ocean away. I have but my scrivener's pay, and I can't leave this place. The British and Indians are nearly at our door. Can you blame me for not being hungry or talkative?"

With a sage look, Bella's eyes swept over her. "Naw, but I think your trouble goes deeper."

With that, she got up and went out. Roxanna nearly went after her to apologize for speaking so harshly, but weariness stopped her at the door. Daylight was dwindling, and she looked past the men playing ball to the house on the hill.

Oh, Lord, You ask too much of me. Please provide a way of escape. I cannot bear the burden of being here any longer.

⁂

"Miss Rowan?"

Roxanna exited blockhouse headquarters and stepped into the path of a sturdy-looking man in fatigue dress. She had seen him before but hadn't paid him any particular mind. Now she looked at him—truly looked at him—for the first time, a tremor of self-consciousness sweeping through her.

"The name's Greer, Miss Rowan. Graham Greer. I was hoping to see the colonel."

She tried to smile, remembering Dovie's plea. "Colonel Mc-Linn is outside fort walls on maneuvers with his men." Truly, she'd hardly seen him the last fortnight or so. She studiously avoided him—and he seemed to be avoiding her, though she knew the coming campaign consumed all his energies. When he was within fort walls, he was always surrounded by his officers.

His hazel eyes registered uncertainty. "Since tomorrow is the Sabbath, I thought I might hold a service, see if anyone wants to come."

Her beleaguered heart warmed to the unexpected words. She stepped out from under the cool eave into the spring sunlight. "A Sabbath service sounds fine."

"Thought I'd better ask the colonel first."

"I doubt he'd mind," she ventured, not caring if he did. "It might be good for morale, especially in light of the coming campaign. And with so many of the men ill of late . . ."

He turned his tricorn hat absently in his hands. "The worst of the fever seems to be over. Mayhap a Sabbath service would be a fitting way to give thanks."

The humbleness in his tone touched her, and she smiled for the first time in days. "I'll see you in the morning, then."

"Aye, say, ten o'clock. Beneath the big elm."

28

A finer Sabbath morning Cass had never seen. The elms and oaks surrounding the stone house rustled like a spring symphony and cast lacy patterns of light upon the ground. Both sky and river shared the same azure hue, and all looked lush and peaceful, almost perfect—so at odds with his present predicament. From one open casement window, he could see a few men milling about the fort's parade ground in the early morning light.

The day before, he'd issued a few passes to the regulars for fishing or visiting sweethearts at Smitty's Fort, but most preferred to keep to their quarters and read or sleep. He'd been drilling them hard of late, and he didn't blame them. Much to their glee, the night before he'd allotted an extra gill of rum to every man, as much to ease their aching muscles as to assuage his conscience at driving them so.

Jehu Herkimer had brought him the first gill, and he felt almost foolish refusing. The look on the officer's face was almost comical, his surprise was so great. "Saving yourself for the better brandy, eh, Colonel?"

But Cass said nothing in reply, one thought skittering across his conscience. *Saving myself for Roxie Rowan.* Not a drop of liquor had passed his lips since the night he'd kissed her. He had only to recall the exquisite sweetness of holding her to

dispel any desire to drink again. Yet he couldn't deny the lure
of it, guilt-ridden as he was. He wanted something to dull his
pain, to take away the everlasting sting of what he'd done to her.

Now, looking down at the fort's confines, he could make out
her unmistakable form crossing the parade ground. The combi-
nation of sapphire silk and lace was hard to miss, but it was the
direction she was headed that was even more arresting. Under
the lone shade tree of the fort—a sturdy if aging elm near the
quartermaster's—Graham Greer waited at a makeshift podium
that was actually a barrel, his head bent over an open book.

A Bible, Cass guessed, in preparation for the morning's service. His uneasiness kindled as he watched her sink onto the
crude log bench nearest Greer, her skirts swirling in graceful
lines along the dusty ground. Though a respectful distance was
between them, Cass felt a fierce protectiveness rise up inside
him. What had she to do with Graham Greer?

No sooner had the question gained a foothold than he knew
the answer. Rumor was that Greer was smitten. Realizing it
firsthand made what Cass was about to do all the easier.

It was a bit past ten o'clock when Cass came down the hill.
Only a half dozen or so men had moved toward the elm to sit on
the makeshift seats for the service. Cass took a back bench well
behind Roxanna, the rising sun beating down with summerlike
intensity on his coat, making his neck bead with sweat. She had
no inkling he was near, though he found it hard to look away
from the gentle slope of her shoulders beneath the rich fabric
of her gown and the little wayward wisps of hair spiraling free
of its pins beneath her straw hat.

No sooner had he sat down than a good dozen of his men—all
officers—appeared. He kept his eyes forward as if unaware of
them, somewhat amused that his presence was more of a draw
than Greer's preaching. The Herkimer brothers sat on either

side of him, and then Micajah Hale took the bench alongside Patrick Stewart. In a few more moments, as if someone had rung a bell, came Johnny with Dovie and—could it be?—the rest of the Redstone women. Even little Abby.

Perhaps a Sabbath service was in order, then. He'd not graced one since he'd accompanied Washington to chapel in Virginia prior to his being sent west. At Truro Parish, where Washington served as vestryman and warden, there had been fine upholstered pews and finer music. Here there was not so much as a single prayer book, and his hands felt strangely empty. As empty as his soul. The admission cut him, left him feeling as vulnerable and exposed as a soldier with a broken musket.

He fastened his eyes on Roxie's still figure, his thoughts adrift. A conversation they'd had weeks before returned to him, gnawing at the edges of his mind just as it had ever since they'd spoken. She'd worn the same blue dress then. Perhaps that is why he thought of it now. As was her habit, she'd been sitting on a bench under her cabin eave that sunny Sabbath afternoon, Bible open on her lap, Abby beside her. She was unaware of him, but her softly spoken words seemed so arresting he couldn't simply pass.

"Who is among you that feareth the Lord . . . that walketh in darkness, and hath no light? Let him trust in the name of the Lord, and stay upon his God."

He made a move forward, and she looked up at him. He was struck by the poignancy of her expression. A telling wetness lined her lashes, brought about by the reading, he guessed, or some internal battle he couldn't see. Concerned, he sat down on the bench beside her as Abby scampered away.

"Isaiah?" he said, looking at the page.

She simply nodded, returning to the text, her handkerchief clutched in one hand.

"I've not read that particular Scripture," he told her. "Not that I remember."

"I've not either, till now."

271

"What do you make of it?"

She looked at him, surprise in her eyes. "Honestly?" When he nodded, she said, "I've been thinking of being hemmed in here, in this fort. And I believe this is simply a dark place where God, in His providence, has placed me."

"You don't feel forsaken, then?"

"Forsaken?" She hesitated, and he sensed her struggle for the right thought. "Sometimes I feel I'm walking in a sort of darkness, as the Scripture says. But now I see I must simply trust Him, keep my eyes on Him, and have faith that all will come right."

He looked out over the empty parade ground with something akin to loathing, and his own misgivings seemed to make a mockery of her heartfelt words. "And do you believe that God has called me here, to this fort, to have the same trust and faith, given my own situation?"

She turned her face to him. "Why should your being here—or your response—be any different than my own?"

"Because I lack your faith, Miss Rowan. Because Providence has indeed abandoned me. Because I feel as a somewhat superstitious Irishman and soldier that I've been brought here to die." Though he hadn't meant to speak harshly, he had, and he saw fresh tears glinting in her eyes.

"Is God not your commanding officer, Colonel McLinn?"

"In a sense."

"In *every* sense?"

He smiled thinly and looked down at the ground. "And as such, He can issue an order and do as He pleases with me, is that it?"

"Isn't it?"

He had no memory of what he'd said in response or the walk across the parade ground in the Sabbath stillness to headquarters. But her words followed him then and now, demanding an answer.

When, he wondered again, had he allowed himself the freedom to doubt God's eternal love and faithfulness? At what point had he discarded the faith he'd held close since childhood? Was God not a part of his life here . . . Richard Rowan's death . . . Roxie's coming? Despite all the turmoil, hadn't he felt a renewed sense of God's presence of late? Especially since he'd confessed to Roxie about her father?

Still, he was unsure of the task before him. She hadn't forgiven him, and it turned him more tense, making what he was about to do all the harder. Was he obeying what he felt the Lord was asking of him this day? Or simply letting his own lovesick heart skew his reason?

He watched as Greer thumbed through his Bible, his fair face a hearty red from so many eyes upon him, perhaps. But when he spoke, it was with a confidence gained from familiarity with the book he held in his hands. Cass thought it fitting that he read from Exodus about Joshua, given the coming campaign.

Though he'd come this morning to set an example, he hadn't expected to find much that would hold his interest, given his agonized thoughts, or at least divert it from the woman who was in his line of sight, completely still, her head bent as if drinking in every word. His admiration for her strengthened in that still instant. Despite the press of present circumstances, the pain and perplexity of the moment, she kept on. Steadfastly. Unswervingly.

Bravely . . . if broken.

Roxanna felt herself sliding toward sleep on the sun-drenched bench. It wasn't that Graham Greer's preaching was lacking. She was simply weary from too many sleepless nights and now succumbed to the warmth and wind of a Kentucke May, the leaves of the lone tree high above rustling like angels sharing secrets. Fortunately, the brim of her straw hat with its lace veil hid her half-shut eyes.

When the benediction was given, she roused herself and said a few words to Dovie before coming fully alert. Behind her, just rising from the back bench, was Cass. The sight brought a sharp pang. She'd not expected him at a Sabbath service. Standing head and shoulders above the knot of officers around him, he seemed about to turn away. She lowered her eyes to collect her lace mitts from the bench before looking up again, acutely aware that he was moving toward her—and every eye was upon them.

"Might I have a word with you, Miss Rowan?"

Resistance rose up inside her. But what was she to say? "All right," she murmured, moving into the shade of the elm.

"Not here. Outside fort walls. A walk, if you will."

Her lips parted in surprise. Under any other circumstances, a walk was a pleasant enough prospect, but venturing beyond fort walls might prove a hair-raising experience. Her bullet-ridden hat flashed to mind, and she gave him a slightly stiff smile. "Does your scalp mean so little to you, Colonel McLinn?"

He glanced skyward, but back to her again. "I've already petitioned Providence and invoked divine protection, ye ken."

She almost said no, but took his proffered arm instead, looking around for the guard. She felt no small inkling of alarm when she realized he'd dismissed them. The dust rose in little clouds beneath their feet as they exited through the sally port into a golden afternoon. Her pulse began a wild, untamed ticking in her throat and wrist. She didn't know if it was the heat or his bold invitation that turned her breathless.

Not one word did he utter as they walked up the hill. Weary, a bit too warm, she found herself wishing he would take her into the coolness of the house, then steeled herself against the memory of what had happened there. As they skirted the west wall and passed into the orchard, they were soon lost to view in the heavily leafed trees. Here apples and cherries had been planted so thick they held the promise of hope and permanence.

He seemed to be scrutinizing the outlying edges of the woods that grew in a green tangle beyond the fruit trees. Was he nervous without a guard? She certainly was, and relief flooded her when he went no further. There he stopped and looked down at her, and she realized in a little heart-catching rush that he meant something more than another apology.

His voice was husky, his lilt molasses-rich. "Roxie, I'm not a man who wastes words, so I'll just say it plain."

When she didn't look at him, he brought her chin up with his hand. Despite her most formidable intentions, the tender gesture turned her to jelly. His face held such an appealing earnestness—and her heart was so sore—she didn't think she could bear being alone with him like this . . .

"I've brought you up here to ask you to be my wife. To share my name and my life—come what may."

For a moment she felt the wind might push her over. All her senses seemed to scatter.

A proposal? Was he . . . jesting? Nay, he was not, and his raw honesty—his audacity—seemed to shatter her resistance. Frantic, she fought to stay grounded and took a step away from him.

"You ask for my hand? On the heels of your confession?" The words reeled out of her, blunt and unforgiving. "Do you honestly think I could conscience being wed to the man who killed my father?"

His eyes darkened with pain. "I'd hoped you would forgive me in time. Your father was like a father to me. I would have willingly—gladly—died in his stead. But there's no undoing what's been done. I'll live with the regret of it till my dying day. I'm asking you to look to the future—"

"Future?" She spat out the word in disgust. "What future?"

"*Our* future."

"We have no future. Why would you even ask—"

"Why?" He took her gently by the shoulders. "Because my head and heart are so full of you I can think of little else. Not

275

the coming campaign. Not the enemy within fort walls. Not even Liam McLinn."

She stiffened and tried to pull away. "Even if my father was still alive, there are too many other things at play. You are, by your own admission, lonely—"

"Lonely, aye, and lovesick—and a great many other things on account of your coming."

She shook her head, groping for excuses. "Circumstances might make me attractive to you here, but put me in a room full of colonial belles and you'd not notice me at all. I'm . . ."

"You're what, Roxie? Plain? Not genteel enough? Unintelligent? A bit lame?"

"For a man of your standing, yes."

A flash of exasperation rode his features. "I suppose your next argument will be that I ask for your hand because I'm beholden to your father on account of his dying wish—because I took his life. Or that I dishonored you by kissing you like I did, and as an officer and a gentleman I'm duty-bound to make things right."

"Yes, 'tis all those things—and more." Heat stung her cheeks, but her voice stayed firm. "We see things so differently, you and I. Too differently to allow for any lasting happiness. Our way of looking at the world—"

"At God, you mean."

"Yes, God. That is the very heart of it—and that is one of the reasons I must refuse you."

He fixed her with a bruising stare. "What kind of God would deny you marriage to the man you love?"

"I—I never said I loved you."

"You didn't have to." He gentled his tone and let go of her. "You care for me as deeply as I care for you, only you do a poorer job of hiding it. You still love me no matter what I've done, no matter how hurt you are. There's no denying it."

Beneath his keen gaze, she felt exposed, as if stripped to her shift. He was referring to their kiss, surely, looking past their wager over cribbage to the wealth of feeling beneath. Only he was contemplating it with far greater calm.

"Roxie, look at me and tell me you don't love me."

She stood as lifeless as Abby's rag doll, her insides twisting. It hurt her to look at him, to see the raw regret in his eyes, the wearied lines of his striking face. She turned away, but he simply came nearer, the buttons of his coat pressing into the soft silk of her bodice as his arms went round her. Her hat, pushed back by their closeness, fell in a lacy heap at her feet. She began to cry, sobbing into her hands, his breath warm against her ear.

"Roxie, I love you beyond all reason, and I'll not rest till you're living in the stone house, sharing my table and bed and all else I own."

"But you're about to go on a campaign . . ."

"Till then we'll take our fill of each other, making many a memory to carry us through the time left to us."

Her dream returned to her in a poignant rush—abed and about to deliver in the stone house—without him. Suddenly it made sense. He wasn't there because he'd been killed on some far-flung battlefield, never having known his son or daughter . . . "What if there's a child?"

"Then I ken there's no better way to leave you."

She rested her head against the fine cloth of his coat, feeling the strong heartbeat beneath. The premonition she'd felt sitting across from him in his study returned with sickening clarity.

"No matter what happens, no matter what's ahead, I'll not leave you wanting," he murmured, his calloused fingers a caress upon her damp cheek. "Congress has promised me a fine pension. With that and what's left of my inheritance, you'll be one of the wealthiest widows in the colonies."

She shut her eyes, the pain in her heart so sharp it seemed his words were naught but a knife.

"Roxie, what do we have in this life—except each other?"

What indeed? He was offering her the world—himself, a

home, perhaps a child. It was all she'd ever wanted, all any woman could hope for. Her new life could begin in the span of a few moments. She would not have to return to her father's crude cabin with all its lonesome ghosts but could stay on the hill, the mistress of the stone house. She could love him wholeheartedly and passionately, without reservation . . .

She took a step away from him and saw a shadow pass over his face. Despite the overwhelming check in her spirit, she said, "You were wrong to ask, to presume I would forgive you—continue to love you. I don't—and I never will."

He studied her, one hand resting on the hilt of his sword, his eyes a swimming blue. With her sharp, careless words, she'd wounded his pride and far more. Yet he stood before her straight and silent and noble. He wouldn't reveal the depth of his hurt. An officer was schooled in many things, particularly stoicism in the face of defeat, even heartache. Her father had been much the same.

For a moment she feared she'd not stay standing. Her grief at their quandary settled over her like a mourning shawl, so cold and heavy it seemed to push her into the ground. She couldn't shake the sense that by refusing him, by holding on to forgiveness, she'd shut the door on her future happiness—and his. The weight of her twenty-eight years seemed to rush in and crush her. Trembling, she bent and picked up her hat and walked away.

At the edge of the orchard, she looked back, but he wasn't looking at her. His eyes were on the deep green woods with their flickering lights and shadows. Perhaps he, like she, was past caring that there was no guard. Let the enemy rush in and wreak whatever havoc they would. It seemed far preferable to a barren life.

She walked down the hill unescorted, heart sinking lower with every step. She didn't know how she summoned the wherewithal to smile and nod at the people she passed on the way to her cabin—as if she'd just returned from a Sabbath stroll, not left her heart and discarded dreams in the orchard. Though she felt utterly broken, she knew he was wounded as well—and she feared the consequences.

Oh, Cass, don't drink your disappointment away. One day you'll see that I was right to refuse you.

Yet even as she thought it, she wished for a little blackberry wine to take away the sting of her own unhappiness. She craved aloneness, yet the parade ground was full of spring revelers singing "Johnny Has Gone for a Soldier" and playing with pewter whizzers and rawhide balls. Beneath the lone elm where the Sabbath service had been held, some enthusiastic betting was going on over a well-watched game of cribbage. The sight nearly made her wince, and she shut the door of her cabin, wishing she could shut away her sorrow as easily.

Benumbed, she was hardly aware of setting her hat aside and making tea. She reached for the cup and saucer, but they were no longer resting high on the mantel, their graceful porcelain lines reminding her of all she'd just forsaken. She took a pewter cup and waited for the kettle to boil, startled when a soft knock came at the door.

Oh, Lord, I cannot face anyone now, especially Bella.

Very slowly, Abby pushed open the door. Her face held a rare pensiveness, her pale features twisted with worry. Without waiting for an invitation, she came inside and slipped onto a stool. Roxanna took a steadying breath.

"You're just in time for tea, Abby," she said, trying to smile. "Sukey can join us if she likes."

In answer, Abby set her rag doll at the table with a little acorn cup, placing its cloth hands together as if saying a prayer. Then she took Roxanna's hands and folded them between her own. The tender gesture touched every raw nerve Roxanna had. With a sob, she sank down on the bench, taking Abby in her arms. Through the emotional storm, she felt a little hand patting her head and shoulder. It was just her and Abby now, and that would have to do.

Thank You, Lord, for a little girl who understands heartache.

29

Cass watched Roxanna walk down the hill, shoulders stooped and steps slowed, as if he and not she had just refused an offer of marriage. Gut instinct told him to go after her, that his hold on her was solid enough she might give in if he asked a second time. But the sting of rejection was too strong, so he shoved sentiment aside and thought of how he'd erred in his asking and might have mounted a better offensive. Despite his best intentions, of not wanting to hurt her from the first, he'd created a double tragedy with his blatant confession and proposal. Her heated words chipped away at any hopes he had of their future together, however brief, and left him hollow, even a bit breathless.

You were wrong to ask, to presume I would forgive you— continue to love you. I don't—and I never will.

So hopeful he'd been that she'd forgive him—accept him—that he'd told Hank to ready the ballroom and his best dress uniform. Best reverse that order, he thought ruefully, before Hank got to Bella and Bella got to the fort.

Entering through the back door, he heard Hank's footfall upstairs, high on the third floor. "Hank!"

"Comin', sir," came the answering call.

Cass met him on the landing, removing his cross belts and

280

handing them to Hank before unbuttoning his uniform coat. "Shut the ballroom down. There's to be no celebration." Though Cass had never said the word *wedding*, Hank had been hard at work ever since Cass left the stone house for the Sabbath service, clearly as confident as he. And now that it was off, he looked as crestfallen as Cass felt.

"You sure, sir?"

"Aye, as sure as the Redcoats are over that river."

"I'm awful sorry, sir—'bout Miz Roxanna and them Redcoats."

"You no doubt saw us in the orchard."

Hank's face crumpled in concern. "I surely did, though I didn't aim to. I was airin' out the ballroom and just happened to look down—"

"I'd be obliged if you didn't mention it—not even to Bella." His stern look reinforced the order.

"Guess a man's got a right to keep his heartache to hisself," Hank lamented.

Shrugging off his coat, Cass felt the damp linen of his shirt clinging to him in places. The day was too warm for wool, but 'twas his angst over her refusal that left him sweating, not the heat. "The course of true love ne'er did run smooth, so Shakespeare said."

Hank hung his head. "You be wantin' some whiskey, sir—or a bit o' brandy?"

"Nay, spirits are a poor substitute for what I want." With that, he passed into his room and shut the door, then in one glance wished he hadn't. He'd walked into a bridal bower.

Flowers spilled out of vases about the room—clusters of redbud and white dogwood in full bloom, and hepatica looking like the sky turned upside down. Fresh linens graced the immense canopy bed, and his best uniform was waiting just as he'd asked. The scent of early summer was everywhere, and the joyous sunlight slanting through the open windows onto the clean plank floor seemed to make a mockery of his misery.

Passing a hand over his jaw, he pondered his next move, then went out and down the curving steps to the sanctuary of his study. Going to his writing desk, he took out a piece of paper and stub of pencil and began to empty his mind of the memory of her. He worked hard and fast as if doing so could expunge his need—a heavy stroke of dark hair here, the thoughtful brow and expressive eyes there, the full, kissable mouth, all contained within the graceful oval of her face.

Finishing, he reached into his breast pocket, removed the locket, and flicked it open. His own rendering was, vanity aside, the superior of the two. He'd captured her just as she'd been in the orchard half an hour before. Vulnerable. Broken. Heartrendingly lovely.

And amazingly resolute.

Leaning back in his chair, he expelled a ragged breath. For the first time in his military career, if not his life, he had no game plan, no counteroffensive. He was left to lick his wounds in private. Roxanna Rowan was proving a formidable opponent. He was more in love with her than ever. And more convinced he didn't deserve her, or her forgiveness, even had she offered it.

❧❧

Come Monday, Roxanna had composed herself enough to sit with her lap desk on her knees and write with a steady hand. As if Cassius Clayton McLinn had merely taken her into the orchard to admire the apple blossoms, not propose marriage. She kept her eyes down lest he see straight to her soul and, in his astute way, discover her conflicted feelings for him had only deepened in the ensuing hours, not dwindled. The fact that she'd lied to him—had used her hurt and anger like a weapon against him—stole her peace. His poignant words returned to her again and again, tearing at her heart.

Roxie, what do we have in this life—except each other?

Even now 'twas nearly more than she could bear. She'd considered telling him she could no longer serve as scrivener and thus escape to the kitchen, but he'd behaved so honorably in the face of rejection she couldn't act dishonorably with him. He'd not been drinking, she knew. The lackluster look brought about by a binge was missing this morning, and she felt profound relief. He was sharp-eyed, terse, and almost unbearably in charge, while she was a quivering mess of contradictions.

Numbly she sat, the officers around her, Cass among them, listening as they discussed the latest reports out of the Ohio country. Despite her heartache, she felt at home in this room, lap desk before her, the scent of leather and smoke and tobacco like old, familiar friends. This was the pulse of frontier life, and she was a part of it. Fort Endeavor's rise or fall depended on the efforts of everyone present, even she herself in her own small way, and she wanted it to survive if only for his sake.

As she sifted sand over wet ink, she stole a look at him. His arms were folded, his chin tilted toward his chest, eyes upon a detailed map of the middle ground spread across his desk. She wondered how he could stand there looking so nonchalant as if contemplating little more than a game of chess instead of the enemy across the river.

The scouts were speaking in low tones, but the news they brought was chilling. Redcoats were amassing in large numbers at the northern post commanded by Liam McLinn—and so were a great many Indians, not only Shawnee but Wyandot, Miami, and Delaware. Fort Endeavor's reinforcements were en route from Virginia but still unaccounted for. There were also reports of some schism among the Shawnee—those septs who wanted war and those who pursued peace. Her head seemed to swim with all the details.

"Even if the promised reinforcements materialize, we're outnumbered twenty to one," Cass told them. "With so many Indian allies among the British, the war will be waged a far bloodier way. No Redcoat commander, not even Lucifer himself, will be able to keep them in check."

Joram Herkimer nodded, face grim. "Recent reports of the British and Iroquois fighting the Americans in the east seem to bear that out."

"I say it's suicide to cross the river and meet them. They'll mow us down," Micajah murmured. "Surely—"

Cass silenced him with a look and gestured to the map spread on the desk. "So you advocate staying put and letting them destroy the settlements instead?"

Roxanna tensed as the next half hour escalated into something of a debate over strategy, Joram and Micajah eyeing one another with barely veiled hostility. It was clear the two men had no great liking for each other. When Cass stepped outside with the scouts, Micajah grabbed the lapel of Joram's coat, tearing free a brass button. It rolled toward Roxanna and she bent to retrieve it. Before she could right herself, a sudden blow sent Joram reeling backward. He missed her but collided with her lap desk where it perched on a stool. Inkpots, quills, and sand scattered in all directions as an orderly rushed to her assistance.

No one heard Cass enter. They were too intent on Joram as he righted himself and charged Micajah like a wounded bull. Cass stepped into his path, blocking the blow, then took Micajah by his coat collar and propelled him toward the open door.

"Out!" he shouted. "Every man present!"

His voice ricocheted round the room like a spent musket ball and sent them all shamefaced and scrambling onto the parade ground. Only Roxanna remained, gathering up the wayward quills and pots the orderly had missed, watching the spilled ink bleed into the wood floor. Cass knelt beside her and made short work of the mess, but she could feel his anger override his calm of minutes before.

Afraid to say much of anything, she did manage, "I can clean it up, Ca—Colonel."

"Cass—or Colonel?" He straightened to his full height, her forced politeness seeming to rile him further. "I will not play these games, ye ken. You'll always be Roxie to me, not Miss Rowan. And I'm still in love with you—and wanting to make you my wife—and I'll be hanged if I pretend otherwise."

"Cass, please . . ." His candor made the heat crawl into her face, and she felt a fresh rush of tears.

"Have a seat," he told her, jaw tight.

She obliged, taking the chair he offered, surprised when he took the one opposite and sat nearly knee to knee with her. She kept her eyes on his hands as he reached inside his coat and withdrew a letter.

Without preamble, he said, "I'm replacing you as scrivener."

Her eyes fastened on his face, his words hammer-hard and hurtful. She heard herself say calmly, "That is your right."

His gaze was like river rock, so cold it seemed he'd never been tender toward her. "A soldier's daughter to the end, aye?"

She didn't flinch. "What would you have me say? I'll not beg to stay."

He opened the letter. "Then perhaps you'll be more agreeable to my second offer than my first."

She realized then how much she'd hurt him by her refusal to marry him, and it softened her toward what he was about to say. Likewise, his voice lost some of its heat, and he leaned back in his chair and looked toward the doorway to make sure they were alone. "Soon after your father died, I dispatched a courier to Philadelphia. I have close friends there—devout Patriots by the name of Alexander and Ruth Hazen. They wrote me back straightaway, but I've only just received their reply."

She took the letter from him, wonder unfolding inside her. Was this the answer to her prayer? The handwriting was a woman's—light upon the page, as fragile looking as lace. Within the elegant prose was an invitation. The words were so heartwarming they hurt her. She scanned past the introduction to the poignant summons beneath.

Alexander and I lost a beloved daughter last year, and all the life and light in our house seems to have passed with her. It would be a privilege to have Roxanna come and stay with us for as long as she likes—for the war's duration, perhaps permanently. We are saddened by hearing of her own loss. Perhaps we could be of some comfort, each to the other . . .

She stopped reading, the words a blur of black ink. He'd replaced her as scrivener. She had a chance to make a home elsewhere. The opportunity to escape this dangerous place was open to her as never before . . . and she felt nothing but a gaping emptiness.

Oh, Lord, is this what You have for me, then?

Eyes on the letter, she asked, "How would I get there?"

"A keelboat from Fort Pitt is due any day with a supply of guns and a replacement scrivener. The captain and crew will take you back upriver. 'Tis dangerous, but safer than staying here, ye ken."

"You want me to go."

"I want you out of harm's way."

"'Tis so . . . unexpected." The words were out of her mouth before she realized their irony. She'd wanted to leave here the moment she learned of Papa's passing, and now, mere months later, it seemed a punishment to do so. The realization left her reeling. "Thank you," she murmured, folding up the letter and pocketing it.

Her mind—and heart—were already leaping ahead to Philadelphia, to a new life, albeit reluctantly. The blockhouse receded, and she envisioned elegant papered walls and a sitting room in the Hazens' fine town house. Music. Books. Dancing. Sparkling conversation. Only she was still a spinster, filled with bitterness over what had befallen her here, her every thought of him . . .

"Roxie."

The empty scene snapped shut, and she looked at him again, obviously unrepentant and bent on sending her away. But his tone was tender, and his eyes, such a startling, soul-arresting blue, held hers as only a man in love could do.

Could it be?

"'Tis best for the both of us, ye ken," he said.

There was no denying this. Once apart, they could get on with their lives . . . forget. She'd go to Philadelphia and he'd return to Williamsburg, or Ireland perhaps, though he might well be hung as a traitor there. Truly, the Hazens' invitation seemed a godsend. She'd think no more about his plans or the future he claimed he wouldn't have.

He stood and his voice rolled over her, crisp in its finality. "I've no more need of you today. I have to discipline my men."

She glanced down at the ink stains on the floor and felt it was her heart twisted and bleeding upon the pine planks instead. Setting her lap desk aside, she stood and forced herself to say, "Thank you for making the arrangements for me."

Their eyes met and held, and then she looked away. For a few seconds she thought he might take back the letter and throw it into the fire. His expression was, for the briefest of seconds, besieged. She tried to translate that look and couldn't, for it didn't match the man she'd come to know. Certainly not the man in charge of the entire western frontier. Seeing him thus shook loose what little security was left in her ever-changing world.

In the golden half-light of dusk as she left the necessary, Roxanna felt someone shadowing her. Taking the lavender-scented handkerchief from her nose, she turned to see Graham Greer standing by the corral where the officers' horses were milling restlessly. Cass's Shawnee stallion snorted and blew as she passed, as if chastening her for the apple peelings she'd forgotten.

"Might I speak with you, Miss Rowan?"

"Hello, Private Greer."

He removed his tricorn and held it over his heart. A charming gesture, she thought, even if he hadn't meant it to be. They'd not spoken since the Sabbath service, though it seemed he was intent on doing just that in the fading light. When he hesitated, she was struck by a latent realization. Was he truly smitten?

Her own throat felt bone-dry, but she managed to say, "'Twas a fine Sabbath service—and well attended."

"I'm afraid it's to be my last."

"Oh?" She felt a strange twist of regret. "Are you leaving?"

He smiled and offered his arm. "*We're* leaving, Miss Rowan. Colonel McLinn assigned a guard to guide you to Philadelphia. I'm personally responsible for seeing you safely to the Hazens' doorstep."

Her steps nearly faltered. "He—what?"

"Half a dozen regulars received orders to that effect today. I have a letter of introduction right here."

"Yes . . . of course." Feeling caught off guard, she tried to summon good sense. Since learning of the Hazens' invitation this morning, she'd been unable to push past her hurt to think of the particulars. Of course Cass would have assigned a guard—he'd not leave her unescorted with polemen of questionable character. "Thank you for telling me."

They walked slowly past the sally port, moving under the deep eave of the commissary that afforded more privacy. She was barely aware of katydids croaking a throaty tune beyond the walls and bursts of laughter erupting from a near porch. A multitude of eyes followed them from every quarter. One thing she wouldn't miss upon leaving Fort Endeavor was the utter lack of privacy.

"What will you do once you see me safely there?" she asked quietly.

"I was hoping you'd ask that."

The conversation had taken an intimate turn. Graham's gaze

held hers in a way only a man with romantic notions would do, and she found herself studying him in a new way. His eyes—were they blue or brown? Why hadn't she noticed how attractive he was? The answer sprang to mind in a heartbeat.

Because she'd been drowning in Cass McLinn.

"I'm thinking of staying on in Philadelphia for a fortnight before making my way back to Virginia," he said.

"I heard you have a farm in Fairfax County."

"Aye, on the main road near Thistleton Hall."

Her heart did an absurd little dance. *Home.* "I know it well."

"Mayhap this is too soon, but I'd be pleased to take you there."

She paused, a bit lightheaded. Since Cass's confession—and proposal—she'd hardly eaten, and now, amidst this turn of events, she felt faint. *Lord, is this my way of escape?* Relief and grief tugged at her so fiercely that tears came to her eyes.

He studied her in the half-light. "If you don't mind my saying so, there's a bit of talk about the fort that you and the colonel have parted company. I wouldn't press my suit otherwise."

She bit her lip and balled her hankie into a fist, glad when they resumed walking. "I'm flattered by your offer, but my life is in such disarray I think I'd best ponder it all before making any plans."

"I understand," he replied. "But if it's any consolation, I've been praying and feel the Almighty has brought us together for a purpose."

Had He? Graham sounded so sure, and she clung to his words like a drowning woman being thrown a bit of ballast. She was about to embark on yet another journey. If she made it to Philadelphia, what then? The Hazens' home shone bright as a beacon in her stormy thoughts. If she was ever to forget Cass, might she meet someone in the city? Or should she simply accept Graham's invitation and return to Virginia?

Oh, Lord, things are happening so fast. Please make the path plain to me.

289

30

Dawn's intrusion through the windows was a welcome sight. Around midnight Cass had been jerked awake by a dream so disturbing it took all his will not to cry out. Sleepless ever since, he'd lain awake in the humid darkness, only to have Roxie rush in and banish the blackness. Roxie with her violet scent and inky hair and soulful eyes. If he couldn't have her, hold her, he could still possess her in the stillness of daybreak and feel his arms around her in sweet recollection.

Lately he'd prayed for God to guide and protect her, to let her go to Philadelphia in safety and peace. Yet without her—without her steadying, comforting presence and her prayers—he felt himself slipping further into darkness. Despite her avowals that she didn't love him and never would, she seemed the last shred of light he had against the coming campaign. His dread of what awaited him deepened by the day.

Liam's malevolence seemed to be reaching across the river, ruffling that smooth expanse of green water, encroaching on his sleep. In his dream he'd faced him, faced his Redcoat army and a great many Indians, his own men having deserted him. Liam was demanding he give an accounting of his sins. Somehow—but how?—Liam knew about Richard Rowan and the men mistakenly shot at dusk. Because of this, Cass was to be stripped of his commission and sent to Ireland in disgrace.

Outside the window a lark trilled, and he reached for the locket he'd taken out of his uniform coat the night before. On the bedside table it lay open, a keepsake Roxanna didn't know he had. Snapping it shut, he felt a despair he'd never known. He was sick to death of secrets.

Roxanna stood up in her garden, lush vines of melons and gourds in a green tangle at her feet. With one hand she steadied a bowl of peas against her hip, and with the other she shaded her eyes against the glare. Lately she always seemed to be looking upriver for the keelboat that would take her east, but since Cass had told her of its coming the week before, nothing except a heron or two had disturbed the water. It flowed green and empty past Fort Endeavor as if taunting her packed trunk and unmet expectations.

Turning, she thanked the guard who'd stood watch as she'd worked, and made her way to the sally port, careful to keep her eyes off the stone house. It was quiet this morning, as Cass had gone downriver on some business at Smitty's Fort. She'd seen him and the guard ride out, leaving Micajah Hale in command. A lingering cloud of dust rose in the wake of a woodcutting detail that had just exited the gates. Inside the fort, regulars were busy about the parade ground and commissary, and it seemed a great many more men were on watch than usual.

All around her, birdsong threaded the warm air and the sky was an unclouded blue. Kentucke was a paradise, she mused, but it still needed an army to defend it. Would it always?

She entered the kitchen, thankful to find it empty, and wrinkled her nose at the smell of burned bacon and greasy eggs. It being washday, Bella and the Redstone women had gone to the river and left the cooking to her and Dovie. She lifted a linen cloth and peered at a giant mound of dough cocooned in a wooden tray, then started shelling peas. Her garden was hardly big enough to feed the entire post, so she named it her officer's garden, giving its bounty to "the chosen twelve," as Bella called them. LeSourd had shot a buffalo, and two huge roasts were spitted over a smoky fire just beyond the back door. Though she disliked the gamey taste, the men seemed to relish it.

Perspiration beaded her upper lip as she finished the peas and began peeling a small mountain of potatoes. Adding some of both to the stew Bella had started, she turned to find Dovie filling the doorway to the dining room, hands full of fresh herbs. Her plump face was creased with concern, her waist so expansive that Roxanna wondered if she might deliver sooner than planned. Or might she be having twins?

"I hear you're leavin' on the next keelboat."

Her expression was so plaintive Roxanna felt a spasm of remorse. Was Dovie hurt that she hadn't shared the news? "I—it's only just been decided." Truly, she'd been so steeped in pain and the suddenness of the plan she'd given little thought to anyone else. "I'm sorry, Dovie. I was going to tell you . . ."

Crossing to the table, Dovie set the herbs down and fingered her apron. "I disbelieved it when Bella told me. I was countin' on you bein' with me when the baby comes."

"Colonel McLinn has made the arrangements, otherwise I'd stay. Things have become so . . . complicated. 'Tis better I go."

Tears glittered in Dovie's eyes, turning her touchingly child-like. "I never thought you'd abandon your friends, Miz Roxanna. You're needed here. I need you."

"But you have Johnny, and Mariah and Nancy—"

"That ain't the same. Everybody says you're helpin' hold this post together, nearly as much as Colonel McLinn. I know you don't believe it, but it's true. Johnny says since you've come, the colonel's a changed man. And that bodes well for the rest of us. If you go, you're liable to take the heart right out o' this place."

"But we can't stay penned up in this fort forever, Dovie. We have to get on with our lives, whenever the opportunity presents itself to leave this place."

With a sigh, Dovie nodded halfheartedly, her gaze searching. "You all right, Miz Roxanna? You look a mite peaked." Raising a hand, she brought the hem of her apron to her brow. "This kitchen's so hot I'd rather be on wash duty down at the river, Injuns or no." Turning, she moved to open the back door wider, securing it with a bucket.

Swallowing down the knot thickening in her throat, Roxanna asked, "Dovie . . . does Johnny ever . . . talk about the last campaign?"

"You mean the one when your pa—and them others—got killed?" When Roxanna nodded, she said, "He don't ever mention it, least to me. But he'd be the last man to speak ill of Colonel McLinn, respectin' him like he does." She perched on a stool, mouth drawn. "Now, Johnny ain't so fond of Major Hale."

"Oh?"

"Got a chip on his shoulder as wide as that river out there, Johnny says. And he ain't too fond of Hank neither."

Raising a handkerchief to her own damp brow, Roxanna said, "Please . . . think no more of it." She began taking out bread pans, greasing them and setting them out by rote. Wordlessly they formed the dough into loaves to let rise, and Roxanna fought the expanding ache in her chest. Finally she said, "Dovie, I'm not feeling well. I'd best go back to my cabin for a spell."

"You go on, Miz Roxanna. I can finish up here."

On her way across the dusty parade ground, she spied Cass coming through the postern gate atop his stallion, two officers and the guard in his wake. Anger flared inside her, hot and bright as a candle flame, only to be extinguished by a rush of relief. Outside fort walls, he was ever so vulnerable. She never felt at rest when he was away.

Especially since she'd removed the protective covering of her prayers.

※ ※

"Keelboat comin'!"

Roxanna heard the regular's hoarse cry and wished she could share in the excitement it wrought. In the sultry May twilight, she watched half the parade ground empty as she stood in the doorway of her cabin. Since the officers were still eating, the regulars were assigned to welcome the boat in. In a few days' time it would take her upriver, once the cargo was unloaded and the relieved crew drank enough rum to brave the trip back east, so Bella told her.

She turned and took in her packed trunk. Already the tiny cabin had an empty, inhospitable feel. Who would occupy it next, she wondered? Whoever it was, she pitied them. She sat down, weary from a long day in the kitchen. Moments before, she'd left the serving to Bella and the Redstone women, overwhelmed with all that faced her. Philadelphia promised a refuge . . . peace. But would she ever reach it?

Dovie's words still haunted her, made her feel she was indeed abandoning them all. Thrusting through her turmoil was Abby's little face—Abby, who seemed on the verge of emerging from her silent cocoon, the only soul who seemed to bloom in this dangerous place. If Abby spoke, Roxanna would be gone and wouldn't witness the miracle.

She left the cabin and joined the soldiers hurrying to the river. But before she was halfway down the hill she sensed something was horribly amiss. The vessel seemed to be limping along, and only one man was standing on the broad deck. Had there been a plague? A fight? One long look confirmed the latter. Pausing by her garden, she could see the devastation littering the keelboat's deck. Goosebumps crawled all over her.

She was barely aware of Cass coming and taking command of

the situation, his calm a startling counterpoint to her trembling. Though no one said a word, she surmised in a few brief moments the truth of the matter. She wouldn't be leaving Kentucke now—perhaps ever.

☙❧

A sheen of perspiration that had nothing to do with the Kentucke heat speckled Cass's brow as he set foot on the riverbank. Everyone seemed to be watching him, gauging his reaction to so much carnage in so small a space. Ginseng and molasses and rum poured forth from hatchet-marked crates and barrels around the fallen men. Flies swarmed in black clouds over both cargo and bodies, and the stench was nearly unbearable.

Swallowing down the bile backing up in his throat, he waded through the water in his boots till he could grasp a hemp rope and help haul the vessel in. The lone man at the tiller regarded him with hollow eyes. Cass had seen that look in soul-sick men after battle and could feel the morale of those watching plummeting all around him.

There was no reason the lone riverman should have been alive—save one. He'd been spared solely to deliver a message. Cass sensed it even before he boarded the boat. Pity stabbed him as he took in the older man's trembling hands and ashen face and noticed he leaned on the tiller not to steer it but to support himself. It took great effort for him to fumble inside his soiled linen shirt and pull a paper free. A sudden gust of wind snatched the missive from the man's bony fingers, and it landed at Cass's feet.

"You're safe now," Cass told him in low tones, retrieving the paper.

The man nodded jerkily and looked back over the deceptively tranquil river. "Mebbe . . . mebbe not."

The scarlet seal of the letter seemed to confirm the dire words. Cass tucked it inside his coat and reluctantly turned toward the bank. His glance landed on Micajah, but he hardly heard his own order. "Bury the bodies and burn the boat."

He glanced uphill and saw Roxie standing by her garden fence. Even at a distance he read misery in her gaze. Turning away, he began searching the vessel, putting together the pieces of this macabre puzzle that held particular significance to him. This was the embodiment of his bad dream—yet another part of the terrible premonition that his life was now measured in days . . . hours. The evil he'd felt was indeed reaching across the river. Every one of his senses, straining with the stench of blood and buzzing insects, told him so.

As soon as he stepped onto shore, the burial detail got to work. He trudged up the hill, careful to avert his face from the woman whose fate was in his hands and who, if he'd had his way and sent her upriver, might well have ended up among the carnage.

Roxanna pulled her gaze from Cass's retreating form and tried to get the attention of the guards who stood as woodenly as the chess pieces in office headquarters, their eyes trained on the river and woods. Finally one did break rank and return her to the fort. Thanking him, she spied Abby just inside the sally port, the chaos of the moment engraved on her small face.

Forcing a smile, Roxanna held out her hand, solaced when the grubby little fingers found her own. Oh, but she was in dire need of another bath. Lately Olympia had been ignoring her altogether, and her red crown of curls was naught but a briar patch. A bit of rose soap and a clean linen shift would soon set her to rights again. 'Twould be a blessed distraction, Roxanna thought, if she could keep from breaking down.

In half an hour's time, she'd heated enough water to turn the rain barrel under the eave into a fine bath. Abby thrashed about in the tub, covered with soapy bubbles, her hair a wet ruby red. She'd recently lost a front tooth, which made her dimpled smile all the more winsome. For the first time since their meeting, Roxanna was almost glad the girl was mute. At least there'd be no fielding curious questions . . . .

Why are all the soldiers hurrying so? Why are big buzzards circling above? Where is Colonel McLinn?

Roxanna took ample time scrubbing her head, not once but twice, picking at the little scalp beforehand. When she was done, the comb slid through the clean, tangle-free curls, and Roxanna threaded a rose ribbon throughout. She was rewarded with a tight hug.

"Would you like me to read you a story, Abby? I have *Aesop's Fables* in my trunk." Roxanna knelt and began scrubbing Abby's soiled dress in the bathwater before wringing it out to dry. "I'll make us some tea first."

Abby nodded and went to fetch Sukey out of Roxanna's sewing basket, then rocked the doll by the hearth. The tea made and drunk, the two of them settled in the rocking chair. With Abby on her lap, Roxanna began to read but could hardly push the words past the knot in her throat. Within moments, Bella came, expression grim. Seeing Abby, she left without a word.

"There goes an old story of a Country-Mouse . . ."

As she read, her mind kept returning to the river. Why such carnage? What had the surviving poleman given Cass that he'd tucked in his coat?

"She visited a City-Sister of hers . . ."

Her voice trailed off as she realized Abby had fallen asleep in her arms. The suddenly still room invited unwanted thoughts. She kept rocking, waiting for a knock or summons at her door. But no one need come and tell her she'd not be going upriver. The facts were plain. Civilization was now beyond her reach. She was locked within the Kentucke territory. There would be no abandoning Fort Endeavor. Yet she felt . . . nothing. Not dismay. Not relief.

Only emptiness.

31

Everyone seemed to be walking on eggshells, Roxanna included. Even at this early hour, headquarters was stifling, the stench of sweat overwhelming. She tried not to think that she might have been well on her way to Philadelphia by now, a replacement scrivener occupying her Windsor chair. But the man who'd been sent to relieve her had been on the ransacked keelboat and was now buried on the hill. She didn't even know his name.

As she finished sifting sand over a document that told of a change in strategy and timing for the coming campaign, she wondered if it was just a ruse to confuse the elusive spy. The men of Fort Endeavor would soon march north, so the dictation read, and invade the middle ground far earlier than planned. Simply penning the words sent a chill up her spine and blunted her anger. If she was ever inclined to believe men reaped what they sowed, the coming conflict was to be Cass's punishment in spades for killing her father.

Stopping the inkpot, she darted a glance at him. There was no denying the strain he was under. Though his handsome face failed to betray a hint of unease, she sensed his deep distress. He was perusing maps with his officers, and Micajah's foot was rat-a-tat-tatting in a nervous rhythm that set her teeth on edge.

Without looking up, Cass said, "Kindly control your foot, Major Hale."

The leg stilled, only to be replaced by a nervous tic pulling at Joram Herkimer's left eye. There was a brief, expectant hush as one of the orderlies brought over an armful of maps. He tripped and jarred the table, spilling the maps in every direction.

Cass looked at the mess and said quietly, "Hobbes, 'tis the third time I've had to clean up after you and 'tis not yet noon."

The orderly shrank at the rebuke and bent to retrieve the maps, bumping his head on the desk edge and overturning a vial of ink. It splashed over the freshly made map Cass had labored over since dawn. In response, Cass brought his fist down on the desk with such ferocity every man jumped.

He uttered a Gaelic curse, his voice lashing them like a whip. "Out—every one of you!"

All scrambled to do his bidding, even Roxanna. But the last officer out shut the door before she could escape, and it was just the two of them in the tense, warm room.

"What say ye, Miss Rowan?"

She felt a bittersweet pang. 'Twas the first time he'd acknowledged her in any way for days. She put away her work, aware of his eyes on her. All she could dredge up from her torn, beleaguered heart was a finishing school rule, and it was little more than a whisper. "Detract not from others, neither be excessive in commanding."

"Guilty as charged."

Guilty of a great many things, she thought, shutting her lap desk a bit too forcefully.

"I apologize," he said quietly, rolling up the ruined map and depositing it in the empty hearth.

She met his hard gaze, rebuking herself for thinking he could have ever loved her, had ever been tender toward her. In that excruciating instant, she saw everything so clearly. Guilt had driven him to offer marriage, not love, and her refusal had wounded far more than his pride. Tears pricked her eyes, and she felt an unbearable, swelling resentment toward him—

And then the door pushed open and Abby stood there.

Roxanna felt a breathless dismay at being interrupted but was amazed that a child's sudden appearance could shift the room's dark shadows. Her reddish-gold hair glowed like a halo in the bright sunlight just outside the door. She looked like an angel, even remembering her manners, not setting foot inside till Cass motioned for her to enter. Then she smiled her wide smile and walked over to the chess board, where she curtsied. The lacquered pieces—staunch rows of British and American soldiers—stood on the mahogany top as if begging for a game to begin.

"I've no time for it today, Abby," he murmured apologetically.

Her little face dimmed like the sun going behind a cloud and strengthened Roxanna's ill feeling toward him.

"I have something better," he said.

Abby perked up again and held out her hand to him with an endearing familiarity. He took it, the hard, lean lines of his face softening as he looked down at her. They went out through the open door, and Roxanna could hear him calling to one of the regulars on the parade ground. Moving to the open window, she watched a soldier lead a pony out of a far corral. Its glossy coat shone a sooty black as it walked docilely through the dust.

Plucking her off the ground, Cass deposited Abby atop the saddled back. She sat as if stunned while he bent to fit her feet into the stirrups and showed her how to hold the reins. "He's your pony and he needs a name. What will you call him?"

The pointed question carried on a warm wind to Roxanna, and she leaned onto the sill, watching Abby open her mouth as if to answer.

Speak, Abby . . . speak. Oh, how she ached to hear the sound of Abby's voice! Was it childishly high or melodiously low? Would it hold a lisp, as she was missing a front tooth?

When her little mouth clamped shut, Roxanna felt a sharp disappointment. Did Cass feel the same?

Holding on to the bridle, he led the pony around the flagpole and magazine a few times, stopping by the quartermaster's to obtain a coveted sugar lump. 'Twas a touching moment, Roxanna thought grudgingly, given he didn't have time for such things, and the state of his temper.

Far across the dusty common, Olympia stood in the doorway of her cabin, half dressed, eyeing the poignant scene. Roxanna felt an urge to go and speak to her, if only to avoid Cass.

As she exited the blockhouse, she could smell meat roasting in back of the kitchen and wondered if Bella needed help. Lately Olympia hadn't been showing for kitchen duty, irking Bella severely, though the other women covered for her. Another Saturday night frolic was just days away, though Roxanna wondered if it would be cancelled because of the keelboat disaster—or Olympia's absences.

As she neared, Olympia regarded her with bloodshot eyes. Stale liquor emanated from her like tawdry perfume, and the lines in her face seemed to have deepened overnight. "I've been meanin' to thank you for seein' to Abby."

"She's no trouble," Roxanna reassured her, looking again at the parade ground. Off her pony now and sucking on a sugar lump, Abby waved a hand at them. Cass, she noticed, had since disappeared, and a regular supervised in his wake. "I was thinking how much life she brings into this fort, even if she doesn't speak."

"Makes up for those of us who got little spark left."

The words were flat, defeated, so unlike Olympia that Roxanna stared at her, new worries dawning. How could she not have noticed how her dress hung loosely on her once voluptuous frame, the pale skin stretched taut over high cheekbones almost skeletal in the glaring light? Had her own preoccupations blinded her to the need in front of her? First Abby's mother . . . and now her aunt.

Lord, is there nothing but death and destruction in this place?

"I didn't realize you were ill. Why don't I speak to the colonel about sending for Dr. Clary?" Roxanna said quietly. She noted the stubborn set of Olympia's jaw at the suggestion. Was she still sore over Cass's callous treatment of Nancy and the deserters? The mere mention of the colonel always got her bristling.

"I doubt he'll send for 'im, but you can try."

Roxanna felt a rush of compassion for her—and fresh ire toward Cass. "I'll see if he's in his office."

Olympia shrugged, and Roxanna traced her steps, aware of a great many eyes on her. Cass's office door yawned open, his officers and the orderlies still scattered. He sat at his desk penning something with furious haste, nearly driving the quill into the paper, she thought. His anger of earlier was still palpable, and the fire in his eyes didn't diminish one whit when he looked up at her. He had no patience for small talk, of course. He seemed to be seething with impatience despite his forced cordiality.

Standing on the opposite side of his desk, she got right to the point. "I've come to ask a favor—if you'll send for the doctor downriver."

He returned to his writing. "Are you ill?"

"Nay . . . 'tis Olympia."

His quill stilled. "'Tis not the doctor she needs. I can well tell you what ails her, though you may not want to know."

"What, then?"

"The French pox."

"I've never heard—"

"Be glad of it." The bruising look he gave her told her exactly what the sickness was—and the indelicate way it was gotten as well.

Heat crawled into her face, and she fixed her eye on the mantel behind him to avoid his gaze. "Won't you send for the doctor?"

"Nay, 'twould be a waste of Clary's time." The words were

spoken with such quiet condemnation they took her breath. "The trouble is one of her own making, is it not?"

"What if it is?"

"You cannot deny she is to blame for such a malady."

"Injurious words are your malady, Colonel McLinn, and far more deadly."

He returned his quill to the inkpot. "Why can I never have an earnest conversation with you without your reprimanding me?"

"Why? Could it be because, though remarkably well-bred, you show a frightful lack of evidencing it? Perhaps I am here to remind you of your manners."

"Or the lack of them, you mean."

She blinked back bitter tears. "Show some decency for Abby's sake, if no one else's."

His face softened visibly. *Ah, that has done it*, she thought. Still, he raked her with cold eyes before shouting for an orderly. She started at the force of his voice, not surprised she was trembling. Oh, but he could be so very intimidating. No wonder the regular at the door looked like a whipped dog.

"You called, sir?"

"Send downriver for Clary."

"Aye, sir. Anything else, Colonel?"

"Tell my officers if they can behave themselves to return to duty. I don't have time for schoolboy antics."

The orderly disappeared and she turned to do the same, but Cass's voice followed her, commanding as ever. "Anything else, Miss Rowan?"

Stiffly, she turned back to him, meeting his gaze reluctantly. Had it only been a short while ago that he'd asked for her hand? Now his eyes held her with such icy regard she felt all the tenderness and heartfelt words of before were naught but wind. Nay, he never loved her. And he was proving it now. The officers were coming in again, meek as horsewhipped schoolboys. Hiding her hurt and fury, she went out.

In the kitchen, Bella eyed her with such intensity Roxanna wondered how much she knew. Might Hank have told her the truth about the winter campaign? Roxanna turned her back as if to deflect her searching gaze.

"Why, you is as stiff as this iron poker," Bella muttered, stabbing the fire beneath the spit just beyond the open kitchen door.

Roxanna relaxed her rigid stance and shifted on her stool.

"Guess you wish you was still leavin' on that keelboat instead of bein' stuck in this here fort."

Amen, Roxanna thought, but she simply nodded and dropped a handful of green beans in a bowl.

"All them rivermen is buried now up behind the stone house at the edge o' the woods. Hank's still helpin' haul rock so the critters can't dig 'em up."

Roxanna shuddered despite the sweat beading her brow. She was aware of the other women shuffling in, Dovie leading the way. All were unusually tight-lipped, taking up their usual tasks with lowered eyes and careful hands.

Bella's voice seemed to snap in the stillness. "Where's Olympia?"

Dovie sniffed. "She's abed."

Bella snorted. "Alone?"

"Bella!" Roxanna's whisper turned sharp. "She's ill, and Dr. Clary's on his way."

"Clary ain't gonna work no miracle," she muttered darkly. "He'll just dose her with mercury like McLinn does his men."

Mercury? Roxanna looked up in question and then wished she hadn't. Bella started in again. "She'll be droolin' black bile before long, right before she goes out of her head completely."

Dovie sniffed louder. "Captain Stewart's in a bad way hisself, already mournin' her."

"He's likely mournin' hisself," Bella said dolefully. "He'll be next." Taking up a sharp knife, she stepped outside to carve a piece of meat off a haunch of venison, leaving the miserable lot of them alone.

Were they all wondering if they'd follow suit? What, Roxanna wondered with growing dread, would be the fate of little Abby?

32

A more macabre spectacle Roxanna had never seen. Holding a frolic so soon after the keelboat's disaster seemed tantamount to dancing on the rivermen's graves. Though she wanted to blame Cass for the indiscretion, she couldn't. He was trying to hold morale together for his men, and she knew firsthand what a little dancing and feasting did for Fort Endeavor.

Dressing for the frolic and helping Abby do the same, she tried to summon some enthusiasm as Abby twirled and hopped up and down. Though speechless, the child communicated bursts of joy with her every move. Bella had indeed outdone herself tonight. From the coffers of the stone house came a remade gown just Abby's size. Roxanna was trying to work a slip of silk ribbon into her bouncing curls, and Bella was exasperated just watching.

"Hold still, Abby-girl! You remind me of a greased pig on market day!"

Since leaving the cabin, Abby seemed to flit about like a butterfly, and Roxanna tried to keep a careful eye on her in the exuberant crowd. A low bonfire burned on the parade ground, and a full moon gave plenty of light. She sat atop a small platform with Micajah and the other musicians, dulcimer on her lap. Across from her, somber and silent, Cass wasn't dancing either.

And the breathless, irrational hope that he'd ask her faded a bit more with every reckless reel. She wanted him to ask if only to refuse him, but he'd not given her the pleasure.

She danced but once with Graham Greer. Though Olympia kept to her cabin, Dovie and Nancy and Mariah went dutifully from one partner to the next, lacking their usual exuberance. Roxanna felt dizzy watching them—and doubly perturbed when Cass disappeared. Unable to sit still a minute longer, she waited till Micajah was fiddling and couldn't follow her to fetch some cider.

But it was Bella who trailed her, face tight with concern. "The colonel wants to see you in your cabin. I'll keep an eye on Abby. Now go."

The vehemence in her tone underscored the unusual request. Cass in her cabin? Why? She raised cool hands to her flushed cheeks and prayed for composure. Would he ask for her forgiveness again?

Moving discreetly to her cabin door, she pushed it open just enough to slip inside, drawing the latchstring in after her. A single taper glinted on the mantel, and Cass leaned against the hearthstones. Self-consciously she smoothed her linen skirt. She felt as conspicuous as the candle in the near darkness. They were alone. The door was secured. Why was she shaking? Why wouldn't he speak?

"Bella said you wanted me." The ill-chosen words nearly made her wince, as did his vehement answer.

"Aye."

He glanced toward the shuttered window, then reached out and took her hand, pulling her into the corner with him. Swallowing a gasp, she leaned into the wall and he let go of her, stooping to loosen two partial floorboards. She looked down, her eyes widening at the sight. Taking hold of the candle, he shoved it closer to the hole, and the patina of a tooled leather chest flashed in her eyes.

"This, Roxie, is your future."

"What?"

"'Tis what's left of my inheritance."

"Nay." She moved back as if bitten, shaking her head. "'Tis yours—your future."

"Dead men have no future."

"But—"

"I'm going to lose my life across that river. 'Tis ordained," he said, inclining his head toward the open Bible on the trestle table, "as if written in your book."

She felt a sudden chill spill over her. "Only God knows the future. Not you—or anyone else."

"Aye, I do know—just as I know the Americans will win the war and Liam will gain the middle ground for the British. 'Tis a certainty I can't explain."

"'Tis reckless thinking . . . no more."

He leaned against the rough wall and looked like he wanted to shake her. "Call it what you will. I'm not coming back."

The candle flame flickered in the warm draft, and she wanted to snuff it out to block the specter of his haunted face. "Are you a seer that you can foretell such things?" Her voice shook with suppressed emotion. "God is bigger than any evil you face."

"*Your* God, Roxie. Not mine."

"He *is* yours, like it or not."

"I like it not." He stooped and replaced the wooden floorboards, then slid her trunk over the spot. "You'd best think hard about your future. I'm merely supplying you with what I can while there's still time."

With that, he turned his back on her and went out.

❦

Cass ended the frolic early, at a quarter till midnight, with two pistol shots fired into the starlit sky. The fiddling ground to a sudden halt, and the dancers dispersed in slow motion, the dirt beneath their feet ground fine as flour. Nary a complaint was heard as he watched his men wander to their quarters. He spied Abby with Bella at the edge of the crowd. Roxanna hadn't come out of her cabin since he'd left her an hour before.

He went round and checked the locks on the quartermaster's and the kitchen and his own office headquarters, wondering if the elusive spy was watching. The lantern was heavy in his hand, and the familiar malarial ache burned behind his eyes. The dread he always felt of its coming shadowed him now. He was in need of all his wits to begin the coming campaign. Nothing must get in his way.

The guard waited by the sally port, and Cass kicked an empty bottle out of his path as he moved in their direction. Fireflies studded the humid air, and his dry throat craved a bit of brandy. He took a last look around before he left, noting Abby had finally gone into Roxanna's cabin and Bella was waiting with the guard. Nothing more needed to be done. He left the fort flocked by his usual entourage, sensing their tension.

How easy it would be for Liam's Indian allies to tomahawk them in the brilliant moonlight. But ease wasn't Lucifer's way. He preferred the chase, the suspense, the intense wearing down of his opponent—like a foxhunt to hounds or a strenuous game of chess. Liam, he remembered, had won nearly every time.

The ornate door opened a crack, and Hank's welcome words cut through the stillness. "Good evenin', sir. Care for a bit o' brandy, sir?"

"Aye, a bottle."

Hank looked surprised, and Cass well knew why. He hadn't had a drop since he'd bested Roxie at cribbage and kissed her so soundly. Wordless for once, Bella eyed him with a strange sympathy as he shrugged off his uniform coat. The dark foyer echoed with the snap of a button as it broke free and rolled beneath a lowboy. Everything in his life seemed to be unraveling, he mused, right down to the clothes on his back.

She moved to retrieve the errant button while he climbed the stair, checking for the locket in his waistcoat but touching Liam's letter instead. 'Twas a sacrilege of sorts to have them side by side. Shutting his bedchamber door, he sank into the wing chair and thrust the paper into the pale orb of candlelight at his elbow.

Beloved brother, 'tis time we meet again.

Swallowing hard, he balled the paper into a fist and threw it into the hearth's cold ashes just as Hank appeared. "Your brandy, sir." When he didn't answer, Hank poured him a glass and left the bottle on the table, dark face creased with concern. "Mebbe it's cinchona you need, sir."

Blast! He could never fool Hank.

"I'm just tired, 'tis all," he lied, yanking off his stock.

The door closed crisply, and Cass passed a hand over his face, which now, at midnight, bore a day's growth. Nay, he didn't need cinchona. He needed five hundred more men and fresh powder and lead from the regiments and supply trains that had yet to materialize. Moving to the window, he looked down at the fort, noting the pale light that seeped through Roxanna's shutter.

Would that she were here instead, uttering words of comfort and encouragement, strengthening him for what lay ahead. Stripped to his breeches, he eyed the brandy again. It wasn't this he wanted but the taste of her kiss—and a clear memory of the spacious, verdant estate across the sea that was only his in ghostly recollection. He'd wanted a home. Children. A settled, decent life. How had it all dwindled to this?

An avalanche of emotion rose up inside him. He picked up the crystal glass with its amber promise and saw it for what it truly was—an empty pledge to dull the pain of what he longed for but couldn't have. Turning toward the hearth, he hurled the glass with a hard arm, and it shattered against the metal fireback, sending shards in every direction. Nay, he wouldn't face Liam muddleheaded and malarial. He'd face him sober and sharp-eyed. Or not at all.

Olympia was dying. Sitting beside her bed, Roxanna tried to pray with her, but she was already out of her head. 'Twas just as Bella had said. Dr. Clary had given her mercury, but the resulting black bile was so horrendous Roxanna begged him to stop. And then, right before midnight, she came to her senses, clutching Roxanna's hand with surprising strength. The other Redstone women huddled nearby, crying and praying intermittently. Abby, thankfully, was with Bella.

"Abby needs a decent mother," Olympia whispered, her voice so ragged Roxanna had to bend her ear to her parched lips to hear. "She needs . . . *you.*"

Me? A shillingless spinster? With no hope of a secure future?

Roxanna opened her mouth to protest, then felt a rush of caution. With tears blinding her, she said, "Go in peace, Olympia. Abby will always have a home . . . with me."

The foolish promise seemed to hover in the air, a sort of bond between them, and a faint smile warmed Olympia's wan face.

"God has forgiven me . . . He's heard your prayers . . . and mine. Tell Abby I love her."

Thankfulness trickled through Roxanna's grief. All was not lost. Olympia knew her Savior. Abby would have a home.

As the minutes ticked past midnight and Olympia took a last breath, all Roxanna could think of was Abby . . . and Cass. In a mere three days he would march.

The next morning Olympia was promptly buried beside the men on the hill and then forgotten, or so it seemed. Going to headquarters, Roxanna could hardly keep up with the activity stirring all around her. Cass—every officer—seemed tightly wound, pulsating with a restless, reckless energy. Was this how men became before battle? His gaze seemed saber-sharp as he surveyed the maps on his desk, and his dictation was no less forceful.

"Every soldier, prior to the march, is to have said accoutrements: a bayonet fitted to his gun, scabbard and belt, a pouch and cartridge box holding twenty rounds of cartridges, one pound powder, fifty pounds of lead balls, and a hundred buckshot."

Save the orderlies, they were alone, but he hardly looked at her. There were so many details to attend to, and his officers were trying their best to do exactly as he asked without risking his ire. To his credit, not once had he raised his voice to them all morning, though they seemed taut as fiddle strings. Strangely, the closer the hour drew for his departure, the more self-possessed he seemed to be.

Yet in the dim light of the blockhouse lamps, Roxanna began to notice a few alarming things. A telltale flush had begun to show beneath his deeply tanned face. And his astonishing eyes were far too bright. He seemed to be fighting some fierce internal battle, winning and losing by turns before her very eyes.

"And finally, every man should have a knapsack . . . a blanket . . . and canteen."

His voice trailed off—a bit wearily, she thought. Out of the corner of her eye, she studied him, her quill still, as he straightened from bending over his maps. So tall he was, yet he seemed suddenly to list, bringing a heavy hand down atop his desk as if to ground himself. In that soundless second, their eyes locked and his subterfuge came crashing down.

Oh, Cass . . . you are so very sick.

She was on her feet, forgetting her bitterness, frightened he might fall.

Heavens, but a wool uniform in such weather is ludicrous— and with a fever . . .

Her fingers touched his blue sleeve, but he jerked away as if she was little more than a pesky insect. "Nay, Miss Rowan."

The rebuff threw a black shadow over her. She'd merely meant to suggest he remove his coat. The warning in his tone returned her to her chair just as the scouts came in, fresh from their foray across the wide river. Their news set her heart to pounding. Liam McLinn and over a thousand British and Indians were poised to march south toward the settlements.

❧

Never before had leftovers remained following supper. To a man, all seemed to have lost their appetite. Their commander hadn't eaten at all. Only Abby, secure on her stool in the kitchen, relished her hominy and gravy and biscuits. Roxanna forced a smile for her sake, glad to see her eating so well after Olympia's passing. The only sign she gave of missing her aunt was clinging to Roxanna and Bella a bit more closely and carrying Sukey everywhere she went, even the necessary.

Last night after Olympia died, an orderly had brought a trundle bed to Roxanna's cabin, and she made it up as homey as she could, with a Star of Bethlehem quilt and a plump pillow. Listening to the soft, snuffling sounds Abby made in sleep, Roxanna felt her spirits sink like stone. She didn't know the first thing about being a mother. And she didn't know how she'd take care of herself in future, much less a child.

Across the room, Cass's tooled leather chest lay undisturbed in its hiding place, offering little comfort. Blood money, she mused. A tidy sum to atone for her father's death. She'd not touch it, no matter how desperate she was.

Thinking of it now turned her more melancholy. She looked up from a stack of just-scrubbed pewter plates, jarred by a resounding thud in the dining room. Bella was already at the serving door, Dovie and Mariah and Nancy right behind her. No shouting or cross words or warning were heard—just the splinter of shattered glass and the heavy thump of overturned furniture.

What on earth . . . ?

Roxanna feared it was the Herkimer brothers and Micajah.

She'd felt their growing animosity for days. Had it erupted all over again? Cass wasn't present, she remembered. His meal untouched, he'd excused himself minutes before and headed up the hill.

Sucking in her breath, she froze as the serving door flew wide open, sending Mariah and Dovie reeling. Abby scampered off her stool as Micajah was knocked backward into the kitchen. Nose bloodied, he picked himself up and flashed them a rabid look before charging back into the dining room.

"Law! Send for McLinn!" Bella cried, wild-eyed.

Dovie disappeared in a flash of linen out the back door, and Roxanna moved closer to peer at the fracas, wiping her hands on her apron, fear rising. Cass couldn't have his officers beat up before the campaign even began. Without thinking, she stepped into the candlelit room, right into the heart of the fray.

"Miz Rox—" Bella's cry alerted her, and she ducked as a stool sailed past her head.

Like angry bulls, nostrils flaring, Micajah and the Herkimers rampaged, oblivious to the main door opening and Cass coming in. Never had she seen him so angry. His face, touched by fever at supper, was now white and tight with fury. He grabbed Micajah by his collar and flung him out the door onto the dust of the parade ground, then turned and punched Joram in the stomach. Joram doubled over in pain, leaving Jehu to mutter some excuse for their behavior till Cass cut him off.

"Two against one is not a fair fight, no matter who started it." With that, he cuffed Jehu in the jaw and sent him toppling backward onto an overturned table. "When the three of you come to your senses, you can clean up this mess—and apologize to the women."

With that, he went out.

Roxanna stood agape.

"Law, if he's thisaway with the ague, that brother o' his better get on back to Ireland," Bella breathed.

The Redstone women had fled, so Roxanna and Bella finished cleaning the kitchen in silence. Distracted, Bella began looking out the door every few minutes, displaying a rare restlessness. "Hank should've been back from Smitty's Fort by now. He always rolls in right before the officers have their supper."

Her words raised the fine hair on the back of Roxanna's neck, and her hands stilled on the kettle she was filling. *Oh, Lord, please not Hank.* Everything seemed to be disintegrating all around them—the keelboat disaster, the enemy marching south, Olympia's death, the officers in disarray, Hank missing. Taken one at a time was daunting enough, but all together, 'twas too much.

"Perhaps he had trouble with that wagon wheel like last time," Roxanna murmured, giving her a reassuring half smile. Abby twirled on her stool, lost in her own childish world, untouched, Roxanna hoped, by the trouble swirling around them.

Shoulders slumped, Bella said nothing and dried a last dish. Pushing down her rising uneasiness, Roxanna hung a kettle from the crane, praying Hank would materialize at the back door. *Lord, please . . .*

Bella eyed her wearily. "Abby and I'll stay put till those three roosters right the dining room and settle their feathers and apologize. You'd best go on back to your cabin. You look a mite peaked to me."

Did she? She certainly felt it. Untying her apron, Roxanna left the kitchen and came round the springhouse to the startling sight of Cass talking to Graham Greer near the smithy. Before she'd taken two steps in their direction, Cass disappeared into the commissary and Graham approached her. She greeted him, conscious of the warm stickiness of the early summer twilight, struck by how still the parade ground was, empty of all but the lookout on the surrounding banquette above. They moved unhindered toward the bench beneath the great elm in the fort's far corner.

"Thought I'd speak my mind before we take our leave," he said matter-of-factly despite his high color. "Somehow a campaign always makes you want to settle matters beforehand."

She simply nodded, wondering about his and Cass's conversation—if it had to do with her. She tried to keep her gaze from straying uphill to the stone house, as was her habit.

He ran a hand over the cleft in his chin, eyes alight. "When I come back from this next foray . . ."

When. His hopeful wording jarred sourly with Cass's fatalistic "I'm not coming back."

"I don't know what your plans are now that we can't go upriver to Philadelphia, but seeing as how Olympia has passed and Abby needs a home, I was thinking the three of us might return to Virginia . . . together."

She swallowed, struck by the simplicity of his proposal, so unlike Cass's passion-filled plea. Yet this might well be the last offer of marriage she'd ever have. Uncertainty made a bubbling stew of her insides. Shouldn't she give him some consideration, at least?

Her voice was soft, rife with reservations. "Will you be leaving for Virginia right after this campaign . . . if . . ."

He took a seat on the bench beneath the elm, inviting her to do the same. "If I return, aye. Have you been praying—pondering my offer?"

She hesitated, knotting her hands in her lap, groping for an answer. With her mind in such turmoil over Cass, she hadn't given it much thought, truly. Graham might not survive the middle ground. But if he did . . . was this the Lord's will for her, then?

Fixing her eye on the firefly lighting on her indigo skirt, she simply said, "When you come back, I'll give you my answer."

At this, he placed his hat on the bench and took her hand. Despite herself, she stiffened, unfair comparisons sluicing through her mind at his touch. Graham was so small. So simple. She could never imagine them well matched in anything—not a game of cribbage, or verbal sparring, or a kiss. He could never bring out the heights and depths in her that Cass did. Yet he seemed a good man, a God-fearing man. Life with him, if dull, would be safe . . . sound. Abby would have a father, a home. Perhaps brothers and sisters. The decision wasn't hers alone. She had Abby to consider too.

"Virginia has always been home to me," she said at last.

33

Come morning, Hank was still missing. The night before, a search party had been sent out by Cass but hadn't returned. A haggard Bella stood in the kitchen after breakfast, near tears and almost shaking. *Why, she truly loves him*, Roxanna realized, *and she'll be devastated if he doesn't come back*. With Bella stripped of Hank's secure presence, Roxanna began to see her in a new, vulnerable light. What would Bella do without Hank? Yet speculating about the future seemed foolish. As it was, none of them could think beyond the fear and dust of Fort Endeavor. The coming confrontation with the British and Indians loomed like a boulder, barring anyone's hopes or plans or dreams.

"Miz Roxanna, would you pray for Hank?" Bella pleaded in the shadows.

"Why, Bella, I've been doing little else," Roxanna said softly, thinking of their near sleepless night.

"I mean out loud—here and now."

Reaching out, Roxanna took one of Bella's dark, work-worn hands in her own and squeezed tight, the words as hard to come by as hen's teeth. "Father, You know what we have need of before we ask, and we need Hank back safe and sound." She hardly heard what else she prayed, her mind was so riddled with other petitions. "And Bella . . . please ease her heartache.

And Abby . . . help her speak. And then there's Micajah's broken arm . . . and a whole army coming against us." She swallowed, fear locking her voice in her throat. She couldn't pray for Cass, though she'd promised to do that very thing.

Tomorrow Fort Endeavor's army would move across the mile-wide river to meet the enemy in the middle ground. To that end, just beyond her door, the fort pulsated with activity. Supply wagons and horses were being readied by every available man within fort walls. She could hear Cass's voice above the din and marveled that he managed to stay atop his fever. Did anyone but she and Bella suspect how sick he truly was? He was now minus one officer in the field—Micajah would stay behind with a remnant of men and nurse his broken arm. The rest of the severely undermanned, ill-equipped army would cross the Ohio and move north before the British and Indians could set foot on Kentucke soil.

Now 'twas noon and she and Bella were in Roxanna's cabin, watching Abby tend to Sukey. One of the regulars had made a little cradle out of mountain ash, and she rocked it with one hand. Roxanna caught the cradle's sweet wood scent as she stood at the door and looked reluctantly at the preparations for battle.

Cass was atop his stallion beneath the flagpole. Though she didn't want to, she lingered on him for what might be a final time. Seeing him thus brought back a string of memories. He looked just as he had when she first caught sight of him on his return from the winter campaign. Though she tried to shut away the thought, one bittersweet recollection led to another. His gift of the teacup and letter. Their first dance. That maddening cribbage game and breathless, unending kiss.

How was it that even now, despite everything, she had to lean into the door frame for fear she would give way? Butterflies flitted from the pit of her stomach to her chest in a woozy dance, and she lay a hand across her bodice as if to still them. Then a layer of anger and regret overrode everything, tainting it all.

Despite the press of preparations—the fact that a dozen or more men needed his attention in the melee all around him—Cass's attention was fixed on Roxanna as she stood in the doorway of her cabin. If he did nothing else this day, he must return her father's locket. The slight weight of it now seemed heavy in his waistcoat pocket, a reminder that he had erred greatly by withholding his confession and needed to relinquish this too, before another minute passed.

Though dust and distance separated them, he had a clear view of her atop his horse and read unmistakable weariness in the slant of her shoulders and unkempt hair. Black tendrils wafted about her solemn face, freed of a few carelessly placed pins. Lately she'd left off wearing her hat, and her fair skin was slightly freckled, her nose sunburned. But her eyes were a brilliant, unforgiving blue—and she was looking straight at him.

Her expression held a hint of the resolve he'd seen in her the moment he'd first met her, when she'd held up that trembling hand as he'd started to tell her about her father, her face so full of pathos it wrenched him even now. No doubt she'd think he'd deceived her doubly by withholding the locket.

With a terse word to a regular to mind his horse, he dismounted to go to her. But as he reached into his waistcoat pocket, it seemed a cold hand clutched his heart. The locket, kept close for long months, now seemed almost a part of him. He hated the thought of releasing it. If he kept it as he longed to do, if only for solace in the difficult days ahead, 'twould soon return to her.

Just as he'd searched Richard Rowan's still body before burial, one or more of his men would do the same to him, stripping him of all personal possessions and finding this, a testament of his love for her. Though she didn't believe he loved her in life, perhaps she would in death.

Thinking it, he hesitated, weighing the wisdom of what he was about to do. The grit of dust in his mouth, the sun making him squint in the golden glare, he made a last move toward her.

Bella moved to stand beside Roxanna, eyes on the gates as if willing Hank to appear. The sun was hot, bearing down with devilish intensity, turning Roxanna's thoughts to watering her garden. But Cass would no longer let her outside fort walls, sending a regular to tend it for her. Too much Indian sign, he said. Yet she craved its greenness and order and peace. Heat shimmers danced with the dust kicked up by the horses and wagons on the teeming parade ground. Even the sky seemed like a square of faded linen from the heat, no longer blue but a stark, bone white.

"Law, but he's down!"

Bella's breathless words pulled her back to the present. *What?*

In a swirl of linen skirts, Bella bolted out the door, and Roxanna went running after her. Was Cass on the ground? There was such a press of soldiers gathering that she couldn't see clearly. Bella pushed past all those broad, sweat-stained backs with a hard hand as the Herkimer brothers called for a stretcher. At the edge of the crowd stood Graham Greer. Roxanna had the uncanny feeling he was more concerned with her reaction than his commanding officer's well-being.

Micajah took charge as second in command, his voice a bit shrill and unsteady, Roxanna thought. "Take him to the stone house, not the infirmary. And make haste for Dr. Clary." With that, he moved to talk to Bella, who, from the look of her, wasn't obliging. She spun away from him and cut through the throng to Roxanna.

Chin jutting stubbornly, she approached Roxanna with renewed purpose. "With Hank away, there ain't nobody to tend McLinn."

"But Major Hale asked you—"

"I ain't goin' to be holed up in that house when Hank comes in." Her shining eyes, deep wells of pain, brooked no argument. "Besides, the colonel's your man, not mine."

Though whispered, Roxanna wondered how many others had heard. Heat inched up her neck in uncomfortable prickles. She didn't dare refute the bold statement. "But I have Abby to tend to—"

"Abby ain't no trouble. You'd best go on up with the Herkimers and the guard lest they have to make another trip."

Folding her arms across her chest, Roxanna tried another tack. "I know nothing about the ague, Bella."

"Well, you is about to."

"And I don't know enough about the stone house—"

"You is a fast learner. Once you is up there, you ain't likely goin' to want to come out. Take some of your belongin's. Sick as he is, this ain't goin' to be a quick trip."

As if this were all part of some grand, prearranged plan, Roxanna saw the guard waiting for her by the sally port through which the stretcher was just exiting. Heart pumping with a wild resistance, she returned to her cabin on leaden feet and stuffed some of her belongings in a knapsack, stooped to kiss Abby, then followed the funereal procession up the hill.

❧ ❧

While Cass was taken upstairs, Roxanna dropped her belongings by the door and wondered where the kitchen was. Without Hank's amiable presence, she felt at sea. The foyer was even grander flooded with morning light than it had been touched by candlelight. To her right was the study, the door ajar. Avoiding it, she walked past the dining room and touched the cool knob of a slightly less ornate door she suspected was the kitchen. It opened invitingly and she stood slightly openmouthed on the threshold.

The large room was painted a bright brick red. Milk-white cupboards with black butterfly hinges abounded, and a huge stone fireplace took up the entire west wall. Tucked just behind this was a narrow stair that ran up to Cass's room, she guessed, and also descended to a cellar.

Crossing to the nearest cupboard, she peered inside. Coffee. Tea. Cocoa nuts. Loaf sugar and spices. Almonds and raisins and olives. A veritable treasure trove.

Next she took in a stone sink with spring-fed water. Bella had told her the house had been built atop a spring, but she'd hardly believed it. Her heart squeezed tight.

Why did everything have to be so perfect?

She could hear the Herkimer brothers talking in low tones upstairs, awaiting Dr. Clary. Reaching into her apron pocket, she withdrew a small tin of cinchona Dr. Clary had supplied after the poisoning and then kindled the hearth's ashes, surprised to find her hands unsteady.

I shouldn't be in this house.

Her dear mother would be scandalized, though in times of war, propriety was set aside for necessity. She didn't want to play nurse. Cass had, in the span of a few weeks, become her enemy, the man who'd taken her father's life. She could never see him any differently. How was she to nurse him with any compassion?

Within half an hour, she'd familiarized herself with everything in the beautiful, practical kitchen, wishing Hank would walk in and render it all unnecessary. But it was only Dr. Clary she heard, his footfall heavy on the stair overhead. She stayed where she was by the hissing kettle, nose wrinkling as bubbling water met bark and made a bitter brew. So lost was she in thought that she wasn't aware of anyone behind her.

"I must admit I'm pleased to have an able nurse," Dr. Clary said, looking her up and down. "With all the trouble pressing in on us, I doubt I'll be back this way in the near future." She turned to take in the hardened, backwoods doctor, his breeches and weskit soiled from riding far and fast. "Colonel McLinn is resting now, but this is a particularly bad attack. My advice is to keep him cool with cloths and administer cinchona if he can keep it down. There's little else to be done."

"How long do these spells last?"

He shrugged. "Days . . . a week or better. He'll likely not die from it, as he's strong as a bull and just as stubborn. But he'll be weak—and out of his head at times. My advice is to find all the firearms in the house and hide them."

The alarm she felt negated the need for her next question.

Scratching his whiskered chin, he expelled a resigned breath. "Sometimes a patient wearies of the cyclical nature of the disease, and a life is lost. I wouldn't mention it, but dire as his present circumstances are, it might seem a palatable option."

She waded through his gentlemanly phrasing to the heart of the matter beneath. Clary knew Cass well. Suicide among soldiers was rampant, second only to desertion. With the fever goading him—not to mention the failed march and the enemy approaching across the river—he might well consider it.

He passed her a brace of pistols. "I found these in his bedchamber. Hide them carefully."

She simply nodded, aware of the Herkimers hovering in the foyer. Within moments they left her alone, and the only sound was the tense ticking of the grandfather clock. Setting the cinchona aside, she bolted the front door and entered the study like a woman condemned. All was just as she remembered—twin wingback chairs, tilt-top table, overstuffed bookcases. On one wall hung a fine Kentucke rifle, the elaborately carved stock a work of art. She took it down, wondering if it was loaded—and where to hide it. A quick but thorough sweep of an unfamiliar, elegant parlor gained her a few more firearms.

Down the kitchen stair she went to the cellar, arms full, forgetting a candle. The plink of dripping water and utter darkness returned her to the kitchen. After lighting a tin lantern, she finally finished her task—having buried the guns under a pile of straw and potatoes before going upstairs to search next.

Should she check on him?

Entering his bedchamber seemed as formidable as crossing the river and facing the enemy. She'd never seen his room, just imagined how it would be, even dreamed of such. Her nocturnal waywardness of months before returned to her in a rush as she climbed the smooth steps. A lingering hint of oil paint. Wedgewood blue walls. A wag-on-the-wall clock. A bed big enough for six people overhung with a crewelwork canopy.

A hint of a smile softened her mood. Papa had always said she had an overactive imagination.

She went into the blue bedchamber before searching the two rooms opposite. No guns within. The stair to the third floor beckoned. Surely there were no firearms in a ballroom. She'd search there later. Best master her fears and face Cass, who was likely lost in the grip of fever.

His door was partially ajar, and she hesitated at the opening.

Lord, please . . . give me infinite grace.

Slipping inside, she blinked—and felt her jaw go slack. The beautiful room seemed to greet her in an intoxicatingly familiar fashion. Her backside connected with the first seat available—a finely turned Chippendale chair. The deep Wedgewood blue walls seemed to mock her, as did the wag-on-the-wall clock above her head. Though the shutters were drawn and the room was shadowed, the immense lines of the bed were plain, as were the bed curtains—not fancy crewelwork but brocade. Only this was in error. Even a whisper of oil paint lingered.

"You look like you've seen a ghost."

Her gaze ricocheted to Cass, planted firmly in the middle of the bed, lying back against more pillows than she could count. Seeing him thus was doubly disorienting, as he was usually on his feet. Taking a bracing breath, she said, "How are you feeling?"

"Given Clary tried to knock me out with whiskey, ne'er better."

She was acutely aware of the distillation of sweat, spirits, and the tang of leather. "You should be drinking cinchona."

"I should be on my feet. Come morning I've a campaign to begin."

"You're delirious," she whispered, getting up and going to him. Placing a hand on his brow, she felt its strange heat. "I've made some tea and I'll bring up some cold cloths."

His gaze shot round the room. "What did Clary do with my pistols?"

"Entrusted them to me."

"The devil he did! I cannot be abed and defenseless. Bring them up from the cellar."

Her eyes widened. "How did you know?"

"'Tis the first place someone would hide them."

Sighing, she gave a slow shake of her head. "Nay, Colonel McLinn. You must prove yourself a good patient before I return them. And thus far you've earned no favors."

"Come now, Roxie, be a good sport."

"Patronizing me will gain you nothing. I'll give them to the British. Now, which will it be? Cinchona or cold cloths?"

He gave her a withering look. "Neither."

"That, sir, is not an option."

His feverish eyes held hers in challenge. "The pistols first. Then some cinchona." Dismayed, she turned away, but he caught her wrist. "Here in my own house I'll say and do as I please."

"If you keep this up, I'll leave."

"Then who will tend me? Hank?"

"Nay, he's . . ."

"I know, Roxie. He's missing. Since late yesterday. Just because I'm out of my head doesn't mean I've lost my hearing. The scouts found his wagon and everything was untouched. But he's disappeared."

Did he miss nothing? Not even she knew this.

He let go of her wrist. "I ken you don't want to be here any more than I do."

Their eyes met again, and she glanced away. Despite everything, despite all the hurt in her heart, she still longed to build a bridge between them, to return things to the way they'd been before circumstances had carved a deep chasm between them. But she couldn't—and he couldn't.

The room was too warm, and she looked longingly toward the shuttered windows.

"You need fresh air," she murmured, but it was she herself who felt the need.

"Not in war time," he cautioned. "Have you ne'er seen an Indian or Redcoat scale a wall?"

She suppressed a shudder, forehead furrowing, and moved to the coolness of the hall. Hurrying to the third floor, she entered a long, lovely room with painted paper and a cut-glass chandelier. Dancers swirled in her imagination across the gleaming walnut floor. Opening a window, she felt a breeze brush her heated cheeks as she looked down at the orchard and then the river. All was green and serene and quiet. But for how long? From here the fort looked small, the soldiers no bigger than nails. Surely the enemy couldn't reach a third-floor ballroom.

Coming back down, she lingered at Cass's door. His eyes were closed, and the feverish intensity of his face had returned. She'd bring cinchona and cold cloths as soon as she could. For now she'd best find another hiding place for those guns.

❦

At half past six, Roxanna heard a dove cooing in the orchard. The big house was blissfully still. The hearth smells of crusty bread and chicken broth seasoned with thyme and pepper wafted to the far reaches of the house. She'd set out a tray with some slices of Cheshire cheese she'd cut from a huge wheel to tempt Cass, along with some cold cider from the cellar. When he awoke, she'd take it up to him. So far he'd slept all afternoon, but she couldn't dismiss the notion that he had meant what he said and would commence the campaign come morning, sick or not. Hours had passed since she'd checked on him, and this second time was no easier than the first.

Up the stairs she went, still full of wonder that his room was so similar to the room in her dream. Night was falling fast, and the house was cast in unfamiliar shadows. But all was peaceful, offering a luxurious retreat despite the turmoil. When she went in to him, he appeared to be sleeping. She rested a hand against his cheek, and the heat of it seemed to singe her palm. A sinking sensation ripened in the pit of her stomach.

Some nurse I am.

Cold cloths and cinchona should have been brought up long ago, though she'd thought it best he sleep. Dr. Clary had left him in his shirtsleeves, and she moved to remedy that, setting her mind against the intimacy of doing so. Fumbling with the glass buttons of his linen shirt, she finally triumphed—it peeled away in a damp layer, revealing a masterpiece of muscle and bone. The sight of so much skin sent her senses scattering. 'Twas a task for a wife . . . a manservant. Hank.

Forcing herself to look away, she turned back the quilted coverlet till only the sheet remained. He murmured a smattering of Gaelic and rolled on his side, oblivious to all she did. Balling up the damp linen, she felt the weight of what she guessed was a watch fall out of the shirt's folds and roll beneath the bed. For a few brief seconds, she stooped and groped about, fingertips touching something smooth and round. When she took a good look, she went to her knees. Could it be?

Papa's locket.

Opening it, she looked down at the girl she'd been at eighteen, the year he'd had her portrait painted. They could only afford a small likeness, but the artist did not disappoint. Nay, he'd flattered her immensely. Was her hair truly that black? Her eyes so blue? But all that paled beside the question her heart clamored to have answered.

Why did Cass have it?

As she tucked it in her pocket, a sliver of pain punctured the joy of discovery. Yet another secret . . . a deception. Turning, she hurried below the stairs to do what she should have done in the first place.

Midnight. All her bread and finely seasoned broth went untouched. 'Twas cinchona tea for her patient—and barely. Even semiconscious, he despised the stuff and knocked the spoon out of her hand repeatedly.

"Cass, Cass," she half scolded, continuing to force the liquid between his lips. She finally gave up and tried spring water instead. His fever seemed to be ablaze inside him, chilling her with all its implications. Here he was, abed, the whole Kentucke territory undefended and on the verge of attack . . . How then, she wondered, could he still vie for control, sick as he was? When he opened his eyes, the fire in them frightened her.

"Roxie." He caught her wrist, stilling the cloth she held. "Let a sick man die, aye?"

But she paid him no mind, dipping the linen in a bucket of cold water and wringing it out till her hands were raw. Her sure, sweeping movements over his face and neck and chest seemed to settle him, and he slipped away from her again. Weary, she pushed stray strands of damp hair off his forehead and whiskered jaw. His hair seemed to flicker and flame in the candlelight, a brilliant russet even in the dark. Too tired to stand, she perched on the edge of the immense bed and gave in to her perennial need to look at him.

Her gaze trailed over his chest, the smooth, muscled flesh marred by scars large and small—an upraised crescent along his side, a pinkish knot on his shoulder. Other smaller wounds now healed but still visible. 'Twas a warrior's body . . . a soldier's. A grudging compassion flooded her. He might have died from such wounds. Many did.

Her pondering gave way to wonder as she glimpsed the boy he'd been. Roguish. Intense. Mesmerizing. Had he been a handful for his mother? Did he resemble his father? And Liam? Did he look just like him? Every heart-stopping detail?

Rising, Roxanna cooled him a final time with the cloths. Intuition urged her to stay near him all night, not risk the twenty or so steps to the bed in the blue room. Her eyes settled on a wing chair, and she sought its cushioned comfort, bringing the candelabra closer. Oh, but she'd forgotten to shut the third-floor windows. Surely he'd been delirious uttering such things. She didn't believe Redcoats or Indians could scale walls . . .

34

She came wide awake at dawn. 'Twas another glorious summer day, the birds bursting with song beyond the tall windows, the shutters unable to hold back the light. And there, standing in a sunbeam, was Abby. Roxanna stared, sleep muddling her senses. Had she left a door unlocked? Such a small child couldn't have gotten in a third-floor window.

Abby was alongside the immense bed, her solemn face in profile. Cass lay on his back in a tangle of bedding, eyes closed, unaware of the little hands reaching out to him. Abby's mouth opened and closed, as if rusty from lack of use. Chest tight, Roxanna sat on the edge of her chair as Abby uttered a single unmistakable word.

"Papa."

Papa? A wealth of fresh pain knifed through Roxanna. Was she dreaming? Hearing Abby's voice at last—so bell-like and sweet—seemed impossible. She felt like an intruder in the room, partaking of yet another secret she shouldn't know. Gripping the arms of the chair, she stood, and the sound sent Abby spinning.

"'Tis only me, Abby," she said soothingly, though her calm words belied her fractured feelings.

Abby threw herself into Roxanna's arms, sobbing into her skirts. Sitting back down, Roxanna gathered Abby onto her lap and tried to shush her, rocking her back and forth, though the wing chair gave no movement. Was she afraid of losing Cass like everyone else she'd ever known? First her mother, then Olympia? And now . . . her father? 'Twas a relationship she'd never once suspected.

A wave of wonder followed on the heels of her hurt. "Abby, you can speak! Praise be, you can! Now tell me—please—how did you get into the house?"

The small, upturned face shone with tears, and she patted her pocket and produced a skeleton key—Bella's own.

"Did you take the key?" Roxanna queried. "Or borrow it?"

But the little mouth was clamped tight even as she gave up the key. From the bed, Cass shifted restlessly. Abby got down from Roxanna's lap and climbed the bed steps, crawling on the high tick to reach him. For a moment Roxanna thought she would perch atop his chest, but she sank down near his head instead, leaning over and kissing him on the nose. He came awake and smiled a slow smile at her.

"Abby-girl." Pleasure faded to confusion as he looked toward the shuttered windows, then searched the shadows for Roxanna.

"What day is it?"

"Tuesday, June 2," she answered.

The day you meant to march.

Drawing Abby near, Cass tousled her curls and then pushed back the bed linens, swinging two bare, well-muscled legs to the floor. Was he able to stand? Hopeful, Roxanna took this as a cue to leave, hurrying down the steps to lock the door Abby had opened minutes before. The study window told her Fort Endeavor was still bustling and awaiting word of their commander. She wanted to run downhill and see Bella . . . ask about Hank. But the sound of a dresser snapping open and shut and the murmur of voices returned her upstairs. She found Cass leaning against the door frame, clearly spent. Her hopes for his recovery dissolved in a look.

"Abby was just telling me how she picked Bella's pocket," he said, as if it was the most ordinary thing in the world.

Was this how she came by the key? Preoccupied as she was about Hank, Bella was not her usual sharp self. And Abby—had she really spoken? The child wrapped her arms round Cass's knee, a winsome smile on her freckled face. The expression was so like his, Roxanna felt a bittersweet pang.

"What's for breakfast?" he murmured.

"Bread, broth," she answered.

He was moving toward the landing, dragging Abby as she clung to his leg, giggling all the way. Before taking the first step downstairs, he scooped her up like a sack of meal and slung her over his shoulder. Roxanna followed, expecting him to weave like a drunkard since he was so ill, but his hand was firmly anchored to the banister.

How on earth did he do it?

He was still consumed with fever—she could tell just by looking at him. But he was up and dressed in an immaculate linen shirt and buff breeches, a creamy stock expertly folded about his neck. Coming to the central foyer, he paused by the dining room door and set Abby down.

"Will you ladies join me for breakfast?"

Abby nodded vigorously while Roxanna glanced at the massive, polished table with its Chippendale chairs gathered round like officers convening. "'Tis so . . . big."

"In the study, then."

She hesitated. The study held too many memories of that other tender time.

He was studying her thoughtfully. "Will you refuse a man's last request, Roxie?"

Last. An ominous word, one she didn't like. She met his eyes, her reluctance plain.

"We could go in here, ye ken," he said, gesturing to the kitchen.

At this, she brightened. He and Abby took a seat at the small worktable with its simple puncheon top and surrounding stools. Reaching for an iron poker, she stirred the fire and set the broth to heat, glad to turn her back on him and get her bearings.

"You look more at home in this kitchen than Fort Endeavor's," he told her.

"'Tis hardly a kitchen, it's so beautiful." She smoothed her apron, wishing he'd look away from her. Everything felt odd and she felt old. Catnapping in a chair all night had left her stiff and sore as an old soldier. But the pain in her heart was far worse.

She took the stool opposite and tried to smile. "We should say grace."

"Aye." He nodded, looking down at Abby.

She turned a sunny face up to him, eyes agleam.

"Abby will say grace," he said quietly, though it was an order nonetheless. Abby simply shrugged her little shoulders, as if it was all a game. Leaning over, he whispered something in her ear.

She echoed with a little lisp, "Be present at our table, Lord . . ."

He bent nearer and she repeated, "Be here and everywhere adored . . . These creatures bless . . . and grant that we may feast in paradise with Thee. Amen."

Roxanna got up, blinking back tears as she served their breakfast. She could handle Cass the soldier and Cass the patient, but Cass the father left her undone. Heads bent and side by side, he and his little daughter dipped their pewter spoons in bowls and ate. Dawn was suddenly flooding the room with a rainbow of light, rifling their vibrant red heads and illuminating every matching feature.

Yes, Cass, she is yours. How could I have been so blind?

But the shock of it wasn't the hardest part. 'Twas knowing that another woman had possessed him in a way she never would and that together they'd produced this enchanting child.

Taking up her own spoon, she tried to eat but was no more successful than he. Only Abby drained her bowl and asked for a second serving.

Sitting across from them, pretending nothing was amiss, was excruciating. The kitchen was far too quiet. Roxanna heard the tick of the hall clock, the rhythm of her own pain-bound heart. From somewhere beyond the windows, a rooster crowed and broke through the birdsong. She was barely aware of the knocking at the front door till Cass started to get up.

She rose with far more ease. "I'll go."

In moments, Bella stood before them, arms akimbo, eyes questioning. Did Bella know about Cass . . . Abby? Abby looked up from her soup as Cass leaned over and murmured something in her ear.

With a contrite half smile, she echoed impishly, "My 'pologies, Bella."

With that, all of Bella's dander disappeared and her eyes turned a velvety brown. "So you finally found your voice up here at the house. I been waitin' a long time for that." Eyeing Cass's plate and bowl, she muttered darkly, "You'd best be drinkin' that cinchona and followin' Miz Roxanna's orders. Miss Abby-gail best go with me."

But what she didn't say was all Roxanna heard.

No Hank . . . no able-bodied commander . . . no sign of reinforcements.

Roxanna saw them out and locked the door behind them, noting the sag of Bella's shoulders and Abby's reluctant steps as the guard returned them down the hill. She found the kitchen empty and her heart gave a queer lurch. Taking the small stair against the far kitchen wall, she found Cass in his room again, atop the bed on his back, boots and all. From where she stood, she could see he was racked by chills, waves of them rippling over him with an unrelenting vengeance. Eyes closed, he was already slipping away from her and hardly stirred when she tugged off his boots. He'd gotten up for Abby's sake, she guessed. And now he'd pay the price.

Later, Bella came to relieve her. Roxanna all but raced down the hill, heart so heavy she felt it would burst. A mass of contradicting emotions left her breathless. She didn't want to leave Cass's side, yet she did. The locket she'd found in his shirt was tucked in her pocket, adding yet another mystery to all the rest—her father's death, Abby's origins, and Hank's whereabouts, not to mention the enemy's.

Micajah intercepted her on the parade ground, and she felt an unwarranted irritation brought on by a near-sleepless night.

"How is he?" he asked, stepping into her path.

"Dr. Clary warned it would be a bad attack. At first he seemed to rally, but now he's out of his head."

"Bella's with him, I suppose."

"For the time being."

"Then there's naught to do but wait. Everything's ready for the march . . . but the commander."

She detected a slur in his tone, and it made her bristle. Her eyes moved from his tanned face to the arm encased in a sling. "'Tis a shame you yourself are unfit for duty, Major, or you might have led the campaign in his stead."

He flushed an angry, indignant red, and she spun away from him, wondering where Abby was, still awed that she was Cass's daughter. Finally she spied her with her pony, chatting with a regular at the far end of the parade ground. The sight softened her angst. No doubt she'd keep Fort Endeavor spellbound for days with her charming lisp.

Shunning her cabin, Roxanna retreated to the kitchen, where Bella had left dough rising and side meat simmering. But the familiar room seemed dank and ugly, such a contrast to the stone house, and it only added to her melancholy. Dovie looked up from finishing breakfast dishes when she entered, her burgeoning stomach pressed against the sink. Mariah and Nancy were missing.

"Miz Roxanna, you look plumb frazzled. Colonel McLinn ain't no worse, is he?"

"Yes, worse. Any word of Hank?"

Dovie shook her head and dipped a final plate in rinse water. "The search party brung his wagon back, is all."

Roxanna felt a jarring loss. Somehow she kept thinking if Hank came back, Cass would get better. Hank best knew how to tend him. "Malaria is a terrible malady, particularly at a time like this."

"With the men itchin' to march, you mean?"

She nodded, lifting the lid on a steaming kettle. Beans and potatoes filled it to the brim. Nearly nauseous, she stirred them, wanting to ask about Abby but unable to push the words past the lump in her throat. Maybe Dovie didn't know . . .

"I sense you got more on your mind than the ague," Dovie said, taking a seat near the hearth. "Care to tell me what it is?"

At this, all Roxanna's reservations came tumbling down. She turned away from the fire and sank onto a stool, wondering where to begin. Inside her head, confusion reigned, and she struggled to broach the matter as delicately as she could. "What do you know about Abby's origins, Dovie?"

Their eyes met in mutual understanding, and Dovie's face grew grave. "Well, I . . ." She paused, clearly pained by the question. "Abby's ma, Bethann, was a real beauty. She hadn't been workin' at the tavern long when Colonel McLinn came downriver with a surveyin' crew. She took to the colonel right off—all the women did. He only had eyes for Bethann, though."

Bethann . . . surveyors. The two words made a stew of her insides with all their implications.

"He stopped by again on his way back up the Ohio and found she'd had Abby. The colonel wouldn't admit she was his, said it could have been any man's. Olympia was in a fury. Only he could have sired a child with a head of hair like that, and we all knew it. Nearly broke Bethann's heart in two. When she died, Olympia said the colonel killed her, not the pox."

Roxanna swallowed past the catch in her voice. "The French pox?"

Dovie nodded. "Same as what took Olympia. When the tavern on the Redstone burned, we didn't have nowhere to go. Olympia heard from the keelboaters runnin' the river that the colonel was down here at Fort Endeavor. She figured if we showed up with Abby, he might take us all in."

The story sounded plausible enough. Only Roxanna didn't want to believe it. She'd thought it was her own pleading on their behalf that resulted in the Redstone women staying on. She guessed Cass had been operating out of guilt even then, allowing them to take up residence.

A new thought pummeled her. Did he have the French pox too?

Dovie rested a hand on Roxanna's shoulder. "I'm glad Abby's got her voice back. She ain't said a word ever since her ma died. But she sure knows who her papa is."

Roxanna looked down at her lap, thinking of the tender scene between them in the bedchamber and then at table. "The colonel does seem to care for her, whether he acknowledges she's his daughter or not." Slowly she stood, fighting an everlasting weariness. "Thank you for telling me, Dovie. I'd best relieve Bella."

Up the hill she trudged to find Bella waiting in the foyer, wringing her hands in an odd, heartrending way. The guard hovered outside, eyes on the river and woods, as if expecting the enemy to burst forth at any moment.

"The colonel's worse than I ever seen—talkin' out of his head and thrashin' about and callin' your name and Hank's. It's plumb more than I can stand."

"Go on back to the fort, Bella," Roxanna said, reaching out to squeeze her hand. "I'll do what I can."

Locking the door after her, she took the stairs in a rush, strangely breathless. Might Cass defy Dr. Clary's predictions and die—or find the guns she'd hidden a second time and harm himself? When she burst through the bedchamber door and saw the twisted bed linens and his restless, sweat-drenched form, her panic soared.

"Coming across the river . . . got to stop them . . ."

She leaned over him as he rambled, and he grabbed hold of her wrist with surprising strength.

"Bella . . . get Roxie . . . tell her . . . her father . . ."

"Cass," she whispered, bending low and laying cool hands on him. "I'm here and you needn't tell me anything. I know about Abby and all else." She was crying now, fear scaring the words out of her. "You mustn't speak . . . please."

Taking a basin of water, she wet a cloth and tried to cool his tortured skin, but he continued to thrash about as the fever's intensity spiked higher. One hour passed . . . two. The clock over the door ticked on endlessly, and nothing she did relieved him. Not cinchona or cold water or kind words. Not prayer, or tears, or all the reluctant love in her heart.

Lord, please . . . help me . . . I'll forgive him everything if You'll only heal him.

After countless hours of wrestling with his confession, she was beginning to understand that her father had died in a terrible accident. When her feelings settled and her faith thrust itself to the fore, she knew it was a part of God's plan. Incomprehensible. Hurtful. But allowed by Him.

She also sensed, deep within herself, that Cass's physical suffering mirrored the distress buried in his soul. He'd cared for her father, and the guilt of what he'd done was killing him. And she . . . wasn't she guilty as well? By withholding forgiveness, wasn't she adding to his grief?

Such suffering pushed her to the very edges of her endurance, made her nearly writhe with him. Hair askew, she dropped to her knees by the bed, too worn to pray, and just listened. Beyond the birdsong and steady ring of the blacksmith's hammer at the fort came an unmistakable impression. *The study.* Resting her damp cheek against the tousled linen of the bed, she waited as the impression pierced her fear and exhaustion once again. Then, against her will, she got up and went downstairs.

The room behind the finely paneled door held a stubborn memory. Of all the rooms in the stone house, this was his—it held his beloved scent, bore his rough yet refined mark, was the most broken in.

Going to a writing desk, she looked down and caught her breath. A Bible lay open to Psalms. *Oh, Cass* . . . Her heart, so sore, seemed rent in two at the poignant sight. Had he been reading, seeking? Realizing he wasn't forsaken?

Opening the polished mahogany top revealed further surprises. Pencil and ink drawings abounded. Mostly of her, done with such exquisite detail tears filled her eyes. The feeling with which he'd worked was palpable, springing from each page with depth and life.

Beneath her likeness were other faces. Abby. Bella. Hank. Cass himself—or Liam? And . . . Cecily? She knew so little about the woman, but this portrait, in vivid Bordeaux ink, told her so much. Cecily was breathtakingly beautiful . . .

Gripping the desk lid, she took in the writing implements and every rich, inky hue—turquoise, tobacco, verde, auburn, indigo. Six turned wood and brass seals. Blue and silver sealing wax. Feeling like a trespasser, she shut it away and faced the bookcases.

Oh, Lord, please show me why I'm here.

There were so many books, the spines of some visibly worn. *Tom Jones.* Dodd's *Sermons to Young Men.* The classic French *Dance of Death.* Several volumes of Irish poetry. A giant tome of black leather with gold lettering demanded closer inspection, but she had to stand on a small ladder to reach it. 'Twas an encyclopedia of remedies, and it hung heavy in her hands.

The big book opened easily, having been marked by a black ribbon. *Malarial fever. Chills. Joint pain. Vomiting. Convulsions. Death.* A court physician had once cured Louis XIV's son with a decoction of rose leaves, lemon juice, cinchona, and wine. *Cinchona bark is most effective in wine.* Was this her answer, then?

Returning to the kitchen, she measured out the despised cinchona before descending the cellar steps for wine. Six drams of rose leaves were easy enough, for Bella had recently stripped two bushes clean. The drying trays were in the keeping room behind the hearth, full of petals and leaves. Bella had talked of making a sachet. But lemon? Lemons were a luxury. Rummaging through every cupboard produced little till she came to Bella's makings for preserves. A packet of dried lemon rind would have to do. Gripping the handle of a steaming kettle, she poured hot water over the rind as a substitute, letting it steep till it turned a deep yellow.

Just what, she wondered, was she resurrecting him for? Battle? The death he claimed would come? A future without him?

She opened a window, heedless of the danger, eyes on the wide river dappled a greenish-gold in the sunlight. A light breeze caressed her face and hair, making her want to lean upon the sill and succumb to sleep, not return upstairs and force Cass to drink.

But the wine went down far better than the water, and he even came to his senses for a few breathtakingly lucid moments. "I ne'er believed you'd be feeding me spirits."

"I have no choice. 'Tis a divine directive."

His smile was more shadow. "The old water-into-wine trick?"

"You *do* know Scripture."

"I'm not the heathen you think I am, Roxie."

"I know," she said, the poignancy of his and Abby's prayer engraved upon her heart. "I stopped believing you were a heathen the moment you taught your daughter to pray."

His eyes, so clouded by illness, turned to blue ice. "Abby's not mine."

She leaned back against a bedpost, wishing she had some

wine herself. "She snuck in here and called you Papa. And Dovie told me everything."

"Everything?"

She swallowed hard, the sordid story bitter to the taste. "How you and a surveying party came to the Redstone tavern . . . and you met Bethann."

"Is that her mother's name?"

She rolled damp eyes and looked away. "You'd do well to remember such a liaison."

"You don't think the British send surveying parties downriver dressed as Bluecoats?"

Her gaze swiveled back to him. "I . . . what?"

"Abby is Liam's child, not mine. Once again you judge me too hastily."

She stared at him, suspended between disbelief and the knot of hurt and confusion festering inside her. Would he explain away her locket so easily?

He went on, carefully and deliberately, his gaze never wavering. "Olympia tried to blackmail me into claiming Abby as my own when she first came here. But I was nowhere near Redstone when she was conceived. I was still in the east serving under Washington while Liam was populating the middle ground."

Heat touched Roxanna's face as she thought of others besides Bethann and Abby. "But Olympia didn't believe you," she murmured.

"Why would she?" His terse tone revealed his disgust. "She didn't know about Liam. She only believed what he told her—that he was Colonel Cassius McLinn."

Shame pinched her. *But I know of Liam and I still blamed you.* All that Micajah had told her returned to her in a sickening rush. Liam—Lucifer—had caused untold trouble for Cass in the east, and was doing so still. How would it be to have an enemy twin masquerading as yourself, doing duplicitous things in your name, perpetuating untold damage?

She sat down on the end of the bed. "Was Liam always so base?"

"Nay, once he—like Lucifer himself—was good. But the war . . . divided loyalties . . ." He was already slipping away from her, wracked by the severe chills that followed the fever, so violent his teeth nearly chattered. "Please . . . build a fire to take the chill away . . ."

A fire in June.

She drew the bedclothes up around him, went to the hearth, and kindled a small fire with unsteady hands, if only to solace him. Having him out of his head rattled her beyond all reasoning. She felt vulnerable and defenseless in this imposing house with this imposing man who seemed naught but a beacon for the enemy.

Her eyes roamed the room, but all its lovely details seemed to blur before her gaze finally settled on the dog irons—twin soldiers—and a balled-up clump of paper in the ashes. She snatched it up and smoothed out its once fine vellum, looking at the longhand so much like Cass's own.

Beloved brother, 'tis time we meet again.

Crumpling it up, the feel of it like poison, she flung it into the fire. Liam was coming. Soon. But for the moment she was almost too tired to care. Another hour passed, and she felt nearly ill from lack of sleep. With a last glance at Cass—eyes closed and still shaking—she passed into the blue bedchamber, leaving the adjoining door open in case he needed her. The room's elegance reached out to her, an inviting cocoon of blue brocade and wainscoting and sunny corners. Climbing up onto the high bed with as little grace as Abby, she collapsed atop the feather tick, half asleep before her head touched one of the pillows.

The bed curtains around Cass were blowing in rich profusion like the sails of a ship. For a moment he thought he was at sea on the vessel *Liberty* that had brought him to America from Ireland. Throwing back the sweat-stained sheet, he found his feet, every muscle protesting from being abed so long. A fire had smoldered out in the grate, and a window was cracked to emit a honeysuckle-scented wind. 'Twas dawn, he guessed, not dusk.

Standing up proved a remarkable feat. He swayed, his aching head adance. Going to the washbasin, he leaned both head and bare shoulders over the porcelain bowl and poured the entire pitcher of tepid water over his upper body. Despite being sick to his stomach from the wine Roxanna had given him, the make-shift bath seemed to ground him. Sluicing off the water with his hands, he pushed back his hair before tying it carelessly with a string and moving through the twilight shadows.

Though he'd not spoken or opened his eyes much of the time, he'd been acutely aware of when Roxanna was or wasn't with him. And she'd left his side hours ago. The clock over the door told him so, as did the ache in his chest. Unable to find the locket, he felt adrift, groping about the bed linens, afraid she'd vanished as mysteriously.

Roxie, my love, where are you?

The blue bedchamber beckoned. He made it to the door and leaned against its sturdy frame, taking in one slender, stocking-clad foot below a petticoat atop the bed's rumpled counterpane. In the semidarkness, turned on her side, all the hills and valleys of her beneath her dress took his breath. She seemed as finely sculpted as a lush landscape he'd once come across at sunset on a march into the middle ground. The same almost holy awe took hold of him, and he wanted to reach up and still the ticking of the clock and stop time, overcome by the brevity and beauty of that fleeting moment.

Oh, Roxie, what will become of you—and Abby—when I'm gone?

Coming nearer, he cast a long shadow over her as she slept. He stood enthralled, hands clasped behind his back. Her hair was all atumble, much like the night he'd claimed his kiss, not returned to its sooty knot but taken down all the way. Did it reach her waist? He hated that he didn't know.

With a soft sigh like Abby might have made, she turned over, eyes still closed, and curled into a ball, her knees almost to her chin beneath her disheveled dress. Before she'd settled again, he leaned closer to brush his lips against her temple in a sort of farewell before going down the hill.

35

Still no Hank. Still a headache and residue of fever. Still dissension among his officers. But the scouts brought some astonishing news anyway. Reinforcements from Virginia were but two days away. And Abby was nearly chewing his ears off with her gabbiness. Having eluded Bella, she stood beside him now, sucking on a sugar lump beneath the flagpole and squinting up at him as if he, not the sun, were the center of her universe. He'd been within fort walls just a few hours, but his mind—and his eye—kept returning to the stone house.

"Where's Mith Roxanna?"

He nearly smiled at her lisp, like she had too much sugar in her mouth. "Still abed," he said.

"'Tis not bedtime, but noon," she piped. With a winsome smile, she held up her sugar cone, licked down to the size of a guinea. "Want some?"

He stared down at her, distracted. "Nay, sugar is bad for soldiers. I ken the quartermaster spoils you."

She dashed a look about, suddenly solemn. "Where is my pony?"

"Having his supper like you should be."

Her face dimpled into a merry laugh. "But I don't eat hay."

Stuffing the remaining sugar in her mouth, she raised her arms

346

and he picked her up, thinking how light she felt, no heavier than a sack of flour. Once in the empty dining room, he pushed open the kitchen door and found a dour Bella piling corn cakes on a platter. Thoughts of Hank sprang to mind, but he pushed them aside. The fierce odor of an unappetizing stew filled the air between them and made his stomach roil.

Bella blinked like she was seeing things as he set Abby down. "Law, but I never expected to see you so soon, sir."

"Miss Rowan may put old Clary out of work."

"Well, I reckon. Where is she?"

"Still abed," Abby said.

"Nay, no longer," came a reply from the back door. Roxanna entered, looking as fresh as he felt stale, her cheeks flushed from sleep. Abby latched on to her skirt like a burr, small face alight.

"I mithed you, Mith Roxanna. There's been nobody to play with save Sukey. But the smithy's dog had pups. He said I could have one if I asked you. I like the brown one. He looks like a sugar lump."

"My, but I've missed a great deal being gone," Roxanna said, hugging her and looking around as if to get her bearings. "But I'm back now to—"

"To get Gab—I mean Abby," Cass said.

Roxanna looked at him, her sudden smile chasing every shadow from the room. "Yes, to get *Abby*," she echoed.

"Gabby's more like it," Bella said, sour mood lifting. "Now let's get ready for supper."

"I'll help serve," Roxanna told her, donning an apron. "'Tis almost time for the officers."

"Past time." Bella glowered. "Major Hale's forgot to call the men—again."

But even as she said it, the summons sounded. With a smirk, Bella passed the platter of corn cakes to Abby and hefted two pitchers of cider herself. "Come along and help old Bella, Abby-gail. Maybe that sweet voice of yours will make my possum stew go down a bit better."

With a wink, she and Abby went into the dining room, leaving Cass and Roxanna alone in the kitchen. This was what he'd hoped for—only he couldn't think of a single thing to say. But simply standing up when he should still be flat on his back and having the woman he loved within arm's reach was enough.

She smoothed her apron, her wary eyes meeting his reluctantly. "You seem to have risen from the dead."

"Aye, 'twas your wine that cured me."

"Nay, 'twas my prayers."

He nodded. "I'm grateful for both."

Her face clouded. "You're still not well."

"Well enough."

"Well enough to . . . ?"

"Lead a campaign." He looked down at her, his voice low and soft yet steel-edged. "But before I go, there's one thing I need to know." She stopped fussing with her apron and returned her full attention to him. "Do you have my locket, Roxie?"

Surprise burst from her blue eyes. "*My* locket, you mean."

He smiled a bit guiltily at the fire he'd kindled in her. "I suppose I owe you an explanation."

Yes, about a great many things, her expression seemed to say. He could hear his officers filling the adjoining room and wished he was back in the stone house alone with her. If they were, he'd ask for her forgiveness again, gamble for her hand a second time . . .

"Colonel McLinn, sir."

Joram Herkimer stood behind him. Never before had an interruption been so unwelcome. He felt all the expectancy seep out of him. Likewise, the lovely lines of her face were touched with regret. She rued the interruption just as much, he realized with a sharp stab of hope. For now, 'twas enough.

❦

Roxanna waited till the officers were mid-meal before disappearing to her cabin. She felt so overcome that Cass was on his feet again, her emotions so raw, that she sought the privacy of her own quiet place. Drawing in the latchstring and closing the shutter, she knelt by her bed, feeling childlike, so tossed about by her emotions her prayer of thanks seemed almost incoherent. But God alone understood the depths of her heart.

Oh, Lord, forgive me for my lack of forgiveness.

Her earthly father, incapable of holding a grudge, would have been shamed to see her struggle so. Tears welled in her eyes, and she blinked them back. She needed to tell Cass what was uppermost in her head and heart while there was still time. She hated farewells of any kind, and this one, while so very necessary, would be more than she could bear.

She slowly got to her feet, her eyes roaming the shadows and coming to rest on a torn-up floorboard in the far corner. Startled, she drew closer to Cass's hiding place. There, just below, was the tooled leather chest—looking the same as she'd left it, or so it seemed. With unsteady hands, she lifted it out and set it on the table. Her fingers fumbled with the buckles and straps, dread ticking inside her, wondering what she'd find.

Holding her breath, she eased back the lid to . . . *emptiness.* Shock coursed through her in icy trickles. What? How? Only a few days ago, the trunk had been full, nearly overflowing with cash and gold coin. While she'd been nursing Cass on the hill, someone had stolen it! Who?

Setting it down, she hurried to the door, hoping to catch Cass before he went up the hill. Abby was just outside, new freckles spattering her delicate skin from the summer sun, eyes more blue than gray today. She clutched her rag doll in the crook of her arm, her small face mirroring Roxanna's own alarm.

"Oh, Abby, I'm missing something. Will you take a note to Colonel McLinn?"

She simply nodded, and for a moment Roxanna feared she'd slip back into muteness. Framing Abby's face with trembling hands, Roxanna said, "Forget the note. Just whisper in his ear. Tell him I need him. Once he's finished his supper, of course."

As if sensing the urgency of her mission, Abby started off at a near run across the parade ground. Little dust devils erupted beneath her bare feet, and her calico dress was a flash of blue. She was running to her daddy, Roxanna mused. Only her daddy was in the middle ground.

Cass's gaze swung to the open door the moment Abby filled it. Pushing aside his pewter plate, he felt warmth suffuse his chest. *She might have been mine . . . she should have been mine.* Same copper curls. Same stubborn set of features. A hearty dose of Irish freckles. Then and there he prayed that Liam's meanness hadn't touched her fresh spirit. Mayhap her mother had been amiable. No matter. Roxie would see that she was raised right.

He looked down the long table, leaned back in his chair, and inclined his head to invite her in. At his notice, her oval face bloomed like a fragile flower in the sunlight. She stepped warily into the shadowed room, where lamplight struck pewter and the clink of utensils and drone of masculine voices made a discordant melody. But on she came with her rag doll, climbing onto his knee to the amusement of his men.

She eyed his nearly untouched stew and half-eaten corn cake, and he said drily, "Go ahead, Abby-girl, have a bite."

But she made such a face his officers burst out laughing and looked askance at their own unappetizing plates.

Placing a soft hand on the ginger stubble of his cheek, she brought his head down till her mouth was against his ear. "Mith Roxanna is sad. She's mithing something."

The innocent words, confusing though they were, sent an icy river of alarm down his spine. Standing so fast he nearly lost his balance, he left the table without a word to anyone, Abby in his arms. Glancing past the east barracks to Roxanna's cabin, he noticed clumps of regulars awaiting their supper and watching him with wary fascination.

"Adams, Miss Abby would like a pony ride," he said to the nearest regular, knowing he needed to meet Roxanna alone.

The trek across the parade seemed strange since he'd been away from the fort for so long. He felt every eye upon him, marveling at his quick recovery—or his boldness in seeking her out. But he wasn't cowed and he didn't care. He would have kicked the door down if he'd needed to, but it was open—wide—and she was just inside, her face drawn with worry.

Her chest rose and fell, and her words were almost nonsensical. "Your chest—all the contents—everything—are gone."

His gaze shot to the corner where the trunk and floorboard were awry, the chest gaping open. He leaned against the door frame, adjusting to the last thing he'd expected to hear.

She stared at him, perplexed. "Who could have taken it? I've told no one—"

"Few secrets are kept in a fort, particularly with a spy on the loose."

Coming inside, he shut the door and drew the latchstring in, casting the cabin in deep shadows. Only a smattering of light filtered through the shutter, and it was aswirl with dust motes. She backed up a bit, lips parting in surprise.

Did she think he might take her in his arms—kiss her?

Standing before her in the dimness, he tried to make sense of the loss. He'd meant the trunk's contents to be her future—hers and Abby's. That alone had given him some solace, had made up in some small measure for his failings—and Liam's. Barring this, he groped for the only alternative he could.

"'Tis not too late to wed me, Roxie. If only in name. For Abby's sake."

Sorrow darkened her gaze. "For your pension, you mean."

"Aye. 'Tis yours for the taking."

Their eyes locked in the little beam of light escaping the shutter crack. She'd never looked more frightened or confused. With a little sob, she covered her face with her hands, and he felt his own chest convulse. Hopelessness hung in the air, poisoning the peace they both craved, the future they were powerless to do anything about. He took a tentative step toward her, unsure of how to comfort her, afraid she might turn away. But when his arms went round her, she didn't resist. The warmth of her, the sweetness of her scent, took his breath away. He held her as tightly as he dared, the inky knot of her chignon just beneath his chin, her tears wetting his coat. He rested his bristled cheek against the silk of her hair and waited. Long minutes ticked by. He could feel them as if they were his pulse, his lifeblood, instead.

Her voice was hardly audible, laced as it was with pain. "I can't marry you, Cass, but I can forgive you."

He bent his head nearer. "How can you forgive such a thing?"

"If God forgave me all my sins, how can I not forgive you?"

He let the gentle words take root, assuaging the rough edges of his regret, and then his thoughts took a sharp turn. Though she forgave him, perhaps even loved him, 'twas not enough to reverse the terrible path he must take. Or secure her own uncertain future.

She drew back from him, her voice resigned. "When are you leaving?"

Spent, he sat down and folded his arms across his chest, if only to keep from reaching out to her again. "Reinforcements should arrive soon, and the day after that we march." He felt bone weary even uttering the words. He longed to say instead, "Let's pledge ourselves each to the other and sail for Ireland and leave this war-torn land." But he was dealing in delusions. Ireland had long ceased to be a safe haven . . . home. The colonies—Virginia—were naught but a shadowy dream. His own mortality met him at every turn.

How vulnerable she looked standing there in the shadows. Tears shone in her eyes, but she managed to say with far more composure and grace than he deserved, "I'll pray for you every time I think of you. I'll keep the prayer you taught Abby alive in her heart till you come back."

He opened his mouth to contradict her, but the words lodged so tight in his throat he couldn't speak. He was days away from death. 'Twas a waste of words to argue otherwise. Rising from the stool, he opened the cabin door and went out.

For several long minutes she looked at the door once he'd shut it and fought the urge to run after him. The locket now seemed heavy in her pocket. *Do you have my locket, Roxie?* He'd gotten it from her father as he lay dying, she guessed, or found it among his belongings afterward. She wanted to know the details—yet didn't. Whatever had happened that ill-fated day, Cass had found the locket and held on to it. Perhaps . . . She groped about for answers. Perhaps he'd kept it close as a reminder of his promise to take care of her.

Not because he truly loved her.

At noon the next day, official marching orders for the army were posted, and the parade ground rang with huzzahs and hur-rahs as the expected regiments from Virginia poured through the gates. A strangely festive feeling permeated everything, which only fueled Roxanna's uneasiness. How could men about to make war be so jubilant? Even Cass seemed unusually lighthearted, perhaps for the benefit of his men, yet as the day wore on she sensed his mood shifting. Inside his simmering headquarters as the June heat swelled, he and his officers went over weaponry, supplies, subordinate command, and the latest intelligence from across the Ohio River.

"Even with reinforcements, our numbers are woefully weak," he admitted, looking up from a detailed map. "'Tis why I've had you report abroad that we have three times the number of the enemy. A phantom force, if you will."

"That may be why they've not crossed the river," Micajah speculated.

"But there's enemy sign everywhere," Joram Herkimer said, eyes on Cass.

"We may well have to revise our strategy," Cass told them. "Instead of a major battle, it seems wiser to stage surprise raids and simply harass their troops to death, Shawnee style."

"There are a number of weak spots in the British defense," Jehu acknowledged, thrusting a finger at a particular point on the map. "Beginning here . . ."

Roxanna was no longer listening. Returning her quill to its inkpot, she tried to ignore the blinding pain in her head. Abby had thrown up her supper in the night, and neither of them had gotten much sleep afterward. Though she seemed fine this morning, Roxanna wondered if all the turmoil and excitement were to blame. Her own stomach rebelled at the thought of the coming meal. Its unsavory odor seemed to cling to the warm, windless air like rancid perfume. Venison stew again, she guessed, and burned cornbread.

"Are you well, Miss Rowan?"

She looked up from the final dictation she was copying to find the officers huddled in a corner and only Cass behind his desk. *Miss Rowan.* Oh, but she preferred Roxie by far. His voice was flat. Weary. Was it her imagination, or had he succumbed to the resignation she sensed weighting him?

"I'm well, Colonel McLinn."

"Bella told me Abby was sick in the night."

"Yes, but she seems quite recovered this morning."

He nodded. "You're at liberty to go." With that, he sat down at his desk and shuffled through a stack of papers without looking at her. "There's no more to be done."

No more . . . ever.

She tried to breathe past the crushing burden in her chest. She willed her eyes to stay dry. 'Twas goodbye. Come morning he would march. There was nothing left to say. He'd confessed and she'd extended forgiveness. Their complicated relationship was at a tumultuous end. Setting her jaw, she gathered up her writing implements and left him as resolutely as he'd left her the night before.

36

The next morning, Roxanna took Abby gently by the shoulders. "I'm going with the army to help Bella and the soldiers. Dovie will look after you while I'm away."

Abby nodded, tears welling, and Roxanna hugged her hard, feeling a rush of emotion threatening her own resolve. It was then she saw the purple medal strung with black silk ribbon around Abby's neck.

"Papa gave me his heart," Abby said, holding it out for closer inspection.

His heart indeed. Roxanna's own heart squeezed tight. The coveted cloth badge, edged in silver braid and earned on some far-flung battlefield, was now faded and fraying.

She knelt down, tears spotting her cheeks. "Keep smiling and talking and praying, Abby. I'll be back soon."

But would she? Everything seemed so uncertain, the cheerful words a lie. As Dovie led Abby away, Roxanna lifted her haversack and canteen, the rattle of departing drums in her ears. Stepping outside, she walked toward the kitchen just as she'd done countless times before slipping through the sally port. No one, save Dovie and Abby, knew she was going. Not Graham Greer. Not Bella. Not Cass. And if she didn't hurry, she'd never catch up with them. With her pistol tucked into her waistband, she hurried across the sun-warmed grass, feeling as sneaky as a deserter. Only her mission was to join the army, not abandon them.

They were a good mile ahead of her, but their tracks were easy to follow, the supply wagons leaving deep, dusty grooves in the summer ground as they hauled their too-heavy loads. The plan to go with them had come to her in the night in feverish fashion, like a bad dream. She didn't want to leave the relative safety of the fort, yet a strong compulsion pushed her forward.

Was it the Lord's leading or her own?

She trudged past the fort's ripening cornfields before plunging into deep green woods. Within their stifling embrace she felt disoriented, hardly able to hear the tat-a-tat of the drums. But she must stay out of sight, well to the rear of the column, unbeknownst to Cass. He'd be in a blistering fury if he suspected she followed.

Astride his black Shawnee stallion, he'd led his men out the front gates an hour before. Standing by the flagpole as he left, she had trouble keeping her eyes to herself. He stood straight as an Indian, a whole head taller than any man present, in full dress uniform like he was going to a fancy ball and not battle. Not once had he glanced her way. *I've no more need of you,* he'd sometimes said after a day's transcribing. And he was proving it now. But he did lift Abby off the ground at the last, accepting the pink posy she offered to tuck in a buttonhole.

Now, after a mere two miles trailing them, she was spent. 'Twas the heat and the constant racket of insects that set her teeth on edge. The very woods seemed suicidal, dappled a dazzling array of greens and golds in the sunlight and wind, capable of hiding untold enemies. Once she thought the army's rear guard spotted her, but she darted behind a giant elm till they were lost from view.

All day she did this before remembering they must cross the Ohio River, and she could hide no longer. Deep and muddy and a mile wide, it might have been the Atlantic. The angst-filled memory of nearly losing her life, of the keelboat captain with an arrow shot through him, almost made her turn back.

She waited till dusk, when low fires flickered like fireflies along the river's south bank and the hum of men's voices and Bella's cooking encroached on her hiding place, before she stepped forward.

"Miz Rowan, that you?" one of the regulars barked, pulling his pipe from his mouth.

"'Tis me, Private Tucker."

"You been followin' us all day?"

She nodded, picking briars from her skirt, sensing his approval.

"I'm mighty glad to see you . . . but I fear the colonel might be of a different mind."

Different indeed. She peered into the darkness, thinking how the men were nearly indistinguishable from each other. Was this how it had been the eve of her father's death?

"Where *is* Colonel McLinn?" she ventured.

"Eating with his officers," he answered, gesturing to a far tent.

"Well, I'll not ruin his supper," she replied, a note of lament in her voice.

He slapped at a mosquito. "I doubt his day can get much worse. We've had anything but an easy time of it since we left Endeavor. Two horses lame and three men sick."

She almost faltered. A fierce longing for her cabin and Abby and the fort's familiar routine came rushing over her. As if sensing her disquiet, he held up his pewter plate. "Care for some victuals?"

Beans and molasses and bread were the offering. Though famished, she shook her head. "Thank you kindly, but I've some things in my pack."

She smelled rum in the air and guessed a gill for each man was in order, if only to cope with the heat and the insects. Bidding him good night, she made her way amidst myriad greetings along the riverbank to where a pale canvas tent loomed like a ghost in dense brush. Bella was in back of it, banging pans and kettles in a fit of temper, her makeshift kitchen sorely lacking. She wielded an iron skillet like she wanted to hit someone with it.

"Bella," Roxanna whispered.

Turning, Bella threw up a free hand in mock fright. "Law, but you're a sight for sore eyes. Can you help me move this here table?"

They spent several minutes rearranging things till Joram Herkimer's voice broke in behind them. "Good evening, Miss Rowan. Colonel McLinn would like to see you inside."

Inside. The canvas tent glowed golden with lantern light and was empty of officers now, save Cass. She could see his shadowed profile against the canvas wall. Word of her coming had flown through the camp like a noisy jaybird, she guessed. She could hide no longer.

Cass lay his quill down and pushed away from his camp desk when Roxanna entered. Stripped of his uniform coat, his dark stock undone, he was still perspiring, and he felt another freshet of sweat at the sight of her. Despite the heat, he saw that she was pale, the pulse in the hollow of her throat apparent. She stood just inside the entrance, hands clasped and face stoic as if awaiting his tirade.

His voice was low and grieved. "Roxie, why in heaven's name have you come?"

Her chin came up. "Why? Because I can't possibly sit at the fort wondering what's befallen all of you." Tears made her eyes shine as she forged on. "There's going to be death, wounds—"

"Aye, and a great deal more. This is no place for a lady. Not even Bella should be here."

"But we are here and can be of use—"

"You're not a help but a hindrance."

Her wounded expression should have checked him, but he was naturally irritable on a campaign, not given to mincing words, and this was no exception. "You confound the best-laid plans by coming here. I asked Graham Greer to remain behind expressly for your future—yours and Abby's."

Her gaze wavered. "Why?"

"I heard of his proposal—and your consideration of it." His tone was a bit too sharp, but he was sick to death of playing this infernal game of not caring when in truth, she was all he thought about. "There's another reason you shouldn't be here. How can I possibly keep my mind on battle when the woman I love is in harm's way?"

At this, she wilted further, though her voice—and her gaze—held firm. "You would think the woman you love would be a support to you by her very nearness—"

"Aye, but only if she loves me back. Unrequited love is not what I'm after."

He'd gentled his tone, but she still looked grieved. In truth, he wanted nothing more than to touch her, to drink in her scent and softness, if only for the time left to them. But they couldn't draw comfort from each other. The boundary lines were firmly drawn, and they seemed as far apart as the enemy.

"You're dismissed," he said without thinking, seeming to wound her further. But he was suddenly beyond caring, riled that his rear guard hadn't detected her in the ten-mile march they'd made that day. Breaking their gaze, he returned to penning a final letter to be given to the Continental Congress upon his demise.

Life on the trail as a soldier, Roxanna decided, was beyond difficult. At dawn, after crossing the river atop enormous rafts beneath a sheen of gunmetal sky, their trek north into enemy territory soon became a blur of dust and heat and tension. Cass insisted she ride at the middle of the procession on a mare flanked by his officers. Seated in the unfamiliar saddle, she thanked the Lord anew she'd had the sense to bring her straw hat. The sun seemed to fry the silk pansies and ribbon atop it but spared her face at least. Up ahead, Bella wore her own battered bonnet and walked.

Danger seemed to pulsate everywhere—in the wall of woods on either side of them, among the shrill racket of cicadas and other insects, in the constant creak of leather and clink of canteens. They were being watched, she sensed, by unseen Indians. Cass rode at the front of the throng—a perfect target for an arrow or musket ball. She kept her eye on him as if she had the power to cover and protect him with her loving gaze—and prayed.

For peace. For protection. For a miracle.

She could see why the land had become a battleground. Birds of every hue and song brought splashes of color to the lush landscape, and the scent of honeysuckle was so strong it seemed a vial of it had been broken open atop the greening ground.

Oh, Lord, will peace ever come to this beautiful place?

At dusk they camped on a high, timbered ridge where the view stretched for miles. She stood beneath the leafy canopy of an old, gnarled oak, soothed by its rustling as a breeze cooled her brow, well away from the heart of camp. She wanted to stay out of Cass's sight. If she was a distraction, she didn't mean to be. Her worry that she was a burden worsened in the twilight. Saddle-sore and sunburned despite her hat, she leaned into the tree's rough trunk and wondered if she might be the first white woman to set foot in Shawnee territory.

"'Tis better appreciated with this."

She turned to find Cass behind her, extending a spyglass. Taking it, she was only too glad to look elsewhere. The pounding of tent stakes back at camp rivaled the sudden pounding of her heart, yet the delicious sensation of his standing so near almost made up for his stinging dismissal the night before.

"There, to your left, is the former site of Chillicothe, the principal Shawnee town," he told her in his low lilt. "And beyond that is the Scioto River."

The spyglass brought things sharply into focus, and she imagined it as it used to be—sapling shelters instead of burned shells, once peopled by an abundance of natives alongside a sparkling watercourse. The setting sun slanted long fingers of light over an immense river valley, and all was a shimmering explosion of color. She felt overwhelming admiration coupled with sharp regret. The country seemed open—without end—and war a desecration in so beautiful a place.

She finally found her voice. "'Tis like Eden."

"Or Armageddon," he answered.

They were shoulder to shoulder now and she let the spyglass down. Long, silent minutes ticked by and she sensed his heart was full as her own, that he was intent on telling her something momentous.

"Just so you know . . . I've made my peace with God, Roxie."

They were looking outward over the beautiful valley, and she took the stunning words in, glad he couldn't see the sudden welling in her eyes.

"When I was a boy, Christ made Himself known to me. I'm a believer. I'd just chosen not to believe for a season. Misfortune turned me cold, and I felt God had abandoned me. But I've since come to my senses. And I'm telling you this because I don't want to leave you wondering."

Her mouth trembled as a hundred questions flooded her head and heart. What had changed? When? Biting her lower lip, she blinked back tears and tried to fashion some response, but when she turned to him, she found she was alone. There was simply the sigh of the wind where he'd once stood—and a gaping emptiness.

The following morning, in less time than it took to load a cannon, Cass and two dozen of his men had launched a successful raid on a British supply train and netted a multitude of guns and ammunition, with no lives lost on either side. These were the tactics he was known for, not the muzzle-to-muzzle old-style fighting with men mown down like hay before a scythe. This Indian-style warfare was the strategy bringing the British army to their knees in the east.

Now, dressed in the detested scarlet uniforms, half his party were on their way with the barren supply train into the heart of Liam's camp to tell a woeful tale. Once there, they'd discover all they could and spread exaggerated reports of Patriot numbers. Cass and his remaining men had just sent the Redcoats driving the supply wagons back from whence they came—naked and barefoot. His officers could barely contain their laughter as the enemy ran east in humiliation.

"Remember," he cautioned from the saddle, "better a good retreat than a bad stand."

Is fheàrr teicheadh math na droch fhuireach. He repeated the words in Gaelic to himself to make a point of remembering as Joram Herkimer maneuvered his gelding abreast of him.

"What's next, Colonel?"

"We're going on a reconnaissance mission. I need to study the lay of the land before moving troops forward."

Jehu rode up on the other side of him. "Is it true what they say, sir? That one Indian equals three soldiers?"

"Aye, Redcoat soldiers, not Bluecoats," he said, retrieving his good humor with a grin.

They chuckled as he trained his spyglass on the retreating enemy. If only sending Liam packing was as easy, he mused.

❧

That night the firelit camp was teeming with Kentucke militia, Bluecoats, and Frenchmen in their distinct blue and white uniforms and melodious accents. Many could speak only broken English, but since they were all devoted to a common cause, it hardly mattered. Standing beside the tent she shared with Bella, Roxanna watched Cass ride into camp and greet the unexpected reinforcements. If General Washington, under Lafayette's persuasion, hadn't spared the extra men, what then, she wondered?

"Oh, Bella, look at them," she marveled. "Two hundred? Three?"

"Ain't near enough," she muttered darkly. "But I'm glad the colonel can make sense of all them Frenchy words flyin' round."

Later, lying on her pallet in the darkness, Roxanna strained past Bella's snoring to hear Cass as he laughed and talked with the French officers in his tent. Though she understood little beyond *oui* and *non*, she felt warmed by their camaraderie. 'Twas obvious he had plenty of catching up to do, being absent from the eastern conflict for so long. Though copies of the *Virginia Gazette* littered the camp, they were old and had been perused till the print was worn away in places.

The next morning they broke camp, moving north just as scouts reported the enemy was advancing south. It seemed that Roxanna prayed with every step, a mounting dread in her breast. Beneath the wide brim of her straw hat, her eyes strayed again and again to Cass at the head of his swelling army. She made sure she wasn't conspicuous, staying shy of the big marquee tent with its distinctive scalloped edges, more than willing to let Bella and the orderlies serve the officers their meals. He had too much on his mind to think of love or lockets or stolen kisses over cribbage. But he—and his staunch avowal of his feelings for her—was all she thought about.

Now, away from the fort, she felt time slipping away from them—every precious second. Eyes down as she performed the most mundane tasks—mending men's garments, cooking, scrubbing pots and pans—she was keenly aware of the deep feeling swelling inside her, a stubborn love that made her look up and linger on him as he checked artillery, drilled his men, and met with his officers. Once, over a flickering fire at dusk, their eyes met. 'Twas the briefest, most intense exchange, but a thousand things were in that look—and she felt as warm and befuddled as if he'd kissed her.

Even after he'd disappeared into his tent she found it impossible to dismiss the set of his shoulders, the flash of his disarming smile, the intriguing way he went from Gaelic to French to King's English without a single stammer before five hundred admiring men. 'Twas difficult to breathe, thinking such things. He had skill, nerve, and endurance in spades, and she was overwhelmed at the thought of being without him.

"What's come over you?" Bella murmured inside their tiny tent. "You ain't heard a word I been sayin' for a full five minutes."

Drying off from a hasty washing in a near creek, Roxanna took up her brush and ran it through the wet strands of her hair. "You were saying how hard it is to cook for an army, and that Frenchmen seem hungrier than Americans."

"Maybe that's why I can't keep my eyes open. Sure will be good to get back to the fort, if we ever do."

Roxanna studied her, thinking of Hank, wondering why she never spoke of him anymore. Had she given up hope of his return? Clearly exhausted, Bella was asleep before Roxanna lay back on her own pallet. High above, the moon was full and bright, drenching the thin canvas above her head with fairy light. All around them, like spokes on a wagon wheel, lay militia sharpshooters, not in tents but in the open. She and Bella were well guarded, and the marquee tent was just a stone's throw away.

The night sounds, so strange at first, were becoming familiar friends—the chorus of crickets, the hoot of an owl, the rasp of soldiers' snores, muted talk from the officers' quarters. She was, after so many nights, able to distinguish the rich cadence of Cass's voice from a dozen or more men. But tonight all was quiet, and the silence seemed to issue an invitation.

Was he alone?

She lay still, fighting a wild desire. She wanted to see him, to break the endless monotony of days with scarcely a crumb of attention from him. *Oh, Lord, I've completely lost my head.* In a crowded camp, she'd have to step over a dozen sleeping bodies before coming to the canvas wall that separated them. Perhaps she should simply go to the necessary . . . get some fresh air.

Sitting up, breath held tight, she glanced at Bella's bony form and then her own. Divested of her stockings, feet minus shoes, she was clad in a dress that was clean if disheveled, though she looked more like a camp follower than a lady. Careful not to wake Bella, she stole out of their tent into the humid night, feeling time was against her.

Stark white moonlight spilled onto her dress as she walked, the earth warm beneath her naked feet, the buzz of crickets humming all around. The door flap of the large tent was open to admit a night wind, and she lingered there half a minute to ascertain Cass was alone before she ducked inside, heart fluttering like a bird against her rib cage. His back was to her as he sat at a field table strewn with maps, a pool of lamplight illuminating articles of war.

For a few seconds she faltered, nearly slipping away as quickly as she'd come. In that rare window of absolute quiet and insight, she glimpsed his crushing loneliness, the immense weight of being responsible for the fate of so many, the dread of the coming day.

She didn't move—or breathe—yet he said without turning round, "I ken you're there, Roxie."

"'Tis only me," she said.

"'Tis enough."

Slowly he stood and turned toward her. Though he blocked the lamplight, every line of his deeply tanned face was suffused with surprise as his gem-blue eyes swept over her. Despite the sultriness of the night, he wore his uniform coat, and his vibrant hair was a deeper red where it lay damp against his temples. And she was reminded once again of how unkempt she was, her hair undone.

His expression turned tense. "Are you . . . all right?"

Her breath was coming in shallow little bursts like she'd run a hard mile. "No," she finally said. Reaching inside her chemise where the locket rested warm against her skin, she withdrew it and held it out to him. For a moment he didn't move, and she felt as mute as Abby had been.

"'Tis yours . . . I want you to have it," she said finally.

She saw the confusion leave his face and understanding take its place. He took a step nearer, extending a hand. She took a step, releasing the locket into his calloused palm. A breath of wind nearly snuffed the lamp then sent the flame leaping bright as daylight. There was no hiding in the shadows now.

He placed the locket on his desk and turned back to her, face full of questions. Her heart plummeted. Would he not put it in his waistcoat like before?

She glanced around the tent, then back to him. Why was it such agony to speak?

"I—I wanted to say goodbye . . . alone . . ."

"Not before five hundred men, you mean," he finished for her.

She nodded, fighting tears.

He swallowed, his voice a bit ragged. "You know we're to move into position tomorrow—for battle."

She nodded again, and the wind gusted, sending several un-anchored papers fluttering from his desk. He snatched at the air and retrieved them, then set the lamp atop them, nearly snuffing it out. The shadows hid her sudden trembling, and she took a step back, bumping his metal camp bed, which was still folded, the linens untouched. He'd been sleeping on the ground among his men in the open air, and she wondered why he wasn't there now. 'Twas nearly midnight . . .

He was still in uniform—that striking rebel uniform that had come to mean something terrible and irreversible to her, with all its dreadful implications. He came nearer, as if waiting for her to explain why she'd come. But the pain pooling in her heart wouldn't let her speak. She simply put out a hand to him instead, fingertips brushing a polished button. Through the layers of wool and linen, she felt the steady pulsing of his heart.

He didn't move a muscle as her shaking hands began pushing his coat off his shoulders. She couldn't bear to have it come between them, nor could she explain her relief as it slipped free and collapsed on the tent floor. Fumbling a bit in the near darkness, she took the locket off his desk and tucked it in the breast pocket of his waistcoat.

His voice grew strained as he looked down at her. "Roxie ... I ..."

She shivered as his hands cupped her shoulders, then fell away like she was fire. In that moment she sensed his hesitation toward her and realized how much she'd hurt him. All her angry words and protestations of the past returned to her a hundredfold, cutting her as they'd surely done him. Though she'd forgiven him, could he forgive her?

"Cass ..."

She placed her hands flat against his chest, then moved upward, tracing the finely tailored lines of his waistcoat as it leveled out onto the sturdy planes of his shoulders. In the deep darkness, her fingers brushed his finely wrought Gaelic jaw, the day's shadow of beard, the queue ribbon holding back his hair. An undeniable yearning swept through her.

Did she ... dare?

Standing on tiptoe, she brought his head down and pressed her mouth to his. Surprise rippled through him—she could feel it—and in answer his hands spanned her waist—warm, supple hands that held muskets and sabers and lethal things but now touched her so tenderly. When he drew back a bit as if measuring his response, she cast aside restraint and began covering him with kisses—sweet, sustained kisses on his mouth and bristled cheeks and chin—till he sat down atop his desk and wrapped her more fully in his arms and kissed her back.

For long moments she didn't know where he ended and she began. He fanned his fingers through her hair, his rough palms catching on its damp strands, murmuring endearments in Gaelic she'd once heard when she was so ill and he'd prayed for her. His kiss deepened and she responded in kind, awash in the wonder that he wanted her. At last she laid her cheek against his chest, feeling the swell of the locket beneath.

Her voice wavered and became a whisper. "I should never have taken it away from you."

His mouth was warm against her ear. "The locket hardly matters. 'Tis you and only you I need."

Yes, but the truth of it had dawned all too late.

Only a man in love would make provision for her as he'd done, for Abby, even sanctioning her marriage to one of his men, a soldier he could have used in the field but he'd kept at Fort Endeavor, all for her future. He'd even humbled himself enough to tell her he'd made his peace with God so she'd not be left ignorant and grieving.

Her voice broke. "You've told me—shown me—you love me at every turn, but I've flung it back in your face."

"You've never known what it's like to be loved . . . truly loved . . . till now." Gathering her closer, he stroked her hair. "I've been thinking of something your father said—that the true measure of love is what one is willing to give up for it. He was talking about freedom—fighting for liberty. But I believe 'tis the same for love as war."

"What do you mean?"

"When all of this is over, I want you and Abby to be happy—and safe. To have a home. Graham Greer is a good man, more farmer than soldier—"

"Nay, Cass . . . please." Putting her fingers to his lips, she shook her head as vehemently as Abby might have done.

"He'll be a decent husband to you."

"'Tis you and only you I need," she echoed.

Gently he took her face between his hands. "Should I return to Kentucke, I'm going to resign my commission. I want nothing more than to live out my days in the stone house with you and Abby, our future children . . ." His voice thickened and nearly faltered. "But those hopes are in God's hands now."

"Have you asked Him for such a thing?"

"Aye, a thousand times over."

"As I have," she whispered. "Perhaps together . . ."

The lines in his face deepened. Had he given up hope? Did he still believe he would die on the morrow? Her heart, sore for so long, seemed about to burst.

Oh, Lord, I cannot bear another loss . . .

He enfolded her hands between his own. "What does Scripture say? 'If one prevail against him, two shall withstand him . . .'"

"'And a threefold cord is not quickly broken,'" she finished softly.

It was a verse her father had oft repeated. *A threefold cord.* Cass. She herself. Providence. And the one prevailing against them? Liam—and too many Redcoats and Indians to count.

37

They moved at dawn, trading the expansiveness of ridge and river valley for dense wilderness broken only by a narrow ribbon of crystal water. Here the woods were suffocatingly close, a green wool blanket of feverish proportions pressing down and turning all to sweat and insect stings and abject misery. This, Roxanna understood, was where they'd wait till they sighted the enemy. Outright battle was imminent. No one had to tell her so. She felt it in the intense vigilance paid to their surroundings, the preoccupation with artillery and orders, the terse murmurs among knots of men.

Desperate to take their minds off what was to come, she and Bella scoured the surrounding woods for berries—rich, ripe berries that stained their fingers purple and would be made into crusty cobblers to fortify the men. Sweat streaming down, Roxanna filled one bucket and then two and soon lost sight of Bella. But her thoughts were so full of Cass she hardly noticed. Their whisperings and stolen kisses of the night before returned to her with such sweet intensity she put a hand to her lips, still able to taste his kiss.

Setting down her bucket, she knelt at a slip of creek, cupping her stained palm for a drink. She couldn't hear the distant camp sounds above the gurgling rush of water and was aware far too late of the sudden shadow that fell over her.

"Miz Roxanna?"

Her head jerked up. *Hank?* Sweat stung her eyes and she blinked. But the man whose moccasins were planted firmly on the creek bed opposite was a half blood—his unnerving features a mix of Indian and white. A British scout?

"Yep, that's her, all right." Hank's voice rang out of the woods a second time.

In confirmation, the man's hands shot out and grabbed her. She went limp, her mouth cotton, before realizing what was afoot. He was half-dragging, half-carrying her toward the familiar voice that was now ominous, his dirty hand clamped over her mouth to keep her from screaming.

Oh, Bella, where are you?

Briars nicked her skirt and bare ankles as her captor tore through the brush, intent on some horses half hidden beneath a blind of trees. Hank was waiting, binding her mouth with a strip of linen, so tight she felt strangled. When her captor heaved her atop his horse, she thought she might be sick. Stunned, she stared at Hank like she was seeing a ghost. Only the ghost was solid and unsmiling and wore a red coat.

They went at a blistering pace as if expecting Bluecoat scouts to waylay them at every turn. With every step Roxanna felt further wrapped in disbelief. Hank . . . a spy. *The* spy. The malevolence behind the tainted cinchona. The robber of the tooled leather chest. And his allegiance was to . . . Liam?

With shock and exhaustion pummeling her, they at last came to the edge of the enemy camp. Dismounting near an enormous tent, she took in more men than she'd ever seen milling like insects over the surrounding ground—so many men and tents and artillery she knew Cass's Bluecoats were doomed. Stomach quaking, she found it hard to stand on her shaking legs, though the half blood's brutal grip braced her. Hank refused to look at her, tending to the horses, while her captor removed her gag and pushed her toward a large marquee tent.

She entered reluctantly, unsure of what awaited, eyes immediately drawn to the sole person inside. Not Liam, whom she dreaded, but a woman in raspberry silk and lace, eating sweetmeats from a silver dish.

Her narrowed eyes swept over Roxanna, and surprise softened her sullenness. "Surely there's been some mistake. This looks like a common camp follower, certainly not the mistress of Colonel Cassius McLinn."

On her lips his melodious name sounded like an oath. The half blood she'd addressed had vanished, leaving them alone, but Roxanna was too intent on staying upright to answer. She gripped a tent pole, her surroundings shifting like she was aboard ship.

"Hank has told us all about you," the woman continued with a slight smile. "And since Liam was anxious for an introduction, we thought to bring you here. I wasn't sure it could be arranged, but Hank rose to the challenge."

Such sarcasm turned the sweltering tent unbearable, and Roxanna sat down hard on a near barrel, the splintered wood grazing her thigh. Lifting the hem of her apron, she wiped her brow with trembling fingers, bitter words pooling in her mouth.

"I'm Millicent Ashe," the woman continued, taking out an embroidered handkerchief and dabbing her own pale forehead. "I'm Liam's . . . well, suffice it to say, I'm an old friend from Ireland." When Roxanna said nothing, she continued, "Pardon my manners. Would you care for some refreshment?"

To Roxanna's relief, Millicent reached for a pewter pitcher and poured water, not spirits, though addled as she was, spirits was what she needed. Crossing the tent, Millicent moved gracefully around half a dozen camp chairs and a large field table before extending the pewter cup. Roxanna thanked her, hardly believing she had. But good manners were so ingrained—and she was so rattled—she hardly knew what she did.

Before she'd taken two sips, a figure appeared at the tent's opening and an officer stepped into the room. But for the scarlet and white of his uniform, the likeness was so jarring tears sprang to her eyes.

Liam.

"Comparing me to your beloved and finding me lacking?" His voice was so low she doubted even Millicent heard, but it was like acid.

She felt heat flood her face, for that was exactly what she'd been doing. Identical, yes . . . yet there was something cold and hard, almost reptilian, in Liam's features. A freshly minted scar pulled at one cheek, marring the generous curve of his mouth. His eyes darted round the tent before returning to her, and she saw they were a rich if rocky blue-gray. Her soul went still. They were Abby's eyes . . .

"Miss Rowan, I presume," he said, looking her over, his assumptions plain. "Colonel McLinn's paramour."

"I'm not"—she struggled past her fear, hating that her voice wavered—"your brother's mistress."

"A pity," he said, taking a camp chair and giving Millicent a half smile. "Such an arrangement does have its rewards."

They were sitting in an awkward sort of circle, just the three of them, and Roxanna could better see Millicent's extravagant gown. The excess of silk alongside her own plain linen was so startling it made her feel even smaller. They seemed to regard her with a sort of amused interest, as if trying to decipher what Cass could possibly see in her.

Her only weapon, she decided, was words. "You'll gain nothing from bringing me here."

At this, Liam's eyes lit up, his voice a lazy, lilting drawl. "On the contrary, I've gained a great deal. Your absence has robbed my brother of more men, as a search party has gone out after you. When you fail to turn up, he'll be rattled indeed. For a besotted Bluecoat commander, such a distraction could prove disastrous."

Roxanna wanted to curse her folly. Whatever had possessed her to follow Cass in the first place? He'd called her a distraction, and she was. He felt such a crushing responsibility for her given her father, might he surrender in order to save her?

The officer before her melted into a puddle of scarlet and white. She was trapped, pure and simple, and if she even tried to run from the tent, she didn't doubt he'd shoot her in the back and hang her from a gibbet for all to see.

He fixed cold eyes on her. "How many men does Colonel McLinn have?"

"More than you," she answered, unashamed of the falsehood.

"Artillery?"

"Six-pounder cannons—too many to count."

He laughed and leaned back in his chair, regarding her with heightened interest. "You're lying."

"What do you expect me to say?"

"You're in love with him, aren't you? Yet Hank tells me you refused to marry him."

"What does that matter to you?"

"I'm always interested in my brother's affairs. 'Twould seem a rustic like yourself would jump at the chance to marry an Irish aristocrat."

The condescension in his tone brought her upright, but it was the sight of Hank just beyond the marquee tent that stiffened her back. "If he is an aristocrat, his fortunes are now in reversal. I'm well aware that what was left of his inheritance has been stolen by Hank and given over to you."

"Aye . . . even you." His face was tight, almost feral looking, setting off little alarm bells inside her. "Since you're here, we might as well settle a few more matters. You've obviously surmised that Hank is a British spy and has been since the start of this war. What you don't know is that *I* killed your father, Miss Rowan, not my brother."

Though every word was enunciated clearly, they might have

been spoken in Gaelic—they made no sense. She simply stared at him, heart pumping erratically, black spots spoiling her vision.

"Hank may have pulled the trigger that day, but 'twas my order that Richard Rowan die. Your father made the fatal error of naming Hank as the spy in his journal. I had little choice."

The words continued—sharp and piercing and utterly unremorseful. She looked away from him, remembering Cass's anguish after the campaign and his heartrending disclosure in the study of the stone house, so different than Liam's own.

"'Twas easy enough to accomplish, given what transpired. A great many shots were fired that day. Hank was standing behind my brother when it happened. And Cass, bless him, has ever been plagued by a keen conscience. He believed it was he who delivered that deadly shot. We were only too glad to go along with the ruse." Leaning toward a camp table, he uncorked a bottle and poured himself some brandy. "I'd hoped that there would be an outcry among his officers and he'd be stripped of his commission and prevented from being reinstated under Washington's command. But alas, his men are a loyal bunch."

Millicent stirred in her chair and sighed. "Ah, the games these brothers play! I'm ready to see it end and get back to the city."

"Soon, my love," Liam said, eyes never leaving Roxanna. "New York will wait for us."

His scrutiny made her stomach knot. Though she lowered her eyes to her lap, he continued to study her as if contemplating how best to use her. She sensed it—and feared it—and felt smothered by panic.

Strangely, there was a telling sympathy in Millicent's voice when she said, "Miss Rowan is tired, Liam. Don't you see?"

Pushing up from his camp chair, he stood. "Till dinner then."

❧ ❧

Amidst the candlelight and crystal of Liam's table, Roxanna thought of Bella's beans and corn cakes. Here, inside another marquee tent between two Redcoat officers, stuffed into one of Millicent's too-tight gowns, she sat in a sort of awed disgust as platters of meat and cheeses and sweets crowded the linen-clad table. Light-headed though she was, she refused to eat a bite, her empty plate shining in silent protest.

Liam sat at the head of the long table, Millicent on his left, with no less than a dozen officers. Roxanna felt suffocated by the unwanted verdigris gown, the stifling heat, the officers' attentions. Chatter and laughter flowed as freely as the wine—long-necked bottles of Montepulcian and Rivesalte—and for a few disorienting moments Roxanna felt they were celebrating a battle won before it had even begun.

"Miss Rowan, I would suggest you try the tenderloin," the officer to her right said in low tones. "You'd fancy you were in France and not the frontier."

"Thank you, no," she replied, taking up a goblet and bringing the lukewarm water to her lips.

"I understand," he said between bites of beef. "If I were an unwilling guest of Liam McLinn's, I fear I'd have no appetite at all."

She looked down at the napkin in her lap, struck by his apologetic tone.

"I doubt our commander means you harm," he continued, finishing yet another glass of wine. "He's at war with his brother, even more so than the Americans, really. Bad blood, you know."

"'Tis a waste of two men," she murmured, "and a good many more."

"Yes," he replied, a wry twist to his mouth. "But you must admit he has just cause. If I'd had my inheritance squandered by an unscrupulous brother . . ."

She turned to him, feeling she'd been jarred by a thunderclap. Seeing her confusion, he leaned nearer, but his words were nearly snuffed out by the conversations all around them.

"Perhaps you are unaware of the exact circumstances. As the eldest son, Liam had the lion's share of the family fortune. Till his brother lost nearly everything gambling. 'Twas a stroke of good luck to have Hank—our spy—return what was left of it." He shot a triumphant glance at his commander deep in conversation with Millicent. "And now he'll be able to settle the score once and for all on the morrow."

The unwelcome words gripped her and didn't let go. What had Bella told her? That Cass was the eldest son by mere minutes, not Liam. 'Twas none but Liam who'd lost all but the little remaining in Cass's trunk, gambling it away between Ireland and England and the colonies in one grand deception after another. Her thoughts whirled and settled like dust devils as she groped for the truth. In the past she'd often believed the worst of Cass. But now . . .

"Your commander is nothing but a sham," she said slowly and deliberately, meeting the officer's gray eyes. "Liam McLinn is the second son of an Irish peer who stole his brother's inheritance after losing his own—and is stealing still. General Washington dubbed him *Lucifer* McLinn for good reason. And you're willing to blindly believe anything he says—even follow him into battle—and die for his lies."

Pushing back her chair, she stood, and the table quieted, all eyes on her as she turned away.

"Take Miss Rowan to her quarters," Liam said tersely, and an orderly at the entrance stepped up to do his bidding.

As soon as she set foot outside, she could hear the empty conversation and laughter resume. Like sounding brass and tinkling cymbals.

⚜ ⚜

She stayed on her knees all night. Sharp stabs of hunger kept her awake, but the dread of dawn was the true culprit. Sequestered inside a tiny tent with only a cot and a canteen of water, she watched moonlight seep under the tightly pegged canvas and wondered where Cass was at that very moment. He'd need a miracle to face his twin and all his men on the morrow.

Her head dipped toward her folded hands in exhaustion as Old Testament images flashed to mind. Joshua and the battle of Jericho. David and Goliath. Daniel in the lions' den.

Forgive me for lying, Lord. She'd greatly exaggerated Cass's numbers and artillery in some ridiculous hope it would make a difference. They needed a miracle of Old Testament proportions. Till then she'd be fasting. Praying.

Toward morning she heard the thunder of cannons. Pushing past the tent flap, she faced her guard, saber-tipped musket at his side, startled when a fine mist touched her face. Fog wrapped pale tentacles around the surrounding maples and sycamores, hovering over the near creek like a second skin. The morning was cooler, accounting for the sudden shift in weather, but quite unusual for June.

"Ain't gonna be any hard fightin' today," the guard muttered.

Tents stood at attention all around them, and she could hear drilling and drumming on a far field beyond. By noon the fog was lifting, and she saw things she'd not noticed before. They were on a ridge, and in the sloping valley to the south, an American flag was flying on a liberty pole above Bluecoat mortars.

She was hardly aware of Millicent coming to stand beside her. A British cannon boomed without warning, spitting a hot ball into a far Bluecoat entrenchment. Dirt sprayed in brown profusion, and she saw a man in homespun fall. Within seconds an officer leaped out of the ditch into the open. *Cass.* Stunned, Roxanna sucked in her breath. He shouted a terse order, enemy artillery erupting all around him.

"There is no flinch in Colonel McLinn," Millicent said with a tight smile, "nor has there ever been."

Her words were lost as Bluecoat sharpshooters took aim at the British gunners, the men frantically working to swab the cannon's hot muzzle before reloading. Roxanna's insides clenched tight as a fist. She had to open her mouth to breathe. And then, like a white curtain coming down on a stage play, fog filled the valley, and Cass and the Continental line were lost from sight.

"What a royal view we have," Millicent remarked, fluttering her fan in the sultry air, her fair features alight with interest.

Roxanna shut her eyes, biting back a barb.

"I can see you think me callous, but war is all I've ever known. My father was a British soldier. I've been surrounded by such all my life."

"And Colonel McLinn was once a friend—an acquaintance— of yours. Have you no feeling for him?"

A smile softened her rouged lips. "I admire him—and pity him. His is a lost cause, as is that of all the Americans." Concern clouded her lovely features, and she looked at Roxanna a bit anxiously. "I've been asked to keep an eye on you. Apparently there's a plan afoot to steal you away."

Hope flooded Roxanna, only to be snuffed out when Millicent produced a silver-mounted pistol. "I shall do my part, of course."

≈≈

Through the fog Cass could hear British drummers beating commands to control the movements of their troops. *Rat-a-tat . . . rat-a-tat . . . rat-a-tat.* Only Providence could have sent such weather, he reflected, and allowed his men to do what they'd done. Under cover of darkness, they'd made a nighttime assault on two enemy redoubts and captured four cannons. When the weather cleared, the enemy would find their own artillery turned on them. From the trenches his men could hardly contain their glee. He tried to smile, to share their excitement, but the expanding knot of anguish in his chest choked out any high feeling.

Roxie . . . where are you?

"Colonel, these Redcoat linstocks are a bit of a doodle compared to our own," one of his artillerymen was saying, examining the long device that held the match to light the cannon.

"Aye, but it fires the same. 'Tis all that matters," he replied, eyes returning to a far ridge now obscured by mist.

He withdrew his spyglass as Joram Herkimer crawled out of the trench to stand beside him. They faced north, staring into a wall of white that gave no hint of altering. His second-in-command's voice was low and tense. "Where do you think Lucifer is?"

"If I knew that, the battle would be half won."

"Where is *she*?"

The honest question felt like a blow. Cass's jaw clenched. "That's the better question."

If it were any other British commander—Gage, Howe, Cornwallis, Clinton—he'd have rested in the fact that they were gentlemen. But Liam's take-no-prisoners policy made him especially dangerous. He'd never known Liam to kill a woman, but he was capable of it and would find satisfaction in it simply because he knew Cass cared for her.

Turning away, Cass began to walk the trench, leaving heavy boot prints in the dry earth. The regulars in the ditch below were smoking pipes in a rare idle moment, awaiting his directive. Before he'd reached the midpoint, Jehu Herkimer found him, his face a contortion of disbelief and disgust. Every muscle in Cass's frame tensed.

"Simmons and Holt are back, sir—with news."

But it hardly needed announcing. The two scouts were barreling through the fog straight toward him, buckskins soiled and chests heaving, though it was Holt who got to him first. "Have a wee listen to this, sir. Hank is behind enemy lines, plain as day—I mean black as night." There were a few snickers as he rushed on. "He's in league with the enemy, he is. Practically lickin' Lucifer's boots. 'Twas him who led 'em to Miz Rowan."

Cass fixed his eye on the scout as the words rolled over him in a punishing wave. He was hard-pressed to keep the sting of surprise and regret off his face. He'd thought Hank dead. Better that than this.

"They've got Miss Rowan keeping company with your brother's mistress," Ben Simmons said quietly. "Can't remember her name . . ."

Cass felt his expression grow more grim. "Millicent Ashe."

"Aye, the Irish lass. They're in a big tent up on the ridge there, waiting for the fog to lift, same as us. All them lobsterbacks are in position on yonder hills—along with them heathen Injuns."

"Good work," he said by way of dismissal before motioning for Joram to summon his officers.

His tangled thoughts swung from Hank to Bella, still so distraught over Roxie. Since losing sight of her in the woods, Bella had been a wreck. Nor would she deal well with Hank's perfidy. They'd lived as man and wife, come west together. Though Hank had been his valet for better than two years, Cass had thought him too acquiescent—and too timid—to spy. But therein lay the deception. Only Hank would have known about the tooled leather chest, have had unquestioned access to headquarters and the stone house. And then there were all those trips to Smitty's Fort for supplies. Again, a perfect opportunity to rendezvous with the British.

How could he have been so blind?

Slowly, like the drawing up of a heavy curtain, the fog began to lift. His officers were around him now, the regulars and militia looking on. He swallowed down his inhibitions, hand tightening on the hilt of his sword as he dropped to one knee on the hard ground. There was a fumbling to snatch hats off heads as his men realized what was about to happen.

He removed his own tricorn and placed it over his heart, now so full he felt it would burst. Flashes of the life he'd hoped to have—with Roxie and Abby in the stone house—cut into his soul and deepened his dread of what awaited him on the other side of that foggy curtain. 'Twas in God's hands, all of it. And he acknowledged that fact now on bended knee before several hundred men who'd never heard him utter anything but God's name in vain.

"Our Father which art in heaven, hallowed be Thy name." Head bent, he hesitated, resurrecting the prayer from a boyhood long gone. "Thy kingdom come, Thy will be done in earth, as it is in heaven. Give us this day our daily bread. And forgive us our debts, as we forgive our debtors. And lead us not into temptation, but deliver us from evil: for Thine is the kingdom, and the power, and the glory, for ever."

A resounding "Amen" was murmured collectively, a chorus of support on all sides, wrapping round and bringing him to his feet. Through the scattering fog a regular was bringing him his horse. The stallion pulled against its harness, hooves adance, sensing the coming conflict. Returning his tricorn to his head, he reached inside his breast pocket and withdrew the locket, touching the tiny spring. Roxie looked back at him in mute appeal.

Deliver us from evil.

38

Roxanna stood to one side of the large tent, its canvas sides rolled up so that it had become an awning. Across from her, Liam was in full dress uniform flanked by his senior officers, Millicent equally resplendent in scarlet silk. All had spyglasses, intent on the action in the valley below. The sun struck the steaming ground with such brilliance Roxanna squinted as she looked south, wondering where Cass was among men no bigger than matchsticks in the distance. Not a shot sounded as the fog rolled back—and then suddenly the air was rent with cannon fire from the British and then the Continentals.

Out of the corner of her eye, she saw Liam's expression shift from smug to startled before giving way to blatant disbelief. He adjusted the spyglass as if doubting his view. "An admirable start, turning our cannons on us," he said slowly, jaw tense. "I suppose we'll let them have a bit of sport first before we mow them down and continue south to the settlements."

Leaning against a tent pole, Roxanna looked to the entrance. An Indian ducked inside, so tall he seemed to block the sun, his bare skin painted a hideous black. He fixed a dark eye on Roxanna before joining Liam at the front of the tent. A second Indian followed. Shawnee allies? She turned away, a chill spilling over her as she made a quick tally of the guard posted outside.

Eight British regulars surrounded the tent, ready to intervene if she so much as thought of fleeing. And oh, she'd thought of little else since coming here.

She sensed Liam and his second-in-command would soon slip away and join the battle below, perhaps take some of the guard with them. That hope kept her from dissolving completely.

Minutes passed, and she felt her composure crumbling bit by bit. She was tired . . . hungry . . . weak. She'd not had a bath in days and could feel vermin making tiny trails over her scalp, perhaps from the infested bedding she'd been given. All the prayers she'd said, poured out of a weeping, anguished heart, now seemed like ashes as evil held sway all around her.

She couldn't stand the smug satisfaction on Liam's face or the boredom on Millicent's or the detached arrogance on the senior officers'. Images of war began colliding in her mind—the acrid stench of gunpowder, the scarlet shimmer of too many Redcoats, the heavy sweating and grunting of men taxed to their physical and mental limits. A line of perspiration trickled from her brow to her chin. Cocooned on this bluff, she was far from the thick of battle, but she seemed to sense Cass's distress, wherever he was, and it seeped into her very soul, weighting her like lead.

Oh, Lord, please help him . . . help all his men.

"Feeling neglected, Miss Rowan? Here, have a look." Liam thrust a spyglass at her, but she refused it, cowed by the sudden flash of anger in his eyes. "Your beloved is down there in case you're wondering—"

"I'm well aware of it." Her wavering voice strengthened and snapped. "Why aren't you?"

"Why aren't I?" He regarded her with amusement, contempt scrawled in every hard line of his face. "As commander, I have countless men to fight in my stead."

"Commander?" The venom in her voice turned every head in the tent. "You're not a commander—you're naught but a coward."

Their eyes locked—his so like Abby's yet hard as iron. She

385

took a step back, but not before his hand shot out and struck her, his signet ring cutting her lip. Blood ran into her mouth and down her chin, and she nearly fell from the force of the blow. No man had ever hit her. The shame and shock of it started her crying, and she sank down hard atop the nearest keg, fumbling for the handkerchief she didn't have.

She was acutely conscious of Liam looming over her, as if debating how to be rid of her, when one of the Shawnee shadowed him, returning his attention to the field. When Liam turned away, she felt a piece of cloth settle in her palm. She brought the soft square of linen to her bloodied lip, as surprised by the Indian's gesture as Liam's savagery.

But this, she realized, was no ordinary Indian. Her eyes clung to him, trying to make sense of his familiarity. His shaved head and paint-smeared features continued to confound her—till she caught sight of his headdress. *Five Feathers?* As if aware of her scrutiny, his dark eyes slid her way again, and he pulled something from his beaded belt.

Papa's watch.

Was he mocking her? Or communicating something more? He turned away, and she shifted her attention to the valley beyond, drawn by the surprise and consternation on Millicent's face. Liam's expression was more veiled, betraying little but mild irritation. Fresh alarm knotted her insides. What was happening out there?

"I told Tarrington to hold the line no matter what," Liam muttered, shifting the spyglass to his other eye.

The gunfire was steady now, occasionally punctuated by the boom of mortars and cannon. Smoke billowed above a melee of fighting men, each side taking and then giving up hard-won ground.

"There are . . . so many." Millicent's voice was like a whisper, but every ear heard, all eyes fastened on the Continental line and the glut of men behind it. Swells of the blue uniforms of the

French and the darker indigo of the rebels seemed to ride like a wave over the scarlet and white. And then, within moments, a red tide surged back over Cass's Continentals till the line of Patriots seemed ground to dust.

Suddenly other officers were pouring beneath the awning now—jubilant and tense and talking all at once—and Roxanna felt all the breath go out of her. The Continental line had broken . . . the Bluecoats were in retreat . . . victory was at hand. Her mind was reeling in such confusion she backed up into a tent corner, lip swollen and still bleeding, wishing the ground would open up and swallow her. Even without a spyglass, she'd seen how many men had fallen. They lay like toy soldiers knocked to the ground—British entwined with Americans in a horrific spectacle of death.

Oh, Cass, where are you?

Liam was smiling coldly, and Millicent's fan was fluttering like a bird's wings against the rising heat. The guard had gathered to observe the action, muskets lax. They turned their backs to her and looked in a different direction, seemingly forgetting about her altogether. She wanted to run away, but her limbs were leaden—and then a dusky hand circled her wrist. Five Feathers stood over her, his fierce face paint masking his intent. Confused, she stared up at him and waited for what would surely come next—only she didn't care. She wanted to die. She wanted to end the burning pain in her head and heart once and for all.

Gesturing for her to be silent, Five Feathers moved her beyond the awning past a line of empty tents, where he crouched and tugged her toward a horse hidden behind a huge sycamore. There in the leafy shade, her shaking legs wouldn't help her onto the bare back. She felt no bigger than Abby when he pushed her atop the stallion, mounting behind her and gripping the reins.

He kicked the horse's sides and they bolted south. This close, he smelled of smoke, his encircling arms hard as iron bars. They flew through thickets and over sun-dried creek beds so swiftly her teeth chattered. Miles of wilderness began to blur, and then her senses rebelled at the thunder of cannons and the stench of black powder.

Would he drop her into the very heart of battle?

Numbness turned to disbelief as they galloped toward Blue-coat tents and the large marquee that reflected the strengthening sun. There Five Feathers dismounted and tugged her from the horse's back, leaving her on shaking legs before riding away. Dazed, she looked back at him, but he'd slipped through the smoke. All she saw was a flash of his horse's tail.

"Miz Roxanna!"

Bella was shouting at her, but Roxanna could hardly hear above the din of battle. Face contorted with disbelief, she grabbed Roxanna by the shoulders, tears running in rivulets down her dark face. "Law, but you look a sight! What have they done to you?"

Roxanna's own eyes filled and nearly spilled over. Her lip was so sore it hurt to speak. "I'm . . . all right. Is Cass . . . ?"

Bella's face seemed to close, as if hiding secrets. Pulling away, Roxanna plunged through a lingering mist of fog, stumbling along an entrenchment, senses straining. Up a hill she ran, hungry for a glimpse of him, unaware she was treading on dangerous ground at the rear of a column. Bluecoats surged just ahead of her, leaving spent cartridges and broken muskets in their wake. Overcome by the melee, she fell to her knees, trying to make sense of her surroundings, fingers digging in the warm grass and dirt, her white kerchief trailing like a flag of surrender behind her.

Bella dropped down beside her, shackling her with a hard hand. "You got to come back to camp. Now!"

From somewhere—in the midst of the fray—she could hear Cass shouting at his men to hold the line.

Her heart, so barren moments before, seemed to burst.

"You got to go back!" Bella shouted above the noise. "For Abby's sake!"

The frantic words seemed to restore her reason. Dazed, she got to her feet and let Bella lead her, returning her to an abandoned camp depleted of all but a few scattered sentries and the sick.

"Now sit down here and stop your shakin' and drink this," Bella soothed, pushing her toward a crate and passing her a canteen of water. "Though what you need is some o' my cherry bounce."

Roxanna took a long drink, spilling water down her dress front. Bella stood so near that her skirts brushed Roxanna's, as if she feared Roxanna might take flight again and she'd have to stop her. The sun was burning her eyes in its downward slant. Absently she guessed it to be three o'clock and wished for her hat.

"When . . . will it . . . end, Bella?" The question was so weary, so strung out, it hardly seemed a sentence.

Bella drew a deep breath. "Lord only knows. Them Redcoats don't like fightin' past dusk. But the colonel and his men come alive at night." Taking back the canteen, Bella's eyes turned searching. "Was that Indian who brung you back here the one the colonel kept locked up last winter?"

Roxanna nodded, eyes on the smoky horizon.

"McLinn was beside hisself when those Redcoats took you. I wish he could see you now. It might make all that fightin' go easier." She took a sip from the canteen and ran a tongue over parched lips. "I suppose you saw Hank. Only you're too kind to tell me so."

Before she could dash it away, a single tear spotted Roxanna's cheek. How much did Bella know? How much should she share? Or hold back?

Bella's eyes turned damp. Head down, she reached into the pocket of a dress blackened with soot and spotted with grease. "Right before we left on this here campaign, I was cleanin' out some o' Hank's things and found this. It's in your pa's fine hand."

The missing journal pages?

Roxanna took the papers, left edges tattered where they'd been torn from the book's binding, and her eyes fell on one telling line.

I fear—I know without a doubt—who the enemy is. Hank.

"Don't know why Hank didn't burn them pages. Mebbe he thought it didn't matter. Mebbe he forgot where he hid 'em—or didn't reckon on me findin' 'em."

"I'm sorry, Bella." The apology, though heartfelt, was woefully inadequate.

Bella swallowed hard and passed a hand over her eyes. "I know you is sorry. You sure look it. It's Hank who should be sorry . . ."

Roxanna looked north, to fighting she couldn't see, and felt tension tighten like a coil inside her. 'Twas absolute torment to sit here while men fought and fell just beyond that hill, Cass among them. But even as she thought it, found the waiting unbearable, a thundering commotion to their right drew their attention. The wounded were beginning to come in, and her heart wrenched anew at the sight.

Following Bella's lead, she began doing what she could— carrying water, binding wounds, whispering words of comfort and snatches of Scripture, praying for those who were beyond all hope of survival. The sun dipped lower, but the gun and cannon fire never ceased, and in time she no longer started at its thunder.

Lord, how long must the carnage go on?

She was so weary she seemed to have slipped into a sort of trance, senses dull, her every movement slack. She hardly heard a new ruckus behind her, nor saw Bella's frantic features as she turned toward the sound.

A few bedraggled officers and Frenchmen were coming into camp, emerging from the smoke into fading sunlight, some so powder burned she scarcely recognized them. Despite the dust, she saw Cass plainly and found her feet. He was on his back atop the litter used to transport the wounded, and she caught but a glimpse of him as he was lowered to the ground.

She had no recollection of how she closed the gap between

them, pushing past soldiers and horses to reach him, but in moments she was on her knees, her salty tears spotting his face. Flecks of powder blackened his tanned skin, and his eyes were closed. A silent cry erupted inside her as her hands hovered over him, desperate to ease his hurt.

Joram Herkimer knelt beside her, his generous shadow offering a sort of shade for the tumult of her emotions. "His horse was shot out from under him and then fell on his leg. I'm afraid it's badly broken. But it's the lead that grieves me."

The lead?

The bullet's path was plain before her eyes. Breathless and shaking, she lowered her head to Cass's chest and recognized a startling absence of blood. Beneath her ear was the torn-up cloth of his uniform coat where the ball had nested—and a dull heartbeat. Frantic, her fingers plucked at the fabric of his waistcoat, fumbling till she pulled the locket free. A ball was imbedded in its face, destroying its silver beauty, blackening her portrait within. It glinted in the sun and made her wince at its reflection. But her heart was strengthening, rejoicing.

Oh, Lord, You spared his life!

His eyes swept open but were marred with pain. "Roxie, go . . . *now.*"

Did he think he was still on the field—in the thick of the fighting? "Cass, 'tis all right. You're back at camp. But we have to get you moved—your leg . . ."

His features relaxed, and he squinted at the sky as if trying to get his bearings. "Listen to the drums. They're in retreat."

Truly, the battle sounds, so distinct minutes before, now seemed a distant echo. The grassy hill kept them from seeing what was going on just beyond. Could it be they'd beaten the Redcoats back?

His hand brushed her cheek. "How did you get here?"

"Five Feathers—he brought me back."

His look was searching, disbelieving.

"You know—the Shawnee with Papa's pocket watch."

She saw his confusion clear and understanding dawn. Looking about, he made a move toward his sword. It lay near him in the grass and she reached for it, then saw the blood marring the tip. Stomach lurching, she left it alone.

Jehu appeared, so winded he could barely speak, his queue undone, his tricorn missing. "They're in full retreat," he panted, eyeing the hill in wild-eyed disbelief. "I don't know how it's possible, but they are."

White-faced with pain, Cass attempted to sit up. "Get me off the ground." Together the Herkimers managed to bring him to his feet.

"Find me a mount," he said.

Joram turned to do his bidding while Roxanna stared open-mouthed at Cass's left leg, now bent at an impossible angle.

"You can't possibly—"

"Watch me," he answered.

They had to help him into the saddle, and Jehu passed him his sword. Returning it to its sheath, he was the commander again, his eye on the hill, scattered pockets of firing just beyond.

He looked down at her, features taut with pain. "Stay here at camp, Roxie."

"Nay," she said, reaching for his horse's bridle.

But he was already turning away, just beyond her reach, his thoughts on the field. She watched him go, still wild with worry, the Herkimers alongside him, Bella shadowing her.

Oh, Lord, please bring him back to me.

❧ ❧

The big bay sidestepped and then lunged forward at the touch of a single spur. Cass rode cautiously, cresting the hill till the valley lay before him like a swath of green silk. There he nearly forgot his throbbing leg and intense thirst and Roxie's entreating look as he'd left her.

As far as he could see, Redcoats and Indians were fleeing, leaving their dead behind, their cannon in the field, a trail of clothes and shoes and broken equipment in their wake. He leaned forward in the saddle, sensing the shock of those around him. In the distance, French officers were riding toward them, leaping over the snaking Bluecoat trench.

They saluted, Gallic faces brimming, and burst into French. He listened, trying to make sense of it all, his officers' faces a puzzle beside him. The French captain withdrew something small from his breast pocket, leaned forward in his saddle, and passed it to Cass. Sunlight struck gold, and he felt a nauseating familiarity. Liam's signet ring.

"Your brother, mon colonel, is dead."

Cass shifted in the saddle, the ring between thumb and forefinger, and kept his expression inscrutable.

"The vile British commander is—how do you Americans say it—suicide?" When Cass didn't respond, he continued on, exuberance high. "Your brother was not in his right mind. He was seeing things—seeing more Bluecoats and Frenchmen than Redcoats and Indians. His officers—they became confused and began to flee the field. Watching it, he put this gun to his head."

He produced a silver-plated pistol. Liam's own. Cass regarded it with a sinking feeling deep in his spirit. What of Millicent? Hank? A bit light-headed, he tightened his hold on the reins. His men were surrounding him now, a great cheering mass of militia and Bluecoats, slapping backs and tossing tricorns into the air. He smiled despite himself, caught up in their jubilance, acutely aware of their bleeding limbs and powder-burned faces.

"Come on, boys," he finally said with a lavish grin. "Reload your pieces and we'll give them a proper send-off."

⁂

Hours later, the shock had worn off and the reality of grave pain set in. Night had fallen, and fireflies winged about the marquee tent, mosquitoes buzzing against the netting of Cass's bed. But he was hardly conscious of anything beyond his throbbing left leg and the hole in his heart. He hadn't believed Liam dead till the French officers had shown him. And then, seized with an unbearable mix of relief and regret, he'd leaned over the pommel of his saddle and retched.

"Another sip, please."

The alluring voice brought him round, and he turned his head. "There you go again, trying to make me tipsy."

Underneath the netting Roxanna sat, trying to slip him sips of rum to quench the hurt of a broken leg and a lost brother. Though she hadn't been present when he'd identified Liam, the poignancy in her face told him she knew all about it.

"They've set your leg," she said. "Ben Simmons is an able doctor when he has to be."

"Where's my locket?"

She gave him a wan smile and looked over at his uniform coat lying across a trunk. "'Tis in your waistcoat pocket, where it belongs."

"All mangled, I'll wager."

"Better that than your heart."

"'Tis glad I am of that." His eyes held hers and didn't let go. Though hours had passed and the smoke had cleared and the din of battle was done, he was still striving to make sense of all that had transpired, still a bit disbelieving. "Roxie, what do you think happened with Liam?"

"His confusion, you mean?"

"His seeing things, aye."

Her face assumed such wistfulness it reminded him of Abby. She was privy to something he was not, he thought. He could tell just by looking at her.

"I think Liam saw things as they truly were—a heavenly army," she said softly. "How else can it be explained?"

"You were praying."

"Yes. But more importantly, *you* were praying."

"Aye . . . but what were *you* praying?"

Tears came to her eyes. "Elisha's prayer in 2 Kings . . . 'Lord, I pray thee, open his eyes, that he may see. And the Lord opened the eyes of the young man; and he saw: and, behold, the mountain was full of horses and chariots of fire.'"

He regarded her with a sort of wonder. She looked down at her lap and he saw her mouth tremble. "I didn't want to lose you . . . to face life without you . . . to have to tell Abby you weren't coming back. So I prayed like I've never prayed before—and fasted—and begged for an Old Testament miracle."

She set the cup down, trying to wipe away the wetness streaming down her face. He reached out to her, her brokenness mirroring his own, tears leaking from the corners of his eyes and running into his hairline. Lying on his back, he couldn't comfort her like he wanted but had to be content with her head upon his chest, his fingers stroking her disheveled hair till hairpins lay like wingless insects on his shirt.

Even on his back with a badly fractured leg, he was acutely conscious of the sweet, womanly essence of her, her winsome vulnerability and strength. He wanted to ask about her cut lip but sensed she had shut that part of her captivity away and would share it with no one, not even him.

Slowly she lifted her head and took up the cup again. He drank slowly as she cradled his head with her other arm.

"Marry me, Roxie." He spoke the intimate words into her ear.

She responded with a smile as color crept into her cheeks. "Best wait till your leg is mended—"

"Wait? If I wait, you just might change your mind."

"No, Colonel McLinn. You have my promise as a good soldier's daughter. Though I don't have any idea who'll marry us."

"I do." He grinned, a roguish twinkle in his eye. "Graham Greer."

39

Fort Endeavor had never been so crowded. Or so jubilant. And Colonel Cassius McLinn had never seemed so humble, Roxanna thought. The victory was heaven's own, and he made no claims to the contrary. Even blockhouse headquarters had a different feel. The door was always open, and French and American officers came and went at will. Even settlers came to pay their respects and hear firsthand what had happened in the middle ground. There was no drilling, no court-martials, just reveille and retreat, and the customary raising and lowering of the garrison flag at sunrise and sunset.

Abby was overjoyed at their return, jumping up and down and spinning like a toy top, so giddy—and gabby—that Bella finally led her away to the kitchen. Roxanna followed, wanting to hold her close and hear what she'd done in their absence, but stopped just shy of the kitchen's back door. Alone with Abby, Bella hung a teakettle from the hearth's crane as Abby asked one tentative, heartrending question.

"Where's Hank?"

There was a lengthy pause, so unlike Bella that tears burned in Roxanna's eyes. She leaned against the wood wall out of sight and waited for the answer.

"Well, Abby-girl, Hank got killed along with them Redcoats.

He ain't comin' back." Bella's voice was heavy, weighted with such fatigue and sadness it was palpable, before rebounding with surprising enthusiasm. "But we got better things to think about, like a weddin'. You know who's gettin' married, don't you?"

"Papa and Mith Roxanna?"

"That's right. And we're all goin' to live in the stone house as pretty as you please. And I get to be the queen of yo' kitchen."

"What's a queen?"

"A fancy lady with jewels in her hair. But I ain't goin' to be that kind o' queen. Just a kitchen queen. And Miz Roxanna's goin' to be yo' mama. Now ain't that a fine thing?"

A delighted, slightly disbelieving smile tugged at Abby's mouth. "Will there be a baby?"

Bella chuckled. "Law, but I hope so. You need some brothers and sisters. Let's just pray they don't all have red hair."

Her smile faded. "Why is Papa hurt?"

Bella sat down and pulled Abby onto her lap. "Why? He got his leg broke bein' brave. But it'll mend in time."

Unlike your heart. Roxanna turned away, a prayer for Bella on her lips.

She'd told Cass of Liam's confession and that it had been Hank who'd fired the shot that killed her father. But Cass hadn't told her about Hank's death. Somehow, perhaps irrationally, she'd hoped he'd return to them a changed man, if only for Bella's sake.

Despite her grief, Roxanna was filled with joy as plain as Abby's in regards to her own future. A bride and a mother to Abby and mistress of the stone house, all in one day.

Standing in the twilight shadows amidst fireflies and a still-scorching evening breeze, she looked longingly at headquarters. Since returning two days prior, she'd hardly seen Cass except to transcribe his letter of resignation, which was dispatched to Virginia posthaste. Though it would be months before he was relieved of command, he had mentally moved beyond its burdens and responsibilities. She could see it in the relaxed lines of his face and the telling shift in his demeanor.

The change brought about a sweet relief. But other concerns quickly crowded in. She wondered if he'd ever walk normally again. The broken leg, Dr. Clary declared, was a grievous one. He'd splinted it and supplied crutches and advised spirits to dull the pain—rum and brandy and whatever else was at hand. But Cass refused to drink. Pondering it now, she felt a profound thanks and failed to hear the footfall behind her.

"Miss Rowan, Colonel McLinn would like to see you," said an orderly half hidden by the quickening shadows. Thanking him, she started toward headquarters, only to have him intercept her, arm extended. "The stone house, Miss Rowan."

She couldn't hide her pleasure at the invitation. Though word of their betrothal hadn't been announced, it was hardly necessary. The news would soon be commonplace.

Up the hill they went, followed by a small guard. Before she'd mounted the first step, the elegant front door was opened by another orderly who seemed almost as delighted as she.

Was something afoot? He showed her to the dining room, where dozens of bayberry candles glittered in a cool draft and the air was redolent with roasting chicken and herbs. There at the head of the table sat Cass, his crutches in stark relief as they rested against a paneled wall behind him.

She paused in the doorway, feeling tongue-tied and flushed. "Colonel McLinn."

"Miss Rowan," he returned with a little smile, as if amused by her mock formality.

The orderly seated her to Cass's left before disappearing through an adjoining door to the kitchen. She surveyed the china and cutlery and crystal spread before her, a vase of crimson roses within arm's reach. A few petals lay upon the damask tablecloth. Reaching out, she fingered one a bit absently. Soft as baby skin.

"Are you expecting company, Colonel?"

"Nay, no longer."

"I'm hardly fit for your fine table," she murmured, though he himself was in fatigue dress. Looking down at her simple linen gown, she was thankful to be clean, at least.

"You've ne'er looked more beautiful to me . . . my bride."

She met his eyes. Her stomach began to somersault. She couldn't think of a single coherent word to say.

"You're lucky I'm wounded," he told her.

"So you can't chase me round the room, you mean?"

"Aye, I can't so much as kiss you."

"There's nothing wrong with your arms—or your lips," she replied a bit saucily. "Just your leg."

"Which should be mended by our wedding day. October, I think you said."

She reached for her napkin and placed it in her lap. "'Tis right around the corner."

"The continent, rather."

At his grim resignation, she laughed. "By then you might have found a preacher."

"I—"

The adjoining door to the kitchen swung open noiselessly, giving them pause. The supper smells intensified as the orderly carried in a tray laden with warm bread, whipped butter, and consommé. Roxanna all but held her breath as the young man set the steaming bowls before them and spilled nary a drop.

"'Tis only the first course, ye ken," Cass said. "There are five more to follow."

Delight flickered through her. "You spoil me."

"You need spoiling." Leaning over, he reached for her hand.

At the touch of his fingers, emotion tightened her throat. She paused, eyes on him and then the candelabra. When she looked at him again, she found his eyes shimmering. Was he thinking of Liam? Hank? The soldiers he'd lost in the middle ground? Or so suffused with thankfulness over being spared he couldn't speak?

"Why not pray the prayer you prayed with Abby?" she said softly.

He gave a brief nod, and together they bent their heads. Though the words had been memorized long ago, she felt his deep emotion. "Be present at our table, Lord. Be here and everywhere adored. These creatures bless, and grant that we may feast in paradise with Thee. Amen."

"Amen," she echoed with feeling, dipping her spoon into her soup. "Who is in the kitchen tonight?"

"A French lieutenant. He's asked to stay on as chef."

"But Bella . . ."

"Bella can be in the nursery."

She was smiling again, hardly aware of what she ate. "With Abby."

"Aye, with Abby." He took a sip of water. Not wine, she noticed. "Did I mention I want a dozen or more children?"

She feigned disappointment. "Only twelve?"

A smile pulled at the solemn lines of his mouth, and he buttered his bread with relish, as if making up for the meager rations in the field. "I was hoping you'd feel the same."

"Twelve children sounds something like an order. We already have one, remember."

"Abby needs brothers and sisters. This house needs life— laughter."

The door reopened, and a second tray, burgeoning with roast chicken and cream sauce and assorted vegetables, was set down. Roxanna's mind was spinning with the intoxicating thought of eating in this beautiful room day in and day out. With a French chef, no less. Only she'd throw back the curtains and let in light and fresh air and remove the hideous elk's head above the mantel—

" . . . our wedding trip."

Her musings evaporated. "You were saying?"

"I thought perhaps we'd travel to Philadelphia, take Bella and Abby. They could stay with the Hazens while we go on to Williamsburg and Richmond and enjoy ourselves."

"But isn't river travel still dangerous?"

"Not with an escort of fifty French riflemen and two retiring officers."

"Who will take command in your stead?"

"One of the Herkimers since Micajah is being discharged."

Taking up her fork, she cut a bite of meat and eyed the artfully arranged vegetables. "You don't want to stay here, then? Honeymoon in this house?"

In the candlelight, his eyes—so wildly blue—softened. "Only if you do, Roxie."

I do. She set her fork down, taken by a sudden whim. Hadn't she learned anything on the march into the middle ground? Life was too precious to tarry. Today was all they had.

"It seems like we're always waiting. For your leg to mend. Our wedding. Your replacement." She glanced at her plate. "The next course. Safety. Happiness. Peace."

Pushing back her chair, she got to her feet. Alone with him in the polished perfection of the dining room, she circled round to the back of his chair. Putting her arms around him, she buried her face in the scarlet silk of his hair.

"Tomorrow," she said.

He went still. "Tomorrow?"

"Tomorrow . . . I will wed you tomorrow."

She sensed his surprise and pleasure as plainly as she felt the frantic fluttering of her pulse.

"You'll wed a cripple," he finally said.

"Then we'll limp down the aisle together, provided we can find a preacher."

His joyous smile turned her heart over and made jelly of her knees. With a deft maneuver he pulled her nearer, well away from his splinted leg. She sank atop his lap in an avalanche of linen and lace, their foreheads touching.

She queried with a joyous smile, "What say ye, Colonel McLinn?"

His eyes glinted with good humor. "I say aye, Mrs. McLinn. Limp on."

Epilogue

Never had the stone house looked so beautiful, felt so at peace. In the gleaming foyer, elaborate swaths of pine boughs were tied with scarlet ribbon, and a hundred candles shimmered and danced each time someone came through the front door. The scent of gingerbread and plum pudding swirled in the air, and the dining room table was set for twelve. 'Twas Christmas Eve, and the house had never been busier or more filled with life. As the French chef performed culinary feats in the kitchen, the portraitist who'd come downriver at the colonel's request held court in the parlor.

They'd only recently returned from the east, enjoying the unending gaiety over the war's end and countless balls and receptions held in the officers' honor. Washington and Lafayette were no longer simply names to Roxanna but real people with loved ones and lives to live now that the conflict was over. Congress had presented Cass with a generous pension for his service and more land than they knew what to do with.

Fort Endeavor was no more. Its oaken logs and pickets had been torn down and reassembled into a spring house, chicken coop, smokehouse, and too many dependencies to name. 'Twas hard to believe a fort had ever held sway. Now snowflakes descended in a wild winter's dance, covering the sloping ground from the house to the river.

"Come here, Master Jack, and hold still so this poor man can make your picture." Bella's voice was lined with exasperation, though her smile stayed bright. With one sinewy arm she reached down and rescued the titian-haired boy from his fascination with the hearth's fire.

Glancing their way, Roxanna resumed retying the bow in Abby's curls. At ten, she wore a replica of Roxanna's dress—a festive cranberry silk overlaid with silver lace, a small string of pearls about her neck.

"Mama, you look beautiful," Abby whispered, stroking one of Roxanna's sleeves.

"So do you," Roxanna whispered back before returning her attention to the whimpering baby in her lap. "A merry heart makes one so."

"Will Henry smile or cry for his picture?"

"Mayhap a bit of both," Roxanna replied, glad to rest after all the fuss of preparing for the sitting. She ran her fingers over her son's silky head—the only ebony-haired child they had—and gave her knees a little bounce to quiet him. Sticking a fat fist in his mouth, he gnawed and drooled over his first tooth.

"Where's Papa?" Jack asked, coming alongside her chair.

"Hiding presents for us," Abby answered with a knowing smile. "If we're polite to Mr. Painter, we get to open one gift before Christmas morn."

At this, Jack wrinkled his freckled nose and contemplated the graying artist across the expanse of carpet as he began mixing paints near a large canvas. "I don't want a gift. I want a musket!"

"So you can be a soldier like yo' papa?" Bella asked, shadowing him.

Blue eyes blazing, he looked up at her with all the bluster a three-year-old could muster. "Aye! So I can order you around and keep you from the fire and make you eat your mush!"

Bella chuckled. "You sound like yo' papa, all right." Her sharp eyes dismissed him and softened as they took in Roxanna. "That baby's goin' to spoil your Christmas dress. Let me take him, and then Master Jack and Miss Abby-gail and me will have us a little treat in the kitchen while you're waitin'."

"Gingerbread!" Jack shouted, leading a charge to the sitting room door, Abby hard on his heels.

Roxanna released the baby, not caring if her fine dress was spoiled, knowing the artist could paint it as he pleased. But Bella couldn't be long without her chicks, as she called them, and Roxanna watched them go, thankfulness—and impatience—flooding her.

Where was he?

Her answer soon materialized in the doorway, causing her heart to somersault. Cass was looking at her, adjusting the stock at his neck as if it wasn't quite right. She hadn't seen him in uniform for years. The buff and blue was as arresting as ever, even without cross belts and weapons. Her eyes lingered on the Purple Heart she'd sewn into the rich blue cloth, the fine lapels and braid on the fancy coat stirring to life a host of memories.

He took the wing chair beside her, just as he had the night of their first cribbage game. They'd played endless rounds since. Reaching over, she smoothed his sleeve, the wool warm beneath her hand. He kissed the back of her fingers, glancing at the artist.

"Seeing you in uniform again . . ." she said, then hesitated. It cast her back to the past, on that first Christmas Eve years before when she'd stood before him and her world had come crashing down.

"I can change, ye ken."

"Why? You look every bit as gallant as when I first saw you. Though I do wonder," she murmured with a hint of a smile, "if you're missing something." Leaning nearer, she slipped her fingers inside his waistcoat pocket, smiling when she touched something smooth and familiar. "Do you have my locket, Colonel McLinn?"

"Aye, I do."

As she pulled out the delicate silver chain, her heart gave a little lurch. 'Twas a locket, truly, but not the marred one of old. This treasure shone of new silver and had a sprinkling of tiny diamonds across its heart-shaped face.

"Merry Christmas, Roxie."

He'd gotten it in Williamsburg, she guessed. There was a fine silversmith there. Cupping it in her hands, she opened it slowly, lingering on the portraits within. Cass was on the left, their three children on the right, all exquisitely captured in miniature.

"Did you paint—?" she began.

"Aye, I did," he answered. "With a little help from the portraitist, Mr. Stuart."

Shutting it, she turned it over. Etched on the back was the beloved Scripture that had come to symbolize their life together—Ecclesiastes 4:12. Her heart was so full she couldn't speak as he unclasped the locket and placed it around her neck.

And if one prevail against him, two shall withstand him; and a threefold cord is not quickly broken.

Acknowledgments

Heartfelt thanks to my wonderful editors, Andrea Doering and Jessica Miles, and the entire editorial team, who always go above and beyond on my books. A huge thumbs-up to Twila and Michele and all of sales and marketing for connecting with readers everywhere. To Cheryl and her inspired art team—your covers take my breath away! Special thanks to Deonne and Donna, who go the extra mile in publicity. I wish I had the names of everyone at Revell whose hands and hearts are a part of this work. Bless you all.

To my readers near and far—you know who you are—you've enriched my life in countless ways through snail mail, email, photos, gifts, prayers, and encouraging words. *You* are the reason I write. That the Lord brought us together is a continual blessing to me each and every day.

Many thanks to Janet Grant and Books & Such Literary Agency for your wisdom, finesse, and ongoing support of my work. When people tell me you're the best, I know it's true.

To Lori Benton, fellow eighteenth-century lover, who read through this manuscript and offered insight and wisdom. You are such a faithful friend—and your beautiful prose blows me away!

To my husband, Randy, and my sons, Wyatt and Paul, who,

during a very busy winter of fiddling, basketball, traveling, and whatnot, created a little library for me that delights my writer's heart! I could not do this without you three. Special thanks to my brother, Chris, for his unfailing support and wisdom, always.

To my dear author friends Lorna Seilstad, Ann Gabhart, Julie Lessman, and Kaye Dacus. You four are a huge blessing!

Also, a huge huzzah to Dr. Carrie Fancett Pagels, founder and moderator of Colonial American Christian Writers, and the history lovers therein, for endless inspiration.

I thank God for the gift of storytelling. It's been my constant companion since childhood and continues to be an unending joy. "As each has received a gift, use it to serve one another, as good stewards of God's varied grace" (1 Pet. 4:10 ESV).

Laura Frantz credits her grandmother as being the catalyst for her fascination with Kentucky history. Laura's ancestors followed Daniel Boone into Kentucky in the late eighteenth century and settled in Madison County, where her family still resides. She is a member of the Kentucky Historical Society and the American Christian Fiction Writers, and is the author of *The Frontiersman's Daughter* and *Courting Morrow Little*. Laura currently lives in the misty woods of Port Angeles, Washington, with her husband and two sons. Contact her at LauraFrantz.net.

Meet Laura Frantz at

www.LauraFrantz.net

Learn more about her books,
read her blog, and learn fun facts!

Connect with Laura on

Laura Feagan Frantz

LauraLFrantz

"You'll disappear into another place and time and be both encouraged and enriched for having taken the journey."

—Jane Kirkpatrick, bestselling author

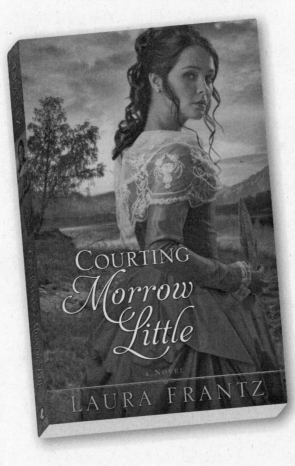

This sweeping tale of romance and forgiveness will envelop readers as it takes them from a Kentucky fort through the vast wilderness of the West.

R Revell
a division of Baker Publishing Group
www.RevellBooks.com

Available wherever books are sold.

"*Laura Frantz portrays the wild beauty of frontier life.*"
—Ann Gabhart

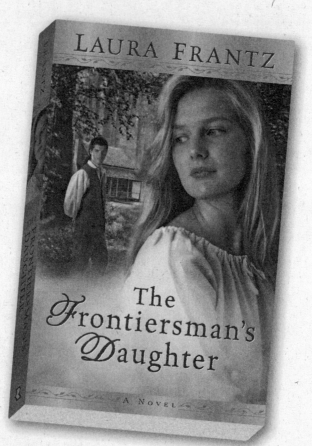

As she faces the loss of a childhood love, a dangerous family feud, and the affection of a Shawnee warrior, it is all Lael Click can do to survive in the Kentucky frontier territory. Will an outsider be her undoing?

Revell
a division of Baker Publishing Group
www.RevellBooks.com

Available wherever books are sold.